ADVAN[CE PRAISE]
FOR *KATH[ERINE'S WISH]*

Katherine's Wish is a beautifully observed novel. Linda Lappin has created far more than a haunting portrait of Katherine Mansfield, that subtlest and most modern of writers—it's as if the unfinished stories, notes jotted in journals or letters suddenly coalesced. *Katherine's Wish* grants the writer's own final wish to give permanent shape to the arc of a life in which the creative and the personal are inseparable. The novel reveals a core truth: that Mansfield's was not so much a creative life cut short as one that flourished so long against all odds.
　　—Alexandra Johnson, author of *The Hidden Writer*

Katherine's Wish, fifteen years in the making, is a dazzling bit of fictional sorcery, conjuring to life the bright and talented swirl of modern society in the 1920s. Katherine Mansfield, John Middleton Murry, Virginia Woolf—these vibrant individuals who created a rich universe such as had never been known before—live in the pages of Linda Lappin's latest novel with a fierceness of energy and intellect and yearning. This novel is a must read, whether you have historical interests per se or only enjoy a story so compelling and moving that there's no putting it down. I certainly couldn't!"
　　—David Lynn, editor, the *Kenyon Review*

The author of two critically successful historical novels, *Prisoner of Palmary* and *The Etruscan*, Linda Lappin turns her gifted hand to fictional biography in *Katherine's Wish*. Short-lived and so poignantly, if not tragically, dedicated to the art of fiction as Romantic poets once lived and died for the Muse, the unconventional Katherine Mansfield is brought to life in this novel of 1918 to 1923, encompassing her marriage to British critic John Middleton Murry, her travels across war-devastated Europe, and her death by tuberculosis at the spiritual asylum in Fontainebleau run by G. I. Gurdjieff. Like the "new biography" of Lytton Strachey and analogous fiction by Virginia Woolf, Lappin's fictional life of Mansfield recreates the ineffable, "rainbow-like" essence of a human being from the inside perspective of three people: Mansfield herself, her traveling companion Ida Baker, and Murry. The factual basis of Lappin's work is scrupulously researched so that the milieu, or social and literary context, seems to come alive, too. Even away from London, in the chapter "Hotel Beau Rivage, 1918," for example, Bloomsbury beckons, heightening the longing as well as the pain of separation.
　　—Wayne K. Chapman, editor, *The South Carolina Review*

Historical fiction of the finest kind; thoroughly researched, faithful to the facts, engagingly written, sympathetic yet unflinching and emotionally convincing in its portrayal of Mansfield, her writing, and personal life, as well as the contacts with Orage and Ouspensky which led Katherine to intentionally spend her final months as Gurdjieff's guest.

—J. Walter Driscoll, editor, The Gurdjieff Reading Guide

Although the story of Katherine Mansfield's short, tragic life is well-known, Linda Lappin has brought to her fictional recreation both a reporter's sense of facts and a novelist's sympathy with human consciousness. Here we find a cast of characters we thought we knew—Mansfield, her husband John Middleton Murry, plus assorted Bloomsbury figures, most notably Virginia Woolf—but we see them in a new light, clear and imagined. Lappin has an eye for both inner and outer detail, for the drama of the ordinary, which of course involves matters of life and death. She has reimagined one writer's life, as well as her early death, with great sensitivity and a feeling for cultural history. She takes us back in time and space to another world and brings it to life for us. Above all, she reminds us why Mansfield, one of our language's great writers of short fiction, deserves our attention."

—Willard Spiegelman, editor, The Southwest Review,
author of How Poets See the World

Praise for
The Etruscan (Wynkin deWorde, 2004)

"Book of the Week" "...captures the fine line between illusion and reality."

—Book View Ireland

"Gorgeously detailed, wickedly fun, *The Etruscan* unburies the nearly lost genre of literary gothic...Lappin explores how the ambiguous text of a woman's life can be thwarted by gender and social position, become lost, and eventually survive."

—Prairie Schooner (University of Nebraska Press)

"An intelligent, atmospheric novel with finely drawn characters and beautiful language and style. It is not easy to put down...this artfully-written novel inhabits a supernatural landscape...Lappin's gift for atmosphere places her among the finest writers of gothic art, not genre."

—The Southern Indiana Review (University of Southern Indiana)

Katherine's Wish

A Novel

Linda Lappin

Based on the lives of Katherine Mansfield,
Ida Constance Baker, and John Middleton Murry

La Grande, Oregon: 2008

ACKNOWLEDGEMENTS

I am grateful to all those who helped me during this project in many ways: offering encouragement and comments, providing materials and useful contacts, furthering my understanding of Mansfield's life and work within the context of her era.

I would like to thank David Applefield, editor of *Frank*, for helping me initiate this project and David Memmott, publisher of Wordcraft of Oregon, for bringing it to print. I would also like to thank Benedetta Bini, Duff Brenna, Natalie Costes, Peter Brook, Wayne K. Chapman, Walter Cummins, Vivienne Emmott Mura, Barbara Hausman, Alexandra Johnson, Thomas E. Kennedy, Christopher Klim, David Lynn, Sandro Melani, Ron Mitchell, Gaetano Prampolini, Ellen Reynard, Francesca Saggini, Willard Spiegelman, Henri Thomasson, and Thomas Wilhelmus, all of whose assistance, encouragement, and inspiration at various turning points in this project were indispensable.

Special thanks go to J. Walter Driscoll for his bibliographic assistance; to James Moore, whose research into the lives of G.I. Gurdjieff and Katherine Mansfield helped guide me in the writing of this novel; and to my husband, Sergio Baldassarre, for his patience and unflagging support.

Sections of this novel have previously been published as:
"Hotel Beau Rivage" in the *South Carolina Review*, Fall Issue 40.1 2007
"A Public of Two," in *The Southern Indiana Review*, Fall Issue 2006
"Katherine's Wish" (final chapter) in *Best New Writing 2007*, Hopewell Publications, 2007
"Katherine's Wish" (selections from Part Two) in *Esercizi di Lettura* SetteCitta', Viterbo, Italy 2005
"Un Anello Per Katherine," translated into the Italian by Sandro Melani, published in *Caffe Michelangiolo*, Sept.-Dec. 2005, Florence, Italy

Thanks also to Lisa Dowdeswell and the Society of Authors, Literary Representatives of the Estate of Katherine Mansfield, for their assistance.

Published by
Wordcraft of Oregon, LLC
www.wordcraftoforegon.com

Cover photo by Linda Lappin
Katherine Mansfield photo: www.clipart.com
Cover design: Kristin Summers, redbat design

Printed in the United States of America

AUTHOR'S NOTE

This book is the fruit of over twenty years' fascination with Katherine Mansfield and fifteen years' active research. The germ of the novel was an essay I wrote, "The Ghosts of Fontainebleau," published in *The Southwest Review* in 2000, recounting a recent journey to the old priory outside Paris where Mansfield died in January 1923. *Katherine's Wish* is a fictionalized account of the last five years of Mansfield's life, and an inquiry into the reasons and relationships which had led her to Gurdjieff's Institute for the Harmonious Development of Man where she spent her last few months. Many primary and secondary sources were consulted in writing this "slice of life," including hard-to-obtain documents generously made available to me by James Moore, author of *Gurdjieff, The Anatomy of a Myth* (Element Books) and *Gurdjieff and Mansfield* (Routledge, Kegan, Paul). A selected bibliography appears at the end of this volume. However, *Katherine's Wish* is a work of fiction—not a historical narrative, and for this reason I have taken liberties to compress time sequences and rearrange a few details in the chronology of some events in order to shape and give pace to the story. My portrayal of the major relationships and events in Mansfield's life, and my recreation of her inner musings about writing, religion, and art are based predominantly on textual evidence. Although I have re-imagined, reinterpreted, and fleshed out some episodes in the characters' lives which have been documented by various—and sometimes conflicting— sources, I have tried to adhere to an overall sense of "truth," rendered, however, as a "mosaic." The novel is faithful to Mansfield's voice and spirit as conveyed through her journals, letters, and other writings. In creating this narrative, a few paraphrases of diary entries and letters written by Mansfield, D.H. Lawrence, and Virginia Woolf have been woven into the fabric of the novel.

For Gerald and Virginia Lappin

List of Characters

Katherine Mansfield   "KM," "KMM," "Katie," "Katya," "Kissienka"

Ida Constance Baker   Katherine's companion, "Jones"

John Middleton Murry   Literary critic, Katherine's husband, "Jack," "Murry," "Boogles," "JMM"

S.S. Koteliansky   Russian literary critic and translator, admirer of KM, "Kot"

D.H.Lawrence   "Lorenzo"

Virginia Woolf

Lady Ottoline   aristocratic London hostess, "Ott"

Dorothy Brett   painter, close friend of Katherine's

Betsy B.   aristocratic writer in love with JMM

Francis Carco   Corsican writer, briefly lover of KM

Alfred Richard Orage   editor of the *New Age*, follower of Gurdjieff, "Dick"

Beatrice Hastings   writer, mistress of Orage and Modigliani

P.D. Ouspensky   disseminator of Gurdjieff's ideas in London

Dr. Sorapure   Katherine's physician in London

Harold Beauchamp   Katherine's father

Connie   Cousin of Harold Beauchamp

Jinny   Connie's companion

Dedo   Amedeo Modigliani

PART ONE

1918

BANDOL: HOTEL BEAU RIVAGE

The train pulled on through the blizzard. Katherine pressed the small of her back against the seat and took short, tremulous breaths to keep herself from coughing. The stuffy air in the compartment was pervaded by the sickening smell of mothballs, perspiration, and wet galoshes, wafting forth from the gentleman in the gray overcoat sitting opposite her. At Calais, he had poked in his head with a hearty, "Alone, Madame?" then bundled in and plopped down before she could protest. He now snoozed blissfully, a newspaper spread over his face, snuffling beneath a map of the latest German offensive, while the pool of melted snow at his feet slowly seeped towards her side of the compartment.

If Ida had been there, she would have shooed him away and dried the puddle, but luckily or unluckily, Ida's request for a visa had been denied and she was forced to stay behind. She was now in Katherine's flat in Old Church Street, watching over Katherine's cat. Murry could not be trusted with such an important task. There was no room for a pet at his lodgings in Redcliffe Road and he was too busy with his new job at the War Office to bother with a cat. To Katherine, Ida's absence was cause for rejoicing. She hoped Murry might possibly be prompted to join her in Bandol—knowing that she was ill and alone while traveling abroad, without Ida's assistance. That was not likely to be soon. Murry's war work was considered vital. It might be months before he could obtain leave. Still, she had begged Ida not to make a second request for a visa and Ida, unwillingly, had agreed.

Outside the snow swirled down through the boughs of skeletal trees. The country road following the tracks was quickly filling in with white. A small fox, or perhaps a hare, bounded across a field, leaving a jagged trail in the snow. Yet the quiet countryside could not assuage Katherine's restlessness. She had been sitting there for hours. She would be sitting for hours more. The train stopped in every station on the line where the engine died with a groan. After an interminable wait, it lurched to life again, jolted forward with a great burst of steam, then inched reluctantly along to the next stop. No one knew the reason for the delay. It was the war, they said.

She yearned for something hot to drink, but the restaurant car was closed. There was not a cup of tea to be had anywhere on the train. That too, because of the war. Whatever was wrong these days, it was the war, and one had to be resigned to it.

Her feet burned; her back ached; her head throbbed. She shifted in her seat to soothe a cramped knee and frowned as she thought that Ida would not be there tonight to massage her painful tendons. How would she manage all those heavy bags? Perhaps it was unwise of her to venture so far into France alone with the war on. But the doctors had insisted she could not weather another English winter without grave risks to her heath. And look at it now! The worst snow storm in over twenty years. Just imagine what it was like in London.

She prayed she would be able to manage well enough. She was, after all, an old hand at traveling, and this wasn't her first trip alone abroad in wartime. She had already challenged the French border officials when she had followed her lover, Francis Carco, to the front three years ago. There in the little town of Gray, she had spent three days in a tawdry pension under a false name, waiting for Carco to knock at the door, as she imagined bullets whizzing by the window. What an adventure! As for Carco! Whatever had she seen in him? He was no war hero, only the postman for a bakery unit, and not even much of a writer. It was only to rankle Murry that she had consented to that rendezvous which had been so disappointing in the end. And then Carco had offended them both by making a caricature of her in his recent novel. That just shows you can never trust a writer with your confessions.

What was Murry doing now, she wondered, scribbling at his desk at the War Office, writing clever phrases for recruitment posters? Or wooing that vixen Lady Ottoline who once claimed to be her friend? Now that Murry was in service to his country, he could not leave England to follow her to France, but he could gad about London, making love to all her so-called friends. Upon her return, she would put an end to all that, by marrying Murry, once her divorce from George Bowden came through at last. What a terrible mistake *that* had been: marrying Bowden on the spur of the moment, simply because he adored her and seemed so well-connected. Of course, that wasn't the *real* reason she had let George rush her to the altar. The real reason had been the fatherless child in her womb, Garnet's child, the baby she had lost later in Bavaria. And that had all been Mother's fault. She would never have miscarried if Mother hadn't sent her to that dreadful spa to get her away from Ida.

George Bowden. How he had worshipped her! The vibrato of his tenor voice had always grated on her nerves, but he had seemed so manly and sophisticated and by marrying him she had thought she might punish and escape her family.

When one is young, desperate, friendless and penniless, half-baked solutions sometimes seem practical, even auspicious. Their marriage had not even lasted twenty-four hours before she had flown the coop with Ida's assistance. They had laughed about it afterwards. Good God, impossible to think that nine years had passed since then.

She sighed and suddenly missed Ida, upon whose dumpy bosom she often rested her small, sleek head. It was going to take all her reserves of courage and energy to see herself through this time alone in France. Courage she had plenty; energy much less. At least she was returning to a hotel where the owner knew her well. Madame Galle would surely fatten her up again on butter and cream, quite unavailable in England with the rationing, and help her replenish her strength. Katherine had written ahead to reserve the same room which she had occupied during her last stay in Bandol just before Murry had joined her there and they had moved out to the Villa Pauline on the edge of town.

She smiled thinking of the villa where she and Murry had been so happy together: the crisp sheets scented with lavender, the gleaming marble floor splashed with sunlight, the mimosa trees out the window frothing yellow in the sea breeze. She pictured the two of them sitting at the breakfast table, surrounded by piles of books and papers; she so seductive in her emerald kimono; Murry looking so dignified in his burgundy-striped silk dressing gown, doing his work; she hers, and the table strewn with egg shells and milk bottles and empty pots of *crème fraîche*. Murry standing before the mirror of the armoire, asking anxiously, "Have they cut my hair too short?" At her negative reply, he had ventured, "Then have they left it too long?" She chuckled remembering this episode, then felt something snag in her chest. The sting of tears astonished her. No one would ever understand why such a scene was her ideal of domestic bliss. And now how much time would pass before she would see Murry again? This trip to France, they had vowed, would be her last trip alone. He had promised her that after they were married, hopefully in May or as soon as her divorce came through, he would never allow her to travel abroad again without him.

The dry air tickled her throat. She coughed with a wheezing, raucous croak, most unladylike, downright disgusting. The drowsing gentleman grumbled and twitched beneath his newspaper. Alone or not, thought Katherine, as she observed the corpulent form slumped across from her; whatever happened, she had a secret friend, a hidden helper, a pistol purchased just before departure on the advice of her father. *My dear girl*, he had urged in a letter from Wellington, *for heaven's sake, get a gun and learn to shoot.* Father was so practical about that sort of thing. Who would imagine that this delightful London lady in her smart cloche and gray tweed traveling suit was packing a pistol in her handbag? She imagined pulling it out now and pointing the polished blue barrel at the snoring gentleman. Catching a glimpse of her reflection in the dark window as the train threaded a tunnel, she nodded slyly to herself. With a flask of brandy in her overcoat pocket and a pistol in her purse, this little New Zealander was ready for anything.

They reached Marseille at one o'clock. Here the sun was out, though the sky was streaked with gray and a mistral was blowing. The station was crowded with soldiers on leave, and peasants transporting baskets of cabbages and onions. Few civilians, even fewer women, milled about, trying to get somewhere on non-existent trains for nothing was running on schedule, and all the signs indicating platforms were wrong. A railway official informed her that the express for Bandol was not due in for another two hours, at least. Not one of the lavatories was working properly.

There were three queues to wait in. One for her ticket; another to check her visa; a third to collect her trunk. Before facing such enervating tests of strength, she craved refreshment, but there was not a speck of food left in the station. The station buffet was cleaned out. There wasn't even an orange vendor or a coffee wagon. There were no oranges because of the war; no coffee, either, of course, and no place to sit down. All the benches along the platforms and all the chairs at the buffet were occupied, mainly by soldiers, hundreds of young men, whose rucksacks and duffle bags were piled in huge pyramids against the station wall. Whenever she saw soldiers, she thought of her dear brother Leslie, dead in the war, whose face once shone among hapless ranks like these. She singled out a few boys to study: rough country lads, their ruddy faces tinged with fear, pocked with gonorrhea. Home on leave from the trenches, she thought, still vertical beneath the sun. They had not yet become names in newsprint, numbers in a ledger, unlike beloved Leslie whose grave lay in a dark wood in France. Tears blurred her eyes as her lips murmured his name. This war was such a waste of youthful virility.

She got through the queues all right, turned her trunk over to a porter, and registered it for the next part of her trip, praying she would find it again once she got to Bandol. Then she dragged her bags down to the end of the platform where the first class carriages would be when the train came in. From here the tracks led out of the station through a depot area where abandoned railway carriages with shattered windows lay on dead sidetracks. Beyond, the black mouth of a tunnel beckoned.

Piling her bags together, she perched herself on top, wrapped herself in her cashmere shawl, a gift from Ida in their schooldays. As she tied the shawl round her shoulders, a few beads of the fringe slipped off to the ground and one rolled over the edge of the platform. She frowned. How was it that Ida had not noticed the frayed fringe and mended it before packing her things? That was the sort of detail she counted on Ida to take care of. Katherine gathered up the loose beads and put them in her pocket, then tied the silken tassels in a knot to keep them from unraveling any further.

Now that she was settled, she decided to dig out her emergency provisions, for she had told Ida to pack some biscuits for her journey. Rummaging through her carpetbag, she found a packet containing a tin of French butter biscuits imported from Normandy, which must have cost five times the price of ordinary English biscuits. Imagine buying imported French biscuits for someone on their way to France. And with a war on! That was just like Ida to have no practical sense and to be so careless with their money. Katherine opened the tin and took out just one. The delicious biscuit crumbled in her mouth, bringing welcome satisfaction. Smacking her lips, she took out another biscuit, forgiving Ida and even blessing her for this extravagance. The biscuits had made her thirsty, but her water-bottle was nearly empty, and she knew she must save the rest for her journey. But she had hardly touched the brandy. She took a discreet sip from the silver traveling flask hidden in the secret pocket Ida had sewn into the lining of her coat. After all, she was alone on the platform, and it was awhile before departure time. She needed a little something. The brandy burned her parched throat and she coughed.

She took out her copy of the *Times Literary Supplement*, shook it open to Murry's latest review, imagining a conversation with him as she began to read. *I do so agree with you entirely, but my darling, why do you praise such dreadful prose?*... Smoothing out a crease in the page, she sniffed the pungent scent of a cheap French cigarette. Looking up, she glimpsed two male legs encased in khaki standing within the rim of her vision.

What now? With all the space on the platform, some fellow had glued himself to her. Wherever had he come from? Perhaps from the maze of tracks just beyond the platform, leading away from the station. She glanced down the platform towards the crowded atrium. She and the gentleman were quite alone.

Why is it women are unable to travel without this sort of nuisance? She liked being looked at by men; she knew she was attractive, but she did not like to be stalked in such a way. She did not want to give him the satisfaction of looking at him directly for he might take that as an invitation. At any moment he would slink over and simper "*Vous êtes seule, Madame?*" offer help or perhaps a cigarette. She held her breath and waited, pretending to peruse the page. The legs inched closer. She heard the man humming under his breath in an insidious manner. If he moved in just another foot or so, she could reach out and give him a chop in the knee. Perhaps he wants to steal my bag, she thought. Clutching her purse with pistol to her breast, she jerked her head round to challenge him, eye to furious eye.

She was startled by the paltry figure leaning on a nearby column. The soldier was not even looking in her direction, but was gazing out toward the tunnel.

The man's face was gaunt with jaundice, his cheeks sunken, his hair a blondish streak plastered to his scalp. One shoulder stooped askew, beneath it dangled an empty sleeve. He turned to stare at her blankly. It seemed to her he resembled someone she once knew long ago, but could not place.

Their confrontation was cut short, for a whistle blew and a train chugged through the tunnel onto the adjacent track. As the great engine shut down, the brakes screeched, and a cloud of soot billowed from the smokestack, filling her eyes and nostrils with black grit. She covered her face with her handkerchief and coughed. This time she felt something rip behind her left shoulder blade. She coughed again, to see if the pain repeated itself, and there it was, a tiny tear in her flesh.

Wiping the soot out of her eyes, she saw the train doors burst open, releasing a mob of soldiers, half-drunk, shouting and singing, pouring down the platform toward the main body of the station. She blinked and glanced again at the one-armed soldier. Puzzled, she saw that the man had gone. She scanned the empty platform and surmised that he must have headed out of the station, on across the tracks.

Headlights glared in the tunnel as another train emerged and lumbered onto the track, belching soot. The express to Bandol had arrived. A small crowd gathered around the second and third class carriages. She rose, collected her things and dragged herself towards a first class carriage, where a handful of people disembarked. As she was about to climb on, there was a sudden uproar down at the other end of the platform near the third class carriages and she was dismayed to see the horde of drunken soldiers now rushing toward her train. The men ran along the platform, pushing people out of the way, jumping up to knock on the train windows, leaping aboard at every door. Horrified, she watched as civilian passengers and their bags were thrown off onto the platform. The soldiers were taking possession of the train, but there were still several carriages between her and the shouting mob. Perhaps they would not invade the first class carriages. She threw her bags on and scrambled up, just as a soldier a few cars down spotted her and bellowed, "*Madame, Arrêtez-vous!*"

The first compartment was locked, so was the second. The men had almost reached her carriage. She could hear the thundering of their boots down the corridor of the next carriage. There was more shouting on the platform. Frantic, she tried the third compartment. The door was stuck, but she put all her weight on it and pushed. She stumbled forward as it swung open, nearly landing in the lap of a young officer sitting by the window with a huge dog at his feet. The dog snapped viciously as Katherine groped to regain her balance, and the officer yanked it back on its leash, giving a harsh command in an unfamiliar language. There were five other men in the compartment, all dressed in officers' uniforms with braided epaulets and with cutlasses lashed to their waists. They looked at her astonished. She saw immediately that they were neither French nor English. For one sickening moment she feared they might be Germans.

"*S'il vous plaît*," she began, fixing her frightened eyes on the man holding the dog. "Is there a seat free? Please, I am not well. I must join my husband in Bandol tonight."

Before they could reply, three French soldiers burst into the carriage and stormed into their compartment.

"This train has been requisitioned. You must get off," barked one, grabbing her from behind by the waist, ready to hoist her off like a bundle of rugs.

Katherine opened her mouth to scream but all that came out was a strangled gasp.

One of the officers in the compartment jumped to his feet and shouted in clipped, guttural French, "That is my wife. She has joined me here for my period of leave. Release her immediately, otherwise you will have me to deal with," and he drew his cutlass with a flourish. The other men placed their hands on their decorative scabbards, and at this signal the dog growled. The fellow holding the dog slackened the chain and the animal strained forward, its black lip curled to reveal formidable incisors.

Katherine felt a thrill of terror as her self-proclaimed husband seized her by the arm, wrenched her from the French soldier and pulled her to his side. There was nothing to do but play the part, although her legs were trembling. She composed her face, bit her lip to keep from crying and tried to look demure as he crushed her protectively to his chest. The rough weave of his tunic scratched her face. She could smell the rank scent of his sweat.

"All right, all right," the scowling soldier grumbled. "But hide her out of sight!" They trampled on toward the next carriage.

As soon as the French soldiers had gone, the officer released his grip, clicked his heels in salute and offered her a seat by the window. One of the men tossed her bags into the overhead rack, kicked the door shut and fastened the lock, while another pulled down the window and jerked the curtains closed.

"Just until we leave the station. They must not see you here," her would-be husband reassured her.

Almost disbelieving this stroke of luck, Katherine leaned back in the seat and closed her eyes, trying to calm the pounding of her heart. Opening her eyes again, she found all six men staring at her with probing eyes. The only thing to do now was to pretend they were not there, at least for a few moments, so that she might define the boundaries of the private space she would be occupying for the next few hours. She began preparing herself for the journey as if she were alone in the compartment.

She smoothed down her skirt and spread her traveling rug across her lap. Removing a scented handkerchief from her handbag, she wiped her forehead and hands. Next she took out a comb and mirror and adjusted her hair. The dog, meanwhile, pushed its nose against her knees, demanding a caress, then dropped at her feet, panting.

Coolly, through eyes half-closed, she observed the men as they, in turn, observed her. She reflected that her pistol would have been quite useless against six men with knives, and a dog. Still, these officers seemed to be gentlemen and were certainly handsome enough. Ruddy blond with Slavic features, they all had that curious Slavic upward cut at the corner of the eyes, a stubble of reddish beard on sculpted cheekbones, soulful eyes and beautiful hands. It had been exciting to be contested by two armies. She allowed her fantasy to elaborate on the experience now that the danger had passed. She was already describing it to Murry in her mind. How jealous he would be!

The train idled in the station for over an hour. With the window closed, a sour smell of sweat and a doggish odor soon filled the compartment. Again she repressed the tickling in her throat and was grateful to the men because they refrained from smoking. Two of the officers spoke French, and all of them spoke German, which she spoke fluently, so time passed quickly in pleasant conversation. They were Serbians on leave. She told them that her husband, Jack, had been wounded while rescuing a comrade from German gunfire and that he was now in a hospital near Bandol. She had left her two small sons with their Aunt Ida in London to rush to his bedside. When they learned she was a war hero's wife, and possibly soon to be a widow, the Serbian officers treated her with due reverence, and she was so convincing that she half-believed the tale herself.

When the whistle blew and the train shunted forward, she peeked behind the dirty canvas curtain and was startled to see that one-armed soldier again, standing right below her window. Yes, there was no mistake. That was the fellow, all right, with the sickly yellow face and the empty sleeve. His eyes met hers with uncanny frankness and he smiled hideously, then brought his yellow hand to his lips to blow her a lecherous kiss. She dropped the edge of the curtain, coughed and nearly choked on the gurgling in her throat. When she finally caught her breath, the train bumped to a halt for five long minutes. Katherine peeped out again from behind the curtain as the train began to move forward. The soldier on the platform had vanished. A thought flashed through her mind and her pulse raced with fear: *Perhaps he had boarded her train!* Thank God with these officers she felt quite safe.

Hours and hours later, finally Bandol. The gallant Serbian officers handed down her luggage and with heartfelt sincerity wished her and her husband well. She almost felt ashamed for having lied to them, but then she was a writer. It was her business to tell lies, as long as they were interesting and did no harm. After saying goodbye to the Serbian boys, she felt alone and vulnerable again. She looked about the busy station, trying to get her bearings. Here too in Bandol, the station was teeming with soldiers, and also with nurses and orderlies, for several carloads of wounded men had just arrived on her train and were being carried off on stretchers and put into horse-drawn carts waiting outside the station. Suddenly remembering the one-armed man, her fear, briefly forgotten during the trip, now took shape again. She scanned the crowd, and to her immense relief, did not spot him. Had she really seen that fellow beneath the window as the train pulled out, or had it been a trick of her nervous imagination? She shuddered thinking of that hideous kiss. Surely she could not have imagined that.

The baggage car attendant informed her that her trunk would be sent on to her hotel the next day, so there was nothing else to do now but find a fiacre and go to the Hotel Beau Rivage. A porter fetched a driver for her, threw her bags on top of the cab, and helped her scramble up. Driving through the town, she saw many changes since she had last been there. There were fewer people about the streets, and many shops were boarded up. Long lines waited outside the bakery. A cart creaked past, heaped high with medical supplies and crutches. Pulling up outside the hotel, she was cheered to see the familiar garden with its waxy evergreen shrubs, pink japonica and lemon trees with ripening fruit. To think it had been snowing on the Channel! She paid the driver, climbed down, and ordered the man to carry her bags into the hotel.

Stepping into the main salon, she saw that the place was not what she remembered. The marble floor was dulled by a patina of dust. A stink of mutton disguised with mint and onions lingered in the air. The front desk was deserted, but from the half-open door behind it came the unconsoled bawling of an infant whom no one seemed to be tending. The child's crying jarred her nerves. She rang the bell and waited, leaning against the wooden counter, fearing her knees might buckle under her from sheer exhaustion. At last a strange woman with a puffy red face appeared at the top of the stairway, wiping her lips with a grubby napkin.

"May I help you, Madame?"

Katherine introduced herself. "*Vous n'avez -pas reçu ma lettre?*"

The woman shrugged. With the war, the mail was always delayed, but she had plenty of rooms, and wadding the napkin into her pocket, she invited Katherine to follow her upstairs. Madame led the way, rattling her ring of keys.

The hall was silent; the great stoves in the corridor were unlit. The floor chilled her feet through the thin soles of her shoes. Her old room was currently occupied by a gentleman traveler, but there was another suitable one next door. This one also had a view of the garden, and was closer to the lavatory. Katherine peeked out through the shutters. Cats prowled amid scraggly bushes. The begonias in Mme. Galle's flowerbeds had been replaced by rows of salad and

19

leeks. The price, twelve francs a day, was far too much, but she had no choice. The other rooms cost more, the proprietress informed her, for running water had been installed in them after the hotel had changed owners. Her room was still at the old price.

Katherine ordered a dinner of broth, toast, and a boiled egg for she could not face the idea of dining on tough mutton doctored with herbs. While waiting for her tray to be brought, she unpacked her carpetbag of the things she would need for the night: her nightgown and medicine bottles, Murry's picture in a tortoiseshell frame, and her little square traveling clock. Arranging these things on the bedside table, she reflected on how they defined her life: the photograph of her handsome, absent lover; the phials of colored pills. She took the gun out of her purse, slipped it into the drawer of the bedside table and turned the key just as the maid arrived with her dinner tray and a tepid hot water bottle. At ten o'clock, too tired to write even a brief note to Murry, she downed the rest of her brandy, and crept between icy sheets. She touched her wool-stockinged foot to the hot water bottle. It felt as cold as stone.

The man next door kept her awake nearly until dawn, for she could hear him coughing and shuffling about through the thin wall. Perhaps he too suffered from weak lungs and like her had come here trying to cheat the winter by anticipating the spring. No doubt he was also an insomniac, and moreover, he seemed to be afflicted by dysentery. At least three times in the night she heard him plodding down to the lavatory, where he produced a cavernous sputtering of sounds which at first amused, then annoyed and at last simply exhausted her. His feet scuffled across the floor as he returned to his own room, jiggled the key, and shut the door firmly. Once it seemed to her that he had paused outside her door and she could hear him breathing. What was he doing out there loitering in the corridor? Waiting for a sign of invitation from a woman traveling alone? How could she bear up under all this? She could not even demand a different room, for the others were all too expensive.

By morning a mistral was blowing. The shutters banged and rattled; the wind whistled through the cracks in the plaster. She opened the window and pushed the shutter back against the force of the wind to see palm fronds flapping and mimosa trees in bud tossing wildly against a livid sky. She stayed inside till noon when the wind dropped, and then ventured out for a walk in town to do a little shopping. There were no cigarettes at the tobacco shop, only cigars. The stationer's was boarded up, so there was no writing paper to be had. There was a foreclosure notice pasted in the window of what had once been her favorite pastry shop. She called at the grocer's where she and Murry used to shop for sundries, but the shopkeeper did not recognize her. The prices were outrageous, much more expensive than London. She dawdled before half-empty shelves, making mental calculations of francs and sous and finally selected a tiny pot of raspberry jam and some almond biscuits for teatime, although she could ill-afford such luxuries. As she stood counting out her coins beside the cash desk, Madame looked up from the *jambon* she was slicing, frowned at Katherine and said, "*Madame, mais c'est vous*...You are much changed. You have not been well."

A boy brought a chair and Katherine was obliged to take her place among a row of flour and lentil sacks slumped against the wall and listen to the town gossip for nearly an hour. So much had changed because of the war, so much had been swept away so quickly. Mme. Galle had died. Her son had been badly wounded. The bread in town had become indigestible because the bakers mixed sawdust in their flour. So many brave young men gone, the music master and the doctor's son. Finally weary of this recitation of catastrophe, Katherine rose to take her leave. The shopkeeper peered at her curiously and asked with a hint of insinuation in her voice, "But this time has Madame come without Monsieur?" Katherine provided a respectable excuse for Murry's absence, as if the war weren't enough, and though she spoke calmly, she felt the blood rush to her cheeks.

Returning to the hotel, she reminded herself that she could expect no letters from home as yet, for it would take at least eight days for the mail to get through. How would she survive until Murry's letters arrived? She stared at the row of empty boxes behind the front desk, at the two tarnished brass keys dangling side by side: the key to her room and to the one next to hers. All the other rooms were unoccupied for only the desperate or criminals travel in wartime. She and the gentleman next door probably had more in common than she imagined. Sooner or later, she thought, as she trod up the stairs, she would have to make his acquaintance and join him in the smoky dining room for roast mutton and haricots with vinegar, of which he was apparently too fond, given his nightly performances in the lavatory.

In the afternoon she tried to work, sitting at the window, propped up on cushions, wrapped up in rugs. After all, that was what she had come here for. For her health, yes, to avoid the London cold, but also to work. Murry had given her a stack of books to review for the literary magazine he edited and her finances depended on those few pennies he promised to pay her per inch. But she hadn't counted on such a nerve-rattling wind. The kitchen maid had no idea how to fix a proper pot of tea and had brought her up a pint of dirty liquid with three tea leaves floating on top, which she had left untouched. After several false starts, she threw down her pen. The flow would not come as she bid it. How could she be expected to hold up through all this? She rubbed her eyes and stared out the window at a scrawny cat slinking through a laurel hedge. She wondered now why she had ever come here alone. Ida would have at least offered some distraction.

Her black mood had descended. The only way to throw it off was to take a walk somewhere. A small amount of physical exertion. Get a bit of air in her lungs. She bundled up, clapped on a hat, and swathed her throat like a mummy. Leaving her key at the desk on her way out, she saw a white envelope sticking out of the box behind the desk and nearly jumped for joy. Murry must have found a way to dispatch letters quickly through the War Office. The proprietress handed her the letter with a smirk, saying, "*Bonnes nouvelles, j'espère.*"

Katherine's face fell as she recognized the childish scrawl. It was only from Ida. She mumbled a response and went out. As she walked down the boulevard, reading her letter, the wind nearly tore it out of her hand.

Katie dear, said the letter, *I have posted this before you leave, so that it will be waiting for you when you get there. Although it is funny, as after all, you are here with me asleep in the next room. It's as if there were two of you. The one here with me and the other far away in Bandol reading this now. I hope you like the surprise.* Love Ida

Katherine was furious. How absurd it was to be loved so devotedly by the wrong person! She crumpled the letter into her pocket and continued briskly down the boulevard, the wind stinging her cheeks red. Thank goodness Ida was not there to torment her.

The wind swept her along, exhilarating her. However the town had changed since her last visit, the landscape was still inspiring with a foaming violet sea, mauve pebbles along the beach, little red boats tossing near the shore, although the gray hulk of a warship looming further out added an ominous touch to the scene. Rounding the curve of the little road leading out of town, she darted down a country lane, skirted a vineyard where dead leaves shivered on the vines, and found her way to the Villa Pauline, where she and Murry had stayed when they had last been in Bandol.

She was sad to see the house abandoned, the pink facade crumbling, the plaster peeling, one dark green shutter banging loose in the wind. Still she had never realized how beautiful it was. Only now, gazing through the gate at the tangled garden, did she understand how much she had lost and how much she still had to lose. She recognized the wrought iron chairs now rusted where she and Murry had once sat discussing Dostoevsky and Chekhov. She pressed her face against the cold iron grille of the garden gate. How was it possible that the villa had gone to ruin in just two short years? A swampy, fetid odor of decaying leaves hung in the air, mingled with the smell of wood smoke from the chimney of a nearby house. She pushed the gate open then hesitated. Perhaps she really did not want to explore any further. It had been a grave mistake to leave Murry in London and come back to Bandol alone. She certainly could not get any work done here with this burden on her heart.

The walk back was further than she remembered. She had to stop to take small cautious breaths for her left lung scorched her chest like a red-hot iron. Lights came on across the bay as she crept down the boulevard back to the hotel.

At the café across the street, the pink-striped awning, not yet rolled up for the night, swelled and flapped in the strong wind. A lone, hatless figure sat at a table along the street, wrapped in a greatcoat, smoking a cigarette. The hair prickled on the back of Katherine's neck as she stared at the man, for it seemed to her she recognized the odd stoop of his shoulders, the limp sleeve, the colorless hair. The one-armed soldier! He had followed her all the way to her hotel in Bandol! He must not see me, she thought, as she dashed across the street, summoning energy from some untapped abyss, and nearly colliding with a delivery boy on a bicycle. Glancing back before pushing through the hotel door, she saw the man squarely in the face. A doubt assailed her. This fellow was fatter and had a moustache. The man rose and shuffled off down the street with a cane. Both his arms were perfectly intact.

It was the wind, she thought, the wind had agitated her imagination and had played tricks on her eyes. Relieved, she went to the desk and demanded her key.

"Madame should not have gone out in this wind," chided the proprietress.

She supped in her room on broth and a boiled egg, then sat at the table by the shuttered window, trying to work, but a gale had begun to blow. With the wind howling and the rain battering the window panes, she almost felt as though she were on a ship miles from the coast. Shelley must have drowned in such a squall, she thought, closing her notebook. There was nothing to do but crawl into bed with her little worn volume of Shakespeare. It was just the night for *The Tempest* or perhaps *The Winter's Tale*. She read for an hour, underlining archaic words to look up in her dictionary the next morning.

Just before she was about to put out the light, something strange happened. She had a little coughing fit, and felt once more that lacerating spasm in her back and shoulder. An unfamiliar tang filled her mouth and she brought her handkerchief to her lips. A small bright red blob stained her handkerchief. She examined the blot. It was not the viscous black color of menstruation, but frothy crimson, yet only a small spot, surely nothing to worry about. Lawrence had told her that he too sometimes coughed up blood. *My dear, it is absolutely nothing to worry about*, she found herself saying aloud in the empty room. But what would she tell Murry if it should happen again? The poor boy would be frightened out of his wits.

Too restless to sleep, she got up and took out Ida's letter, read it again by lamplight and sighed. How silly and yet how thoughtful. Dear Ida! She smoothed out the creased page, lay it on her breast, put out the lamp and finally fell asleep just as she felt Ida's letter slipping to the floor. Long after midnight, she sat up with a start. Had there been a noise at the door or had it been a dream? The moon shining in through the slats of the shutters cast a ladder of light across the floor. The noise was repeated, a scuffling sound in the corridor right outside her room. Staring through the moonlight at the door, she saw the brass handle move slightly.

She unlocked the drawer of the bedside table, took out the pistol and pointed it at the door. Finger on the trigger, she sat bolt upright, her back pressed against the cold brass rail of the bedstead. The handle jiggled again. Her heart was hammering in her ears and she nearly gagged on her own fear, but still she managed to cry out, "*Qu'est-ce que vous voulez?*" Throwing off the covers, she climbed out of bed, leapt to the door and thrust it open with a bang.

There was no one in the corridor, but the blue smoke of a cigarette swirled up in the beam of a lamp still guttering at this late hour along the hall. Beneath the door of the next room, a thread of light shone upon a strip of worn red carpet. She stood there listening, alert to any sound, but heard only the silence of a sleeping hotel. Then the gentleman next door coughed once, discreetly, as if to signal to her.

Stepping back inside, she shut the door firmly, turned the key twice, then looked round the room, in search of something to bar the door with. The oaken bedside table was far too heavy for her to manage, but the armchair would do very well. She dragged the chair from its corner by the window and pushed it up against the door, then fell into bed exhausted.

A bold ray of sun breaking through a chink in the shutter awakened her early in the morning. Outside, the wind had finally dropped. The bedclothes felt clammy, a few strands of dampish hair were stuck to the nape of her neck. The woolen singlet beneath her nightgown clung to her bosom. Damn! She had been sweating in the night again. Sitting up in bed, she noticed the chair against the door and acknowledged with a sigh that last night's episode had not, alas, been merely a dream, after all. She got up and moved the chair back to its original position, although the effort made her arms ache. Slipping back under the covers, she lay in a doze, half-listening to the sounds around her. Footsteps down the corridor. A clanging in the pipes. A tinker passing in the street with his cart. When the maid pounded on the door to wake her at ten o' clock, Katherine got up again, threw on her dressing gown, unlocked the door, then sank into the armchair, as the maid set down her breakfast tray and burst open the shutters to a flood of sunlight.

Taking the tray with toast and eggs and tea in her lap, she began eating eagerly, amazed by her own appetite. This time the tea was more palatable than yesterday's dishwater. Her hunger was a good sign, she thought, and she knew she must eat to keep up her strength. The change of air must already be working its magic.

After breakfast she hobbled down the stairs, for her knees and hips were stiffer than usual, and out to the garden, carrying a bag containing her rugs, books, and papers. She intended to make headway with her work this morning. Madame had arranged a wrought iron table and chair for her in a sunny nook, but to Katherine's displeasure, she saw no cushion had been provided to protect her from the damp chill of the metal chair. Going back up all those stairs again was quite out of the question.

Madame was nowhere to be seen. Katherine looked up at the windows, her eyes searching for the maid who appeared a few moments later in a window below Katherine's room, laying bedclothes to air over the windowsill. "*Mademoiselle...*" Katherine cried out, and waved, but the girl hurriedly stuck her head back inside, pretending not to have seen her. Why are servants in foreign hotels always so elusive when one needs something? It must be part of their training, she thought. She would just have to do without a cushion. Folding a rug in half, she lay it on the seat, sat down, and settled into her chair. Despite this protection, she could feel the cold in her thighs and buttocks shooting all the way up her spine. She sighed. Her rheumatism had made her even more sensitive than the princess and the pea. Only thirty years old and nearly a cripple.

Her table and chair were set beneath an arbor where the old wooden lattice sagged under the weight of a jasmine vine already covered in thick buds so early in the season. A few tiny white blooms had opened prematurely, releasing their sweet spicy scent to the tepid, welcoming sun. Watching in delight as yellow and black bees droned among the flowers, she reflected how extraordinary it was that her illness, though debilitating her physically, had given her the power to truly *see* the things around her. A leaf, a teacup, an edge of lace on a curtain acquired a sheen, a volume, an intricacy they did not previously possess. This brought to mind impressions of her childhood, when she used to sit happily on the ground in the garden of their house in Tinakori Road, back in Wellington, watching for hours as a line of ants trekked along the edge of an aloe spear. Had she known such happiness since then? There was a radiance in the sunlight then. *Where has it gone, the glory and the dream?* Sometimes a high fever brought the same sharp-edged vividness, and once, under the influence of drugs, she had experienced something similar, when Aleister Crowley had given her hashish cakes to eat and afterwards she had sat on the floor arranging matchsticks in geometrical patterns all afternoon. Yet even that had only been a shadow of what she felt now, while watching a sparkling dewdrop slide down a lily stamen. The act of observation was so intensely absorbing, she felt as though she were enclosed in a dome of light that blocked out all other impressions.

But she must now take up her books, for in order to keep on schedule, she had to complete one review by lunchtime. She had promised Murry to send three reviews by the end of the week. She took out the packet of three books from her bag. She had not even had time to open the parcel before; slipping out the first volume, she read the title and groaned. Another boring domestic novel about modern couples wounded in their sex.

Why must she waste her time and energy reading and actually writing about worthless books like these? The reason, of course, was a simple one with which she could not argue. She needed the money to cover her expenses while traveling abroad, and everything cost so much more than she had expected. Still, if she had a truly worthy companion, a man like Virginia Woolf's husband, Leonard, she would not now be required to squander her precious energies in such menial tasks. Did Virginia know how lucky she was to have a man whose devotion to her allowed her to work? A man like Leonard Woolf, so wise and witty, suave and urbane, so gentlemanly and solicitous, and so unlike Murry, who drove Katherine like a slave over those reviews and for whom she was now required to sacrifice part of her own allowance in order to pay back the printers debts on his magazine. A man so easily taken in by flighty females with heaving, fleshy bosoms; a man who did not even know, until she herself had taught him, how to peel and eat an egg properly in public! What sort of a man was that?

Then again, in all sincerity, she knew she and Murry would never change places with Virginia and Leonard—an odd couple they were in the end. Her friend Gertler called the Woolfs: "Joseph and Mary" and indeed that grave epithet seemed very fitting. Virginia was so passionless and as cool as a slab of alabaster. The sex act aroused no feelings in her whatsoever, as she had once candidly confessed to Katherine, not even revulsion or distaste—just disinterest. She could not understand why people went on so about it, let alone why they allowed their lives to be ruled by it. In this regard, Virginia was so different from Katherine for she could not thrive without physical affection and was as keen for sex as a savage. Yet Leonard, indeed an attractive man, loved and desired Virginia, stood by her, and ministered to her through thick and thin.

She remembered now their first dinner together in Richmond. For months she had wanted to meet Virginia, as she had so admired her novel *A Voyage Out*, but the aristocratic Woolfs dwelt within a realm far removed from the world to which she and Murry belonged, with their bedsitters and printers debts. Then Lytton Strachey had taken a fancy to her, and had intervened to organize a meeting, and a week later they had been invited to dinner at the Woolfs' home one Friday evening in January.

Sleet as fine and penetrating as needles hissed on the pavement, drummed on the taut, stretched silk of the umbrella that Murry held over her head, as they dashed out of the station, late, as usual, for their dinner engagement. Hogarth House was just around the corner from the Richmond station, so Murry had sensibly insisted there was certainly no need for a cab, but by the time they reached the imposing brick house on Paradise Road, they were soaked through. Dinner could not be served until they had dried themselves a bit by the fire, and servants had come and gone with armloads of warm towels.

That night the dinner had been fine filets of plaice smothered in a creamy yellow sauce with herbs accompanied by heady Alsatian wine. The silver was so beautifully polished, Katherine could see the reflection of her eyes in her spoons and knives. The cook herself had brought in the dessert: a trifle of chocolate, mint, and rum, which everyone had praised. Virginia's cook, Nelly, was a buxom matron with a red face, primly attired in a stiff black dress, a starched white cap and a lace-trimmed apron, just like a governess in a Victorian storybook. If only there were a Nelly in her life. Those chafed but competent red hands turned out endless banquets of roasts, scones, gravies and apple tarts, all for the pleasure of her mistress, who, Katherine imagined, began the mornings by giving orders to her staff with all the authority of a queen. *There will be twenty-five guests for dinner. For breakfast, I should like strawberries and cream. Please serve the coffee at eleven. I am not to be disturbed until then.* How different from Katherine's own household where very often the only help was Ida: Ida burning the cutlets or scorching the toast or boiling the eggs till the yolk turned green, and Murry sitting there staring in stony reproach at the food on his plate, saying not a word.

Over dinner they had talked about Katherine's work and Virginia had told her that she and Leonard had decided to buy a printing press to publish their own books, and those of their friends. Katherine too might contribute a book to the list. At this news, Katherine had felt a prickling of pure envy. In Virginia's writing she found such a serene and unruffled freedom, as though she were undisturbed by disappointment or distraction, always safe and at peace under her own roof, surrounded by comfort, with her man at her side; while Katherine had to manage with unheated bedsitters, tea at the ABC, and an ambivalent and reticent Murry. Now to Virginia's cornucopia would be added her own publishing house. Her life was complete in all ways, except, perhaps, that she had no children of her own and had to make do with her nephews and nieces. One need not enjoy sex to produce offspring and yet Virginia and Leonard had none forthcoming, as far as Katherine could tell. Perhaps things between the Woolfs were not as ideal as they seemed. Even Ida, she imagined, would sooner or later have to marry and have children and she and Murry would play aunt and uncle. And how *did* Virginia manage without physical passion? Could she really be as frigid as she appeared?

Physical passion indeed had become a great problem for Katherine, when it had never been so in the past. She had always felt free to express and satisfy her desires with whomever she chose, but now that her health had become more delicate, Murry seemed to have grown colder in that way towards her, yet she yearned for him more strongly than before. Sometimes before falling asleep, she would evoke the warmth of his body lying upon hers, the scent of tobacco and cologne on his skin, and the cold, smoky smell of his hair when he came in from the street in the evening. She still dreamed of giving him a child, but the doctors all agreed that she could no longer bear children.

The pen fell from her grasp and rolled under the table. With a shock she realized she had been sitting there over half an hour dreaming, hardly aware of an icy chill that had begun to blow ever so slightly against her neck, where a gland now throbbed. She pulled her shawl tighter, then leaned over to retrieve the pen. Sitting up again, she heard footsteps on the path behind her, and Madame the proprietress's voice rang out gaily,

"A visitor, Madame! A visitor from England!"

Katherine drew in a sharp breath, imagining that Murry had come, but from the tread of thick-soled shoes crunching impatiently along the gravel, she knew it could not be her future husband. Murry never hurried on any occasion, if he could avoid it, but always walked at a solemn, easy stride. Certainly he had never rushed towards her with such impetuosity. A voice breathy with excitement called out her name. It was Ida.

Katherine stiffened in her chair; her face turned crimson. Without deigning to glance at her visitor, she said, "I told you not to come."

"Oh Katie, I couldn't bear to think of you here alone. I promise I won't get in the way."

Katherine, her face still averted, opened her book and pretended to read.

"I am afraid, Jones, that is impossible."

"And I'll be here to do any errands you need. Going to the post office, shopping, helping with your laundry so you needn't send it out."

Katherine was suddenly aware that the proprietress still hovered nearby behind the thick fronds of a palm, watching with smug amusement this meeting between the two English ladies. What was she doing there, eavesdropping in the shrubs, when surely she knew not a word of English? Turning to the woman, Katherine ordered her to serve her lunch on a tray in her room. When the proprietress had sidled back down the path, Katherine unleashed her fury upon Ida.

"We agreed you were not to come this time. I am quite well and I do not need your assistance."

Ida, silent, stared down at her scuff-toed shoes.

"So tomorrow you can just get back on the train and go home."

"I have brought you rum babas from Paris," said Ida meekly, proffering a squashed brown paper bag which Katherine declined to take.

Ida stuffed the bag into her overcoat pocket and broke into tears. "Since Jack couldn't get leave, I thought you might need help."

At the mention of Murry, Katherine relented, observing Ida as she wiped her eyes with a grayish handkerchief. "Did he give you anything for me?" she asked.

"He sends you his love."

Katherine's mouth tightened. "No letters? No books or parcels?" She checked herself from saying, "No money?"

"He said he would be sending out a new parcel of books by the end of the week. He said I should help you by copying out all your articles for you, if you need me to."

Katherine considered this briefly. Ida's secretarial help just might make her work easier. "Very well. I suppose you may stay until ..." She did not say, "until Jack comes" — for she knew now that Ida was here, Murry would not be coming until perhaps the spring, if at all. "Until as long as necessary. But what has become of the cat if you are here?"

"Oh Katie, I am sorry to say, Jack let him out the front door, and he just bolted. I looked everywhere but couldn't find him. We suspect he has been adopted by the neighbor's children, and may be held prisoner in their garden. Jack promised to investigate and write you immediately."

Katherine sighed. One leaves one's home in other people's hands, and everything goes to the dogs. Murry himself was probably now prisoner in someone's bedroom—Lady Ottoline's—she could imagine it very well. She had seen Ottoline make advances to him in the gardens at Garsington on the pretense of showing him a vegetable plot.

"I'll be having lunch in my room, Jones, and then I am going straight to bed."

"Shall I accompany you for an afternoon walk?"

"No, not today. Yesterday I wore myself out by walking too far. But you may join me for tea in my room later on."

"Oh, Katie, thank you so much. I promise to be as discreet as possible."

Ida leaned over and touched her lips to Katherine's cheek, and this time Katherine did not turn away.

"My goodness, Katie! Your cheek is like ice! You are going to catch a chill out here, I think. Let me help you carry your things inside." Ida quickly gathered up the books, papers, and rugs, and helped pull Katherine up from the chair. Getting up, Katherine felt a sharp pain in her hip, but managed to stifle a cry of discomfort.

Ida chided, "You know you shouldn't sit outside without a proper cushion."

As they exited the garden and entered the wide glass doors, Katherine uneasily surveyed the tall flight of stairs leading to the upper floors and took a deep breath, as though before a dive.

"Jones, I must ask you a question."

"Of course, Katie, what is it?"

"How much money have you brought?"

"A bit."

"We're going to need every penny."

Pausing at the desk where Madame the proprietress stood studying a ledger, Katherine ordered, "Lunch for two in my room, please," and leaning on Ida's arm, headed for the stairs.

. . .

Ida sat at a desk in the dark hall near the entrance, going over Katie's accounts, adding up the columns of figures with sheer dismay. Was it possible that an extra cup of milk at breakfast could cost so much? Not to mention the extra servings of cream, *confiture*, meat, and fresh fruit? That to launder and iron three chemises, ten handkerchiefs, and two nightgowns could be so expensive? Aside from the robbery of the hotel food and services, there were the other expenses as well. Katie's medicine. Her stationery. Stamps for her correspondence. The blood oranges from Seville delivered daily by the grocer's daughter for Katie's tonic. No fewer than six or seven oranges a day, squeezed into a dark pulpy nectar. Now that Ida was here, preparing Katie's orange juice tonic for her mid-morning refreshment was one of her important tasks, along with supervising more nutritious meals with the hotel cook. Left to herself Katie could live indefinitely on boiled eggs and toast, if only in order to have fewer distractions from her work, for having to decide on what to eat was a time-consuming chore. Then there were the flowers. When Katie sat down to work, she demanded that there be flowers on her desk. But what nerve to charge so outrageously for a spray of mimosa or a single, slender iris probably plucked from the hotel garden. What was this about twelve francs for embroidered baby bibs? Gifts, Katie had explained, for a friend's baby not yet born. The young girls here in Bandol did such beautiful embroidery. Katie's explanation had not fooled Ida, who knew of the secret stash of baby things Katie kept hidden in pink tissue paper at the bottom of her trunk, dreaming of a child that would never be born, for Katie, they both knew, could no longer bear children. And the ceramic candy dishes and the crystal vase? More extravagances she could not resist, precious knickknacks for her future home with Murry. He posed no objections when Katie squandered all her money on collectibles, but Ida had a horror of all these fragile china and crystal objects that must be packed to perfection and lugged back across the Channel until Katie found the real home she yearned for. If anything got broken it was always Ida's fault. Katie had already chosen a name for the house where she and Murry would live as man and wife, once her divorce from George Bowden came through and they had had time to find a suitable place. They would call it the Heron in honor of Leslie Heron Beauchamp, Katie's beloved brother who died in the war. Then Ida would have to take a furnished room somewhere, hopefully not too far away, and make do with afternoon teas with Katie, and an occasional dinner party. Ida did not relish the idea of the Heron in the least and was glad that Murry was too busy with his own work to go house hunting while Katie was abroad.

She turned the pages of the leather-bound account book in despair. Would Katie never learn to manage her money? Ida too felt so inadequate and she sometimes made the most awful mistakes. Just last night, she had ordered a fried egg for dinner. It wasn't on the hotel menu, but she had wanted something plain and thought it would cost less than the more elaborate dishes listed. Katie had finished her own *pot-au-feu* long before Ida's dinner was served. Visibly exhausted and doubtless wanting nothing other than to go upstairs and crawl into bed, she kept staring at the empty place setting before Ida.

Then at last, a platter had been brought with an enormous *soufflé omelette* made with at least six eggs, which had cost three times more than any of the other dishes. Ida had been so famished she ate the whole thing, while Katie looked on disgusted.

The omelette had been delicious, but Katie had been furious, and rightly so, Ida now realized after glancing through Kathie's accounts and roughly calculating how little money was left. Murry had sent not a penny for all the reviews Katie had done, and she could not draw on her allowance as it had been pledged to pay back a debt to the printers on behalf of Murry's magazine. Unless Katie's father came forward with more funds, she—they—would soon be penniless. But Katie was too proud to ask her father for any more money, fearing he might discover Murry's insolvency and decide to interrupt payment of her allowance altogether. Mr. Beauchamp did not quite approve of Murry. The two of them could live on credit at the hotel for awhile longer, she supposed, but then? Until Murry delivered promised funds they were at the mercy of the hotel proprietress and the greengrocer.

But Katie was working on her own stories again, perhaps a little too feverishly, and this cheered Ida's spirits for it made life with Katie so much easier. Work was the only thing that distracted Katie from her spells of depression and ill-health. Ida did not mind the long hours of solitude she spent away from Katie's company while Katie was working. It was enough for her to know Katie was there in the next room, sitting hours at her little cramped table, with a fur muff around her feet, and a hot water bottle lashed to her spine, reading or writing furiously. It was Ida's task to make sure that she was not disturbed, and to see that the necessities of the day could be tended to without Katie having to lift her head from the page.

31

To Ida's mind, their daily routine here in Bandol was perfect. If only it could always be like this, that would be her view of Heaven. She helped Katie dress in the morning and brushed her shining, fragrant hair. Even Katie had to admit how expert Ida had become at this chore, after her recent job as a hairdressing assistant in Hampstead. They breakfasted in Katie's room, after which Katie demanded to be left alone to write, in the garden, weather permitting, or in her room. Ida would discreetly withdraw to pass the morning hours, walking along the seafront with her cape flapping in the wind, or more frequently, doing errands for Katie like going to the post office or the stationer's. Ida had found a stationer's shop way across town with the loveliest notebooks and fine blue writing paper that Katie adored. It was quite a walk, and she had to pass a tavern where the *patron*, a fat little Frenchman with a gleaming, bald head and a dirty white apron spread across his paunch, called out to her from the doorway as she hurried by, inviting her inside. What did this man want from her? Although she never deigned to look at him, the baldness of his head fascinated her. How did his head get so shiny? Perhaps he rubbed oil on it—and this seemed so silly that Ida had to press her lips tight to keep from laughing out loud as she marched past, her eyes fixed on a distant point up ahead. This was a trick Katie had taught her in their schooldays. A faraway look coupled with a steady stride was guaranteed to make one invisible to men when wandering the streets alone. Katie knew other tricks, too, such as how to make every single head turn when one steps into a room, but Ida had no use for those things. She hated to be observed by strangers. Being looked at by a man was nearly as bad as being flayed alive.

Once the danger was past, and the *patron* had grumbled a word and gone back inside, she slowed her pace and enjoyed the walk. When all the errands were done and the packages secure in her little furry bag made from a worn squirrel skin, she visited the haberdashery not far from the stationer's, where, despite her execrable French, she had made the acquaintance of the elderly woman who kept the shop. For nearly an hour, she would dawdle over the trays of lace trimmings or silk embroidery skeins that the old lady pulled out to show her, and bob her head as the woman chattered on amiably, though she understood less than half of what the woman said. She always came away from the shop with a little packet containing some bit of lace trimming for Katie's underwear or a new fine lawn handkerchief for Katie although they really couldn't afford such luxuries. Still Ida would rather go without meat for herself in order to buy Katie the niceties she deserved. She knew how fine Katie desired to be, down to the most hidden details: the silk bands around her stockings, the lace on her chemises, the lavender sachets with which she scented her nightgowns. Few people except Ida herself, Katie, of course, and Murry, had had the privilege of touching those secret silk wisps and ribbons.

Ida always made sure she was back before noon, when Katie took her tonic even if she had to run half the way with her long hair flying behind her, and then the decrepit old men with brown faces like wizened potatoes, lined up outside the cafés would laugh with toothless grins as she hurried by. Then there was just time to see to some small task for herself in her room like rinsing out stockings or sewing on a button before it was time for lunch. There was always a button missing from her blouse or a thread hanging, or a hem half-unstitched, and Katie would sternly reprimand her for being so untidy. Katie believed a woman should be perfect, but Ida never managed to look her best. Something always marred the picture: bitten nails or scuffed boots or a grease spot on her collar. But it couldn't be helped, and she prayed that Katie would not love her the less for her imperfections.

Sometimes they lunched in the dining hall, but generally they had lunch in Katie's room. Katie's stomach was queasy these days; she couldn't bear some of the stronger kitchen smells, like cabbage or pork. After lunch they rested, each in her own room and Ida allowed herself to take a delicious half hour nap. Katie never slept in the day. She lay beneath the covers with a pile of books, reading voraciously. In the afternoons, when Katie felt up to it, they took a walk sometimes as far as the sea. Katie loved the sea in all seasons. She would stand in rapture, eyes closed, hair blowing, oblivious to the bitterest winds, following distinct melodies which Ida could not discern. Katie could hear woodwinds and cellos in the roaring of the sea, but all Ida heard was a pounding and a crashing and a breaking up of stones.

When Katie was well enough, they dined downstairs, retiring early for cigarettes and cognac in Katie's room, though Ida did not really care for either. She indulged only to keep Katie company but they were both quite happy to avoid the obligatory after dinner chatter one must make in hotels, though there were hardly any other guests at all, except for an elderly gentleman, and an occasional traveler who came for a night. Ida assisted Katie's preparations for bed, and helped her slide in between the bedclothes, for the maid tucked the covers in so tightly turning down the sheets was like prying open a clamshell. Sometimes Katie needed her legs or shoulders massaged, then after a chaste kiss on the cheek, Ida returned to her own room, to wait an hour or two, listlessly turning the pages of a book until the hotel was silent. Once the way to the lavatory had been trod by any other guests on their floor and their shutters had been closed; keys turned; lights in the hall put out, Ida would steal back to Katie's room, carrying her pillows and blankets. Katie unlocked the door at her signal—a tap-tap so soft that not even the gentleman next door could hear. Once inside, Ida locked the door, and pushed the armchair up against it for Katie feared nocturnal intruders, and the night before Ida's arrival, someone had attempted to enter her room, probably by mistake.

Arranging her pillows on the floor by Katie's bed, she made a sort of nest for herself where she would spend the night, ready to spring to Katie's aid should Katie call out for her. She always made sure Katie was fast asleep before she let her own eyelids flutter shut in sweet exhaustion. Waking early, way before dawn, her back and shoulders aching from the hard, damp floor, Ida would tiptoe back to her own room and collapse into her narrow little bed till the maid roused her at ten. It was so rare now for Katie to invite her beneath the covers as she once did long ago in their schooldays. This was a loss to which she was not completely resigned. The memory of those thrilling hours, the touch of Katie's fragrant skin smelling of orange blossoms and musk, the warmth of her body pressed close in a passion Ida had so reluctantly welcomed and then even more reluctantly renounced, had not yet faded entirely from her yearning body. That memory was like the warmth lingering in a stone when the sun has slipped behind a cloud. But sometimes still now, Katie would let Ida take her head in her lap and stroke her hair when she had fever or was rudely awakened by a nightmare. After all these years, Katie was still tormented by night terrors, and Ida's presence was the only thing, besides Murry's own, of course, that soothed her. Ida doubted Katie had ever shown Murry this vulnerable side. Ida's nightly visits were a secret they had shared since they were girls. And nothing, not even Murry himself, could ever change that.

What would life be without Katie? There would be no poetry or joy, but only the dreary business of getting on, of shuffling along the gray sunless corridor that was her life, leading from nowhere to nowhere. Other women in other houses in brightly lit rooms had husbands and children to cherish. Sometimes, while traveling with Katie, when their train pulled away from a station, hurtling past rows of modest houses illuminated in the dusk, Ida tried to imagine herself in one of those stuffy sitting rooms with faded floral wallpaper, serving tea to a brood of children, sitting next to a portly husband, a respectable-looking man with a moustache and a brown corduroy suit. But she could not hold the picture in her mind for long. Ida knew nothing of men. Their largeness, their whiskers, their smell, their hairy hands, alarmed her. The only men she really knew, besides family or work colleagues, were Katie's acquaintances and a couple of fellows from Rhodesia, cousins of childhood friends, to whom she wrote charitable letters now that they were in the war. She had never been kissed on the mouth by a man, and frankly she could not imagine anything more disgusting. Her own father had smoked cigars, and even kissing him on the cheek after he had been smoking had been nauseating enough. How Katie had laughed when she had confessed that to her. But she had been kissed by Katie years ago—a brushing of Katie's lips with inebriating sips of breath. Katie's mouth, as soft as a thistle, had sipped and sucked and teased every inch of her skin till she glowed from within and cried out in an unimaginable joy and Katie had smothered her cries yet again with another kiss. And she had given herself up to it with a groan, her heavy body had fallen lax beneath Katie's fervor. Had it been wrong to yield to Katie's desire? Katie's mother certainly thought so. Mrs. Beauchamp had tried to separate them forever by having Ida's father call her back to Rhodesia and by sending Katie to Bavaria for a cold water cure, guaranteed to wash out unhealthy tendencies in women. But there had been no need for such drastic measures, for soon after Katie simply stopped wanting her that way. She had quickly found a new lover in Bavaria, Floryan, a young Polish student. Not a word had been spoken about this change of feelings, but a coldness had descended between them, and ever since then Katie seemed even to shun her touch at times.

But what was she doing here, dreaming of Katie's kisses? There was still a small pile of bills from the chemist to be entered in the accounts. She recorded the figures in the proper column of the account book, lay down her pen and sighed. She glanced at her watch. Four o'clock. The hotel was quiet at this hour in the afternoon. The blinds were drawn in the west window, the hall was half in shadow. The proprietress was out on an errand, her little cubicle behind the desk was locked. From the kitchen came the smell of buttery pastry baking in the oven. Katie was still resting. Around five o'clock, she would go up to fetch Katie for their afternoon walk.

Why was it that all these hotels looked alike? Wherever one traveled: France or Switzerland or England, one seemed to end up in the same sort of place. There was a huge broken clock, a pile of old newspapers, and a tarnished copper pot holding forlorn umbrellas. There was always the head of some slain animal staring with vacuous glass eyes from above an unlit hearth. This one was a massive boar's head. Its flaring nostrils and sanctimonious frown reminded her, ludicrously, of her father, the deceased Colonel Baker, whom she could not bear to think of without a spasm of guilt and sorrow. He had committed the unpardonable, the unspeakable, he had put a gun to his head and blown his brains out in order to save himself from loneliness. Wretched, ungrateful daughter that she was, abandoning him to that remote farm in Rhodesia, to follow Katie around Europe. A lump came to her throat, and she choked back her tears. Her first loyalty was to Katie, whatever that might cost her.

She heard a noise on the stair. A faint rustle, a light step. She looked up over the tops of her glasses straight into the mirror at the foot of the stairs, and saw Katie stealthily descending in her stocking feet.

"Katie, is that you?" she called, "I've been here going over the accounts and it seems to me that you, I mean we, have been spending far, far too much. How much are we paying for milk a meter? How silly of me! I meant to say, a liter?"

She rose and went to the bottom of the stairs to meet Katie who had stopped midway down to slip her shoes on. Katie was dressed to go out, wearing her camel hair coat and a brown cloche, but no shawl.

Ignoring Katie's attempt to sneak away undetected, Ida said only, "Shouldn't you be wearing a warmer coat if you're planning to go out?"

"I'm just going out to sit in the garden in a sunny spot, where it is quite warm, out of the wind."

"No, no. That will never do. Let me run up and get you something warmer."

"Please, Jones, I don't need anything. Please don't trouble yourself."

"It's no trouble, no trouble at all!" cried Ida and she bounded up the steps two at a time, nearly knocking Katie over in her haste.

Katherine watched Ida hurry up the steps and disappear down the corridor as she called, "Wait right there until I come back with your coat!" A key rattled, a door banged. A baby somewhere began to scream. Katherine imagined Ida attacking the wardrobe in her room, and pawing through her clothes looking for a Suitably Warm Coat. She had no intention of waiting for Ida to return. She flew down the stairs, out the door, through the gate and along the street. She had managed to run half a block before Ida appeared at the hotel gate, holding up her fur coat and wailing Katie! Katie! like a banshee, while windows all along the street snapped open and a dozen heads poked out to see who was making all that noise. Katherine turned a corner and made straight for the seawall. With reckless fury, she hurtled down the steps and out across the yellow sand. She looked back, relieved to see that Ida, wisely, for once, had not followed. Then she was forced to stop and catch her breath for her heart was pounding wildly. She paused, chest heaving, and stumbled towards the sea.

The sand was so damp her suede shoes were soon soaked through and doubtless ruined. Grit had insinuated itself under her stocking in between her toes. The wind penetrated her coat. Admittedly it was chillier than she had thought, and she hadn't intended to leave the hotel garden at all, much less take a walk on the beach, but she certainly couldn't turn back now and give in to Ida's insistence. She had to hold her own against the Mountain that continually threatened to bury her under its weight. Living with Ida was like living with a potential landslide that could be set off by the tiniest pebble. She was likely to smother her to death with her over-solicitousness. *Katie dearest, where is your coat? Katie darling, where is your hat? Let me feel your forehead. You must have a temperature. Did you remember to take your medicine?* Far worse than Mother had ever been. Not that Mother really had ever seemed to notice much about her, except the things she disapproved of. "I see you are still fat as ever," had always been Mother's favorite refrain.

Mother. The very word pained her. Mother was so perfect. So unapproachable. Nothing Katherine did was ever good enough for Annie Beauchamp. So be it! Katherine faced the sea now and let the cold wind blow straight through her to chase away these dreary thoughts.

Today the sea was a dusky periwinkle blue streaked further out with cobalt. In the cold, bright sunlight strong gusts of wind blew a glittering spray across the surface. A healing scent of pine wafted down from the blue hills encircling the bay. She sipped the air lightly, taking it gently into her lungs. It was thrilling to be out here in the elements, the only soul on the beach. Looking out at the clouds rolling across the horizon, she could almost imagine she was back in New Zealand again, eleven thousand miles away. The beach was strewn with litter from the recent storms: bottles, frayed bits of rope, bloated dead fish, and even the carcass of a large rat, which despite its foul odor, she examined with interest, stirring it with a stick. The process of death did not disgust her and as a writer, she needed to acquaint herself even with the most unpleasant things.

She walked as far as a pile of rocks jutting several yards out into the water, closing this arc of the bay. The glistening surface was blistered by limpets and barnacles, tufted with long hairs of pale green seaweed undulating in the tide. Tiny crabs scuttled in and out of crevices with every slap of the waves.

Beached among the rocks and debris, something gleamed, attracting her attention. She bent down to study it, nearly soaking the hem of her skirt as a wave washed in. On a mound of kelp lay the decapitated head of a china doll, the blue paint of its eyes chipped away; its maenad hair threaded with seaweed. Katherine was delighted with this discovery. Just last night she had finished rereading *The Tempest* and now cradling the doll's head in her hand, she sang to herself Ariel's song: *Those are pearls that were his eyes. Nothing of him that doth change but doth suffer a sea change. Into something rich and strange.* Why was it these words thrilled her so deeply, chanted softly to herself before the booming sea?

Her sea change would be getting well again. She breathed in the sting of salt sea air. She could taste health in the raw brine and damp. Gently she set the doll's head down and it spun back into the sea in the undertow of the tide.

On her way back down the beach, she found herself in the full force of the blustery wind. She pulled her collar tight round her throat with one hand while holding down her hat with the other, her face tilted down to avoid the swirling columns of sand. She knew now that she would most certainly regret ignoring Ida's sensible advice. Struggling with little shuffling steps against the cold blasts of wind, she looked up and saw that she was not alone on the beach. A tall man in a ragged military greatcoat was stumbling along the strand toward her, puffing a cigarette. With a rush of nauseating terror, she recognized the fellow from the train. He was almost upon her now. She could not flee from the dreaded encounter. Her heart pounded in her ears and veins. But the man trudged past, greeting her with a sidelong glance from behind his turned-up collar. She stopped to calm her breathing and a spray of sand blew into her face. This wanderer did not in the least resemble the fellow from the train. How could she have imagined such a thing?

It really was ridiculous to have such irrational fears. What would Murry have said? That soldier at the station in Marseille, as horrible as he had been, had really been harmless: a poor, sick fellow, even more ill than she was. It had only been her nervous excitement that had made her feel he was somehow an enemy. She had even been afraid of the innocuous elderly gentleman who occupied the room next to hers at the hotel. To think she had nearly shot him when by mistake he had grabbed the handle of her door while groping his way back from the lavatory, probably to keep from collapsing in the hall. A few days later, one evening at dinner with Ida, she had spied him in the dining room, a shrunken old man with folds of yellow skin dangling under his chin and an old-fashioned dress shirt with onyx cuff links like one Father used to wear to the Bank of New Zealand's Christmas ball. Imagine, a poor, wheezing, senile monkey like that frightening her! Now that Ida was here she saw how silly those fears were. But why was it so impossible to find a balance when she was alone? As she climbed back over the seawall, she saw the beachcomber scrambling over the rocks where she had just been, his red scarf fluttering like a banner in the wind. He crouched down to retrieve something from the sand and put it in his pocket: a rock, a shell, no, Katherine thought, as an inexplicable shudder rippled across her shoulders and down her spine. He had pocketed her doll's head.

Katherine sat at the table by the window in her room, writing a letter. On her desk, a bright explosion of mimosa sprays in a vase and a small half-eaten box of chocolates, both gifts from Ida. Katherine's cheeks were flushed and she felt unaccountably restless this evening. Her chest and back ached. She must have taken too much sea air that afternoon. Ida sat nearby in the armchair, reading Galsworthy, and chuckling to herself in a most annoying way. They were waiting for the girl to bring their tea. Every five minutes, Ida would read a passage aloud and ask for her comment. It really was too much to bear. Katherine's throat tickled, she coughed with a painful, almost barking sound. A salty taste filled her mouth and she brought her handkerchief to her lips. There it was again: a bright blob of blood, more copious, more obscene than before. She coughed a second time, and there was more. This time she knew she had to tell Ida.

Katherine rose slowly, walked over to Ida and dropped the bloody handkerchief onto the page of Ida's book. Ida looked up at Katherine's stern, worried face, then, puzzled, glanced at the spotted handkerchief. It was the one with the little pink embroidered swans swimming around the corners which she had bought for her at the haberdashery.

"Katie, your lovely handkerchief. Shall I launder it for you?"

"Jones, how can you be so stupid? Look at this! Don't you realize what this means?"

Ida frowned and studied the stained fabric. Her eyes widened.

"Oh Katie! Was this when you coughed?"

"We must find a doctor immediately."

"I'll go at once," said Ida, rising from her chair.

"Take this and wash the blood out. It looks as though I have taken to butchering sheep in my room. If Madame sees it, she'll turn us out of the hotel."

It was after eight o'clock when the doctor, accompanied by Ida, finally came to examine Katherine in her room, where she lay half-wilted in her nightgown, worn out by the wait. Hours seemed to have passed since Ida had gone to fetch him. A squat little Englishman smelling of cognac, with bulging eyes like coddled eggs, stepped into the room and announced his name. Dr. Winsley was dressed like a proper dandy, with yellow suede gloves and a silver-headed cane. He listened to her back and chest with a stethoscope, scrutinized her sputum through his monocle, made detailed notes, and then pronounced the words Katherine most feared: Consumption, though at an early stage.

"I must return to England," she said as Ida helped her fasten up the buttons of her nightgown when the examination was over.

The doctor put away his stethoscope and rinsed his hands in the porcelain basin on Katherine's dressing table. Drying them on a fresh towel Ida supplied, he turned towards his patient with a sickening smile. His breath reeked of cognac.

"But Mrs. Murry, with this war on, travel is all but impossible at this time. The border is closed at present. It is a miracle you and your friend are here at all. And in any case, I could not possibly allow you to return to England. It would be most unwise to expose yourself to any further strain. The air here will do you good, at least until late spring, when indeed you shall have to leave, for the warmer spring temperatures are conducive to fevers. Something which a woman in your state," he paused now and beamed at her, "should definitely avoid. Take advantage of the rich diet here in the Midi. Butter, cream, milk, fresh fruit, are all indispensable to you. Furthermore," his eyes lingered over Katherine's bosom, "in the warmer mornings, you may expose your chest to the direct rays of the sun. That alone, with proper rest, should help considerably."

With this advice, Dr. Winsley took his leave of her, gallantly kissing her hand and promising to rush to her aid at any hour of the day or night, should he be needed. Then Ida accompanied him downstairs.

Stepping out into the corridor with Dr. Winsley, Ida heard a clock somewhere in the hotel striking ten and realized they had missed their dinner and would have to go to bed hungry. It was too late to get anything from the kitchen now, and she would rather not disturb Madame. Perhaps Katie still had some biscuits from teatime left in her room. Beside her, Dr. Winsley was descending the stairs rather uncertainly, clinging to the banister. She prayed he might make it all the way down without stumbling and breaking his leg. Luckily, the proprietress was not at the desk when they reached the hall. She had retired for the night, but the little door behind the desk leading to her rooms stood slightly ajar, which meant she was still awake. Ida hoped that she had not noted the doctor's arrival, for Katie did not want her to know that she was ill.

Accompanying Dr. Winsley outside to the front steps, she offered to pay him thirty francs for his services, but he waved her hand away with a tipsy gesture of reproach, assuring her it had been a pleasure to assist her charming friend. With an exaggerated bow, he swaggered down the hotel steps, out through the garden and into the street, swinging his cane with such vehemence Ida feared it might fly straight out of his hand and strike someone on the head.

Madame, in a threadbare dressing gown, shabby night cap, and shawl, emerged from the door marked *Privé* into her cubicle at the front desk as Ida stepped back into the hotel. She had indeed taken note of the doctor's arrival and departure, for she scowled at Ida with suspicion. It was clear she wanted no illness in her hotel.

Ida blurted out the phrase Katie had instructed her to say to reassure the woman. "It's only a little cold— *Seulement un petit rhume.*" Hearing herself pronounce *rhume* like the English word "room," she blushed.

Madame had understood well enough. "*Très bien,*" she sniffed.

Wishing to avoid further interrogation, Ida trotted briskly up the stairs. Looking back, she saw Madame still standing at her cubicle, staring up at her.

"*Un petit rhume, hein?*" said the proprietress with ironic emphasis, hands on hips.

"*Mais oui, Madame,*" replied Ida and she scurried down the hall to her own room.

Bending over the basin on the dresser, Katherine rinsed her face with cold water and pushed a wet compress to her swollen eyelids. Patting her face dry, she observed herself in the mirror. Ida must not see that she had been crying; it would only make things worse. What was needed now was action and not tears. She sat down to the little table and penned a few lines to Murry: *There's something I have to tell you. The fact is. It's worse than we thought. I can't leave here until the end of April or maybe May. I couldn't bear the strain of traveling. I have a touch of fever and I've coughed up a bit of blood. Not much, it isn't dangerous. But, the doctor... there's an English doctor here—says I must be careful. This is a terrible set back, I know. But don't worry darling. The slave is here to do my bidding, and I really can manage and can hold out as long as I know that You are thriving.* She reread her words, then wadded up the paper and tossed it into the wastebasket. This was not the right moment, the right tone, Murry would only worry. Where, oh where, was Ida? She crawled back into bed and waited for what seemed like hours until Ida knocked.

"Thank goodness you've come, Jones! I don' t think I'll ever be able to sleep tonight."

Ida began her nesting preparations. "Well, Katie," she said, spreading her blanket on the floor, "the doctor did say it's only at the beginning, and that if you take good care of yourself, you'll come through this just fine. It could be worse, you know. You could be..."

"Yes, I might be blind, deaf, and paraplegic besides..."

"Katie!"

"Jones, can't you see that I mustn't be ill! Because of Jack. I can't be ill away from Jack. I think I'd die if I had to spend any more time away from him. And Jones, suppose this thing gallops!"

Katherine burst into tears. Ida sat on the bed beside her, took her in her arms and stroked her hair. Katherine let herself be briefly petted and squeezed, then wriggled out of Ida's grasp.

"Jones, we can't stay here any longer. I must return to London at once and find a decent doctor."

Ida frowned. "But the border is blocked. Without a medical certificate, they won't give us our traveling papers! And Doctor Winsley thinks you should stay in France."

"I will send for him tomorrow. I must convince him, whatever it takes and I think I know. That doctor seems to have taken an unprofessional interest in me. If necessary, I shall turn it to my advantage!"

Ida looked shocked, but did not reply. She got up and resumed rearranging her bedding on the floor.

Katherine crushed a pillow to her breast and groaned, "Oh, Ida, why must my life always depend on irrelevant details like medical certificates and postal strikes?"

"Try to get some sleep now."

"I'll never sleep tonight."

"Shall we play a little game of Patience just to relax your mind?"

"No."

"Shall I read to you? A little Galsworthy?"

"I am not in the mood just now."

"A massage then for your shoulders."

Ida knew that a massage always worked to soothe Katie, and indeed at this suggestion, Katie obediently stretched out on her stomach with a little sigh, and closed her eyes. Ida came to the bedside, bent over her and began to undo the long row of tiny pearl buttons down the back of Katie's nightgown.

"Careful of the buttons, Ida. You'd think I was a bun and you were picking out my currants."

She moved the soft flannel aside to expose the firm, pale flesh of Katie's back. The shoulders were sharp and bony, the rib cage as fragile as a child's. She fondled the nape of Katie's neck, then bent down to plant a timid kiss there. "You've lost more weight, Katie," she whispered.

"Don't talk, Jones, just massage."

Katie seemed to be melting into her hands as Ida stroked her soft flanks, then began a systematic kneading of every inch of flesh from her buttocks upwards. Katie grunted with pleasure and buried her face in the pillows. Then to the left at the base of Katie's spine, Ida's fingers discovered a slight swelling. She pressed it cautiously and Katie cried out in pain.

"Jones! Are you mad? "

"There seems to be some sort of swelling here. A growth!"

"What do you mean, a growth?" Katie demanded, propping herself up on her elbows and turning to glare furiously at Ida.

Ida's fingers prodded the area more insistently and Katie winced.

"No, I mean, it's just a swelling of the muscles, you know. Probably from tension. Not a growth. I am sorry. I shouldn't have used that word."

"Button me up immediately, Jones. You'd have me dead and in my coffin."

"How can you say such a thing!"

"Put out the light now, please, and let me get some rest."

. . .

Summoned by Ida, the doctor arrived the next day at three o'clock, stumbling from his dinner, smelling of cigars, his lips still wet from drink.

Katherine had arranged the room for his arrival, two chairs pulled before the fire, a bottle of fine cognac on display, flowers on the mantelpiece, Murry's picture tucked away, the shutters tightly closed for privacy's sake. Anxious Ida had been banished to her room. Katherine was dressed for her role, however much it disgusted her. She wore a fine black gown with lace sleeves and a yoke of lace covering the bodice, black lace stockings, and Mother's pearl earrings. Her lips and cheeks were artfully rouged and every inch of her skin had been perfumed with vanilla and orange blossom water, a scent no man could resist, or so she had once been informed by a Parisian *demi-mondaine*.

"My dear doctor, aside from this unpleasant discovery, other important concerns force me to return to England immediately, " she said, pouring out two shots of cognac and handing one to the doctor who had settled in a chair by the fire.

"Most unwise, my dear lady, most unwise," he said, accepting the glass with a smile.

"As you know, I am an author of some repute, and there are vital questions I must address with my publisher," she injected a tone of authority into her voice as she paced before the fire, glass in hand, half-imagining herself as a character in a Chekhov play. Standing before the fireplace, she could feel the flames on her bosom and throat.

The doctor swirled the golden liquid in his glass, and held it a moment to his ruddy, pock-marked nose.

"Nothing is more vital than your health, surely," he said at last, lifting his glass in a toast.

Katherine touched her glass to his and met his eyes as he took his first sip. This cognac had been bought with her last few francs, and she prayed that it would have the desired effect. "I am convinced that returning to my own home, with servants and family to care for me, I will be much better off, than here, alone, in this hotel."

He reflected, sipping meditatively, as though testing the quality of the cognac. It seemed to meet his approval, for he said, "That is a point in your favor. But think of the journey. And it is not easy to obtain permission to travel with the advancing of the Germans."

"Of course, I need a medical certificate to obtain a *laissez- passer* for myself and my companion. That is why I have asked you to come." She stepped toward him, her eyes fixed on his face.

"But, Madame, why do you wish to leave the south of France? The climate is so much more salubrious here than in England. But perhaps it is because you are lonely. You are a young, beautiful woman, no doubt of a passionate nature, stricken in her prime by a dreadful illness, and you seek consolations. You should allow yourself to be consoled, dear lady. In your condition comforts and affection are necessary." He swilled down the cognac in his glass, put it down on the hearth and reached out to clasp her hand.

"Your hand is frozen Madame," he said enclosing her hand in his clammy fingers.

She smiled as sweetly as she might manage despite a sickening feeling in her chest, and took a step closer.

"Of course you are right, doctor. My passionate nature... This illness has been a terrible shock." She let the words die away in a sigh, then closed her eyes and threw her head back like Isadora Duncan, overcome by a sense of the absurd.

He gripped her hand with firmer pressure. She opened her eyes and glanced aside into the flames to stifle her laughter. The scene *was* comic, and yet how desperate she felt! She steadied herself now for the delivery of her next line. "If only you knew how important it is to me, I should be indebted to your kindness forever," she said, glancing back at him with burning, haunted eyes. It was an expression she had perfected over the years, knowing its effect on men. Then with coy submission, she looked down at the carpet, held her breath and waited.

He pressed her hand to his lips for a long moment, closed his eyes as though listening to distant music, then said, "Very well, dear Madame, you have convinced me. I shall prepare the certificate tomorrow. Perhaps you would come for an intimate lunch. Just the two of us, then I'll hire a carriage and drive you along seaside."

She offered no resistance as he pulled her to his lap. A shiver—this time untainted by disgust—flickered up her spine as she quite involuntarily imagined the two of them in his carriage. As his hand brushed her cheek then dropped to her breast, her nipples prickled beneath her black lace bodice. She was shocked by the violence of her physical response. Her lips parted to emit a soft groan, her legs shifted so he might lift her skirt to trace the silken bands of the tops of her stockings, then touch her once fleetingly between the thighs.

"No... I must have the certificate tonight," she whispered, shifting again to dislodge herself from him. He removed his hand. "We must not waste time. There will be a long wait for the application, you see, and my companion must take it to the Consul in Nice in the morning."

The doctor acquiesced with a sigh.

"Here, you see," she said, "I have pen, ink, and paper all ready," and she broke away from him and went to the writing table.

He rose, crossed the room to Katherine's table, sat down, and took pen in hand. She stood over him as he wrote, with her hand lightly resting on his shoulder, dictating the document she required, spelling out every other word. Kathleen Mansfield Beauchamp was in grave, urgent need of medical assistance and must return to London to consult her personal physician.

When it was done, he pulled her roughly to him. Fumbling with the jet buttons of her bodice, he bared one breast to the firelight. She reached for her glass, gulped down a last sip of cognac, snapped her head back, and swallowed a little laugh of bitter triumph. What would Murry say to see her now?

PARIS

She sat before the window of the Café Mahieu, smoking a cigarette, staring out at the brightly lit boulevard, contemplating the blackened skeleton of a bombed-out building right across from the café. Just two nights ago, this quarter had been hit by Big Bertha, the German's super-*Kanon*, which, for weeks now, had been launching its bombs on Paris every eighteen minutes. Stripped of its front wall, a honeycomb of rooms and corridors was exposed. Amid the charred rubble and broken glass, a few forlorn, recognizable fragments of domesticity had miraculously survived the blast: a straw-bottomed chair, a chamber pot, a cast iron stove, while in the tall plane trees lining the street, rags of colorful garments hung entangled in the branches covered with a flickering of green buds. A pink chemise, a green tie, bits of fabric and paper like festoons left over from a celebration. Old men and small boys picked through the rubbish heaped along the street, searching for anything salvageable: a nail, a roof tile, a scrap of metal, the wheel of a baby's pram.

It was amazing how the Parisians reacted to Big Bertha. At the first ear-splitting squeal of the warning siren, people scattered to safety, then came the sputtering and bursting of the bombs, the ground shaking and glass shivering to shards. An absolute quiet reigned for a moment afterwards and then the streets and cafés filled up again, as people went about their business. If you were not caught in the direct vicinity of the explosion, you were safe, but there was no telling where the next shell might hit. Every action: stepping out to buy a *baguette*, stopping beneath a lamp post to tie your shoe, crossing the street to avoid a puddle, might signify safety or certain death.

At first she had allowed herself to be caught up in the panic. She had heeded the hotel proprietor's warnings and had risen shakily from her bed in the night, with a fur thrown over her nightgown and her feet in slippers, to follow the others down into a freezing cellar. There she had waited out the dawn in that human-packed, airless space stinking of wine and sweat and other foul human odors, while around her the men smoked like fiends, and she feared she would suffocate. After three such nights, far more dangerous to her health than any German cannon, she and Ida had decided they would rather die like ladies in their beds upstairs in the hotel than be asphyxiated underground like rodents. The next time the siren had sounded, Ida had come to her room, pulled down the shades, and lay down quietly next to her in the dark. When the building shook and the windows rattled and glass broke out in tinkling crescendo along the street, Jones had given her her hand to hold.

Dear Ida and her attempts to comfort! As if she were afraid of dying. No, not Katherine, not anymore. That fear had left her when her brother Leslie died.

It was only the thought of Murry that made her care whether she went on living or not. Murry and Murry only. If Murry should cease to care for her, nothing would make sense any longer. Even now, sitting here in this café while around her strangers murmured softly over glasses of *pastis*, she felt oddly detached from herself and from the life she had lived up until then. It was as if the past were something one could shed and leave behind, like a coat left hanging in the wardrobe of a hotel to which one will never return. Out the window, a gust of wind swept a pile of leaves and rubbish along the street. Old selves, like dead leaves, blowing about in the wind.

Despite the present danger of Big Bertha, she realized how lucky she was to have escaped from Bandol, from that dreary hotel, and from that slithery reptile of a doctor. Murry would have died rather than see her behaving thus—really like a whore—there was no word other than the Biblical one to describe her behavior. Encouraging that beastly fellow to fawn on her with his foul breath, kissing and fondling and reaching under her skirt, while he kept murmuring "Dear lady, it is no trouble at all." How was it he had not been afraid of contracting her disease?

She had, of course, done worse things in her life. And what options did she have? This was a war—on all levels, and the bombs now devastating Paris were indeed a confirmation of that fact. Her fate now rested in the hands of the Consul, to whom she had presented her certificate yesterday. If he decided to authorize her request, then she would be granted a *laissez- passer* and could leave France. If not, she must head southwards again. In any case, the war was not going well, and for the moment civilian travel had nearly ceased, except for extreme emergencies. She prayed that the Consul would consider her case in that light.

Murry had, at least, delivered, and had sent a modest sum of money, a ridiculously small amount for all the work she had done, and far less than he had promised. But that was so typical of him. She and Ida had pooled what was left of their cash, paid the hotel bill, bought tickets and fled Bandol. In the rush, Ida lost her suitcase at the Bandol station. They had been required to stop in Marseille and present her certificate to the authorities. Marseille was like a nightmare: a maze of dirty market streets near the station, full of screeching parrots in cages and toothless hags selling paper cones of rancid walnuts, and swarthy little beggar boys tugging on her skirt, clamoring for coins. Then, with permission granted, they had found their way back to the station and had boarded another train for Paris, where they were now lodged in relative comfort for the time being at the Select Hotel. They were down to fifty francs. With that they would have to pay for food and lodging and tickets back to England. How would they manage if the line at Amiens did not hold and her departure for England were delayed?

Faintly a siren whined far away in another quarter. The *garçon*, drying glasses behind the bar, stopped, listened intently, and exchanged an uneasy glance with Katherine. The chatter in the café instantly subsided. The few people at the tables turned their heads to the window in expectation. There was a dull boom in the distance. The ground trembled, the glasses clinked along a shelf behind the bar; then, silence. Katherine drew in a sharp breath as the conversation stirred up again around her.

She looked out at the street, now filling up again with people and checked her watch. In a half hour she would have to be on her way, but first she must make a telephone call. This was no pleasant task, for she had to hit someone up for a bit of cash, and she still wavered. Should it be Carco or Beatrice? She ordered another coffee and lit another cigarette. She had just been to Cook's for her post, but there were no letters, and the Cook's man had informed her that a postal block had begun, and that although a few bags of mail might straggle through in the coming days, by the end of the week the flow would stop altogether. So if more money did not come from Murry in the next two or three days, they would be stuck again unless they could find another source of funds. That meant borrowing from someone, and the only friends she had in Paris were Beatrice Hastings and Francis Carco, if "friend" were an appropriate term for either of them.

She could do without that harpy Beatrice's help. It was certainly no loss if Katherine ever saw her again. Remembering their last encounter three years ago in Paris brought a tightening of disgust to her throat. There had been an awful party at Beatrice's flat in Montparnasse. It was supposed to have been a tea party, but by the time she arrived, almost everyone there was already drunk. Beatrice's lover at the time, the painter Modigliani whom everyone called Dedo, was in an outrageous state, lying on a couch, tippling from a bottle of rum while discussing painting with Max Jacob and with a pile of zebra-skinned pillows which had equally captivated his attention. Beatrice, who had drunk perhaps twice as much rum as her madcap Italian lover, bared her breasts and danced lasciviously with everyone present. Katherine had danced too, with an intriguing young woman, who had pale silver blond hair. The blond girl pressed her bosom tightly against hers and whispered in her ear that she had just married, but alas, had not found the satisfaction she desired. They might have gone on dancing together all night and confiding to each other about the disappointments of men and marriage had it not been for Beatrice, who rudely separated them, claiming that it was time Katherine danced with her. With a vague smile, the girl slipped without demure from Katherine's embrace, as deftly as a silk shawl slipping from one's shoulders and Katherine watched regretfully as her dancing partner was enfolded by other arms. Beatrice then swept Katherine up with her long bean pole arms and whirled her about in a stirring tango, but having drunk too much to keep time properly, Beatrice kept treading on her toes. Everyone snickered into their drinks at what a fool Beatrice was making of herself, but she hardly noticed as she steered Katherine about the smoky room. Poor Beatrice, once a splendid beauty, swan-necked, with firm high breasts, and a defiant sparkle in her eyes. Now after a few short years in Paris and God knows how many gallons of absinthe, she had become even more haggard than Modigliani himself, with deeply etched wrinkles around her eyes, a sagging bust, and a pot belly. She reminded Katherine of a pirate's mistress: all that was missing was an eye-patch and a parrot. As they danced, Katherine turned her face away from Beatrice's reeking breath and stepped over a body or two sprawled insensible on the floor. Beatrice clung to her with amazing strength, and she had to struggle as with a drowning woman to keep from being pulled down. When the music stopped, Beatrice held her fast, peering into her face with glassy-eyed malice. "Tonight, I want you to sleep here with me," she croaked, and with sudden impetus, glued her lips on Katherine's mouth. This was too much for Katherine to stomach, and she had pushed Beatrice away rather too forcibly and Beatrice toppled backwards, crashing to the floor, flop onto her *derrière*.

Dedo roared with laughter and Beatrice, enraged, had seized his half-empty bottle of rum and hurled it at Katherine. The bottle just missed her head and smashed against the wall, shattering into a thousand shards, leaving a large wet stain on the wallpaper. How she had managed to escape that evening, Katherine hardly knew, stumbling half- blinded by furious tears, down the stairs and out into the street, where she had discovered it was nearly dawn, far too late and far too early to return to her hotel. She had waited for the cafés to open, walking up and down along the Seine, stamping her feet in the freezing damp, watching boatmen loading up their barges, as they called to her with lewd alacrity, mistaking her for a streetwalker. She later found that she had left a silver cigarette case and her best pair of black lace gloves at Beatrice's. Her former friend had no doubt disposed of these things by burning them in some sort of black magic rite learned from Aleister Crowley. That had been her exit from Beatrice's life and she certainly couldn't go weeping to Beatrice now, begging for money, although she knew Beatrice received a generous income from her South African family and could well afford to loan her a few francs.

That night in Montparnasse had not been her only battle with Beatrice. Theirs had always been a stormy friendship, ever since they first met in the editorial offices of Orage's magazine *The New Age*, where Katherine had first published her stories. Once, after insulting one of Katherine's short stories, Beatrice physically attacked her, and they had ended up clawing at each other, circling round Orage's desk, ripping off each other's necklaces and pelting each other with purse chains. When he tried to intervene, Orage nearly slipped and broke his neck on the scattered beads, which kept turning up for weeks afterwards, no matter how many times the floor was swept. And yet, in the past Beatrice had befriended her at some very difficult moments. One dreadful winter Orage and Beatrice had nursed her back to health after an attack of influenza. Another time, Beatrice had found a reputable doctor to help her out of a most distressing condition. As a young writer just starting out, Katherine had admired the sardonic wit displayed in the pieces Beatrice wrote for *The New Age*, and for years they had copied each other's prose style; Beatrice had even copied her hairstyle, claiming it was Katherine who had imitated her. Heaven knows in what wretched state she must be now that Dedo had deserted her for a schoolgirl hardly sixteen years of age. She had heard rumors that Beatrice was madder than ever and went about Paris with a live duckling in her shopping basket.

That meant she must go to Carco, whom she had heard was in Paris on leave from his military duties. She dreaded the idea of contacting him again. She had destroyed his letters months ago, determined to wipe him from her memory forever, after what he had done to her: portraying her as a vicious prostitute in his thinly disguised roman à clef, *Les Innocents*. And to think she had found him so alluring at first. Life is so ironic. One finally musters the courage and energy needed to pronounce a sacred vow, "Never again shall I see that man...." only to discover that circumstances drive one to repeat one's worst mistakes. She knew the telephone number of his flat by heart; she had stayed there for a few days the last time she was in Paris. Rising from the table, she went to the telephone located behind a checked curtain near the lavatory.

The number rang at least a dozen times and she was about to ring off when at last a voice, husky with sleep, replied. Carco was not at all surprised to hear from her, or to learn she was in Paris. Probably her presence had already been noted by their mutual acquaintances. He hesitated slightly when she asked if she could come at once, then with a hint of reluctance, agreed to see her. That was his way of playing precious; it was a ploy she had used many times with him as well.

With the last few coins in her purse she paid the taxi driver who delivered her unscathed to Carco's apartment not far from Notre Dame under a rain of falling shards as Big Bertha boomed in the distance.

She sat on a maroon velvet couch, her slim fingers clasped around the stem of a wine glass, sipping the well-chilled champagne Carco had proffered. They spoke French as was fitting for two former lovers, such a civilized language of nuance and suggestion. Their romance had begun after Murry had engaged him to give her French conversation lessons while they were staying in Paris years ago, and she still took pride in showing him how well she handled his language. Her eyes took in the familiar room: the walls of books, the dimming antique mirrors in ornate gilt frames, the fusty opulence of Louis XIV furniture, all telltale signs of his solid bourgeois tastes. But the pink silk pyjamas tossed on an armchair, the empty bottles of *Pernod* lined up by the door, the clutter of books and papers on every table clearly testified to his claims to be a genuine intellectual of the avant-garde—to which his extraordinary collection of paintings also bore testimony. It was truly an impressive collection. She gazed up at the wall filled with modern paintings, these too in heavy gilt frames. An addition had been made since she had last come here: a magnificent nude by Dedo. How was it that shrunken little unshaved fellow could produce such startling paintings?

Carco stood with his back to the bookcase, with that easy, youthful manner of his, laughing at her with shy, burning eyes of liquid black. His pliant mouth, so easily twisted to a sneer, was smiling at her; the gold bracelet on his plump wrist glittered with each womanish gesture. She had once imagined their relationship to be one of cat and mouse, with herself in the role of the insatiable feline and Carco as the toy she might torture or delight according to her whim. Now she saw that in her new condition, these roles had been quite reversed.

Carco was telling her about his new painting. Modigliani had given it to him to thank him for an article he had written praising his work, which had been published in Switzerland. It was the first positive article that had yet appeared, for so far poor Dedo had only met with scorn and humiliation. The police had even closed his recent exhibition at the Weil's shop, for there had been a public outcry over Dedo's far too realistic portrayal of his models' pubic hair. What bourgeois obtuseness! But in five or ten years, that painting would be worth a fortune, Carco proudly concluded.

Katherine felt inadequate when asked to judge paintings. She could only say whether she liked a painting or not, and whether she felt that the artist had been successful at rendering his vision. This painting was indeed extraordinary. A woman standing, naked to the waist, full breasts and hips, a tawny fuzz of pubic hair, blond hair rippling to her shoulders, one eye sharply defined, the other left unfocused. It radiated an erotic energy that Katherine found overwhelming. The woman was as bold and complete as a tiger, yet not aggressive, like Blake's Tyger, radiant with energy, more a goddess, perhaps, than an animal. She was a woman of a sort Katherine had never met, had never seen. In her there was no coyness or studied seduction; she was not a man's exaggerated idea of a woman's sexual nature, but rather expressed a wholeness of being which could not be contained. Like Eve before the fall. If only Lawrence could see this painting, she thought. This was the feminine ideal he had been seeking, and perhaps this was how he saw his wife Frieda. Is this then what virile men expect their women to be like?

And Carco—how would he have fared with this goddess of pleasure? He had been an ineffectual lover, despite his boyish appeal, and very selfish, although they had once spent an enjoyable afternoon in bed, laughing like idiots and smoking and almost setting the bedclothes on fire. The sex had been at best mediocre, over in a matter of seconds. The most thrilling part of their rendezvous had been her adventure of crossing into the front to join him, though neither one had ever really been in danger. Carco's military duties consisted in delivering letters to a bakery unit. She had probably seen more bombs in those few days in Paris than he had seen during the whole course of the war. What she remembered most fondly was watching him afterwards, kneeling naked by the fire in their little room at the pension, poking the dying embers back into a flame. He had seemed so at ease in his nakedness in a way Murry could never have been. Heavens, how *English* Murry could be about such things! Carco had offered some relief, but their encounter had not been satisfying. And then he had gone and done the unpardonable. In *Les Innocents,* he had revealed her sexual secrets to the world, her misgivings about Murry, and other intimate matters which she had confided in a moment of abandon. Anyone who knew them even slightly could have recognized his portrait of her. He had made her the laughingstock of all Paris and London. She had sworn she would never forgive him, but now there she was sitting on his sofa.

She drained her glass, felt the bite of champagne against her palate, closed her eyes and imagined the bubbles dancing to her brain. It occurred to her that she really did not enjoy the taste of champagne. Then, opening her eyes again, she turned her intense gaze upon Carco, and summoning her courage, launched her request for a loan. Suddenly, she found herself explaining far more than she had intended. About her coughing. The abominable, frog-eyed doctor. The flight to Paris. Her fears for the future. Murry, *again.* All the while she was amazed with herself for pouring her heart out to this man whom she really did not respect and who had published her most intimate woes to the world. Finally, averting her face from his and looking down at the carpet, she half-whispered the word "consumption" and had to stifle a cough for her throat had gone dry. Glancing up, she saw Carco staring at her with a horrified expression and her mouth snapped shut.

He is thinking, she realized, *that I may have given it to him.*

Carco took a wad of francs from the drawer of his scrittoire, counted out a sum and lay it on the table before Katherine. She stared at the bundle. It must be more than three hundred francs. She had not expected such generosity, but could not decide whether her prevailing sentiment was relief or shame. She felt the color rush to her cheeks, and looked down at the carpet again.

"I am deeply distressed for your illness and unhappiness. Please let me know if there is anything else you need," said Carco uneasily.

"I promise I shall repay you as soon..."

He frowned and gestured in irritation as if waving away a fly, she thought.

The broad brown forehead puckered beneath the slick black hair, a crease like a sneer appeared at the corner of his mouth. He was ugly, really, she thought, truly ugly.

She slipped the money into her little black clutch bag and clicked it shut with resolution, feeling even more like a whore than when she had let the doctor fondle her in return for a medical certificate. Surely she had never sunk so low as to beg money from a former lover. Why did Murry allow her to find herself in such predicaments? All because, in the end, he was so tight-fisted when it came to money. What sort of a man was that? Tears came to her eyes as Carco accompanied her to the door. Stepping close to embrace him, she was shocked to see him flinch. She stepped back again astounded. He did not want her to stand too near, to breathe near him. Was this the man who had written so tenderly to her, *"With each day that passes, I love you all the more."* Gently he took her hand—his felt soft and rubbery like a mannequin's—said goodbye, and in a moment she found herself alone on the drafty, unlit stairway.

Outside, it was twilight and a soft rain had begun to fall. Music from an accordion tumbled from the doorway of a café across the street. Katherine was still stung by shock: Carco had both rescued and insulted her. Is this what she should expect now from all her friends? She darted across the street and hurried into the café to wait out the shower, her eyes fixed on the lights burning in the windows of Carco's apartment. If he should come out, she would accost him, accuse him of his lack of delicacy and feeling. But the lump of cash in her clutch bag dissuaded her. It felt solid like something she could count on. Carco's gift would see her and Ida through. Back to London, back to Murry's arms.

. . .

She sat on the berth in the ladies' cabin, playing two-handed Patience with Ida who was perched on a steamer trunk squeezed into the narrow space beneath the porthole. They had come down from the lounge early after dinner, exhausted by the trip to Calais, but the ship had not left port. At last there came a creaking and roiling of chains; the engine roared and the ship began to move. A strange peace descended upon her as she gazed up at the porthole, where an uneven line of gray sea appeared. After all the anguish of the last few months and weeks, she and Ida were on their way to England. One by one, she turned over the well-worn cards, putting hearts on spades and studying her sevens while Ida babbled on happily about new dress patterns. In just a few hours' time, she would be safe with Murry again, and soon they would be married.

Later she lay in her berth and watched Ida standing at the tiny sink stained brown with rust and salt, brushing her hair one hundred strokes, looking as worried and worn as a harried servant. Thinking back over these weeks in France,

Katherine felt appalled at herself for how she had treated Ida. Where did all the hate and anger come from? Sometimes she thought she would gag on her own venom. How *did* Jones put up with it all? Ida did not deserve to be treated so, but there was no controlling her own wrath. It was like trying to peddle a bicycle up a very steep hill with a huge snake entwined around her body, squeezing out her breath. Was there no way to free herself from its clasp?

PART TWO

LONDON: 1918

THE SOUTH KENSINGTON REGISTRY OFFICE

The officiating registrar was balding with yellow skin. A slight bulge of goiter showed above his throat, proving to be a distraction for Murry as he stood at Katherine's side, waiting for the ceremony to begin. His eyes kept returning to that swelling of flesh, as though it were a sign he had yet to decipher. He and Katherine, thank God, were still a handsome couple in their prime, with no such visible disfigurement.

Murry was well aware of the distinguished figure he cut with his monocle and his salt-and-pepper trousers, still he felt a bit self-conscious, hoping no one had noticed that his cufflinks had been ingeniously twisted from two snips of wire from a ginger beer bottle. That morning he had mislaid the only pair he owned, twin opals in a gold setting, a gift from his mother when he first went to Oxford, and he had had to invent a quick replacement before bicycling over to the South Kensington Registry Office where he and Katherine were about to be married. He stared at the calendar on the wall behind the registrar's desk and reflected that this day May 3, 1918, might change not only his life and Katherine's, but the whole course of English literature.

He felt oddly abstracted from himself. What was this filter between himself and himself, between the intention and the act, between his mind and his body as it moved through the motions required for the occasion? Quite unemotionally he reflected that the cause of his dulled reaction was the vague but lingering uncertainty about the step he was now taking. O, he wanted Katherine and at the thought of her pale nakedness shining in his bed, his knees quivered. By this rite, she would be his forever. He worshipped Katherine. She was all things to him, as no woman had ever been or could ever be again. She was a tiger, driven by ambition, spurring him on to follow her galloping stride. She was a child of the purest heart clinging to his breast for protection, and the thought of her vulnerability made his chest expand so as to embrace the whole room where they now stood. She was a princess of unrivaled sensibility. She was doubtless the most intelligent woman in England and one of the greatest writing talents of her generation. And he was the one who had discovered her— not counting Orage, who had published only her immature first efforts—when he had published her story *The Woman at the Store*, perhaps the most brilliant story of the decade, in his magazine *Rhythm*. Their lives and fortunes could not but flourish in connection with each other. Literary history would honor their names. For this, marriage was not necessary, perhaps, but they had longed to be married for years, and at last, just four days ago, Katherine's divorce had gone through. Katherine's singing teacher had exited forever from their lives.

Murry had never quite understood why Katherine had married George Bowden and then left him the next day with their marriage unconsummated. He put it down to the inexperience of youth. He himself had been and was still far more deficient than Katherine in passionate experiences. He thought briefly of his first *amour* in Paris to whom he had lost his purity, and hoped it was not unseemly for a man to remember his previous affairs with women on his wedding day. Marguéritte, the lovely French country girl, with her plump bosom packed into a tight bodice with dozens of tiny, exasperating hooks to undo, and an unfashionable black velvet hat trimmed with limp cherries to match her bright lips.

The most enduring memory of Marguéritte, was, of all things, those cherries on her hat, trembling above her ear as she laughed too eagerly at his bad jokes in the café and swung her black-stockinged leg back and forth under the table. With some effort he could evoke a few details of what happened later in her little room above a bakery shop: the snap of her garter as a stocking rolled down, the flash of a white leg and full flanks as she slipped naked beneath the sheets, the smell of the shuttered room afterwards, a lamp guttering on a dresser crowded with forlorn photographs of country relatives, her childlike voice asking, "*Tu n'es pas triste?*" The coitus itself, a hot, breathless blur, had been all too brief to be worthy of recall and afterwards he had indeed felt *triste*; it had not been what he had expected at all. Still, he believed then that he loved Marguéritte, and might well have married her. Her gamine earnestness would have charmed his mother. The two of them would have formed an invincible alliance against him and would have tied him down to some second rate clerical job, forcing him to give up *Rhythm* and his literary career. If that had not happened, it was because he had cruelly abandoned her. Hunched over in a train on his way back to Calais, he had gulped down sobs of guilt after their farewell at the station. He had not told her he would never return. Her letters arrived at Oxford for months afterwards, but their spelling mistakes brought a lump to his throat and he had been unable to reply. Then Katherine Mansfield had come into his life, stepping out of a taxi into a foggy December night in Hampstead.

The dinner party where they met had been arranged at his request. After publishing her short story, intrigued by her style, he had spent an afternoon standing before the shelves at Dan Rider's bookshop in St. Martin's Lane, devouring her new short story collection, *In a German Pension*, cover to cover; as he couldn't afford to buy a copy of his own to take home and read. A friend of his was acquainted with her and promised to introduce them by inviting them both to dinner. He hardly knew what to expect as he hurried towards that dinner engagement in Hampstead. The writer of those stories possessed a wiry toughness, a withering irony. How was it possible that such powers of astringency could be embodied in the petite, demure girl in gray who arrived late that night to the dinner party? Her dress, almost nun-like in its plainness, was adorned with a single red rose, but the black stockings and silver shoes she wore were those of a coquette. Pixie, waif, seductress—it was impossible to identify the species of female to which she belonged. She changed before one's eyes, and was always alluring. At dinner, over plum soup, she had amazed him with her knowledge of Russian and German literature, praising authors he was ashamed to say he had never even heard of. By the time the after dinner whiskies were drained, he knew he must not lose touch with her, and to his joy, as they said goodbye in the street, she invited him to tea, promising brown bread and cherry jam.

Her flat at Clovelly Mansions in Gray's Inn Road had been bare of furniture, with bamboo mats on the floor instead of carpets, and a big stone Buddha with a dish of flowers set before it. There was only one armchair in the sitting room, which he was obliged to occupy while she knelt like a geisha at his feet on a purple silk cushion and poured their tea into Japanese bowls and buttered him a piece of bread. The talk flowed on for hours and he found himself confessing his doubts about his future. He wasn't cut out for Oxford or for the civil service, the two careers his parents had envisioned for him, and Katherine had encouraged him to leave Oxford, strike out on his own, and continue his editorial and critical work. A week later he had moved into the extra room in her flat, and the most remarkable period in his life ensued. He did not know then that the room he had taken previously belonged to Ida, an unshakable companion from whom she would never really part.

For months he and Katherine were as chaste as brother and sister, and yet did everything together. Every night they read aloud to each other from their work, then shook hands, and retired to their separate rooms. Katherine was soon dissatisfied with this arrangement. "Why don't we become lovers?" she had asked one night after dinner. She was snuggled in the armchair, he sprawled on the floor. He contemplated her question. The idea had never even remotely crossed his mind, though she was devilishly attractive to him. He rolled on his back, waved his legs in the air, and studied the worn heels of his shoes. "It would spoil everything" he had replied at last, lowering his legs to the floor. For hadn't sex spoiled his love for Marguéritte by making her think she could claim him and his future somehow? Why couldn't a man and a woman just really be friends, close, loving friends, as he and Katherine were, without sex having to come into it? That was what he believed he thought, and for awhile Katherine accepted it.

They had been so poor in those days. To save money they bought penny meat pies every night for dinner and then had to go to a pub to wash away the rank taste of tainted mutton. Then one evening, something happened at the pub which changed their lives forever. There was an old tart, Lil, a fixture around the place, always sitting half-drunk at the same table, facing a fly-specked mirror which reflected a row of whisky and seltzer bottles behind the bar. One night they had caught Lil staring at herself in the mirror, but she was not aware that they were watching. The sadness and horror of her naked self-confrontation, the expression in those eyes had been harrowing to behold. To Murry it had been like a blow in the stomach. In Lil's eyes he had seen the awfulness of life. Sordidness, corruption, the certainty of decay and death, the absence of all comfort. A thought riveted his brain before he looked away—*This is life*: an aging, drunken, pock-marked whore with sagging breasts and rotten teeth. A chill had seized him that he could not banish. He and Katherine had both come away shaken. They had both felt the same desolation in Lil's glance, and the only remedy to that loneliness was to cling together. Returning to her dreary flat, he thrust himself into Katherine's arms and wept unabashedly. She put her mouth to his and her tongue slipped in between his lips, astonishing him with its forward curiosity. They stumbled towards Katherine's room, nearly knocking over a lamp as they collapsed onto the bed where they tore each other's clothes off. After they had made love, he knew that they had formed a bond which nothing could destroy.

No, he had not wanted sex with Katherine at first, but destiny had joined them and now he could not live without it. She was so uninhibited at times, she made him blush. Wherever had she learned to give such pleasure to a man? He dared not even imagine the shadowy lovers who had lain at her side. Yet he had never satisfied her. He had never truly possessed her. Rather, it was Katherine who possessed and satisfied him. Did that matter? A man like Lawrence would roar that it mattered greatly and thump the table with his fist, thundering that he must not let Katherine lead him by the nose.

Katherine, fragile as a leaf, stood at his side, clutching his arm. She had come back from France with a new perfume, what was it called? She had also come back weighing seven stone seven, and coughing into her handkerchief every five minutes. It was a most alarming habit that made the flesh prickle on the nape of his neck. He had hardly recognized her when he went to fetch her and Ida from the boat train on their return. She was thin as a stick and looked as though she had just been released from some awful prison. She swayed slightly when she walked, like a lily too heavy for its stalk, weighted down with raindrops after a cloudburst.

Ida was not here today, which was some relief. Ida—Katherine's shadow, Katherine's slave—was one of those bothers one must learn to live with, like a cumbersome piece of inherited furniture one is always banging into, but which one cannot bring oneself to throw away and which never really finds its proper place in one's house. Today Katherine must have banished her, or perhaps she was working her shift at the airplane factory in Chiswick. For her witness, Katherine had chosen her half-deaf painter friend, Dorothy Brett, who stood behind them with her brass ear trumpet tilted towards the registrar. The ear trumpet gave Brett a slightly Nordic look, like a Viking maiden. Murry could hear her breathing, her breasts rising and falling, breath after breath: soft, regular, soothing. He fancied he could feel the warmth of Brett's breath behind him, coming in delicate gusts right into the middle of his spine. What was it about her that attracted him against his better judgment? But how caddish of him to be thinking of Brett at the very moment he was being wed to Katherine.

He reached into his pocket for the ring, to reassure himself that it had not fallen out while he was bicycling along the street. The ring felt startlingly cold, as though dipped in ice water. It had been Frieda Von Richtofen's wedding ring from her first marriage and she had given it to Katherine four years ago on the day she and Lawrence were married, when he and Katherine had served as their witnesses. Lawrence would approve of what they were now doing. He believed marriage was the key to human existence, and that no man can amount to anything without a woman behind him. When a man loves a woman, she keeps him directly in touch with the unknown. That was how Lawrence put it: *in touch with the unknown*. Lawrence felt pulled toward the unconscious depths of life, those caverns measureless to man, those deep abysses of the soul shot through with unearthly gleams. The slender figure of Lawrence, sickly and pale, swam naked through that darkness, joyful and unafraid, urging them all: Frieda, Katherine, and himself to follow into the mysteries. Frieda needed no encouraging. Off she leapt into the teeming black waters, ploughing through the waves with her plump, pink arms. But he and Katherine hung back on the shore, unwilling or perhaps unable to imitate the dauntless swimmers.

He had disappointed Lawrence, he knew, many, many times with his indecision, with his fear of life, as Katherine might call it, his inability to act. Take for example Lawrence's plan to found a community, the order of the knights of Rananim, first in Florida, and then on a South Sea island. It had begun as pleasantry: they would all go off to an island and create a colony which Lawrence decreed would be founded on the principles of communism, on pride and wealth, but not on poverty or sacrifice, and on the joyous fulfillment of the flesh in all strong desire. Its symbol was to be a phoenix rising from scarlet flames against a black background. For hours they sat around drinking ale, discussing how it would work and who would come: Frieda, he and Katherine, of course, Aldous Huxley, and Kot. Only married couples would be allowed to come, and old bachelor Kot would have to be assigned a suitable mate if he wished to join them. The extraordinary thing was that Lawrence actually believed in Ranamin, not as an intellectual exercise but as a feasible plan, and had been crestfallen when with the outbreak of the war their interest had subsided. To appease their disappointed friend, he and Katherine had gone to Cornwall to live near Frieda and Lawrence in an attempt to create a smaller, more intimate colony, as Lawrence desired. But Katherine had hated the dank tower with mottled walls and mildewed mattresses Lawrence had found for them to live in. She had soon become ill, and the experiment had lasted only a month before they both escaped, leaving Frieda and Lawrence to squabble and bicker and pummel each other to their hearts' content.

Still, he marveled at his luck at enjoying the companionship of the two most original minds in England, aside from his own, of course, Lawrence's and Katherine's. For *Sons and Lovers* had proven Lawrence was as much a genius as he or Katherine. There were moments when Murry longed to leap into the waters of the Dark God and go thrashing after Lawrence, and emerge from the sea with his body soaked and tingling upon an island untrod by human foot since the days of Caliban. But Lorenzo and his brooding deities were even more possessive than Katherine. Lawrence had begged Murry to seal their friendship with a ritual exchange of blood, and had been mortally offended when he had declined this primeval sacrament. One could not say "no" to Lorenzo without taking one's chances. No doubt if marriage existed between men, Lawrence would have insisted on marrying him.

Marriage between men! Another extraordinary thought. It must be the uniqueness of the occasion that put such bizarre thoughts into his head. A man doesn't marry every day. A slight pressure from Katherine's hand called him back from his musings. He noticed that the registrar's mouth had moved to speak, but he had not caught the words. He had also, most surprisingly, begun to perspire around his collar. The mouth above the goiter spoke again, and this time he heard quite clearly. He knew what to reply, *I do*. It was done, as simple as that. Katherine murmured her own reply in a soft breathy voice, more like the rustling of flowers. At the given signal he slid the ring on Katherine's finger. How loosely it slipped on, threatening to slide off again. But she clenched her fist to keep it tight, and her knuckle went strangely white, like a drowned cadaver's.

The ceremony was over. Katherine squeezed his arm with firm intention, the registrar handed him a pen. He must sign his name in the registry. John

Middleton Murry he wrote with dash, remembering to round off his strokes properly. It was a handsome signature indeed. His mother and father had always been proud of his penmanship. But they were not proud of Katherine. They could not bear her, and he still shrank with shame remembering the day his mother and his aunt had come to Katherine's flat in Gray's Inn Road to take him away from her, and he had pushed them out the door in a fury, shouting *Leave me alone, you women!*

Why was it that he felt no joy but only a sense of uneasy dread as they were ushered out of the office, and another couple was shown in after them? The most immediate problem was what to do with Katherine now that they were married. There wasn't room for a wife in his digs on Redcliffe Road so Katherine had agreed to go to Cornwall for a time with her friend Anne Estelle Rice, while he worked out the details of the lease on a house they had seen in Hampstead. Katherine had dubbed it the Elephant, as it was painted gray and was much larger than they needed. It was also far more expensive than they could afford, not to mention the expenses of decorating and furnishing it. That would just about finish him financially, if Katherine's father didn't come through with some extra funds. But cagey old Harold Beauchamp was stingy with his daughter, especially considering that he was probably the richest man in New Zealand. Lawrence had once asked Murry outright why he did not allow Katherine to support him, imagining, as everyone did, that she received a more generous allowance from her father than the two hundred pounds she actually received, which was certainly not enough for food, lodging, taxis, books, doctors, and the many luxuries Katherine could not do without, from lavender silk corsets to Russian cigarettes tipped in gold paper.

Lawrence had urged him to chuck his magazine and take Katherine to live in Europe, perhaps joining them in Italy, or wherever she liked. The two of them could subsist frugally enough on her allowance, and content themselves with an itinerant life dedicated entirely to writing. If a woman really loves her man, Lawrence had tried to persuade him, she'll be happy sleeping on the floor and doing her own housework. But he could not let Katherine sleep on floors now that she was ill.

Out they stepped into the gray street. The London traffic jostled about him and for the first time that morning he felt extraordinarily awake. In the little square, red tulips nodded in a flower bed. Katherine, still clinging to his sleeve, coughed with an unpleasant gurgling sound. Brett pushed a branch of lilac blossoms into Katherine's arms and kissed her. Then turning to kiss Murry, Brett shoved her breasts against his chest, but he only frowned and lifted his chin above her hair which gave off an exciting animal-like smell, nothing at all like Katherine's floral fragrance. Rigidly he stood, resisting Brett's throbbing warmth. He was a now a married man, and the jealous woman at his side was Mrs. Middleton Murry, a diagnosed consumptive.

2 PORTLAND VILLAS

The dark green gate swung open upon the tiny square of garden and Katherine ventured inside, noting with approval the pink and orange dahlias ablaze near the front steps and the wrought iron lantern artfully placed so that it would illuminate the pear tree at night. Sliding the key into the lock with a quiver of excitement, she pushed opened the front door to 2 Portland Villas on East Heath Road. She stood for a moment in the quiet hall, eyes closed, and listened to the stillness of this as yet uninhabited house. After months, years, of bedsitters, hotels, borrowed flats, and train stations, this was home.

The workmen had finished just that morning. A smell of fresh paint quickened in the sunlight filtering in through the tall windows. With pleasure, she inhaled the odor of crisp muslin and of newly laid carpets. She had come early, a full hour before Murry was due to arrive, to breathe the atmosphere of a house not yet come alive. As her eyes surveyed the premises, a flicker of joy shot through her along with a shiver of disbelief. Tomorrow they would take full possession of the house.

This silence was so rich, untrodden, unsullied, like new snow, tingling and invigorating. But how to preserve this sense of expectancy, of life finally opening up, this quiet anticipation of joy and peace that a new house always brings? There was something almost sacred about one's first impressions of a new house. She went now from room to room, examining every detail. Yet she could not shake the feeling that she was almost an intruder.

She sighed in satisfaction. The pearly gray stairway leading up from the hall with its maroon carpet and gleaming brass carpet rods were just as she had envisioned. She imagined herself descending those stairs in her purple taffeta dress, coming down to welcome guests in the dining room where the table would be laid with her fine Italian china, brass bowls heaped with bronze-skinned apples and pears, red wine sparkling in decanters all deployed upon the embroidered tablecloth she had bought in Bandol. She conjured a scene of laughter and firelight, the mellow glow of cognac in a snifter as Murry lifted it to his smiling, sensuous mouth. Her husband would be so proud of her and the home she had created for them at last.

She went down to inspect the white kitchen, admiring the black and white checkerboard tile floor and the woodwork in Wedgwood blue. A few boxes of their kitchen utensils had already been delivered and were stacked against a wall. The other boxes would be delivered the next morning. She examined the new iron cooking range and imagined a full-bodied cook dressed in a white cap and apron, standing before the flames, vigorously stirring giant, bubbling pots of jam and custard, nodding and frowning judiciously while her mistress dictated the menu for that evening's dinner party. Here, at last, she might have a Nelly of her own!

With some effort, she climbed back upstairs, dallied in the dining room, peeked into her study, then into Murry's. The towering book shelves were empty, ready to be filled with his immense library, the library of one of England's most important critics, coupled with her own. Why, between them they must own over a thousand books! She smiled at the chintz sofa. This feminine penchant of Murry's for chintz was so curious. Most men hated chintz, preferring leather or sober tones of velvet, but Murry had demanded chintz and so chintz it was. She had picked out the floral pattern for him.

She labored up to the next floor, clinging to the railing, on her way to see the bedrooms. Her heart was pounding, surely more from excitement than exertion. She and Murry were to have separate bedrooms, of course, like all civilized couples. That was necessary because she was ill, but it wouldn't always have to be that way. For the moment, however, she must not share his pillow or drink from his cup.

Murry's dressing room and bedroom were papered in pink, again, a rather curious choice, but he claimed the color was restful to the eyes. Katherine's rooms were oyster white. Lastly she paused on the threshold of the small bedroom wedged between her own room and Murry's, contemplating the effect of the fruity chintz curtains against the sage green walls. If things had gone differently this might have been the nursery, cluttered with teddy bears and rocking horses and Mother Goose prints and pale pink or blue trimmings. But instead, this was to be Ida's room if she should decide to come and share their lives, for indeed she had not yet given Katherine her final decision. It was just like Jones to keep her on the edge like that, playing precious, making her have to coax and beg and stamp her foot. She had asked Ida to come tomorrow afternoon to see the room; surely by then she would have come to her decision. If Ida agreed, she'd have Murry go over in a taxi to Eyot Villa, the boarding house where Ida had been living with the other girls from the airplane factory, to collect Ida's things.

Imagine Ida working at an airplane factory! She had tried her hand at a good many things, poor girl, brushing hair and giving facials, accompanying sick old women, and now this factory, laudable enough, with the war effort, but it was time they faced the fact that the best thing Ida could do with her life was to continue doing what she had always done, helping her. She was certainly ready to pay anything Ida asked, within reason, of course, for her invaluable services and Murry agreed one hundred per cent.

EYOT VILLA

Ida handed the tea to her visitors in the sitting room of Eyot Villa, a cheery but tawdry lodging house pervaded by the smell of scones baking, bad drains, and boiled potatoes. Mrs. Sally, the housekeeper of Eyot Villa, had prepared a sumptuous tea table for Ida's guests, as this was perhaps the last occasion on which she would be receiving visitors there at the boarding house now that she had given notice. After much agonized reflection, Ida had decided to accept Katie's invitation to go and live at the Elephant and keep house for the Murrys. Indeed, how could she do otherwise when Katie demanded something of her? She had just been discussing these prospects with her three visitors, all of whom, it seemed, were determined to dissuade her: Dolly Sutton, a childhood friend now living in London, Mr. Gwynne, her employer from the factory where she had been working for several months, and Robert Wilson, two years younger than herself, distant cousin of a childhood friend, whom she had met returning from Rhodesia four years ago, and who was currently in the army. She had been corresponding with Robert since they met, writing dutiful letters to a man in the trenches who might not ever make it home again, and had even knitted him a scarf. Now that he was in London on leave, he had come to fetch her several evenings from the factory and twice they had walked along the river all the way to Kew. His increasing attentions flustered her. She had not expected to see him again, and preferred an epistolary relationship to one in flesh and blood. But knowing he had no friends in London, and would soon be going back to the front, she humored his request for company. Mrs. Sally encouraged his coming round for tea. She liked having young men in her house.

"My dear! You! You are going to keep house for the Murrys!" crowed Dolly in her usual high humor, and she laughed till Ida blushed bright red.

Robert frowned as he took his first sip of tea," I am sure Ida will be a fine housekeeper. I have no doubts whatsoever about her capabilities."

"Nor I," said Mr. Gwynne, helping himself to a piece Mrs. Sally's seed cake. "At the factory she has proven herself to be most capable, reliable, and industrious."

"I did not mean to cast doubts on her capabilities," apologized Dolly, "but I have known Ida ever since we were girls...and I know how hard it will be for her..."

"I, too, wonder if I shall be up to it. But I have decided to give it a try."

Mr. Gwynne sipped his tea pensively. "I still believe Mrs. Murry would be far better off in a sanatorium. These home cures really never work. Your friend will need constant medical attention and expert care. If she's consumptive and in a bad way, you will be nursing her day and night."

"Mr. Gwynne is right," said Robert, "You will be sacrificing your youth and your independence to an invalid."

"I am ready to do what I must to help Katie get better."

"But that is exactly my point," said Mr. Gwynne. "There is a very good chance she may not get better at home. If you really wish her to improve, you should insist that she go to a sanatorium."

"Think of your own life, Ida. You will be giving up a well-paying job with Mr. Gwynne," said Robert.

"And as for the girls here at Eyot Villa," piped in Mrs.Sally, as she swept in from the kitchen with a tray of scones fresh from the oven, "they will miss her so."

"You are so attached to Katherine," mused Dolly, stirring more sugar into her tea, "and I suppose you could never be happy far from her. Your mind would never be at rest knowing Katherine were ill and in need of care."

"That is indeed how I feel," sighed Ida, grateful that someone had understood her feelings. "I am duty-bound to help every way I can."

"Well, you'll have to learn the secrets of good housekeeping," said Dolly, reaching for a scone.

"To say nothing of how to make roasts and pies!" Ida cried, trying to inject a brighter note in the conversation, for she was quickly tiring of these people's judgments concerning her relationship with Katie. "I am hopeless in the kitchen. But Katie says we may soon have both a cook and a daily. Murry will be earning quite well, and we shall have servants. My duties will be organizational."

Dolly reached over to pat Ida's hand. "I am very glad to hear that, my dear."

Mr. Gwynne pushed his cup and saucer away, took a small package out of his pocket and placed it on the table before Ida. "The girls at the factory asked me to give you this."

Ida turned her surprised gray eyes upon Mr. Gwynne who nodded to encourage her.

"Go on open it!" urged Dolly, "I'm sure it won't bite."

"I wasn't expecting ..."

"A small token of their ... of our... esteem."

Opening the package, Ida gave a small gasp of delight as she discovered a gold watch inside. No one other than her father had ever given her such a valuable present. She knew the girls must have pinched pennies for months to afford it and she hardly felt worthy of such an expensive gift.

"Oh, I can't accept such a ..." she began, but Mr. Gwynne firmly pushed the watch into her hand. Ida removed it from the package. The inscription engraved on the back brought tears to her eyes: "To our dearest Ida" and she allowed Dolly to fasten it around her wrist. Shyly she extended her hand toward Mr. Gwynne and then toward Robert so they might admire the watch.

"I hate to lose such a fine worker, but you can always count on us if you are ever in need of job."

Ida smiled, overcome by such good fortune and such generous friends. She couldn't wait to show the watch to Katie.

"Let me see that watch again," said Robert, seizing her wrist. Pretending to examine the watch, he pulled her hand to him and pressed it flat against his heart. Beneath his flannel shirt she felt the muscular plating of his chest and the vital thumping of his heart within, which quite terrified her. Astonished, she jerked her hand away, shocked that he dare display such physical familiarity with her in front of Dolly and Mr. Gwynne. Yet neither one appeared to have noticed and Robert seemed put off by her brusque withdrawal.

Conversation then turned to the topic of the day: the news that the war would soon be over. They were all making plans for after the war. Ida was silent; she had already told them too much about her own plans. Mr. Gwynne and Robert talked of financial matters and investments, which did not interest her in the least. As he elaborated on business opportunities in Rhodesia, Robert kept glancing at her with an especially eager look which puzzled her. She was anxious for them all to be gone, for she was truly tired now and wanted to be alone.

Soon enough Mr. Gwynne and Dolly took their leave, while Robert remained seated at the table. Even when Ida rose to take away the tea things, he still made no sign of going.

In the kitchen, Mrs. Sally, busy with the preparations for that night's gravy, chided her for leaving her gentleman waiting alone in the sitting room.

"He is just a friend, Mrs. Sally, nothing more," said Ida, piqued, as she piled the dishes in the sink. All the girls at the boarding house considered him her suitor.

"You think so, do you? He has come around to Eyot Villa to see you nearly every evening for a fortnight."

"That's only because he doesn't know anyone else in London."

Mrs. Sally clucked her tongue in disbelief. "Dear girl, there are many more things in life you need to learn than how to make a good pot roast. A fellow doesn't come round to see a girl if he isn't interested in her."

"I am sure you are wrong." Ida felt her cheeks grow hot. She did not like to contradict her elders, but could not bear this sort of teasing.

"Go on out to your guest, Ida."

Ida reluctantly joined Robert in the sitting room, where he sat slumped in his chair, playing with a toothpick. As she entered the room, he snapped the toothpick in two and jumped up. "I must be going now Ida, it's late. I have to see a bloke about ordering some machinery for my farm."

Ida nodded. "Will you be staying in London much longer?"

"Does it make a difference to you?" he asked bitterly.

This uncharacteristic rudeness startled her. "You know how much I enjoy your company."

"Walk with me out to the gate, then, " he commanded.

She obeyed, perplexed, wondering if he had taken offense for being left alone for five minutes in the sitting room after she had cleared the tea table.

But Robert seemed to have other things on his mind. As they stood at the gate to the street, his eyes were fixed on a distant point. Abruptly he turned to her and said, "Ida, there's something I must talk to you about. But tonight I'm not free. Shall we have dinner together tomorrow evening?"

"Not tomorrow, Robert. Tomorrow will be Katie's first night at her new house and she has asked me to join them there for dinner. Perhaps another evening."

Robert huffed and grabbed her arm. She was shocked by the rough urgency of his grasp. No man had ever touched her like that. She tried to pull away, but he held on tighter.

"Ida, I beg you to reconsider, for your own good. Do not go and live with that woman!"

"But Robert, why not?"

"She will devour your life."

" How can you say such a thing!"

"She uses you, exploits your good nature. She insults you."

Ida shook her head, "You don't understand."

"I have your letters Ida, written in despair at her ill treatment of you. Her selfish and outrageous demands!"

Ida was aghast. What impression had she given him in her letters? Sometimes, it's true, she used those letters to let off steam when she and Katie had quarreled. But obviously he had read more into them than she had intended.

"It's true that sometimes I am not as patient with her as I should be. When Katie is angry, she can say such cruel things, as perhaps I wrote to you in rasher moments. But I have come to understand that it is her illness that makes her behave that way. I didn't realize that fully before. "

He let go of her at last. "Ida, there might be other opportunities in life for you."

"Working in Mr. Gwynne's factory?"

"You might marry, have children, have a home of your own."

She mumbled an inarticulate reply and looked off down the street.

"I am speaking for myself, Ida. If I haven't spoken out before it was because everything was so uncertain, with the war, with my financial situation and my brother's debts. Now I am nearly clear of all that. I am free to take on the responsibilities of a wife and family. I have always felt, ever since I first met you," he seized both Ida's hands in his and squeezed them hard, " that you would make a fine wife."

Ida's mouth dropped open and her hands went cold. A marriage proposal was the very last thing she had expected from Robert Wilson. Her eyes scanned the street for fear that someone might see them in this intimate pose and get the wrong impression. What if Katie or one of her friends should walk by at that moment? She tried to free her hands, but the strength had dwindled in her fingers.

Robert clung harder as he continued, "It will take another year for me to settle the family property, if you will wait that long, and then we can go, if you like, to Rhodesia, and take over my brother's dairy farm."

At last she wriggled her hands free and found her tongue. "Marriage! I am very fond of you Robert, but I have never thought of you as anything more than a friend. I am sorry if I have led you to think otherwise. It was certainly not my intention."

"Please take your time to think it over. I am offering you a new life, Ida. Your own life. Not a secondhand one as handmaiden to an invalid."

"But Rhodesia! I could never leave Katie and go so far away. And I don't think I would like living on a farm." Flustered she stepped back and brushed a lock of hair away from her face. Nervously she watched the street. It was time this encounter ended. She spoke the cruelest words that sprang to her lips: "And in any case, I am not terribly fond of cows."

Robert colored. "Your relationship with that woman is unhealthy," he blurted out.

"Katherine is like a sister to me. More than a sister. And I to her."

"Your attachment is unwholesome, Ida. People say ..."

She stared at him, aghast at his forwardness. A scowl had replaced his eager, boyish look. "People say?"

"People say that she has corrupted you!" he said through his teeth and glared at the ground.

Ida blanched with shame and fury. No one had ever insulted her so. Without reply, she fled back through the garden, and up the steps into the house, leaving him standing at the gate to the street.

2 PORTLAND VILLAS

With a silvery ring of her bicycle bell and a squeal of breaks, up pedaled Ida to 2 Portland Villas, over an hour late. The underarms of her blue serge dress were soaked with sweat, her forehead perspiring, and her eyes still felt as puffy as a toad's from crying all night after her meeting with Robert. Katie stood waiting for her out on the front step, wearing yellow gardening gloves and frowning, her arms full of pink hydrangeas. Ida greeted her with a huffy hello, jumped off the bicycle and banged the gate open. She tossed her bicycle against the hydrangea bush, crushing a branch of clusters and scattering a few tiny blooms to the ground. Katie shrieked, swooped to inspect the damage, then ordering Ida to wipe her feet, shooed her into the house. She had not seemed to notice Ida's distress, saying only "My goodness, Ida, your hair is so disheveled and there is a snag in your stocking. Please tidy yourself up a bit before Kot comes for my Russian lesson."

Kot, or Koteliansky, was one of the few of Katie's literary friends whom Ida was allowed to meet when he came to visit. Otherwise, she was kept out of sight, or at most, allowed to serve the tea.

But today Katie seemed to be in high spirits, eager to show Ida their new house. Taking her by the hand, she led her through the rooms, pointing out the pretty details she had arranged herself. A lace trimming on a curtain, a candy dish from Bandol, an old Arabian embroidered silk shawl transformed into a lampshade. Upstairs she showed her Murry's room, then her own, and lastly the room she had set aside for Ida's use. Opening the door with a flourish, Katie invited her to enter her new room.

The sage green and lemon walls, the fruity chintz curtains, the coverlet of lilac and cream all took Ida's breath away for Katie had combined her favorite colors with delicacy and skill. By the window stood a table with a handsome writing case of Spanish leather. "For your correspondence and for the household accounts," Katie explained. Ida caressed the smooth cowhide of the case which must have cost a fortune. The shaggy fleece on the floor by the bed was from Katie's bedroom in New Zealand. On the dresser were a lamp with a bright yellow shade, a dark blue bowl of hydrangeas from the garden, and a photograph of the two of them wearing straw hats and black ties, taken years ago at Queen's College. Ida remembered the day it was taken very well. That morning in Regent's Park in 1903, she had sworn to be Katie's confidant forever and never to betray her. Now fifteen years later, she was proud to have kept her word.

A tall window overlooked the garden, offering the same view of the heath as Katherine's room next door which was connected to hers by a door half-hidden by the wallpaper, as if to emphasize the secret interdependency of their lives. On a window seat, cushioned to match the curtains, all green and gold and summer, Wingley, the new household feline, was curled. At Ida's approach, the kitten stirred, yawned, and stretched out a tiny paw to her, soft and pink as a raspberry dipped in milk.

"What a beautiful room, Katie, I don't know how to thank you."

"So your answer is yes!"

"It hasn't been an easy decision to make, Katie."

"I realize that. And I know how hard it was for you when we were in Bandol and Paris, but you see Jones, I know I am cruel and angry and intolerant and absurd sometimes, and I hate myself for being so, and yet I just can't control it. It's partly the anguish of being ill, and partly the physical discomfort. I am always in constant pain...whether it's my back or my joints or my lungs. That can't justify my behavior, I know. But for the sake of our long friendship, I beg you to forgive me in advance when I am impatient and spiteful and hateful."

Ida was deeply touched. There was no need to explain anything. "Of course, Katie, I forgive you... I mean there is nothing to forgive."

"So you *will* come. I *do* need you, at least until I am well again. And Jack wants you too. He is so fond of you and sincerely respects you. I know with you here I shall get well again."

Katie was gazing at her, eyes brimming with eager expectation. Ida wanted nothing more from life than to stay at Katie's side forever, but her conscience rankled, remembering Mr. Gwynne's advice. She took a deep breath and said, "Katie, I was talking yesterday to Mr. Gwynne."

Katie's face darkened. "The fellow from the factory? What has he got to do with anything?"

"Mr. Gwynne, my employer. I had to give notice, of course, I couldn't continue working at the factory and be your housekeeper at the same time."

Katie nodded and eyed her with suspicion.

"He's always been very kind to me. He gave me permission to leave when I joined you in Bandol, and then took me back again the moment I returned, for which I was so grateful."

"So you mean to say that you are reluctant to leave your present position at the factory?"

"Well, I was getting on rather well and did make lots of friends. The girls there even gave me this gold watch," she thrust her wrist out to show Katie the watch, but she did not deign to glance at it. Ida took another deep breath and continued. "But what I meant to say was that I have come to regard Mr. Gwynne in a fatherly sort of way and to look to him for advice."

"And what was his fatherly advice in this case?"

Ida balked, but, knowing that it was better to say things straight out than beat around the bush with Katie, she bumbled on, "He thinks you should go to a sanatorium."

"Go where? I knew it! You and your Mr. Gwynne would have me put in a loony bin!"

"Not a loony bin. A sanatorium. That's a place for people with consumption."

"I know what that word means! You want me to die! You know very well I could not survive ten minutes in such a place. Even Doctor Sorapure has said so! And you have the nerve to suggest such a thing? Out of my sight, you monster!"

There was no escaping Katie's fury. Ida knew she should never have mentioned Mr. Gwynne, but could not take it back now and was forced to go on, "All he meant was that sometimes home cures are not very effective. For your own good, he suggested that a sanatorium might help you get better faster."

"And pray tell, since when does Mr. Gwynne practice medicine? I shall choose my own doctors, thank you."

"I only say this, Katie, because I am concerned about your health, and I want you to get better. Of course I will come and stay if you have decided that a home cure is what you must have. I will do anything you ask of me."

"Anything I ask of you? I want nothing of you if it is not freely given. Nothing indeed. I hereby withdraw my invitation. There is no place for you here."

Katie strode over to the window seat, scooped up Wingley and stalked out again, slamming the door so hard a crack appeared in the plaster molding. Another door opened and slammed shut again down the hall and the grating noise of a key was heard, vehemently being turned in a lock.

Ida found her way down the stairs and out to the garden, where she sank to her knees beside Katie's yellow rose bush and began blubbering like a child. She knew her sobbing and sighing were only too audible to Katie inside, and doubtless to all the neighbors, but could not stop herself. After a time, the gate to the street clanged open. A man's soft voice said, "Ida?" Footsteps crunched down the gravel path, and two polished brown oxfords and a pair of immaculately creased gray gabardine trouser legs appeared before her. She looked up and there stood Kot, looking like a friendly bear in gold -rimmed glasses, carrying a satchel. Beneath his herringbone jacket, he wore a white Russian tunic trimmed with red braid.

Kot squatted down beside her on the gravel. "You and Katherine have been quarreling again."

Ida nodded.

Kot removed a handkerchief from his breast pocket and handed it to her. Ida wiped her tears and blew her nose sonorously. "I must look a fright," she sniffled.

"Indeed you do. But no matter. Tell me what has happened."

But where to begin? How to tell him about Robert and Rhodesia and being corrupted by Katherine and then being rejected by her? The most she could tell Kot was Mr. Gwynne's suggestion that Katie go to a sanatorium and Katie's reaction to it.

"I have already given notice at the factory and at the pension. And the girls there even gave me a gold watch as a present. Now, if Katherine doesn't want me, what will I do? I'll have to go back to Rhodesia."

"Nonsense. Of course, Katherine wants you. And you must try to understand how terrible the suggestion of a sanatorium must sound to her ears, after these months away from home and from Murry, especially now that they are married and have taken out the lease for this house. You can imagine how much all that must mean to Katya and how shattering it would be for her if she should be deprived of it. Still, secretly I agree with Mr. Gwynne, a sanatorium might be the best suggestion for her physical health...perhaps, but not for her soul. And Katya's very headstrong. As you know."

Ida nodded so glumly Kot laughed in his high-pitched almost womanish laugh. Despite his apparent sternness, Kot had always treated her with gentle irony, and now he touched his high forehead against hers.

"Come now, dear Ida. Listen to an old man's advice. Katya needs you. God knows, she needs us all, even more than she realizes. Come into the house with me."

"Katie will just chase me out again, in a fury."

He straightened up, went to the door, and rang the bell. The front door opened just a crack and Katie peered out at them. She greeted Kot then opened the door a little wider.

"Jones, it isn't healthy to sit out like that on the ground. Why are you behaving like a child of eight? There are tea things in the kitchen. Come on in now, be a good a girl, and fix us all a cup of tea. "

Relieved by this sudden change of status, Ida rose, dusted off her skirt, and sniffling into Kot's handkerchief, she followed him into the house.

. . .

Sleepless, Katherine listened as owls hooted across the heath. Her sister's telegram was tossed beside her on the bed, amid a pile of newspapers and books. She had read it now a hundred times, unable to believe the news: Mother was gone. She had passed away during an operation without regaining consciousness. Katherine had not even known that her mother had needed an operation. Her family kept her cut off whenever anything important happened. It was a wonder her father remembered to continue her allowance—as paltry as it was. And now so unexpectedly, they had written to say that Mother was dead.

How was it possible that she had sensed nothing that day? There had been no omens, no clouded uneasiness. All Katherine had felt were her ordinary aches, pains and worries. When Ida's father died, Ida had known, *she* had had a presentiment. Dear dull Ida, as sensitive as a stone, had felt *something*. Jones had come to her one morning, to report a queer dream she'd had that night, in which her father was shouting out to her from across a dark lake, but she could not catch a single word. She had dismissed Ida's anxieties with smug skepticism, telling Ida that she had merely eaten too much chocolate cake at teatime. Then two days later, a telegram arrived from Ida's sister, describing Colonel Baker's awful suicide—a gun to his head—the very night Ida had had her dream. No mere coincidence that had been, Katherine realized. Ida had experienced a genuine flash of second sight. But as for herself, the writer, the poet, the one with the musical gift, so keenly perceptive, she had felt nothing the moment her mother had passed from the earth. She had merely gone about her business that day, unawares, impervious to any inner revelation or anticipatory grief.

Why wasn't Jack there to hold her now, to comfort her? Lying in bed, she kept listening for the clanging of the gate, for the click of the door latch. Despite the delivery of the black-bordered telegram from her sister that afternoon, he had not put off his dinner engagement for the evening. Jack was about to become editor of the *Athenaeum* and he was out this evening to discuss those plans with the publisher. She realized how vital the editorship of such an influential journal would be for Murry's career, for their future, for everything they hoped to accomplish together. Yet, could he not realize for once how much she needed him near? Imagine dining out when your wife has just received such crushing news. But that was just like Murry to go ploughing on ahead with his own affairs. When Leslie had been killed, he had gone off to write in his diary, mulling over the meaning of mortality. Leslie. The name died away on her lips with a sob. Jack had not tried to comfort her, not really, after her brother's death.

She sat up now and stared at the armchair near the bed, closed her eyes and tried to picture Mother sitting there, looking bemused in a pink 1890s style tea gown with a choker of pearls around her neck. This was a trick she played sometimes, calling up people from the past and conversing with them for hours on sleepless nights in lonely hotels. Sometimes it worked with people she didn't even know, even with characters from Shakespeare, and once, only once, had Chekhov graced her with his presence, complaining about the price of vodka, speaking impeccable but heavily-accented English, sounding, actually, rather like Kot. Dearest Leslie, so handsome in his soldier's uniform, dead now nearly three long years, was a frequent visitor to these late night séances. Grandma, too, came often to tell her stories of New Zealand and seemed so real that for an hour or two Katherine was transported back to her cozy room in the house on Tinakori Road with the calico curtain billowing in the breeze. Only when she reached for the little pelican statue made of seashells Grandma held out to her did the image blur and fade, leaving nothing but a halo of bluish light around the empty chair, eerily reflected in the mirror above the bed. But tonight, try as she might, it would not work with Mother. The chair remained empty, illumined by the half-light of the garden lantern shining in the window.

She lay on the bed and hugged a pillow to her breast, thinking back to one of Mother's visits to London, just after she had scandalized the family by marrying George Bowden and leaving him the next day. Dressed in a sophisticated black linen suit and a shiny straw boater, she had invited Mother to tea at her bedsitter in Beauchamp Lodge where she had found rooms after deserting her hapless husband. Mother's first words when she had opened the door had been, "Plump as ever, I see!" Then stepping inside, she had dashed the hat off Katherine's head, ordering, "Give that to the chambermaid." She had cringed before Mother's disdain, but thinking back on the hat, she had to laugh. Mother was right, it was a perfectly awful hat, and they had immediately gone out shopping to buy her a new one and then had gorged themselves on cakes and tea and strawberry jam.

Despite her commanding manner, Mother's childlike spontaneity could be so winning at times. Once she had rung up father at the bank, calling him out of an important board meeting just to tell him how happy she was with their new house. Father loved that about her, and his greatest compliment to Katherine had been to point out her resemblance to her mother. They were really so alike, Katherine had to admit, and how she admired Mother's courage, especially in the latter period of her life. Her mother had loved life and lived more deeply than any other human being she had ever known. Perhaps that's why Katherine loved Lawrence so, he too had that ebullient passion for living. His roots went deep into life. Katherine shared that passion, only perhaps the hardships and loneliness she had endured had somehow veiled the ardor she felt. Its flames no longer flared out to the surface to warm the people around her, but burned deeper into her work, like a steady coal flame. That quiet joy was Mother's legacy.

What was inexplicable was that the tears would not come despite the numbness in her chest. It was a chill and solemn feeling that would not soothe itself in tears. She considered the eleven thousand five hundred miles to New Zealand, her long years abroad, Mother's rare letters, even rarer visits. All this had made her mother less real somehow, and every departure, every separation was like a small death. Yet she could never have stayed in New Zealand with Mother.

Mother never understood the most important things about her. This business of writing meant nothing to her. Mother was convinced that a happy woman; a serious woman needn't bother herself with such scribblings. There was something unseemly about selling stories to magazines, and what's worse, putting in details about one's family. And then there was Ida. Mother could not understand that her friendship with Ida was part of her. And she wouldn't have lost Garnet's baby if Mother hadn't sent her to Bavaria for that cold water treatment. She still had nightmares in which a fiendish green-faced nurse doused her abdomen with cold water spurting from a black rubber hose.

There—that was the latch. She glanced at the clock: it was after one. Stealthy steps on the stairs. A board creaked. Now he must be standing in the corridor. Footsteps advanced almost to her door, and she wanted to cry out " Jack, darling do come in a minute," but did not. No, he must come to her of his own accord, of his own desire. She lay listening, lips pressed tight. The steps retreated, the door to Murry's room opened and shut, and then the house was silent. She lay awake awhile longer, straining to catch some sound but heard only a branch tapping against the window. Sometime before dawn, she rose, tiptoed to Ida's door and knocked softly.

"Ida," she said, "I can't sleep, I'm so distraught. Please come."

. . .

At the sound of the doorbell, Ida hurried up the steps from the kitchen to answer, but Murry, passing through the hall, opened the door himself. Hearing him exchange a few curt words with a fellow, she surmised it must be a tradesman come to the wrong entrance, and headed back to the kitchen where she had left the kettle boiling. Slipping on a smudged apron, she began to cut the cake for tea and was quite astonished when Murry called down to her, "Ida, there are some gentlemen here for you."

Her few friends never visited her here with Katie and Murry, so it must be someone from the factory, she thought, perhaps something had happened with the machinery; there had been an accident! Alarmed, she ran up the steps in her soiled apron and cautiously approached the doorway where Robert Wilson and another burly fellow stood crowding the threshold. They were both in uniform.

"Robert," said Ida unpleasantly surprised. "You might have warned me you were coming." Quickly pulling off the apron, she wadded it upon a shelf in the hall and smoothed her hair.

"These *gentlemen* are friends of yours, I take it, Ida?"

"Robert is an old friend from Rhodesia," said Ida uneasily. She did not like the subtle stress Murry had given to the word, "gentlemen."

Robert introduced the other man as his friend, Marshall, also from Rhodesia, in London on leave. Thinly disguising his irritation at their intrusion, Murry said with false alacrity, "Well, don't just stand there, Ida, show them into the sitting room."

Recovering her composure, Ida said, "We were just about to have tea. I hope you'll join us."

"That's very kind of you, but I really have come just to say goodbye. I'm off to the front tomorrow."

Ida stifled a gasp, which must not have escaped Murry's notice, for he cast her a quizzical look and said, "I insist then, that you *must* stay."

She frowned, hoping Robert would be discreet enough to make no reference to their previous conversation or to his marriage proposal, which she had not taken the least bit seriously.

"Who was that at the door?" trilled Katie from upstairs.

74

"Just a couple of gentlemen for Ida," Murry called back, "they're staying for tea."

"Gentlemen?" said Katie appearing at the balustrade. "For Ida?"

Ida's spirits sank. She would end up having to tell Katie the whole story of Robert's proposal sooner or later. Katie was a merciless interrogator, and she had an uncanny way of reading Ida's most secret thoughts. Katie always had to know all, down to the most intimate and embarrassing details, which she picked over with relish, like a carnivorous bird. Katie descended the stairs now, her silk frock rustling, a hint of amusement upon her mask-like face as she inspected Ida's gentlemen, like a scornful duenna examining a maiden's suitors before a ball. Ida knew well how Robert and Marshall must appear to Katie and Murry's eyes. She blushed for Robert's large red hands with bitten nails, for the sharp colonial twang of his vowels. She introduced the men to Katie, and while Katie and Murry ushered them into the sitting room, she went down to fetch the tea.

Trapped in the role of hostess, stuck behind the tea trolley, Ida observed Murry's feeble attempts to draw the men into conversation. But Murry would never be able understand unliterary fellows like Robert, soldiers and farmers who enjoyed life out of doors, rarely opening a book. Robert, brooding and taciturn, would not be wooed by Murry's inane chatter and Marshall was too shy to utter more than a brief comment on the weather. In the end, Murry simply filled up the silence by jabbering away, eager to impress his visitors with his knowledge and intellectual superiority, talking about a recent literary debate in the newspapers which could not interest them in the least. Even Katie seemed to realize how patronizing Murry must appear to her guests, and tried to rescue them by enquiring with more genuine interest about their experiences in the war. But somehow Murry seized every pause to deflect the conversation back to himself.

Ida did not expect Robert to put up with Murry's attitude for long, and soon enough, once he had drained his cup, he thanked his hosts, and announced it was time to leave, but he made the mistake of asking Murry's advice on the shortest way to the station. Murry, hopeless with directions, suggested a perfectly absurd route, and Katie duly corrected him. "Not left, darling, They must turn right, head down to the square, and take the second road on the right."

"Nonsense," said Murry huffily, insisting his was the shortest way. As Katie and Murry bickered, a hideous sneer appeared on Robert's face. Ida could see that he found the Murrys perfectly disgusting. He put an end to their argument by jumping to his feet and stalking out with an abrupt "Goodbye and thanks," not even pausing to shake hands. Marshall mumbled an apology, grabbed his hat, and followed suit. Out they went, through the front door, leaving their hosts speechless with amazement. Murry looked as though someone had smacked him in the face.

"Wait!" called Ida and dashed after them out through the garden, gravel flying beneath her feet as she ran to the gate. Here Robert stopped, turned to Ida, hands on hips. Timidly, she offered him her hand and was surprised when he took it, though his grip crushed her fingers.

"Thank you so much for coming, Robert. Take care of yourself. I hope you don't feel badly about..."

"Oh come on, Ida!" he barked through his teeth, dropped her hand, and turned away with a shrug. "Let's get out of here," he said to Marshall, and the two men stormed through the gate.

To her despair, they turned left.

"No, no," she cried, running after them, "to the right."

Robert wheeled round, his face purple with rage. "For God's sake, Ida, I've really had enough of the three of you. You and that lesbian and her bloody pedant of a husband!" and without a further word, they rounded the corner.

Stunned, Ida stared after them, then burst into tears. Not wanting to confront Katie and Murry, she lingered in the garden and tried to calm herself by picking a few shriveled leaves off the hydrangea bush. When half an hour later she had regained her composure, she stepped back into the hall. Katie and Murry were still standing there, arguing about the quickest way to the station.

"I must say," said Murry, as Ida came in, "those were rude chaps."

Katie had found Ida's apron on the bookshelf. She held it up and examined it as if it were contaminated with some dread disease. "Heavens, Ida, is this the proper place to leave your dirty laundry?"

Ida snatched the apron from Katherine and hurried upstairs into her room where she threw herself on the bed and buried her face in a pillow. More tears flowed of outrage and shame, injustice and regret, but when she rose to rinse her face in the clean, cold water of the basin on the dresser, the strongest emotion that remained was relief. Surely she would never need see Robert Wilson again, and she could quite do without his letters.

. . .

Katherine, pale with lips pressed tight, sat in Dr. Sorapure's surgery, while he proceeded with the painful treatment of draining an infected cyst in her neck.

"Think of the infinity of the stars," he said, penetrating her skin with a sharp steel needle. "It will not hurt quite as much if you do."

Katherine winced and drew a deep breath. "Yes, I can quite see the stars. I assure you, I have been contemplating them for several weeks now."

A faint smile appeared at the corner of the doctor's mouth. "Think of the endlessness of God's mercy." Once again, the needle struck through her inflamed flesh.

She gripped the edge of the bench where she sat half-reclining, and said, "I envy your faith."

Sorapure had finished now. When he turned away to wash his hands in the sink, she sighed with relief.

"Have you no faith of your own?" he enquired.

"I must quarrel with the idea of a personal god. I think science makes it impossible for an educated person nowadays to believe in organized religion. But don't think me a complete infidel. I know there is *something*. Oh yes, something, but what? Something infinitely distant from me."

Sorapure studied her with kind eyes, offering no comment, and made a note in her clinical record. He was, she thought, an excellent doctor, and would have made perhaps an even better priest. As much as she admired him, she wished to provoke him, as she always did with men she found attractive. And he was a young, attractive, vigorous man, with blond hair and an intense cerulean gaze. His beautifully-shaven cheeks shone with eau de cologne.

"Do you believe in ghosts, doctor?"

Sorapure raised an eyebrow.

"Sometimes at night when I cannot sleep, I project my own ghosts. My beloved brother. My grandmother..... I see them, sitting right before me, there on the rocking chair. And I listen for hours as they chatter to me of the past. It is for them I write, you see. To make them live again. But I do not know if it is they who have sought me out from the dead, or if it is my own imagination that projects them there before me. What would your churchmen have to say about that?"

"The imagination is a spiritual faculty," he said, taking out his stethoscope. "It can vanquish time and space. It can heal or destroy. Only you can know where your visions lead you."

Touché! Yes, he had offered a deeply thoughtful and truly provocative reply, nipping her pride with the swift sting of wisdom. This quality of his made her admire him all the more.

He listened to her heart and lungs with his stethoscope, frowned, and looked her full in the face.

"You are going to tell me that the situation is grave," she said turning to the opaque window of the surgery and pausing to listen to the traffic rattling in the street. She stared at a row of dark brown and blue bottles on a shelf below the window, then at the steel and glass instruments laid out on a trolley beside them. "Whenever I climb a flight of stairs, I feel that my heart is about to explode. The pains in my joints and back impede any freedom of movement. Lying in bed at night, I wake up and find my legs locked and I simply can't move, and unless I sit up, I cannot breathe. Another specialist, Dr. Ainger whom my father arranged to examine me, has suggested I go to a sanatorium, immediately. He believes the home treatment that you have prescribed will not be effective."

"I certainly agree that another winter here would be fatal for you, Mrs. Murry. Adequate rest and diet are essential and the pure mountain air of a Swiss sanatorium could only be beneficial."

"Yes, but in sanatorium, they would not allow me to work. To write. And it is my writing that keeps me alive. And of course my husband. To be deprived of those only sources of joy and comfort would spell my doom. I couldn't bear it. I might as well be dead already."

"You are a strong and determined woman, Mrs. Murry. I have come to realize how much your writing does indeed sustain you. This is not the first time we have discussed the benefits of a sanatorium, which are many. But the anxiety of living in such an environment might be detrimental to your state and outweigh the benefits you might enjoy. Therefore, I do believe that a home treatment is still worth a try, as long as you follow my instructions to the letter. Unless, of course, you have begun to have second thoughts."

"By no means."

"Then I recommend that you avoid all forms of emotional agitation and arrange to spend the next five winters in a warm, dry climate."

Katherine laughed. "As if the two were compatible: abandoning my home and husband while avoiding agitation. Not to mention the worrisome expense of traveling abroad."

"Could not Mr. Murry accompany you?"

She shrugged. "Oh, for a few weeks, I suppose."

"There is your friend, Miss Baker."

"Of course, there is always Ida. What would I do without Ida?"

. . .

The house was dark when Murry returned, but the light in the garden had been left on, illuminating Katherine's pear tree, laden now with firm green fruits, still acerbic to the taste. He opened the door, and switching off the garden light, made his way upstairs, along the corridor, towards Katherine's room. Passing Ida's half-open door, he could hear her snuffling into her pillow. Katherine's door was shut. He opened it now and stepped into the close and sickening darkness where Katherine lay like a wraith in her white nightgown, her mouth covered with the mask of an oxygen cylinder, every breath, a whir and a wheeze. Her eyes were closed, but he knew she was not asleep. He sat down on the edge of the bed. Should he speak to her or remain silent? A patch of moonlight shone down on the rug. He stared at an arabesque in the rug's design, tracing its pattern with his eyes. At last he sighed and she lifted her hand to acknowledge his presence. He patted her hand reassuringly, stroked the smooth pale skin of her forearm just once, then withdrew his hand, thinking as he did several times a day: Should she die soon, the memory of this moment would be intolerable. He rose, murmuring, "Goodnight, Katherine darling," and retreated to his room.

He lay in bed, aching for Katherine's body beside him. He had not touched her again since she returned from France with Ida. How could anyone expect him to continue like that forever? He was a young and healthy man, after all, and Katherine was now, yes, he must face facts, a hopeless invalid. Who could blame him for seeking comfort in another woman? It had not been easy to resist all temptation while she was away, when there were so many women ready to enfold him in tender arms, eager to smooth the thinning hair from his temples. Yet he had withstood all this, never yielding to his own desire, to his own need, for Katherine's sake. But now Brett, he feared, was falling in love with him, and perhaps he was falling a bit in love with her, too. She had even taken a house in Pond Street near theirs, and these last weeks had been a constant presence in the house. For lunch, for tea, for cocktails, for dinner. Surely Katherine would not fail to notice Brett's eager flush when he entered the room.

It was absurd. He loved Katherine and yet here he was thinking of Brett's young strong body, her soft, full breasts brushing against his chest. Katherine had given him his freedom to have experiences but he knew how much she would suffer to discover he had been dreaming of making love to such a close friend. Up to now he had only sat on the heath with Brett, gazing at hundreds of tiny daisies peeping through the grass, discussing Michelangelo, though it was tiresome to hold long conversations with her, because of her ear trumpet. It required him to lift his head at a certain angle, and shouting into it was certainly a deterrent to more intimate contact. But then Brett had put the cumbersome horn aside, and had woven a wreath of daisies to put around his neck, and when she had smiled at him, with her eyes glittering with lust, he had longed to push his face between her breasts and taste the sweat beading on her freckled skin. Yet that had not happened, though he might have seized her then and pulled her to him. Thinking of Katherine waiting at home had made him as shy and helpless as a schoolboy. Damn! It was all too cruel.

. . .

Murry poured out two glasses of whisky and offered one to Koteliansky, who sat, legs crossed, in the battered leather armchair with Wingley on his knees. That had once been Ida's armchair and was a remnant from her Rhodesian home. She had given it to Katherine years ago to furnish the flat in Clovelly Mansions. Now unsightly and encumbering, with its springs poking out through the seat and tufts of wool stuffing trailing out from underneath, its upholstery clawed to shreds by generations of Katherine's cats, it was so comfortable, she would not part from it. For years whenever they moved house, it had followed them like some decrepit but faithful pet. Awaiting to be reupholstered, it had perhaps found a momentary resting place in Murry's study, for surely, with the lease he had signed and the fortune they had spent on repairs and redecoration, they would not be moving again for some time. How ironic: now that he had finally found his wife a home, they must scrape up the funds to send her abroad every winter for the next five years. He prayed that the Beauchamp family would come to her assistance. Katherine's father had a cousin in France who ran a nursing home for rich English patients. She might be convinced to take Katherine in for a period. Still he hated the thought of having to send her so far away.

"Terrible news, Jack," said Kot, sipping his whisky. "You must be shattered."

They had been talking about Katherine, of course, about Sorapure's confirmed diagnosis: rapidly advancing consumption in her left lung. She had just spent a fortnight locked in her room, breathing with an oxygen cylinder, but now the fever was down, and she was up and about. Life was progressing "as normal," but there were plans to be made for the coming winter. Murry swilled down a long draught of whisky, savoring the warmth in the pit of his stomach.

" Sorapure says that she will pull through, as long as she gets plenty of rest, eats well, and avoids English winters. I shall be packing her off to the South of France every winter for the next few years, that is until she's better."

This was a lie of course, the lie they had all tacitly agreed to. Katherine would *most certainly* be well again in a few years' time. Murry presumed Kot guessed that Katherine's state was grave, but he had sworn to himself he would never speak the truth to anyone, and he did not elaborate now. They would all have to play the game as long as it lasted. What a bitter turn of fate: just married, new house, career on the upswing, and a tragically ill wife. People would think him a cad if he ever voiced such thoughts, he knew, he could confide to no one, not even Katherine. He saw himself alone on a block of ice drifting further and further from safety, from conviviality, from life.

"But Katya is a strong one, despite her physical weakness. She is strong in her soul," Kot consoled him.

Oh yes, Katherine was strong, far stronger than he, and Murry admired her for that. It was her strength which had drawn him to her so powerfully. They were really so alike. He shared her determination, her ambition, her fierceness and ruthlessness. *The two tigers*, that was the nickname they had received from their friends, but compared to Katherine, he was a mere house cat, and still had much to learn from her.

"Dr. Ainger, a specialist her father sent to see her, has recommended she go to a sanatorium. But Katherine has refused, and Sorapure does not believe it is necessary, as long as she winters abroad in a proper climate."

Ainger had been very discouraging, if not downright alarming, about Katherine's condition. He claimed there was a patch on Katherine's left lung as big as an adult hand, and a smaller spot on her right one. If she did not go immediately to a sanatorium, he warned she would be dead within three years, at the most. Certainly he viewed her situation as far more imperiled than did Katherine's physician, Dr. Sorapure, who promised recovery with a home cure and winters abroad. After Dr. Ainger had gone, he and Katherine had sat there together in her studio, brooding over the doctor's gloomy pronouncement. Then Katherine had looked up at him and the frozen expression in her huge eyes somehow unmanned him.

"He says I should go to a sanatorium. Is that what you want me to do?" she had whispered.

"No, of course I don't think you should go."

"Do you think a home cure will heal me?"

"Yes, of course, you will be healed."

But did he really believe it? How could he be required to decide whether she should go or stay? Should not that decision be taken by Katherine herself? By Doctor Sorapure? By her father, even? Yet Katherine expected him to make this decision for her. Which doctor should one believe? He must act and yet could not act for he had no idea what he should do. No one, and most certainly not Kot, could understand the depth of his despair, caught as he was in the web of circumstance. He downed another draught of whisky.

A smell of burning meat invaded the room.

"Jack, can you smell smoke?" said Kot abruptly breaking into Murry's reverie, his great nose quivering as he sniffed the air.

"Good God," cried Murry, "Ida's cooking this evening. We had to send the cook away this morning, as she had been helping herself to the gin." He opened the door and called out, "Ida! What's burning?"

At this behest, Ida, looking harried, appeared up the steps from the kitchen in a dowdy floral dress, apron, and slippers.

"Ida, must I call the fire brigade?"

Ida glared defiantly. "It was just a scrap of suet fallen into the flame."

"For God's sake, open some windows." He shut the door nearly in Ida's face.

"She seems an unlikely housekeeper," said Kot, "but she adores Katherine so."

"Katherine insisted on having Ida. An arrangement I might have done without. But they are devoted to each other. And Katherine does need company and care. But I believe we will be hiring some more competent staff soon."

"Isn't Katherine coming down?" asked Kot.

"I shall see what's keeping her" said Murry. Putting down his glass, he stepped out into the hall where the smoke of singed suet still lingered. He coughed, glanced up, and there was Katherine at the top of the stairs. She was wearing a white dress with lace sleeves and green stockings, and looked as spring-like as any pastoral bride. The white dress gleamed on the dim stairway. It fit a bit looser about her bosom and hips than it once did, but she still had a charming figure. Since her return from France she had put on weight again, thank God, and looked a little less like a starved war-refugee or victim of torture. Yet her face was leaner now, her eyes brighter. She cast a long, penetrating look at him and he smiled back so tightly his cheek hurt, for he strained to keep his mouth from trembling. Swallowing a half-formed sob, he said only, "There you are. Kot is waiting."

One hand poised on the banister, she descended the stairs slowly, as though each step were a test of strength. Her dress rustled softly. Never once did she take her eyes off his face, and he obediently returned her gaze, but not its intensity. He could not give her that, and his eyes darted aside before she reached the bottom of the stairway. She stepped into the square of afternoon light filtering in through the hall window and gave him her hand, soft and frail as a leaf, finely veined in blue. He pressed it and the force of his desire for her welled up inside him. How he had yearned for her all those weeks she had been away! Why had she gone so far away from him? He longed now to pull her to him roughly, to cover her with kisses, to sink his head against her breast, but dared not. No, now he dared not touch her. Several times a day he even cleaned his hands with eau de cologne after spending time in her presence. Once when Ida had caught him doing that, he had blushed with shame. He let go Katherine's hand.

Katherine was smiling at him with that knowing way of hers, as if she could read his thoughts, her head tilted to one side. There was a keenness about her now, an edge. Every word they exchanged seemed to hold a double meaning. Laying her hand on his sleeve, she drew him firmly to her side, then leaning on him ever so slightly, shuffled into the study.

Kot set the kitten down and rose to his feet as Murry led Katherine into the room. Peering at her from behind his gold-rimmed glasses, he grinned like a friendly bear, his eager affection for her beaming forth from his swarthy face and body. It was a love so full and rich Murry nearly felt crowded out of the room by its radiance. He found Kot such a funny fellow. Working together on translations of Chekhov with him, Murry had come to know him better. Kot was such a pedant, and so fastidious, a stickler for precision, quibbling over every word, and, then, over every penny owed him for his work. Lawrence claimed he adored Kot, but behind his back called him a chattering magpie, in

Murry's opinion an exact epithet. Murry did not like Kot much, but did not fear him, or any other man, for that matter, as a rival. Katherine charmed everyone she knew. She stirred such devotion in all her male acquaintances, slipping into their confidence as easily as a child... or perhaps a snake, fascinating them with her supple, sinuous movements, her beseeching eyes, her ribaldry, her musical laughter. Then there was her other, hidden side: the brooding, the fears, the cold distances and the inscrutable silences, which Murry knew only too well. Indeed, he alone knew the real Katherine and was privy to all her unpleasant and despicable sides, of which there were many. Not even Ida could claim to know her as he did.

Kot's eyes followed them as Murry led her to an armchair near his desk where she fairly collapsed, choking back a rasping cough. At the sound, Murry turned to the bookcase and pressed his handkerchief to his lips.

"I brought Jack those finished Chekhov translations," said Kot, settling into his chair again and indicating a pile of papers on the desk. Katherine glanced at a thick manuscript and nodded. Then Ida appeared in the doorway, to announce that Brett had arrived and that dinner would shortly be served.

Dinner was no culinary success. The cutlets were tough and slightly scorched, and the pudding tasted burnt. They'd have to hire a new cook at once, Katherine mused, Murry wouldn't stand for this sort of thing for long. Afterwards they withdrew to his study for a drink, but she felt too weak to stay up chatting for long, and soon said goodnight. Kot too rose to take his leave. Ida offered to walk him out to the gate, while Brett and Murry stood sipping drinks by the bookcase. Murry leaned over her ear trumpet, shouting about Rembrandt. Before going upstairs, Katherine stepped into her study, looking for something suitable to read in bed, but nothing quite appealed to her. Remembering Kot's translations, she thought they might serve the purpose, and headed back to Murry' s study. Through the half-open door, she heard his soft laughter and Brett's little grunting replies. What *can* they be going on about all this time? Katherine wondered. Conversations with the hard of hearing are generally limited in duration, yet Murry had been jawing all evening into Brett's ear trumpet. As soon as this thought flickered through her mind, she was ashamed of having such coarse suspicions about dear Brett, who, next to Ida, was her closest friend. Cautiously, she peered through the opening in the doorway and saw Brett and Murry standing close, almost touching, drawn by a subtle magnetism. Brett's ear trumpet, needless to say, was abandoned on the desk. That was all but it shocked Katherine deeply. She thought she might call out to Murry or signal her presence with a cough, then sweep through the room and snatch up the papers, but she could neither turn away nor dash the door open. She could only stand in the grip of some chill fascination and watch the scene unfold. Brett, obviously tipsy, stepped closer to Murry, who was grinning down at her in a horrid way. She pushed herself up on tiptoe, propelled her breasts up towards Murry's chest and touched his lips with her own half-open mouth.

Katherine's heart beat wildly as the blood rushed through her body, igniting the entire surface of her skin, but she could not pull herself away or even make a sound; the spectacle was too captivating. Murry did not enfold Brett in his arms but only stood woodenly, smiling his horrible smile, shaking his head.

The front door shut behind her and Ida came in from walking Kot out to the street.

Ida seemed surprised to find her still up, standing in the dark hall, spying into Murry's study. "Katie, I thought you had gone to bed."

Katherine stepped back from the door. "No, I thought I would fetch a book, but I suppose it's rather late to sit up reading. "

"Shall I fetch it for you?" Ida glanced quizzically toward the study door.

"No," said Katherine, placing her hand on Ida's arm and giving her a monitory squeeze. "There's no need. Please don't bother. Goodnight, Jones ." Kissing Ida goodnight, Katherine hobbled up the stairs.

Ida rose in the gray light. She had been up way too late again, talking with Kot the night before and after he had gone, there had been the washing up to do and a hundred chores to complete so as not to leave the house in disarray for the next morning. Brett had still been there in Murry's study, chatting with him when Ida had gone to bed, and now she wondered if she was still in there, stretched out on the chintz sofa, for they had all had a bit too much to drink.

She rinsed her face in cold water, tugged a comb through her wild hair, and pinned it up. Slipping on her old factory uniform which she always wore when cleaning house, she reviewed her morning schedule. First she must check to see if Katie were awake, prepare her breakfast, and take it up to her room on a tray. Next she must dust all the rooms, upstairs and down, and do the carpets and floors. Thank goodness it was warm now and Katie did not need a fire lit in her room. Then she had to tidy the study, put fresh flowers in the Japanese vase next to Ribni, Katie's little Japanese doll, fill the ink well, and polish the brass lamp, so when Katie came down, everything would be in order, ready for her to write. At nine o' clock sharp, Katie would come downstairs, shut the studio door, allowing no intrusions, and work furiously until lunchtime. Today's schedule would be more hectic than usual for Ida as there would be guests for lunch: the Lawrences were coming and Katie wanted everything perfect for her friends.

She tapped softly on Katie's door and opened it. Wide awake, Katie smiled at her from the bed, the covers strewn with a dozen books and copies of the *Times Literary Supplement*. Ida knew that meant it had been a sleepless night. Katie's wan face and forced smile confirmed this.

"I have been listening to the most extraordinary bird. Can you hear? What do you suppose it is?"

Ida listened obediently and said, "Why, it's a lark."

"Don't be silly. It can't be a lark. Listen, there it goes again. It must be something rare indeed."

Ida closed her eyes and pretended to listen. She despised these games Katie obliged her to play. "A nightingale still awake perhaps?" knowing full well it wasn't.

Katie sighed. "No use asking you, Jones, I suppose you couldn't tell a songbird from a crow."

Ida's cheeks burned with shame. She hated appearing so stupid before Katie, but it was part of their unspoken pact.

Katie took no notice. "I've decided on the menu for today. For lunch with Lawrence we must have roast beef, glazed carrots, and a trifle."

Ida cleared her throat peremptorily and said "The shopping was done yesterday and it will be watercress soup, veal cutlets and onions, green beans, and rice pudding."

Katie sniffed. "Not really what I had in mind, but whatever you wish will be fine, Ida. You're the cook."

Ida acknowledged this small concession with a bow and turned to leave, but Katie said, "Don't go just yet, Jones, I want to ask you something."

Fearing that Katie wished to add something to the menu, Ida paused in the doorway, frowning, worried that there would be no time to do any more shopping.

Katie patted the bed. "Do sit down. And shut the door."

Ida obeyed reluctantly. Sitting on the edge of the bed, she looked at Katie in dutiful expectancy, but Katie averted her eyes. She gazed down at a corner of the counterpane and stroked the smooth pink satin fabric.

"Jones, in those few days before you joined me in Bandol, did you see much of Jack?"

"Not much. I was so busy at the factory, and he was at the War Office. He gave me some papers to type for him, which I did gladly."

"Did he mention that he had been seeing Brett during that time?"

"Seeing Brett?" Ida pretended not to understand, but she had seen how Brett's face flushed whenever Murry was near. What were they doing there together so late in Murry's study last night? Could he stoop so low as to betray Katie's trust under her very nose? She bristled at the thought but she must protect Katie.

"For dinner or for other engagements?"

Ida shook her head and said firmly, "No, not at all."

Katie sighed. "I think Brett and Jack are falling in love with each other. Even worse they may be having an affair."

"Nonsense!" Ida rose to go but Katie seized her sleeve and made her sit down again.

"I caught them last night in an intimate pose. I must say I am not surprised. With me in this condition...but here in my own house! Of course, I admit, she would make a perfect wife for Murry. She'd pose no competition, and she is so docile and subservient. Indeed, he really should marry her after I am gone. Can you think of anyone more suited to be Murry's wife and slave?"

"Don't say such things, Katie. I can't bear it when you talk of dying, even facetiously."

Katie turned her face to the window. "We'd always promised each other we'd let the other free. I wouldn't want to be a drain on his happiness. But I don't think I could go on living if Jack should stop..." Here Katie stifled a sob, "What if Jack doesn't want me anymore?"

"I'll always be here for you, Katie, whatever happens," she said, reaching out to take Katie's hand.

Katie jerked her hand away. "You! You have nothing to do with anything! You always drag yourself into every corner of my life. Can't you leave me a little privacy? A little something of my own? I swear one of these days you will eat me whole."

Ida felt a sudden blow to her chest as Katie's fury exploded upon her with full force. She gasped for breath, but it seemed her lungs had collapsed and all that came out was a hoarse, inhuman croak.

Finally her voice returned as tears streamed down. "How can you say such things, Katie?"

Now seemingly contrite, all vehemence spent, Katie sighed and looked down at the counterpane again, tracing a rose pattern with her finger. "Oh, Jones. That's not what I meant to say at all. You will forgive me. You know I can't live without you, without you and without Jack," and leaning forward she took Ida's head between her arms and pressed it to her breast.

Katherine stepped into the dining room to see if all was ready. Ida had set the table with her best china and crystal and at the center had placed a tall blue vase of flame-colored, hot-house lilies and a silver tray of ripe figs, pale green and glossy purple. Yet the arrangement of the figs did not quite satisfy Katherine's aesthetic sense, and while waiting for the Lawrences to arrive, she amused herself by rearranging them into a perfect pyramid, so that the different nuances of green and purple would be visible all at once, while subtly evoking the darker maroon tones of the carpet. No one would notice but herself, she thought. She was not only a writer, but an artist of life, and this room was her canvas to fill with color and light.

She stepped back to admire the overall effect of her creation which would have made a worthy still life for one of her painter friends. She had spent a small fortune on these figs and flowers, but she would go to any expense to please a dear friend. And Lawrence—Lorenzo as she preferred to call him, given his enthusiasm for things Italian —was more than a friend. He was a kindred spirit, one of the few men in England with whom one could really talk about things that mattered: about love and about the soul, though at times he was rather too insistent at enlisting them in his impossible schemes. Take the community they were to found in Cornwall two years ago where he had installed her in a drafty old tower overlooking a boulder-strewn beach and a bleak, gray sea. Yes, they had lived as cheaply as he had promised on fresh eggs and berries and mutton stew, but the fog and cold had reduced her to a bundle of swollen bones. What had been worse was the constant, unavoidable intimacy with Lawrence and Frieda, who, in their good moods had preached to her about the joys of sex till she was ready to gird on a chastity belt, and in their bad moods viciously attacked each other, especially when Lawrence was in one of his black states of negation. Those had become all the more frequent ever since *The Rainbow* had been censured and burned, and his scorn for England had become a poison exuding from every pore of his body. His mirth was infectious, but his ire could wither the leaves on the bushes as he passed.

The bell rang and Ida appeared with Katherine's guest. Lawrence was alone; Frieda was in bed with influenza. That suited Katherine well enough. At times she could not bear Frieda's company. Lawrence himself looked gaunter and paler than usual, or perhaps this was the effect of the ruddy beard he had adopted of late which made him look a little like a mournful Christ in an Italian fresco. He had just returned from Cornwall and had a dozen stories to tell all at once about cuckoos and periwinkles and foxgloves and his rambles across the Cornish countryside, but when the clock struck a quarter past one and lunch had not yet been served, Katherine grew nervous and lit a Russian cigarette. She had instructed Ida to bring their lunch at one o'clock sharp. They must keep to schedule, for Lawrence had to catch a train in the early afternoon. Hearing Ida's heavy tread in the corridor, Katherine called through the open door, "Ida, lunch is late."

Ida bustled in with a carafe of water and a bread basket on a tray, nearly colliding with Lawrence and splashing water over the carpet.

"My dear Miss Baker," he cried, "I have already had a shower-bath today."

"For heaven's sake, Ida, be careful."

"No harm done," said Lawrence, amused at Ida's clumsiness, sweeping the tray from her hands and putting it on the table. "The table is only set for two," he said. "Aren't you joining us, Miss Baker?"

Ida darted a timid glance at Katherine, saying, "Katie likes to discuss work alone."

"You are not a servant, a slave, perhaps, but not a servant. Katherine, she must set herself a place."

"No, I mustn't really. There are things in the kitchen I must tend to. "

"You are sure?"

Ida nodded.

"I shan't insist, then," he said and he and Katherine sat down to the table.

Ida slipped back to the kitchen.

Examining the figs, he chose one and lifted it to the light streaming in through the dining room window. "You should be ashamed of yourself. Treating Ida like a servant! Your dinners with the Wolves and Bloomsberries have gone to your head."

"Oh, Lorenzo, she doesn't mind. And our conversation would be far beyond her. I am so anxious for good talk and you are one of the few who can provide it. I crave your conversation and I am so jealous, I do not wish to share it with anyone. Not even my darling Murry."

Lawrence grunted at the mention of Murry. Katherine knew that he and Murry had begun to drift apart. He demanded too much of his friendship with Murry. Lawrence yearned for a strong, physical bond, but Murry was far too intellectual for physical closeness with a person of his own sex. Katherine suspected that Murry's sidling away had disappointed Lawrence more deeply than he had let on. Lawrence had hoped to become a sort of neutralizing force in their lives. That, she surmised, must have been the rationale behind the Cornwall community, in Lawrence's eyes. By forming strong bonds between them: she with Frieda and Lawrence with Murry, they would have created a neutralizing pole that would have allowed the tensions of their respective marriages to be released in a healthy manner. They would somehow have become, to Lawrence's mind, complete as human beings, while forming a perfect society of four. The idyll had not lasted very long. Katherine had never believed in it and Lawrence himself had spoiled it with his uncontrolled rages, but he still tried to exercise a power over them through his dogmatic judgments and often sanctimonious recommendations concerning how they should live and work and think. Though she resented his forced entrance into her most private affairs, she had to admit that very often enough much of what Lawrence said made sense. He had a way of penetrating one's most hidden thoughts and wishes, stripping off the masks behind which one hides even from oneself. That was what made him such daunting and yet fascinating company. Lawrence believed in the value of friendship and of deeply sharing life's experiences with a community of like-minded souls. Whether he had drunk the milk of paradise or tasted the gall of hell, he held his brimming chalice out to one's lips—determined that it should be shared—whether ye will or no. Today, despite the many struggles he was facing in his attempts to abandon England, he was in excellent spirits.

Lawrence took something from his pocket and astonished Katherine by snapping open a knife. The blade gleamed in a ray of sunlight as he peeled the fig he had plucked from the tray.

"This is an Italian knife, given to me by a genuine cont-a-dino, a peasant fellow who befriended us when Frieda and I were roaming the hills round Lerici, and we took shelter in a barn during a thunderstorm. We met this fellow who had been out tending his cows. We shared our repast of bread and cheese and he made us a present of this knife, a fine addition to our traveling *kitchenino*. All *contadini* carry a knife like this one, a tool to be used in a thousand circumstances."

Yes, she could just picture it. Lawrence and Frieda sitting on a haystack in a barn: Frieda in a peasant's dress with little tufts of hay in her hair, and Lawrence wearing a floppy, broad-brimmed white linen hat and carrying a rucksack holding only his painting gear and a change of socks, eating bread and cheese with an Italian peasant. How she would have loved to travel to Italy with Lawrence, but she knew she could never catch up with Lawrence and Frieda, who swam naked in the sea in winter, scrambled up mountains at twilight, boiled eggs over campfires for their dinner, and slept on the bare floors of flea-infested inns, thinking it all great fun.

Katherine watched admiringly as Lawrence peeled and ate another fig, savoring the soft sweet flesh with eyes closed. Here was man who was not afraid of life. His presence, when he was in a good humor like today, filled her with joy.

"And how is our beloved Murry?" he asked after Ida had brought the watercress soup.

"Murry has been behaving like an adolescent."

Lawrence snorted and attacked his soup. "One does so love a tangle."

"With Brett."

"Aha! And a very interesting, triangular tangle, indeed," Lawrence put down his spoon and leaned forward on his elbows, ready to enter into one of their probing discussions concerning men and women in the modern era. His eyes glittered mischievously above his goat-like scruff of beard. To Katherine he looked exactly like an embodiment of Pan.

"You know we promised to allow each other absolute freedom."

He pierced her with a sidelong gaze and a devilishly wry smile.

He is thinking that this is a lie, she thought. *I would never really let Murry free. I would always bind him to me somehow.* She reflected on this a moment and confessed to herself that it was true.

Lawrence resumed eating his soup. "You two keep stretching the bonds that tie you to breaking point. Soon enough they will snap in your faces. What you and Murry do not share is the instinctual harmony of man and woman."

"Instinctual harmony? Is that what you share with Frieda?"

"We share the wholesome harmony of sex, a throbbing, naked intimacy."

Katherine grimaced, remembering the sight of Frieda streaking across a field in Cornwall, her bosom jiggling like an undercooked pudding, her skirts flapping, as she shrieked, "He'll kill me!! He'll kill me," with Lawrence, his face all green, bellowing "Bitch! Bitch!" after her, while brandishing a frying pan. An hour later, the scene had been reversed. Frieda roaring with frying pan in hand, and Lawrence fleeing, terrorized. Later, when it was all over, he had sat before the fire, hemming Frieda's skirt. Instinctual harmony, indeed.

"The problem is that Murry cannot be a real man with you. You are far too mental, too intellectual for him. You keep Murry on his toes when he would so much rather just relax and be himself. That is why he is attracted to women like Brett. Her deafness adds to her allure. She is a simpler sort of soul, softer, more spontaneous and direct. He need not always think of clever things to say, as conversation, I dare say, isn't the focal point of their relation."

Katherine bristled. She would let no one but Lawrence speak to her in such a way. That these men found Brett attractive, with her grimy neck and her teeth unbrushed, was unthinkable. Still, his analysis of Murry was acute.

"And you must accept solitude as an inexorable condition of being an artist. You must go into your solitude deeply to discover your own world. But you do not accept this fully. That is another part of the problem. You do not consider yourself complete without Murry, but in actuality, your relationship with Murry is really only a sort of accessory experience. It is not an integral part of yourself. But you do not wish to acknowledge this fact. But the real problem, my dear Katherine, is not Brett or Murry or even yourself. The real problem is England. This place is killing us all. It is killing our soul. This underworld with its purgatorial hordes shuffling through the fog! I'll tell you, present company excluded, the only sane and healthy people in England at this time are Frieda and *moi-même*. And we must all of us escape, if we wish to survive and save our souls."

He looked her level in the eyes; his own eyes were grave and urgent. She felt this too very strongly. She must leave England in order to survive, and not for her health alone.

His tone turned jocular as the meal progressed, and Ida came and went as discreet as a ghost, whisking the dirty plates away and serving the pudding.

"If only you had all listened to my advice, and we had found our South Sea

90

island and had established the kingdom of Rananim!"

"My dear Gonzalo, you have never been to a South Sea Island, but I have. I fear life there would not be as ideal as you seem to picture. I am sure the climate and the food would not agree with you at all."

Lawrence snorted. "As soon as they have endorsed my passport, which as yet they have still refused to do, I intend to set out on my search for our island paradise, near Ceylon, or perhaps off the coast of Mexico. You shall all see that I am right."

"I shall be leaving soon, too. The doctor has ordered winter in a sunny climate. I have not yet decided where. Italy, or perhaps the Midi. *Oh, for a beaker full of the warm south...*"

Lawrence did not smile at her Keatsian recitation. He considered her sternly, then said, "Your illness stems from a deep imbalance in your inner nature, from a lack of harmony between your body and your mind. You surrender yourself to things you do not really believe in and which are not worth a moment of your time. There is a lie in your soul." He peered at her with strange malice and his words cut deep.

Though touched to the quick, she pondered. It was uncanny: this very thought had struck her of late. Perhaps the source of her illness was not merely physical. From what secret depths did it spring? Was there, perhaps, *a lie in her soul?* The very words made her shiver. Like the sin against the holy Ghost, it was the one thing that God might never pardon. She reached for a black fig, split it open, and sucked out the dark red pulp, but she could not swallow it and had to spit it out, for the soft, viscous flesh had begun to ferment.

. . .

Katherine sat in the garden, wrapped in a shawl, taking tea with Koteliansky. A bundle of papers lay in her lap for they had spent the afternoon working on a translation of some of Chekhov's letters, and had stepped out to the garden for a cup of tea. A sharp September breeze swirled up a pile of yellow leaves, raising a low cloud of dust along the ground.

"You cannot imagine how much this little garden means to me," Katherine said, leaning back in the striped pink deck chair and admiring a row of chrysanthemums, bright russet and yellow, planted along the garden wall. "Every season is like a gift. I love every weed and cricket, every leaf and twig. Yesterday I had to scold Ida for pulling up my dandelions."

"Poor Ida, she makes such efforts to please!"

"Ida, my blessing and my curse." Katherine sipped her tea pensively, then put down the cup and glanced through the papers in her lap. "I will take these translations with me to work on in Italy this autumn."

"Yes, it would mean much to me to bring out a book together, bearing both our names." He took her hand and leaned forward, his face eager, as he solemnly intoned, *The Letters of Anton Chekhov translated by S.S. Koteliansky and Katherine Mansfield.*

Katherine smiled at Kot's devotion. He could be content with so little. Her hand rested, small and inert, in his powerful grasp.

"Ida will be accompanying you, I trust?"

Katherine nodded. "And Jack too, at first, at least until I'm settled. I am so relieved he will be coming. I could not bear to leave him here in Brett's clutches."

Kot cast her a quizzical look.

"Haven't you heard that my beloved husband and Brett may be having an affair?"

Kot clucked in disbelief and shook his head, "If that is true, Murry is a fool," he said.

Katherine flashed a wicked smile and tickled his palm, saying, "It's a pity we were never lovers, Kot, you would never have treated me so."

"Never," said Kot, abruptly dropping her hand, "but do not forget, it is you who rejected me. Bid me come and I am yours forever. "

"Ah," said Katherine with a wry smile, "the gallantry of bygone days."

They exchanged a long gaze and Katherine found herself on the verge of tears, touched by the force of Kot's love for her, a love she could never return. It was not that Kot was unattractive. Tall, vigorous, sinewy-limbed with high chiseled cheekbones in a gaunt face and a thick bush of black hair, he seemed to her the virile incarnation of a Hebrew prophet. But his eyes were set too close together, his nose too prominent, his skin a shade too swarthy for him to be considered handsome by English standards. There was something hungry and wolfish about him. He had a predatory look, even though he was the kindest of men. Kot was deficient in the refined male beauty that drew her irresistibly. Why should beauty be so important in a man? And yet it was. Her brother Leslie had been as beautiful as a rose with the morning flush on it. Murry was beautiful with his lean shanks, well-modeled shoulders; his smooth, perfect features; his hazel-green eyes, his ready smile. Murry possessed masculine beauty in the classical sense. An ancient Greek sculptor might have rendered him in marble. Yet between them, she was man and he the woman; she the wooer and he the beloved. And how he eluded her; how he disappointed her. And his lovemaking, still after all those years, so tedious. A drunken stranger knew how to touch her breasts and give her pleasure better than her own husband. And Kot? Here was a man offering true devotion, true communion, the things she needed most in order to be healed. But she could not accept his love. Physical intimacy with him was out of the question. Even the thought of seeing him naked frightened her. She, a tigress, afraid of nothing, was afraid of this man's ardor.

She picked up a page and began to read, then glanced up to watch a falling leaf.

"I feel so close to Chekhov. I don't why. He is so immensely pure. I don't mean that in a sentimental sense but in an artistic and spiritual one. I am so thin and insubstantial in comparison. I know I must strive higher if my work is to have any lasting value."

Leaning forward and plucking Kot's sleeve, she said, "You will not laugh at me if I ask you a serious question. "

"Laugh at you? By no means, Kissienka."

"Kot, do you believe in God?"

"You ask a Russian Jew if he believes in God?" Kot threw back his head and laughed.

"You promised you would not laugh at me!"

"I am not laughing at you Kissienka," and he recited a few verses in sonorous Hebrew; then, for her benefit translated, *"Where were you when I laid the foundation..."*

"I knew you would not answer me seriously. Yes, Kot, I believe ... *not* in what the church calls God... but in something greater than myself. I have glimpses when the glass turns clear and I see myself in all my smallness and pettiness and vanity, and frankly I am appalled, and yet these moments give me hope that there is a more objective truth one *can* seize upon, somehow. There is a *self* that dwells apart, detached, which is not the me, the Katherine you see sitting here. Or which is not *only* the Katherine sitting in this chair. Here I am discussing philosophy with you or with Sorapure in such a serene state...and there I am squabbling with Ida over where the spice box has been put or how the crease in my chemise has been ironed, or furious with Murry because Brett thrusts out her bosom whenever he walks past. The tiniest irritations can make me explode, destroying my concentration for hours, sometimes for days. In that, I am exactly like Lawrence. Horribly like him, in fact. How can one take oneself seriously if one behaves in such an irrational manner? All this keeps me from doing any serious work."

"My dear Kissienka, these are the contradictions of being human."

"Human indeed! I wonder. Now, Chekhov, there was a man: deep, rich, fertile. I think he would understand what I am trying to express, though I know I have made absolutely no sense. I often feel like the clerk in some shabby hotel whose owner has absconded, distributing room keys to the many unruly guests, each one of whom has some claim to my name and identity."

"Perhaps you feel this way because you are ill. You must dedicate all your time and efforts to getting well again."

" Lawrence says my body cannot be healthy if my soul is sick."

"And is your soul sick, Kissienka?"
Katherine did not reply.

PART THREE

Autumn and Winter, 1919

OSPEDALETTI

The hotel manager stood smiling in her doorway, wringing his hands in false sympathy. With a properly deferential grimace, he announced, "I am terribly sorry, Madame, but a few of our guests have complained about your... coughing. I am afraid you cannot stay here any longer."

Katherine listened, her face set in stony resignation, remembering how Francis Carco had flinched as she stood on tiptoe to offer him a grateful kiss. That gesture of alarm, that shrinking back from physical contact with her, had now become all too familiar to her, for she had seen it repeated many times, by strangers, by her friends, and even by her husband. By everyone, it seemed, but Ida. And there would surely be more of it to come. Even her old friend, Gertler, had joked when he learned she was ill, "Don't tell me you've got it too? Is it like they say? Do you really cough up blood?" and had laughed in her face.

It was unfortunate that Murry had just left San Remo and returned to London. The manager would never have dared chase her from the hotel as long as Murry had been there. But women traveling alone are subject to endless insults and vexations which Katherine knew she could ill-afford. The manager had obviously waited until Murry had gone before turning them out.

"Understanding that this may have caught you unprepared," he went on, "I would be more than happy to lease you, for the whole period of your stay, a lovely villa in the hills around San Remo, equipped with all modern comforts, for a very modest price."

The price he quoted was twice the hotel rate, but Katherine nodded, as she had no choice. After a brief discussion of details, she signed the lease he held out to her and pocketed the keys to a villa in the nearby town of Ospedaletti. When the manager had gone, she sat in an armchair, brooding, supervising Ida as she packed their trunks.

"I can't really believe that he has turned us out because of my cough," she mused. "Perhaps he has found someone willing to pay double what we were paying for this room. It's an awful hotel, anyway. The other guests at dinner look exactly like cadavers newly resurrected. I am glad not to count myself among them any longer."

Ida assented, then went downstairs to settle the bill and send the porter up for their luggage. Katherine would follow shortly.

Heads turned as Katherine stepped out of the lift and crossed the hall where the hotel guests had gathered to chat before lunch was served. Monocles glared, newspapers rustled to a close, fingers scrambled for a handkerchief as she passed through the room. *They are all thinking: there she goes—the sick woman, the pariah—* Katherine thought, striding, head high towards the front desk. Before she reached the glass doors where Ida stood outside waiting with the baggage, she was seized by the most painful coughing fit she had as yet suffered in San Remo. Thank God, no telltale blood spurted out onto her handkerchief, although she felt her cheeks go scarlet as she strained to quell the spasm. When at last she had recovered, the manager greeted her with a stern smile, took her arm, and whirled her out to the street. A harried Ida dispensed tips to waiting hands and then they climbed into an antiquated little cart drawn by a decrepit white horse decorated with red ribbons and silver bells.

As the cart jogged away from the hotel, Katherine asked, "Do you think the bells are intended to warn people of my passage?"

Ida stared uncomprehending.

"They tied bells to lepers in the middle ages," she explained.

"Katie! All the horses here have bells."

Katherine observed other carts and carriages jangling down the street. This time she had to admit that Ida was right: the quaint decoration wasn't meant for her alone. Sighing, she asked Ida how much the hotel bill had come to.

Ida took the bill from her purse and handed it to Katherine.

Katherine's face flushed after a cursory examination of the bill. "Jones, have you gone mad? What is the meaning of this extra charge for hotel services?"

"Something necessary," said Ida glumly.

"Have you broken something again?" Katherine accused. "Or have you been ordering oysters and hot chocolate or sending out laundry without my knowledge? Remember, it is I who pay the bills, after all."

"No," Ida said sullenly, "it is nothing of the sort."

"Then I demand to know why I have been charged a full third more than the agreed price?"

Ida mumbled an unintelligible reply, infuriating Katherine even more.

"I didn't understand you Ida, would you please speak more plainly?"

"Fumigation!" Ida hissed through her teeth and looked away as the horse clopped along the cobblestones. The bells tinkled merrily as they made a left turn.

"Fumigation?" Katherine repeated blankly, then the meaning of the word sank in. They would have to disinfect the room after she had stayed there. "And they charged me for that?"

Ida nodded.

Enraged, Katherine wadded up the bill and threw it on the floor of the cart.

Ida retrieved it, smoothed it out, and slipped it into her purse, along with the other accounts.

The insult faded from Katherine's mind as the cart rattled round the curves above the town of Ospedaletti, three miles from San Remo and their villa came into view, perched atop the hill. She had time to savor the charm of their approach. The Casetta Deerholm was a modest little white chalet with a red-tiled roof and a large verandah, nestled in among olive, fig, and tamarisk trees. Several levels of terraced slopes descended beneath the house where thick tangles of bougainvilleas cascaded over the walls in a bright pink froth. Connecting the house to the terraces below was a steep staircase cut out of the cliff, bordered with lavender and rosemary bushes, zigzagging down as far as the sea.

After the cart had climbed midway up the curving road, Katherine ordered the driver to stop. Scrambling down unassisted and summoning strength, she ran a few steps up the nearest staircase. Behind her, Ida sprang to her feet in the cart, shrieking, "Katie! Come back at once! You can't manage all those stairs."

There were still two flights to climb before she reached the top, but Katherine felt quite sure that she could make it. Leaning on a balustrade overlooking the sea, she called out breathily to Ida, "You drive up with the baggage. I am feeling so much stronger now that I am determined to make it up these steps, however long it takes." Gripping the wooden railing, she dragged herself up a few steps more.

Although alarmed, Ida knew there was no calling Katie back from this foolish enterprise. With misgivings, she told the man to drive on, her anxious eyes fixed on Katie in case she collapsed or needed assistance. But somehow, perhaps through sheer willpower rather than physical strength, Katie had conquered the first ramp. Now sitting on a stone bench at the top of the ramp, she waved her hat to Ida as the cart crawled past, rounding the last loop of the road, up towards the villa.

Soon the cart pulled up outside a little two-storey chalet, by no means the full-fledged villa the hotel manager had described to them, surrounded by trees and flowering shrubs. Standing in the doorway to greet Ida's arrival was a peasant girl with a blue-checked dress, a red apron, and a long plait of black hair, who looked hardly more than fifteen. Ida surmised this child was the maid, for the

97

"villa" had been let with a complete staff of servants, including a gardener and his wife who would take care of the grounds during their stay. Katie's plan was to remain here all through the autumn and winter. In May, Murry would join them and Ida would have to find rooms in town or perhaps return to England.

As the driver unloaded their trunks and bags, Ida followed the girl through a narrow entryway into a bright, well-scrubbed kitchen where a row of copper saucepans, beautifully polished, gleamed above the fireplace. In one corner was a wood stove where a huge copper tea kettle sat ready to boil. Below the window was an old stone sink and a low shelf stacked with pretty cups and saucers. The table was spread with a homespun hemp cloth, on which were deployed a jar of marigolds, a loaf of brown bread, and a slab of pale yellow butter. Ida smiled knowing that Katie would surely appreciate this kindness, for she would be thirsty and famished by the time she reached the house.

Seizing the kettle, Ida found it empty. She approached the sink and turned the bronze tap, but it was bone dry. Not even a trickle of water could be coaxed forth. Puzzled, she looked round the kitchen, searching for another source of water. Her French was dreadful—she knew—yet she usually managed to make herself understood. She asked the girl, who had been standing in a corner, watching her, why there was no water. The girl smiled shyly, shook her head, and tapped her ears to show that she could not understand, for, as it turned out, she spoke no French or English but only Italian, of which Ida knew not a word. Indicating first the kettle, then the sink, Ida mimed the act of drinking from a glass and then washing her face. The girl laughed and pointed at a tin pail by the door and then out a side window. Peering out, Ida gasped when she saw a trail leading down the hill behind the chalet to a pump.

Needing no further instructions other than the dismay in Ida's face, the girl grabbed the bucket and dashed out. Through the window, Ida watched her skipping down the trail, swinging the bucket as her plait swished from side to side. Thinking she should light the stove for the kettle, Ida checked the scuttle, but there was no coal or charcoal for the stove, or even any logs. She found a tin of matches on a shelf near the stove. This, at least, was full.

Wondering if there were a storage room or a closet where fuel was kept, she inspected the rest of the house. A small sitting room with a sofa and a fireplace opened off the kitchen. From here a flight of steps led up to a tiny bedroom and dressing room. That was all. There was no bathroom, of course, but in the bedroom was a washbasin, a chamber pot, and a zinc tub neatly tucked behind a folding screen. As she came back downstairs, Katie burst in the door, panting and perspiring, yet as gleeful as a child. Ida was amazed that she had managed to climb the ramps so quickly, but that was just like Katie to muster unexpected quantities of physical strength when something had captured her enthusiasm.

"Jones! Jones! I know I shall love it here. I shall sit all day in that splendid garden and write and write and write. Oh Jones! The view! The air! And the flowers. Have you ever seen a lovelier September? I know I shall get well here. But now," she glanced at the table, "I am longing for a hot cup of tea as sailors long for rum!"

Ida said, "I have sent the girl down to fetch water from the fount so that I can boil the kettle for our tea."

"You mean to say there is no running water in the house?"

Ida shook her head. "And no bathroom. Only the usual amenities."

Katie approached the sink and turned the tap. The pipes groaned and hissed, but no water gushed forth.

"So, all "modern comforts" does not entail running water, here in Italy?"

"And I can't find any fuel to light the stove." Ida sat down to the table. Folding her hands in a gesture of resignation, she looked up at Katie, waiting for her to decide what they should do.

Katherine drew a deep breath. They had been told the house would be stocked with all necessities and she had paid dearly for them. But even a pot of tea seemed to require enormous efforts of organization. "I saw the gardener poking about and introduced myself. Go and see if he will bring us some wood *immediately*."

"But I don't speak Italian!" Ida objected.

"Then bring him to me!"

Ida fetched the gardener, a sallow little man with shiftless eyes and a battered cap, who spoke coarse but fluent French. He informed them that they would have to call the woodman the next day to purchase a load of wood. Seeing that they were without fuel, he would be delighted to loan them a few logs for the evening, but the ladies must come down and fetch the wood from his pile themselves. He had a bad back, he explained, and patted that part of his anatomy with a convincing grimace. The boy who did the heavier work had already gone home for the day.

Katherine accepted the gardener's offer and dismissed him, dispatching Ida with a basket for the wood. Then when the maid returned with water, she inquired in her broken Italian where they might buy fresh eggs, and learning that a neighbor down the slopes kept chickens, sent the girl off to obtain a half dozen eggs for their supper.

Dusk fell as Katherine waited for Ida and the girl to return. She sat shivering by the window, looking out at the twilight. The colors of the sunset were almost too glorious, too gaudy for her taste, possessing an alien radiance. The trembling violet clouds shot through with golden gleams, the curdled pinks above a somber sea, reminded her of a cheap illustration depicting the martyrdom of some poor

Spanish virgin, with whom she did not intend to identify herself, at least not for now.

A steamship, all its lights ablaze, moved slowly across the horizon, a bar of yellow light in the gloom. She thought of Lawrence. Had he set out now for Ranamin? With all her heart, she wished him success in finding a land of sun which would heal and nourish him. Studying the modest domesticity of her little chalet, she smiled, thinking that Lorenzo would have approved of the place. It had that real feel of peasant life not unlike the cottages in Liguria he had described to her, where he delighted in the simplest task, from scrubbing a floor to shredding oranges to make his own marmalade. She had made the right choice in coming here. The isolation of the Casetta Deerholm would surely be more conducive to her work than any hotel setting.

Remembering Lawrence in one of his good moods, so boyish and merry and affectionate, had given her a fleeting sense of comfort, but as the minutes ticked by, the lights twinkling down in the village filled her with a dull, unpoetic melancholy. In similar circumstances elsewhere, she might have recited a few lines of Wordsworth and let her spirit swell out with the grandeur and beauty of great poetry. But perhaps that was just a pose. The truth was that she had been driven from a hotel of waxen, convalescing corpses, who considered *her* too ill to share *their* company, and perhaps they were right. Her world was made less of poetry and fine feelings than of medicine bottles and pills. The truth was that she would be alone here with Ida for days and weeks and months to come with no comfort other than her work. There were reviews to write for Murry. There were Kot's Chekhov versions to polish. There were her stories seething in her head that she must get down on paper. But could anything fill the anguished void she sensed at moments like this, alone in an unlit room at dusk as shadows deepened around her? She knew that here she would be put to the test, and she could only win through by putting Lawrence's advice into practice. She must give herself wholly to her work, with an artist's true dedication, while accepting solitude as a necessary condition of her life. Lawrence was right on that account.

Soon enough both Ida and the girl returned, but the few logs the gardener had given Ida were green and soggy, and would not burn. The stove would not light. Nearly a whole box of matches was consumed before they managed to make a fire in the fireplace, but the chimney did not draw properly, and the house filled up with stinking smoke, irritating her cough. They boiled their kettle and fried their eggs on a trivet right over the coals, as if around a campfire. After dinner, Katherine could not even have a sponge bath; there was hardly enough water to wash their hands and faces before bedtime. Ida could not venture down the steep trail in the dark to fetch more, and they had already sent the girl home.

It was nearly midnight when she tumbled into bed at last, too tired even to write to Murry, but the sound of the sea was soothing, and a single star blazing in her window cheered her, and seemed to say that despite these silly hardships, all would be well.

. . .

Opening her eyes, Katherine stretched her body still swathed in a double layer of mosquito netting and savored this moment of awakening. She had slept a delicious full night's sleep, lulled by the sound of the sea. This had been the first and only full night's sleep since they arrived in Ospedaletti a week ago, for up until last night the midges and mosquitoes had been a torment that nothing could assuage. Within twenty-four hours of their arrival, Katherine's arms and legs had been covered with dozens of bulbous swellings. Whatever remedies they tried: verbena, kerosene, salt water, nothing took away the sting. In bed the mosquitoes were enough to drive one mad. More than once, she had called Ida in the night to defend her from the insects that had penetrated the gauzy tent around her bed. But last night, Ida had finally solved the problem by shrouding Katherine's whole body in a cocoon of netting, and though her wrappings twisted uncomfortably and restricted her movements while in bed, she had managed to sleep the whole night through. Moreover, she had not coughed even once. Struggling out of her swaddling, she reached for the little brass bell at her bedside and called down to Ida, "I'm awake now, Jones! Please bring up my tea."

Receiving no response from downstairs, she rang more insistently and shouted, "It's nearly nine o'clock, Jones."

All was silent below, so Katherine climbed out of bed, slipped on her dressing gown and shuffled downstairs. There was no one in the kitchen and the stove had gone out. She called for the maid, but there was no reply, so she knelt beside the stove, seized a poker, and began to stir the coals. Her efforts were of no use; the coals were too cold to be coaxed back into flame. The scuttle was empty. No matter how much charcoal or wood was brought, it seemed to run out almost immediately. You'd think that Jones munched lumps of charcoal at teatime along with her bread and butter.

Annoyed, she sat in a chair, pulled her dressing gown tighter about her breast, and waited for Ida or the maid to come and light the stove for her breakfast. She had begun the day feeling rested, filled with a sense of exhilaration, ready to get down to some serious work, and now, just fussing with the stove had exhausted her and had sapped her of the delightful energy she had felt surging through her veins upon waking.

Where *was* Ida? She was never there when needed most. Her patience with Ida was beginning to wear thin again, and she dreaded the scenes that inevitably followed when she could no longer control her nerves. In only one week, Ida had broken a glass pitcher and a fruit plate while leaning against the sideboard, and these broken items would have to be paid for. And when Katherine had unpacked her trunk of books, she discovered that in their haste to leave the hotel in San Remo, Ida had mislaid one of Kot's precious Chekhov manuscripts. She hadn't yet had the courage to write and tell him what had happened.

The door opened and in banged Ida, sloshing a pail of water in each hand, her face red and puffy with effort. As she plunked down the pails, water splashed out onto the freshly scrubbed tile floor.

Katherine coolly contemplated Ida's torn sleeve and mud-spattered skirt. "You shouldn't have to carry the water up by yourself, Ida. We have a maid whose wages for this month have been paid in advance."

"She didn't come this morning and there was not a drop of water left after your bath last night." Ida mopped up the puddle on the floor and poured some water into the kettle. Stepping outside again, she returned with a bag of charcoal and began to stoke the stove. Katherine sat down at the table and waited for breakfast to be prepared. Soon the stove was roaring and the tea kettle singing.

"Is the maid ill or has she run off with a fiancé?" Katherine asked, sipping her tea.

"She told the gardener to inform us she would not be returning. Money owed her may be given to the gardener and she will come to collect it from him."

"Money owed her? We don't owe her anything! *Au contraire!*"

"It seems we owe her for a week's supply of fresh bread and butter, at least that is what I understood the gardener to say."

"But we did not order that bread and butter. I assumed it was a gift."

Ida shrugged and began to tidy up the kitchen. While putting away a basket of eggs, one fell to the floor and shattered.

Katherine stared at the broken egg on the floor and sighed, "We must find someone to replace her. You cannot do all the housework yourself."

"If we manage to find someone. They don't seem to take kindly to the English here," said Ida, mopping up the egg.

"She must have heard me coughing the other night. Perhaps she saw the blood on my pillow. She's afraid to stay here in the house with me." Katherine paused to reflect upon this daunting reality. In less than a fortnight she had been thrown out of a hotel and deserted by her maid.

"The woodman has just come," said Ida, pushing aside a lock of blond hair from her eyes and slipping out a piece of paper from her apron pocket. "Here is the bill he has left us. I suppose he will want to be paid once he has finished unloading the wood."

Katherine glanced out the window and saw the woodman's boy piling logs and bags of charcoal and pinecones by the verandah door. Examining the slip of paper Ida held out to her, she noted in alarm that in one week the price had increased by ten percent.

"Can they all be such vultures? Ready to pick my pockets clean before they go for my eyes?"

. . .

Returning from the weekly shopping in San Remo, Ida, gripping her walking stick and loaded down with parcels, sat very still on the omnibus, squeezed next to a peasant smelling of sour wine with a large basket of very ripe cheese in his lap. The driver steered with a nonchalant flair, chattering to the women in the front seats, and sounding his claxon at every bend in the road. As the omnibus rounded the hairpin curves, Ida braced herself and muttered a prayer beneath her breath, for the front wheel skirted the very edge of the precipice and she found herself looking straight down at the plunge and flash of blue beneath her.

The omnibus set her down at the bottom of the hill, than roared off again in a cloud of dust. She labored up the slope in her sturdy shoes, swinging her African walking stick, humming a rhythmic melody to assist her in the arduous climb. She had almost got used to it now, after hauling heavy cans of water up from the fount three or four times a day.

The fur bag across her shoulder was full of treats she had bought for Katie: oranges, lavender pastilles, a little packet of chocolate, stamps and stationery, and some handsome leather buttons to replace the ones missing from Katie's overcoat, but there were no letters for Katie today, as there had been none yesterday, or the week before, or even the week before that. It was no good telling Katie that the Italian postal strike was to blame; that had ended days ago. In response to the lack of letters, Katie's mood had gone from anger, to bafflement, to grim despair. Murry was not thinking of her. He had not written in over a month. He had not sent the money he had promised, or the *Literary Supplements* she craved. Ida could not understand this. Could he really be too busy to write? Did he not know how much Katie depended on his letters? And Katie's birthday had come and gone with no word of greeting from Murry.

A little girl in braids walked by, driving a white cow along the pretty little path lined with pink cyclamen. Ida smiled and said "Buon Giorno," the only Italian words she felt comfortable saying, but the girl glared at her and spat on the ground, jeering "Eengleesh. Eenglessh!"

Ida frowned and hurried on. This was something she could not get used to. The Italians here seemed to hate the English. In town, the shopkeepers kept her waiting and charged her more. The woodman cheated on them and the gardener was rude. Once a little boy had even thrown a stone at her while she was getting off the omnibus, but luckily his aim was poor.

Katie was not in the house when Ida came in. She put down her parcels and went out to the terrace where she found Katie wrapped in a blanket like an Indian squaw, looking out at the horizon. A chill north wind swept a parade of fleecy clouds across the sky.

"Can you hear the oboes and violins in those waves, Ida? This sea is a whole orchestra to me. Can you smell the tang of autumn in the wet sand? Soon it will be winter and the sea will be all melancholy bassoons and rolling kettledrums."

It was a perfect metaphor in Ida's opinion. "You're such a poet, Katie."

There was a long silence as they watched the drifting clouds overhead and listened to the sea. Ida waited for Katie to ask the question she asked whenever Ida returned from town.

"No letters, I take it, Ida?"

Ida had come to understand that Katie's restraint was only a strategy to delay her disappointment. She had had to train herself to keep from trilling out "No, Katie, nothing today," until Katie had first asked.

"There's been a strike, you know. The postal service here is so unreliable."

"Yes, but I have written him twice and even three times every single day, not to mention over a dozen telegrams since we arrived. And what has he sent in return? Two letters. Two short, miserable letters, saying nothing about what he is doing and how he is feeling. I suppose he is too busy dining with Ottoline and making love to Brett. And then there is the question of money, Jones. We're running low on funds. We simply must have those ten pounds I asked him to send. And it is not a loan, but an advance payment. He is ignoring my request. Imagine knowing your wife is ill and needs money and you ignore her and what's more, you have an income of eight hundred pounds a year."

"I'm sure you'll get a letter from Jack soon," Ida lay her hand on Katherine's shoulder.

Katherine stiffened at her touch. Ida let her hand drop, then ran back into the house to put the kettle on.

. . .

The ticking of rain and the hiss of sleet against the windows awakened Katherine in the night. She sat up and lit the brass lamp at her bedside. The black window was spangled with raindrops. The whole house seemed to be filled with the booming of the sea. It was almost like living in a lighthouse. Yet the sound of the waves which had been so soothing to her in their first weeks in Ospedaletti now made her restless and irritable. With the advancing of autumn, the tide level had risen, and the waves rushed into the grottoes carved deep into

104

the cliffs below where they crashed and echoed with a ceaseless, hollow roar. Never again would she live by the sea in winter.

She touched her forehead. She was feverish again and her pillows felt hot and damp in the chill room. Beneath her nightgown, her sweat-soaked singlet clung to her breasts. Her cough had returned worse than ever over the last few days; tonight her lungs burned and ached, producing a low bubbling sound every other breath. Writing to Virginia Woolf that afternoon, she had joked she wished she had been born a crocodile, the only animal, says Sir Thomas Browne, that does not cough. It was easy enough to put on a brave face in a letter, but the reality was far different.

The clock struck four. Where was Murry at this moment, she wondered, reaching for the little sponge on the bedside table to wipe her forehead and neck before extinguishing the lamp again. Was he in bed asleep at the Elephant, or curled up beside Brett in her bedroom? How remote their little house in Hampstead seemed to her now. Sometimes, trying to lull herself back to sleep when she woke in the middle of the night like this, she made the rounds from room to room in her imagination, as if to memorize its details forever. She saw herself standing before the mantelpiece in her bedroom, winding the little shepherdess clock, as she used to do every night before bedtime; then she was in the bathroom, sitting on the edge of the tub, the mirrors all dripping with steam, and Murry floating naked and languorous in the bath, smiling up at her, reaching up to peel the towel from her body, gently pulling her in on top of him into the delicious hot water.

A dog barked down the slope and the vision faded. She tossed beneath the covers, her heart racing but could not re-evoke the scene and lay sleepless for what seemed an eternity. Hearing the first cock crow across the hills, she knew she would remain awake till dawn and her nostalgia deepened to more somber thoughts of annihilation. It would be very easy for her to die here. People died every day of her fever and influenza; she might never see Murry again.

Since she had been here in Ospedaletti, sunrise after sunrise had found her awake thinking of death. It was such a strange sensation. Sometimes it felt so close, as if a barrier were down and she could so easily slip over to the other side. Sometimes it was a Keatsian sensation, a rich, numbing sweetness, smelling of rain on a ploughed field. Other times it was like a quiet, restful wakefulness which made her feel certain that despite everything, there was nothing to fear. *The dead aren't really gone from us,* Lawrence had said to comfort her when her brother died, *they watch over us and help.* Yet that certainty vanished at the slightest interruption, and the old worries and fears swarmed in to devour her peace. Why was Murry so silent? Had he at last deserted her for Brett, or for some other woman? And yet, the last time she had returned from France, they had sworn they would never be apart again. In the bleakest moments she was convinced that it was all over with Murry now.

She reached for the notebook and pencil always ready on her bedside table, and scribbled a few lines

Who's the man as cold as stone
to leave a wife like you alone?

At nine o'clock the next morning, she shut the door and sat down to write. The only solution to loneliness and disappointment was work. Work was the only consolation for the new state of things. Writing was a second breath, a second chance. Ever since her last really successful story, *Je Ne Parle Pas Français*, she had gained a clearer idea of where she needed to go. She must not hold back out of false modesty or propriety. She must tell all; she must deposit her few grains, her residue of truth. She must not fear that friends or acquaintances might recognize themselves in unflattering portraits. How wrong they were when they accused her of using them for copy. It was not their personalities, not as specific individuals, anyway, that she wanted to describe now, but rather types, situations, conditions of existence in which anyone at a certain moment of their lives might recognize themselves, if only for an instant. There was nothing personal about it. No jibes intended. No axes to grind or laurels to bestow. No praise; no blame, just a situation containing the whole drama of a human life, captured in a single moment.

But why was it so hard to get things down on paper? Her ideal would be to produce one complete story a day, but something always posed an obstruction: an uncomfortable chair, a cramp in her neck, a noise out the window. Yet if she could just remain there a few moments longer with her pen poised and her mind receptive without eagerness or strain, the obstacle vanished. The valve would open to release a rush of words like water from a long-trapped spring. It gushed forth with such impetuosity, she needed all her strength to channel it before the flow stopped abruptly and left her hunched at her desk, depleted, holding a pen as heavy as a lead weight.

This new story began with an impression of Murry standing in the doorway of their hotel in San Remo, turning and twisting his signet ring, a characteristic gesture of Murry's, almost a signature of his indecision. Scene after scene spun forth with the motion of the ring twisting on his finger. Ida banging the stove door downstairs then filling the kettle for tea; the inane singing of the gardener at his work, picking the olives; the smell of smoke from the defective chimney, all faded from her consciousness as the story took shape and she was transported back to the hotel garden in San Remo. There among the palms greenish-gold against the blue dusk, amid the bougainvilleas heaped on trellises in a magenta blaze, she pictured herself for what she really was. A sickly thin woman in a loosely fitting dress, her shoulders and throat bandaged in wool scarves; a peevish invalid clinging to her husband's arm. Murry, her numb, bewildered, tragic slave.

At one o'clock, Ida tiptoed into the room, bearing a tray with soup and toast, but Katherine could not allow herself to stop until three o'clock, when weak with hunger, she let the pen drop from her hand, and devoured the cold food. When Ida returned later to take away the tray and bring a brazier of hot coals and a pot of coffee, Katherine dared not even look up from the page, for fear of breaking the thread of words spinning from the nib of her pen. She could hardly write fast enough, and was anxious she might not get it all down in time before the vision dwindled. Ida brought a dinner tray at eight o'clock, and at ten took the untouched food away.

The clock was striking a quarter past midnight as she finally pushed her chair away from her desk. Her legs were so cramped and shaky, she could hardly stand up. Her whole body ached with cold: her legs, her lungs, every joint and every bone, but she felt buoyed up by a sense of triumph. She brought her fist down on the desk with a satisfying and resonant blow, like a magistrate passing judgment. *The Man Without a Temperament* was the best thing she had written yet. To be a real writer at last! Nothing could compare.

. . .

Ida stared down aghast at the shards on the floor. While making Katie's bed, she had bumped against the bedside table and Katie's expensive German thermometer, indeed the only thermometer she had brought from England, had rolled off onto the floor and shattered into bits. There would be no hiding this from Katie who had been running a low fever over the last few weeks and religiously measured her temperature every evening and every morning. To make things worse, today was Saturday, and there would be no replacing the thermometer until Monday afternoon, at the earliest.

The more Ida tried to be careful, the clumsier she became. It was like a curse. No matter how hard she tried to do the right thing, say the right thing, behave as Katie desired her to behave, she always managed to do the just the opposite. Would she never learn the knack of pleasing Katie? As she swept up the glass fragments, the scattered beads of mercury darted away from her broom as if animated by a wicked will of their own.

She heard Katie's soft tread on the wooden stairs, but was not in time to conceal the contents of the dustpan before she stepped into her room.

"What have you broken now?" she asked calmly, peering into the dustpan in Ida's hand, where drops of mercury quivered like tears amid bits of glass. "Oh Ida, not my thermometer!" She shook her head in disbelief.

Ida winced. Katie's quiet rages were far crueler than her shouting rages.

"I am not made of money, Ida, although you seem to think I am. How are we to get on here if you keep on breaking things?"

She turned away, took a book from a shelf, and headed back down the stairs, pausing to say in a hushed but firm voice that made Ida tremble inwardly, "The day is rapidly approaching when you and I must part ways forever."

. . .

Katherine sat alone at her little table upstairs, wrapped in rugs and swathed in a mosquito net, writing. It was a chill, gray day. Livid clouds like blots of ink hung low in the sky and the wind rattled the windows and moaned in the chimney. It was astonishing how quickly the weather had changed from golden autumn to this dreary cold and damp, and yet the temperature was not low enough to kill the mosquitoes and flies that swarmed indoors in search of warmth. Ida was in San Remo for the day. Katherine had obliged her to leave the house, for after the debacle of the broken thermometer, she demanded solitude and silence.

There was no putting up with Ida any longer. Her breaking things. Her inane conversation. Her appalling ignorance. Her maudlin tears. Her suffocating care. At times she was convinced that Ida prayed for her to get worse, so that her help might be even more indispensable. Even Ida's physical presence was revolting with her hang-dog expression and her fat legs, always so untidy with her hair uncombed, threads hanging from the loose buttons of her blouse, smears of coffee or chocolate at the corner of her mouth. And her appetite! She would no doubt soon literally eat them out of house and home, after which, having devoured all the cutlery, tablecloths, and furniture, she would start in on Katherine and gobble her down morsel by morsel. The other night she had even dreamed she had murdered Ida. What bliss! But such plans could never be enacted. She could not possibly dispose of the body unassisted, and who could she ask for help? Despite all those layers of fat, Ida would never burn. Yet Katherine could not indulge in such feelings for long. Her old guilt returned, like a bloated corpse surfacing in a bog. Was it not partly her own fault if Ida was so unkempt and exhausted and unhappy and slavish? Had she destroyed Ida's happiness forever?

A substitute for Ida must be found. In their more lucid moments, they both agreed that they could not possibly stay together any longer, alone in such isolated circumstances, but the anti-English sentiment in the village was so strong Katherine doubted anyone would be willing to work for her. News had spread through the village that she was consumptive. One woman had agreed to come, but at three times the wages of the maid who had left them, which

Katherine could not afford. If no suitable companion-maid could be found, then she might consider sending Ida back to England and going to stay with her father's cousin, Connie, and her companion, Jinny, who ran a nursing home in Menton just over the frontier. There she would be surrounded by comfort and care, but her liberties would be restricted, her work interrupted by chatter. Jinny and Connie were well-meaning, but not really her own sort of people. Ida of course was not her sort of person, either, but at least Ida respected her work. Moreover, both Connie and Jinny were zealous converts to Catholicism and Katherine feared they might not be discreet.

The morning passed in quiet concentration as her pen scratched across the page, no intrusions to disturb her. After lunching on a soup Ida had left warming on the stove, she smoked a cigarette and as she was settling down to work again, she heard most distinctly the crunching of footsteps on the gravel around the house. She glanced at the clock. It was only three o'clock: too early for Ida to return, and she had not heard the melodic claxon of the omnibus as it roared round the curve below. Visitors this way were rare on a weekday morning. Not even mail was delivered out this far in the cold season. And today, the gardener and his wife had gone to the market in San Remo to buy plants and would not be back till late.

The footsteps persisted around the back of the house. She went to the window overlooking the rear and as she stood surveying the grounds, the front doorbell rang. She went to the window on the stairs giving out over the front door, but the roof above the entrance obstructed the view, so she opened the window and called out in Italian, "*Chi è?*" When no one answered, she called out in French, "I am sorry, but I will not open unless you identify yourself!" There was no reply.

She surmised that the village children were playing a joke on her and sat down to her desk again. The noise was immediately repeated: footsteps on the gravel to the rear of the house, followed by a long, insistent, syncopated ring of the front doorbell. She banged open the upstairs window and shouted out again sharply, but no one responded. Unlocking the drawer of her bedside table, she took out her pistol and hurried down the stairs, intending to fire the gun in the air to discourage her intruders.

With a shock of terror, she found the front door wide open, then noticed that her favorite camel hair overcoat with the fox fur collar which she always left hanging on the rack by the door, was gone. Bounding out the door, she was just in time to see two gypsy boys, each with a bundle of rags on his shoulder, making off with her coat. Scrambling over the terrace walls, they disappeared across the hillside. She was lifting her arm to fire a monitory shot in the air when a dreadful thought flashed through her mind. *There might still be someone in the house or on the grounds.* She glanced warily around the apparently empty garden, trying to swallow her fear, peering behind the bay laurel bushes and cypress trees, wondering if she were being watched from some hiding place. Where would she be safer—indoors or outdoors? No one could hear her if she screamed in either case, and it was too cold to stand outside and wait for Ida to return. She would surely catch pneumonia standing out here without a proper coat and wearing slippers. *If only she had not sent Ida away for a silly broken thermometer.* There was nothing else to do but go back into the house and make sure no one was inside. The gun shook in her frozen hand as she advanced into the kitchen, her heart hammering in her ears. The only sign of something amiss was an open drawer where the cutlery was kept, and a puddle of milk on the table where a milk bottle had been overturned. Luckily the gypsies had not found the secret place behind the sideboard where she kept their stash of money. Stepping into the sitting room, she saw that one of the windows giving onto the verandah had been forced open. The thieves must have come in through that window and slipped out again through the front door. She closed the window and made sure the door to the verandah was locked and then began to check if anything else had been stolen. A pair of kid gloves and a silver-plated ashtray were missing from a table in the entrance hall. Steadier now, she mounted to her bedroom, then, assured no one was in the house, came down again. Drawing a chair up by the front door, she sat exhausted, eyes closed, chest heaving and bubbling with each breath, still clutching the cold revolver in her lap, waiting for Ida to return.

At five o'clock the omnibus stopped at the bottom of the hill and a disheveled Ida descended after wandering aimless hours in San Remo. Yet she hurtled up the hill in exhilaration, swinging her walking stick, for she bore not only the usual bread, milk, meat, and a new thermometer, but also a surprise for Katie. This time there were two letters: one from Murry and one from Katie's cousin Connie in Menton, and even a little packet from Murry, all postmarked over three weeks earlier. She prayed these missives might cheer Katie's spirits and help make amends for Saturday's quarrel, for Katie was determined to send her away. She could not bear to think of parting from her, even though things between them had never been so strained.

"Katie, Katie!" she cried, flinging open the door and almost stumbling over Katie, slumped in a chair in the entrance, ashen pale. She looked up at Ida with haunted eyes and Ida noticed the gun.

"Jones, thank God you're back. I have been frightened nearly out of my wits."

Ida stared in horror as Katie recounted the robbery of her coat.

"Think of it, Jones! They could have done me God knows what harm."

Ida suggested putting new locks on the doors and windows, but Katie shook her head. They could not afford such expenses.

In those long hours of waiting, the stove had gone out and Katie begged her to light it again, for she had caught a chill sitting in the draft from the door. Ida lit the stove, then put away the groceries. Pulling the letters out of her bag, she handed them to Katie.

A childlike eagerness glowed in Katie's face as she took the envelopes. The terrors of the afternoon seemed momentarily eclipsed. While Ida prepared tea, Katie sat by the stove, opening her mail, following a precise protocol. She always saved Murry's letters for last, so she might savor every word without distractions. First, she tore open the slim brown parcel, discovering a silver spoon wrapped in pink wrapping paper. "Oh look! It's my birthday present from Jack," she said, holding it up for Ida to see. "The most perfect silver spoon. Can't you just see me spooning custard into the mouths of my future Murry boys? What a wonderfully sweet thought. Dear Jack. He knows how I yearn for us to have a child together. This spoon is a token, he's thinking of it too."

Ida grunted with misgivings. Katie should not indulge in such morbid fantasies.

Next Katie opened the letter from her cousin Connie. After skimming down a few lines, she cried excitedly, "Father's coming for a visit! They're driving down to San Remo and would like to stop in for lunch.... On the 12th of November! Oh Jones, that's tomorrow! Father is coming tomorrow! When in heaven's name was this letter posted? It must have been held up because of the strike. How will we manage lunch for five on such a short notice? You must rush back to town this afternoon before the shops close."

"It's too late to go back into town now. I'll have to go tomorrow morning at seven."

"That's far too late, Jones, you must go with the omnibus at dawn, and be back here by no later than half past nine, if we're to have everything shipshape by lunchtime. We'll need more wood to get all the fires blazing and we'll have to polish this place from stem to stern."

Katie began to pace up and down the kitchen, scrutinizing every detail of the room. She stopped before the fireplace to observe the row of copper casseroles hanging from iron pegs above the mantelpiece. In these weeks of use, they had lost their ruddy glint.

"For example, those copper pots don't wink and gleam like they should. You must work harder to make them shine. They're one of the picturesque touches in this little house, and I do want them to see me flourishing and in lovely surroundings."

Ida glared at the pots. She had scoured them for hours with sand from the hillside, but had not achieved the desired effect. There would be no time for anything tomorrow except the most essential shopping and cooking. Katie would just have to make do with that.

Katie began pacing again, musing out loud about the menu, "And we will need a pastry from the *pâtisserie*. A little tart with apples or pears should be suitable for the occasion. And the gardener must find us some salad in a sunny spot not yet spoiled by the cold. You know how father loves salads, a little valerian and rocket would do just fine."

"Today the butcher asked for an advance on our meat bill."

"Well, give it to him."

"And the pastry cook also wants to be paid."

"You're right, Jones," sighed Katie, reaching for the worn satin clutch bag in which their Italian money was kept hidden in a niche behind the sideboard. She took out a few banknotes and spread them on the table, studied them with a frown, then turned to Ida, her face flushed.

"Ida, how much money did you take from here last week?"

"What was needed to pay the woodman and the girl from the laundry."

"But we've hardly more than the equivalent of twelve pounds left, unless you have a fortune in coins jangling in your pockets."

Ida scooped out a handful of change from her pocket and showed it to Katie. The coins hardly amounted to more than a few lire.

"I hope," said Katie sternly, glancing at the unopened letter from Murry. "I hope he has remembered to send me those ten pounds I told him we needed." She ripped open the envelope, read a few lines, then crumpled it in her hand. Her face was livid.

"He's very sorry but he can't spare a penny right now. Even if I promised to repay him immediately, he could not lend me anything. He repeats that I must not forget he is very nearly bankrupt. And he has sent me a copy of his bank statement to prove it! Really, Ida. How can he be so insensitive? Other men support their wives."

She threw the letter into the stove, took the pile of banknotes from the table - recounted them, and handed half to Ida, saying, "Take this Ida, take it all if you need. Pay whatever bills there are to pay, and buy all the essentials for tomorrow's luncheon. Don't be stingy. Splurge! I intend to entertain my father in high style."

Ida sat up reading on the divan, where she spread her sheets and blanket every night. Now that the weather had turned cold, the tile floor in Katie's room was too chill for her to sleep on. Every night after Katie had gone to bed, she pushed the divan to the bottom of the stairs, to better guard access to Katie's bedroom. Anyone wishing to go upstairs would have to climb over Ida's sleeping body or murder her first. It was nearly midnight. A cricket droned somewhere near the stove, behind the scuttle. Katie had gone to bed exhausted, partly from the day's misadventures and partly from her excitement over Mr. Beauchamp's arrival the next day. Soon Ida would put the lights out and go to sleep. How close the roaring sea sounded, as though it could wash their little chalet away with a powerful slap of a wave. She imagined the two of them treading water in a fast current, their nightgowns billowing in the sea swell, Katie drifting further from her reach.

A large pale green moth fluttered about the electric lamp casting eerie shadows on the wall. Ida felt her eyes closing, her head nodding off to a doze, when the rustling of bushes out the window caught her attention, and instantly her nerves were alert. There was a loud thump overhead as if someone had jumped onto the verandah roof and the whole chalet shook. Katie, awakened, whispered hoarsely down the stairs, "Jones, did you hear that? They've come back!" Then came a scratching noise from the verandah roof.

Katie hobbled down the stairs, gun in hand, and climbed over the divan where Ida sat tensely, listening.

"Ida, do something!" Katie commanded, and she handed Ida her revolver. "You're a better shot than I."

Ida's father had taught her to shoot properly in Rhodesia, and she had once saved a beloved puppy from a rat snake. Ida gripped the gun, crossed the verandah and stepped out into the dark garden, screaming, "*Qui va là ?*" With her arm as cold and rigid as an iron rod, she fired three shots at the sky.

There came a bloodcurdling screech, and a huge tomcat, unhurt but terrorized, leapt from the verandah roof to the ground, and scuttled away through the hedge.

Stunned, Ida watched the cat dash off down the slope. "It's all right," she called out to Katie. "It was only a silly cat. Thank goodness I didn't shoot him."

Katie came outside in her dressing gown and they both began to laugh with delicious release, for it was the first laughter they had shared for weeks and weeks. Katie put her arm around Ida's waist, and they stood admiring the moon, half-full, high above the sea glinting like oil in the silvery light. Then, arm-in-arm they went back inside, and although it was well after midnight, they put the kettle on for tea.

Next morning a bright sun had returned and it was just barely warm enough for Katherine, bundled in a jersey and two cardigans, to take the air in a sheltered place, curled up on the chaise-longue with rugs and blankets while Ida, who had returned from her early shopping trip to town, prepared lunch. Katherine sat staring down at the sea, with a book in her lap and one hand in her pocket. Her lungs and back ached that morning; every breath produced a rumbling sound deep within her chest. Around her the olive leaves shivered in the keen air and, in the stronger gusts, a few purplish olives left unharvested fell to the ground one by one with a soft thud. Across the tidy plot of grass was scattered the fine white down of a cotton plant that had burst its seedpods in the night. Far out at sea, a fishing boat tossed upon the cobalt waves. She watched it moving further and further away, a dark speck upon the horizon, black like a spot on a lung.

She sighed. Soon Father would be there to rescue her from solitude, if only for a few hours. Her fingers touched Murry's silver spoon which she carried in her pocket like a talisman. With this sweet little spoon, she might have fed Garnet's baby, the baby she lost years ago at the age of twenty-one. It was useless to dream of other babies now. Sorapure had explained that she had had an illness and she had been left barren. This was yet one more detail about her past that Murry did not know. Only Ida knew the truth. They could always adopt a child, perhaps, when she was well again. But when would that be? Sorapure said nothing was incurable, it was only a matter of time before the body healed itself. But that was just it! How much time did she have? A doctor she had seen last week in San Remo had told her that the large spot on her left lung had shrunk; there was only a small spot at the apex. He recommended she spend as much time outside as possible, breathing in the balsamic air and avoiding chills and mental strain. If she kept on like this, he claimed, she had a very good chance, ninety-nine percent, of leading a normal life again. But why did she feel so feverish at night? There were days when she could venture all the way down to the bottom terrace, ramble into town, peek into a shop and ride the omnibus back home again. But there were other days when she rose at noon, lay all day on the sofa, and retired for the night at six o'clock with a dozen hot water bottles strapped to her back and chest.

She had begun to count the days until she could return to England, though that was still months and months away. It was funny how one was always waiting for something. For someone to come—Murry, father, Ida. For a letter to arrive. For her fever to go down. Yet the letter longed for, the meeting dreamed of, the journey ended, the reprieve from illness, never really brought the promised joy. She could make a book out of those interminable periods of waiting. Her whole life was crowded into their parenthesis, and she seemed to look down upon herself from above as the moments flowed into a pool where time's motion ended.

Gazing down upon the red-tiled rooftops of the town, she noted a motorcar speeding up the road. A great shining car, engine purring, was mounting the curves as smoothly as a hawk in an upward draft. The claxon trumpeted merrily at each bend in the road. It could only be Father, although he was a good two hours early! Rounding the last curve, the great silver vehicle made straight for the chalet and rolled to a rambunctious halt in the drive, its tires screeching on the gravel. Doors shot open and out tumbled Connie and Jinny in the most extravagant traveling attire: wide-brimmed hats with plumes, furs, veils, and fluttering scarves. Behind them, Pa appeared, looking even from this distance older, grayer, stooped, though he still cut a massive figure in his overcoat, his face shadowed by a stylish fedora.

Pa! Pa! She cried and ran across the yard. It had been years since she had called him that. He preferred to be called "Father." Did he too slink back imperceptibly as she threw himself into his arms? She blotted out the thought, for the joy and comfort of being held by such strong arms was almost overwhelming, and his smell, so manly and reassuring mingled of cigars, cologne, and camphor, took her back to childhood. She found herself weeping. The tears that would not come for her mother now flowed copiously. She wept for her mother, for her father, for Leslie, for herself, for Murry, while her father held her close, murmuring soothing words. Gently disentangling himself from her embrace, he held her at arm's length. "That's enough, child. Let's have a look at you," but his eyes did not smile as they searched her face, and she saw him blink away a tear.

Connie and Jinny, still standing near the car, looked on awkwardly at this reunion. Katherine turned to welcome them and they came forward, veils and scarves trailing in the strong wind rippling through the olive trees. They all embraced. Taking her father's hand, she led them towards the chalet.

"You are much earlier than I expected," she said.

"The driver made good time," said Harold Beauchamp.

"What a lovely drive down on this crisp autumn day! But it is much colder here than in Menton. And what a chill breeze," said Jinny hugging her shoulders against the wind.

"I hope, dear, that we have not inconvenienced you by arriving too early," said Connie, "Your father was so impatient to set off and see you."

Katherine smiled at her father's impetuosity. When he got going he was like a locomotive. Nothing held him back. In that, they were alike.

"No, not at all. Ida will probably have an attack of hysterics. But there is at least a chance that she won't overcook the meat. You see," she felt obliged to add, "we have no servants and Ida is my cook and bottle-washer."

"No servants, my dear?" asked Connie, staring up at the little chalet. "How do you manage?"

"We have had no luck keeping any servants but the gardener. There are very strong anti-English feelings in the village here. We have been subject to all kinds of unpleasantness."

"Nothing like that in Menton. They adore us there," said Jinny. She pronounced the word in the English fashion, "Men-tone," nettling Katherine's nerves. You'd think that after so many years in France, Jinny might have learned to pronounce the language properly.

"And how could they not adore two such adorable ladies as yourselves?" teased her father. Connie and Jinny laughed appropriately; Connie with her girlish giggle; Jinny with a toothy neigh, and they all went into lunch.

Connie was a stout woman of seventy years with a neat gray chignon and soft brown eyes. She favored frilly blouses in pastel colors and broad-brimmed hats trimmed with fur or feathers. There was an old-fashioned daintiness about her. She smelled of fresh starch and patchouli and orange blossoms. Jinny, a more energetic type, was six years younger than Connie. Her full bosom was always buttoned into tight-fitting bodices with high collars in stern shades of blue and gray to accentuate her intense blue gaze. There was something horselike about her, and it wasn't just her laughter. She was efficient and strong and cheerful and so independent, unlike Cousin Connie. But those were the qualities that made Jinny such an excellent nurse. For years she and Connie had been companions and business associates, running successful nursing homes first in England and now in France.

As they sat crowded round the kitchen table, Katherine could have blessed Ida, despite her many faults. The lunch she had prepared, if long on onions and short on chops, was tasty and appreciated. The salad was crisp; the bread and butter fresh; the wine heady; and the pastry superb—though Katherine hated to think how much they had spent to feed her guests. Even Ida's mindless conversation about the ingenious shapes of Italian pasta and her passion for Galsworthy were just the thing to keep the dear old ladies entertained while she tried to talk more confidentially to her father. There was a painful issue to discuss: her yearly allowance must be increased; her medical bills and the expenses of living abroad were more than she could handle on two hundred pounds a year. And she really wasn't earning very much with her stories yet. But Father had a sixth sense when it came to discussing finances. He always managed to deviate the conversation before the subject was actually touched upon. Now when he pulled her close again and peered ruefully into her face with a gruff, "Tell me the truth now. How are you getting on here?" she thought she had her chance.

Father rubbed his hands together and said, "It's very cold here in Ospedaletti. I don't think it is a suitable climate for you. How much are you paying for this pasteboard dollhouse?"

When Katherine told him the rent, he snorted in disapproval. "And is that son-in-law of mine gainfully employed yet?"

Katherine blushed. The few times her father and Murry had met, they simply did not get on. Father had interpreted Murry's shyness as sheer rudeness. He had never understood Murry, and Murry had made no attempt to communicate with him. She felt obliged to defend her husband by saying, " He is now making eight hundred pounds a year as editor of the *Athenaeum*, and will soon be one of England's most celebrated critics."

"Glad to hear it," he remarked with finality, patting her arm. Clearing his throat, he addressed the ladies across the table. "Well now, shall we go for a drive?"

Chagrined, Katherine realized that all talk of financial matters had ceased before it had even begun. Once again she would have to ask Mr. Kay, the director of Father's bank, to intervene on her behalf; or perhaps she might ask Connie to have a word with her father.

Ida, left with the dishes and tidying up, lingered wistfully in the doorway as the others bundled into the car.

It was such a luxury to glide, wrapped in fur rugs and propped up on silk cushions, down the slopes in her father's motorcar, and then to plough through the narrow village streets where chickens clucked along the roadside, and the laundress, bearing a basket of linens on her head, stopped and turned to stare. While winding down the road from Ospedaletti, Father shouted instructions to his Maori driver, producing chocolates, lozenges, tangerines, and even a flask of cognac from the pockets of his overcoat, passing these treats left and right to the ladies, all mellowed after a rich meal with wine, although they felt a bit woozy on the curves. On the drive down, Katherine, mischievously wanting to challenge Jinny's ladylike propriety, entertained them with a sailor's ditty that was not quite off-color, and Father surprised her by booming along with the refrain. Smiling out at the world from behind the thick windows through which the sunlight streamed, she felt invulnerable for once. If she had remained in New Zealand, life would have been like this, perhaps, surrounded by comforts. But hadn't Mother been suffocated by too many luxuries?

Katherine had rejected all that in the name of Art. How grand it had all seemed then, coming to London at the age of nineteen to start a musician's career. But she had no talent, and had soon sold her cello for three pounds. Then she had discovered her gift for writing stories and Dick Orage had launched her into literary London. Through him she had found her mission, her vocation. Nothing satisfied her so much as writing. But it was such a solitary chore to sit cramped at a table with an eggcup full of ink, nursing words from a pen. Had it been necessary to give up so much for that?

Heads turned as they drove through San Remo. A little girl threw flowers at the car. The chemist, who happened at that moment to be crossing the street outside his shop, recognized her in the car, and she nodded to him through the window, like a queen from her cortege.

They stopped for coffee and cognac at a café in San Remo, then drove on through the countryside, pulling over near a field, where they all got out with blankets and rugs and more coffee in a thermos her father had had filled at the café. There they sat among the tall swaying yellow grasses in a sunny, sheltered spot, sipping coffee and smoking. Father, sitting on his campstool under a linden tree, chewed a fragrant cigar while Connie wandered across the field and frightened a friendly cow that tried to munch her scarf. Jinny and Katherine basked together on the coach rug, eyes shut, faces tilted up to the sun. It was wonderful to feel part of a family, part of a tribe. Then Jinny opened her eyes and gazed at Katherine, and Katherine said, " Isn't this bliss? To sit here like two lizards in a patch of autumn sun."

Jinny lay her gloved hand on Katherine's arm. "Even in the chill shadows of winter, God's love shines down on you, if only you will open your heart."

Jinny's swift attack, although not entirely unexpected, had still caught Katherine unawares. She did not wish to be impolite, but she did not want to be proselytized. She had her own quarrel with God for giving her consumption and it was not a subject she desired to discuss with Jinny, or with anyone at all.

Further attack on her agnosticism was luckily avoided, for her father stirred, grumbling about the late hour, insisting they drive on. He rose from his campstool, disappeared for a few moments, then rejoining the party spread out on rugs in the field, he uprooted a handful of late daisies and handed them to Katherine. Then they all piled back into the car.

On the journey back, Katherine was exhausted but happy. She snuggled against the cushions, clutching father's daisies to her breast, staring out the window at the hills, fields, and sea all enveloped in dusky blue. Connie seemed pensive; Father napped; Jinny, up front with the driver, sat very straight and prim as if wanting to give the poor Maori chap a lesson on how ladies sit in cars. Katherine wondered if she had tried to convert him to the Roman Catholic Church on their drive over from Menton.

It was quite late by the time they returned. Ida had lit the stove and had the tea kettle steaming, but Father refused to stay any longer, and demanded they drive back immediately to Menton. Crowded into the tiny hall of the Casetta, they said their goodbyes. Father, tapping his foot, was anxious to be gone.

"I will leave you a little treat," he said, reaching into the breast pocket of his overcoat. She was sure he was about to present her with a small wad of cash, but instead he drew out his silver cigarette case, counted out five Castles cigarettes, and left them next to the wilted daisies on the coat rack shelf. Sweeping Katherine up in his arms, he murmured fondly, "You little marvel. Get well soon. You know you're so much like your mother."

He crushed her head to his breast with rough affection, and Katherine sobbed. Then he pulled away, said a cordial goodbye to Ida, and on the excuse of checking the motor with his Maori chap, stepped out the door.

"There, there" said Jinny, patting Katherine's arm. "Don't let's spoil a lovely afternoon with tears. "

Connie clutched Katherine's hands and thanked her for the luncheon, then turned to Ida to compliment her on her cooking. Addressing Katherine again, she said, "It really is far too cold here. And windy. This house is full of drafts. It's also so isolated here. You must come to stay with us in Menton. Both of you. You will never get better as long as you are here."

They were gone.

Katherine stood at the window, lit up one of her father's cigarettes and watched the car drive away.

"Do you think we should go to Menton?" she asked as Ida set the table for tea. "I hate the thought of having to uproot again and I do adore this house."

"This house is a wind trap," Ida replied. "You know what the doctor said about avoiding chills. And your cousin does say it's warmer there."

"But in Menton there would be no privacy and how could I write? Besides, I know that Jinny, as kind as she is, has in mind to make a good little Roman Catholic of me."

"Well, you may have to go there in due time," said Ida, "Miss Fullerton has left her rug here," and she held up a Jaeger traveling rug Jinny had left in the kitchen.

Katherine took the rug and draped it round her shoulders. It was thick, warm, and very chic. An excuse, she thought, as she caressed the fleecy fabric, Jinny has left us an excuse to pay a visit to Menton.

MENTON

The last bags were piled into the waiting motorcar where Katherine sat wrapped in the Jaeger traveling rug left behind by Jinny during her visit in November, over two months ago. Ida pulled the door to the chalet shut with a bang, slid the key into the rusted letterbox and ran towards the car, her hair flying in the wind. Once again they were escaping and there was no time to lose. Ida climbed in; the driver started up the engine and they rolled down the white gravel road coiling round the wild hillside. Katherine did not look back even once at the little white house with its garden of olive and fruit trees or at the terraced slopes with their tangled shrubs of rosemary poised above the boiling sea. These last few weeks in the Casetta Deerholm had been a nightmare to which she now intended to put an end.

Just a few days after Jinny and Connie had visited with her father, Katherine had fallen ill with pleurisy again and had lain three weeks in bed with a fever, listening to the wind moan, wondering if she would come out of this alive, while Ida ministered to her with her usual blundering attentions. The weather which during the week of father's visit had seemed to presage an early spring, had turned into the bitterest of winters. There had been yet another postal strike in Italy, and the only news that had reached her during those weeks, was, preposterously, a letter from her sister Chaddie, informing her rather matter-of-factly that Father had remarried an old friend of their mother's.

The news had left her speechless. How could he have done such a thing so soon, with her mother hardly in the grave? Father had sat there at the table next to her in the little chalet, holding her hands in his, calling her my pretty and my sweet, and once had even seemed on the verge of tears, recalling her likeness to her mother. Not one word had he uttered of his future wedding plans. Amazing how shallow some people can be, even one's own father. But that just shows you, Katherine mused, that you can't expect anything from anyone.

In those long agonizing weeks, the solitude at night had been unbearable. Lying awake till dawn, going over the past, she was assailed by strange moods till she thought she might go mad. This is what the dead must do throughout eternity, she thought, mull over the past till its heavy swirling eddies finally dissolve to mist.

After yet another row with Ida, she had decided to accept Connie and Jinny's invitation to stay with them at Villa Flora in Menton, but by the time she was well enough to travel, the anti-English crisis in San Remo had precipitated. A local girl had been raped by an English sailor, and in revenge an Englishman had been assaulted on the street. Now decent English people were afraid to walk the streets at night. Last week, the hotel manager had driven all the way out to see them, urging them to leave the area at once, for they were too easy a prey on that isolated hilltop out in Ospedaletti.

Katherine was eager to be gone, but it had nearly been impossible to find someone to drive them to Menton. When Ida had gone to get their visas in San Remo, she had managed to round up this fellow from somewhere. He was cousin to one of the cooks at the hotel from which they had been turned out. A small, shrewd-looking fellow with a dark, wizened face and a heavily waxed moustache, he had canny glinting eyes and wore a gold ring on his little finger. He probably worked as *contrabandiere*, running illegal goods across the border. What's more he stank of cheap cigars, but he spoke tolerable English. One look at him told Katherine he would squeeze money from her purse like water from a soggy sponge.

The car rumbled through the narrow streets of the village, nearly scraping the walls of buildings on either side at every turn. People stopped to watch them pass by, but this time there were no cheery salutes or little girls in pinafores, tossing flowers at the windshield. To the contrary, a boy picked up a stone and threw it at them, and soon a shower of stones hailed down, bouncing off the bonnet as the car ploughed on. As they drove on through San Remo, familiar shopkeepers shook their fists from shop doorways. When the vehicle was forced to stop at a corner, a rough-looking drunk pushed his snarling face against the window on Katherine's side, terrifying her, for she thought he might try to drag her from the car. Their scowling driver pushed right on by, throwing the man off balance. Stumbling back to the curb, he shouted a curse behind them.

"I wonder why they hate us so," said Ida, looking back at the drunken man who stood clinging to a lamp post.

"England wishes to ruin Italy," intoned the driver in a gloomy voice.

"But that is untrue," Katherine protested.

"England has made Italian lire worthless."

Katherine groaned and stared out at the gray, glimmering sea. She knew nothing about economic politics. It was not wise to become entangled in an argument of this kind.

At last San Remo was left behind and they were on the main road to Ventimiglia, following the coast. Thick clouds hung over a choppy sea and the strong wind shook the palms along the seafront, whipping the ragged fronds in all directions. Katherine sank back against the seat. It would be an easy drive along the coast, if there were no unforeseen delays at the border. She reached inside the pocket of her coat where their passports were hidden in a small blue satin bag, to reassure herself that nothing had been forgotten. She glanced at her watch. It was just past eight o'clock.

Then, at a junction where a side road led off towards the mountains, the driver turned off the main road and headed inland. Puzzled, Katherine leaned forward and enquired, "Why are we changing directions? Aren't we going through Ventimiglia?"

"It will be unsafe to take English ladies into France from Ventimiglia. We must go through the mountains."

"Through the mountains? In the winter, in this weather?" She looked up at the sky. Heavier clouds were piling in. Here on the coast they would only bring dense rains, but above five hundred meters in altitude, they were sure to bring sleet and possibly snow.

"If the lady wishes to go to Mentone, she must go through the mountains."

"I will not hear of it."

The car choked to a halt. The driver turned round and challenged her with a sneer. "Then I not take the ladies to Mentone."

"Why not?"

"Police might not let you through."

Katherine hesitated. This might be true.

"But the way is longer. It will cost you more."

Katherine's eyes narrowed as she pressed her lips tight. If only she were a cat, she thought, this would be the moment to spit and scratch.

"Through the mountains the distance is three times more. But I make you pay only twice. Six English pounds."

Ida gasped at the sum.

"I expected as much," mumbled Katherine to Ida. "How much money have you got in your purse?"

Ida checked her purse. "Just enough Katie, and not a lire or a franc more."

"All right," she assented. "The important thing is that we get there by nightfall."

Not a car passed on the way up. There was not a soul to be seen. The road was clear in most spots, but ice encrusted the curves in shadow. Just one slight skid and they might plunge into an abyss. Midway, an omnibus overtook them, honking its claxon and nearly running them off the road. Ida gripped the back of the driver's seat and kept her eyes closed for most of the trip. Katherine sipped the tea in her thermos and gazed out at fields strewn with boulders emerging through patches of dirty snow. After an interminable climb, they had reached the pass, and the driver pulled over to the side of the road.

With eyes still shut, Ida asked, "Are we there?"

Katherine surveyed the jagged peaks against the billowing clouds. Wind buffeted the car.

"Not quite."

Opening her eyes, Ida asked anxiously, "Why have we stopped?"

"Perhaps we're out of petrol."

"Only a minute," said the driver, climbing out with an apologetic grin, and walking round to the back of the car.

Perplexed, they watched him through the rear window, but with an angry sweep of his arm, he motioned them to turn back around. Then they heard him urinating behind the car.

Ida blushed.

A ribald remark flitted to the tip of Katherine's tongue, but she restrained herself. It would not do to irritate the driver in these circumstances.

The man got back in and started up the car, but the motor coughed and died with a dismal, grating rasp.

After three vain attempts to start the car, he got out and opened up the bonnet. As he bent to examine the engine, the wind nearly tore his hat from his head. Katherine and Ida huddled under Jinny's traveling rug, observing the scene with consternation. When he went round to remove a tool box from the boot, Katherine's heart gave a start. This was a very bad sign. It might take ages to repair the engine. She looked up at the sky again. A few silvery flakes glinted in the air, and the thick bank of cloud promised more. If they should be caught in a snowstorm, it could prove to be very dangerous indeed. The road was deserted. No one would be foolish enough to come this way with a storm brewing.

They finished the tepid tea in the thermos and snuggled closer. Katherine's teeth were chattering. Gloved in suede, her fingers were ice and her toes stung in her high laced boots. They stamped their feet against the floor while the driver sputtered and cursed, rattling his iron tools beneath the open bonnet. The wind was blowing harder now, rocking the car and whistling through the fissures beneath the doors. Then the sky opened and the snow came pelting down.

They watched the man walk along the road, and with hands on hips, scan the distance in both directions, looking presumably for some source of help. As he trudged back to the car, Katherine read the worry in his hardened face.

"If only we hadn't stopped. We may end up freezing to death here," whined Ida.

Katherine glanced at Ida's frightened eyes and felt a spasm of sympathy for her friend, with whom she had shared so many moments of danger: earthquakes and violent storms, the German bombardment of Paris, sea squalls and rough voyages. Ida, so practical and stolid, sometimes fell apart at times like these, and it was up to her to maintain the general calm. Indeed a sudden clarity had come upon her. Perhaps it was the effect of too much tea stimulating her brain, or of the biting cold, but Katherine surprised herself by feeling lucid and self-possessed, with an eerie feeling nudging at her mind: the conviction that she had lived this moment before and had come through unscathed. It was all so familiar, the frozen landscape, the wind whistling and battering the car, the man tinkering under the bonnet, she had seen this all before, perhaps in a dream. Poor Ida here beside her, with a knitted scarf bound round her head like a veteran's bandage, with her two little squinty eyes, poor Ida, so tiny beneath these looming peaks. How odd to find that they had somehow exchanged places. It was Ida who needed her tenderness and care. It was Ida who needed her protection.

"It will be all right. I know it's not my time yet," Katherine whispered, leaning over to kiss the tip of Ida's cold, red nose.

Ida threw her arms round Katherine's neck and sobbed, "Oh Katie, I wouldn't mind dying if it weren't for you. But if it must happen I'd rather it be with you than anyone."

"That's a comforting thought," said Katherine, wrestling free from Ida's grip. "But I assure you I have no intention of freezing to death here."

"Oh Katie, forgive me! What I meant to say was..."

There was a rap on the window. The driver, snow dusting his coat and moustache, glared at them and ordered, "The Signora must start car while I fix engine."

"Start the car? I haven't the faintest idea of how to start the car," said Katherine.

The man repeated his request and went back round to the front of the car and bent over the engine. "Start car!" he cried.

"I'll try," rallied Ida, "My father took me driving once."

She got out, climbed into the driver's seat and seized the steering wheel with a look of dubious determination. At the driver's repeated command, a dreadful wrenching sound was heard and the car lurched forward. The engine coughed once and died.

"*Dolcemente. Dolcemente.* The signora must not press foot so hard," shouted the man from under the bonnet, "*Ancora! Ancora!*" he urged.

Ida bit her lip and started up the ignition again while Katherine said a silent prayer, imagining sparks flowing through the wires to the engine. This was a mental exercise Dick Orage had taught her. Oil the wheels with the mind when something mechanical doesn't work. It seemed to help for this time the engine caught. The car jolted again, the engine choked twice and then began turning over smoothly.

Her face flushed with pleasure and relief, Ida kept the motor running till the driver got in again and resumed control. She climbed back in beside Katherine and they embraced to warm themselves as the car shunted forward and skidded off down the snowy road. Katherine rested her head against Ida's shoulder and gave her an affectionate squeeze, "Once again, my dear Jones, I must confess. You have saved the day."

No sooner had they set off again, the clouds thinned and the snow dwindled to a few flickering flakes in the frosty air, and in less than twenty minutes they found themselves at the border checkpoint.

Icicles hung from the roof of an empty sentry box where a ragged French flag stiff with ice drooped on a flagpole. The driver got out and lifted the wooden barrier across a gravel road. As they drove into France, Katherine gave a sigh of relief. She never wanted to return to Italy again.

The weather improved by degrees as they crawled down the endless curves, and by the time they had reached the bottom, the sun was still shining.

Jinny and Connie were out on the front lawn outside their villa as the car drew up. Connie, a thick afghan tucked around her, was stretched in a chaise-longue, with a pile of illustrated magazines on a table beside her and a small Pekinese dog curled at her feet. It looked as though she had been lying there waiting all day for them. Jinny, wearing a garden apron, was pruning shrubs. A formal garden of clipped boxwood hedges surrounded the front lawn. Beyond those verdant walls rose the imposing Villa Flora, not as grand as Ottoline's Garsington Manor, but after the Casetta Deerholm, Villa Flora appeared to Katherine's eyes to be exquisitely aristocratic. As Katherine struggled out of the car, Jinny put down her shears and ran toward her, the little Pekinese bounced behind, yapping at her heels.

Snatched up in Jinny's arms, Katherine began to weep for sheer release and Jinny wept too. "I feel as though I have come through a cataclysm, up from the frozen bowels of hell," Katherine said, catching her breath between sobs.

"But the Lord has delivered you safely into our hands at last, dearest

Katherine," soothed Jinny.

"Yes," said Connie, now approaching," welcome my darling," and she put her arms around Katherine and Jinny for a long embrace, while the dog continued barking at their ankles.

After paying the driver with the last of the cash and supervising the unloading of the luggage, Ida came forward to greet Katherine's cousin and her companion with awkward formality. The visitors were ushered onto a heated verandah where coffee awaited them. Arrayed on a polished, glass-topped table were a coffee service of gleaming silver, little dishes of cakes, chocolates, and sandwiches, bowls of fragrant violets, and a flask of Grand Marnier liqueur. Seeing such luxuries, Katherine burst into tears again and only managed to calm herself when Jinny scooped up the little Pekinese and plopped it into her arms.

While Connie served her guests, Ida recounted their adventures: their escape from an angry mob in Ospedaletti, their sinister driver, the car stalling in the mountains, the sudden blizzard, while exaggerating the dangers they had faced and the heroism of her own role. Jinny and Connie looked aghast as they followed the tale.

Although upon her arrival Katherine had felt on the verge of collapse, the sweet rich coffee and orange liqueur soon revived her spirits. As Ida rattled on to Jinny and Connie, Katherine fondled the little dog Chin-Chin and observed her cousin and her companion.

How she envied these two older women whose lives seemed free of any material care. They could enjoy the solid comfort of each other's company and were not bound by necessity, by shortage of funds, by illness and calamity to stick together. Connie leaned on Jinny the way a woman leans on a man, and yet in no way was eclipsed by her younger companion. They were both complete and independent creatures. Their contentment was manifested in the perfection of every detail of their domestic life together. How far removed from her own friendship with Ida. She and Ida were just like a pair of worn-out, mismatched shoes.

What a toll her illness had taken on their relationship. She knew she must be grateful to her for all her sacrifices, and yet she felt the burden of Ida's devotion like an albatross around her neck. Jinny and Connie could have no idea what they had just been through in Ospedaletti where the mere necessities of life— water, fire, food—had been an ordeal which she could never have handled alone. But now all that was over. That was Italy. This was France, the most civilized country in the world. Here she was sitting in the fading sun, surrounded by women who cared for her and wished her well. She almost felt like a butterfly fanning its wings upon its favorite flower, were it not for the cough that grated in her chest. Her recent attack of pleurisy had weakened her left lung again, just when it had seemed to be improving.

From the verandah, they moved to a sitting room facing the formal garden, where a fire burned briskly. Two huge red marble urns, which looked as though they were veined with blood, glowed on either side of the mantelpiece. A chandelier dazzled overhead, casting dancing patterns of light across the thick red carpet. After more coffee and cakes and chatter, the twilight deepened. Katherine stifled a yawn, and swept the dog up in her lap again. It was time Connie showed them to their rooms, so they could have a rest before dinner. But one thing perplexed her. Looking out through the darkening window, she could see that their bags and trunks had not been brought in and were still piled out front near the porter's lodge, where no doubt the evening dew had begun to settle on them. "I think I'd like to have a rest now," Katherine announced when a pause finally occurred in the one-sided conversation Jinny had been holding with Ida, who looked piqued and tired. "It has been a rather trying day."

Jinny and Connie exchanged a glance. Connie said, "Yes, my dear. We shall have our driver take you immediately to the sanatorium."

Katherine sat up rigidly and ceased petting the dog, allowing it to scramble from her lap back to the floor.

"We were lucky enough to arrange a room for you at the Hermitage, the most luxurious and exclusive sanatorium here in Menton, with first rate medical care and excellent food," said Jinny.

"But I thought I was going to be staying here," she glanced around the gilt-trimmed room, and nearly sobbed at the thought of being torn from it and transported elsewhere in the dusk.

"There's been a change in plans," said Connie.

"Was this Father's idea?"

"I'm sorry darling," said Connie, "but we also have another patient staying here at the moment, an English lady. When she heard that you were...ill...she was reluctant to stay on. It will only be for a week or two until she goes back to England and then you can return here. We are sorry if this is an inconvenience for you, but it can't be helped, and I'm sure you understand the delicate position we are in."

Katherine nodded woodenly. Would she ever get used to being shunted off to corners? Connie's predicament was obvious. The English woman was a paying guest. She was not. But who would pay the bill for the sanatorium? Katherine's own funds, for the moment, were exhausted. Ida had given their last six pounds to the driver, who had then demanded a tip which had not been granted.

Jinny attempted an encouraging smile. "Don't be disappointed. It's only temporary, I assure you."

"But Ida cannot stay with me in a sanatorium."

"No, of course not. Ida may stay here in one of our rooms. We will come to see you every day. Never fear."

There was no opposing Jinny and Connie's carefully worked-out plan, and Katherine was too weary to protest. She meekly allowed herself to be ushered out of the room by Jinny and a maid who wrapped her in one of Connie's old furs, and quickly settled her in the back of Connie's car, with all her luggage piled in the boot. Ida waved forlornly from the brightly lit verandah as the car drove away.

While Jinny accompanied Katie to the Hermitage, Connie showed Ida to the room she was to occupy while Katie was in the sanatorium. It was a large, lovely room, all gray and silver, with a balcony facing south, and a writing desk with cut-glass inkstand set before the window. The only traces of color were a little sofa with gilt legs, upholstered in rose brocade, and a soft burgundy carpet. The spotless white coverlet on the bed was of the finest Spanish satin.

Ida felt out of sorts at the Villa Flora, unsure how she would hold out alone against Connie and Miss Fullerton. Connie would surely be a perfect hostess, putting her at ease, but she didn't trust Jinny Fullerton at all, and her suspicions were confirmed when later, before dinner, Jinny, upon returning from the Hermitage, came to her room for a little talk. She sat on the bed, smoothed an invisible wrinkle in her skirt with a withered hand and said, "I do hope Katherine won't be offended by this change of plans?"

"I am sure Katie understands. I only hope I am not imposing on you both by staying here in her stead."

Smiling, Jinny shook her head. "Nonsense. We are pleased to have you. We are sorry to disappoint Katherine, but in our opinion, a brief stay at a sanatorium can only do her good, especially after those months in that drafty chalet, which was certainly not suitable for winter habitation."

Ida looked down at the carpet, which for a moment became a watery red blur through her tears. These past weeks had been absolutely the worst time of her life, and surely also of Katie's. She had done all she could to help Katie, but had not prevented her from falling ill. Katie had coughed up quite a bit of blood during her fever, too, and had made her promise she would say nothing of this to Connie or her companion.

Miss Fullerton seemed to read her thoughts, for she said, "We believe Katherine is seriously ill."

Ida gave an involuntary sob and fumbled in her pocket for a handkerchief.

"Your devotion to Katherine is touching."

"We have been friends since our schooldays."

"Yours is indeed a rare and special intimacy."

Miss Fullerton was staring at her with a peculiar, knowing smile. Where was she leading? Did she want to know whether she and Katie were, as Robert Wilson had said, as Katie's own mother had suggested, *corrupted*? Why did everyone seem to care so much about this? And what about Miss Fullerton herself and Katie's cousin Connie, were they *corrupted* too? She blushed at the thought, and felt her ears go hot.

"Tell me," Jinny went on, "How do you get on with Mr. Murry?"

"Very well, of course. You know I was living with them in Hampstead as housekeeper and companion before we came abroad."

"You must be on intimate terms with him as well."

Ida nodded, mistrustful of Jinny's intentions. And indeed her next comment was. "We were wondering if there were perhaps some sort of strain in their marriage."

So, that was it. Miss Fullerton wanted her to betray Katie's confidence and reveal intimate details about her life with Murry. Did she take her for a simpleton?

"I am afraid I don't understand what you mean exactly. The strain of being ill perhaps? Of being forced to spend much time apart from the person you are most fond of?"

"Yes, but we have been wondering, and Harold, I mean, Mr. Beauchamp, has been wondering, why he has not come abroad with her this time?"

Ida looked away and said, "Mr. Murry is very busy with his work which is very important. He could not come with her and so they asked me to come. He hopes to join her soon."

"Don't think I want to pry into Katherine's private affairs. You know we will soon be taking Katherine in as our patient, and knowing the details and problems of a patient's personal life can be of great assistance in helping them get better. And we all want that for Katherine, don't we? I only asked you this question because we have heard strange stories about Katherine's behavior."

"Perhaps this is something you should discuss directly with your patient, then, and not with me. I assure you that Katherine and her husband adore each other, and that's all I know."

Miss Fullerton gave her a long steely look, then with a pursing of her lips and slight shrug of her shoulders, took her leave, informing Ida that a maid would summon her when dinner was ready.

. . .

A stately cypress tree dominated the view from her window. Far off stood the mountains bluish and pale, dusted with snow, pink-tipped at sunset. Along the tidy gravel paths where old men and women in dressing gowns crept, accompanied by pretty young nurses, little white narcissus had sprung up in clusters.

Katherine certainly could not complain about her new surroundings at the Hermitage. It was just as Jinny had described, almost supernaturally clean and luxurious. Aside from this view of the mountains, her room also could boast of the most comfortable bed imaginable and a big writing table set in the west window in the sunniest spot. Breakfast was served in a cheerful room heated by a huge ceramic furnace. The oh-so-efficient doctors made their rounds after breakfast. At their bidding, she stretched out on the bed, while they poked and pressed and tapped and listened, as doctors will do, pricking her *derrière* with knitting needles, shaking their heads and noting things down, then prescribing the same useless drops, injections, and cataplasms as always. She did not really expect much from any doctor's method anymore, but there was a charming Swiss nurse who answered the bell at any hour of the day or night and whose sprightly manner at least provided some entertainment.

The company was what one expected. Warmed-over corpses freshly resurrected by Doctor Frankenstein stalked the halls and gathered in the dining room, eyeing her viciously through hollow-eye sockets. Compared to them, Katherine was a picture of health. It was astonishing how such a skeletal crew, waxen-faced with arms and legs like walking sticks, had the energy to produce so much noise. Yet their voices shrieked and boomed, their footsteps pounded down the corridors, their doors slammed all night long. She stuffed cotton in her ears and swathed her head with a wool scarf to deaden the noise, but she could not sleep, and in the end the night doctor had to give her a good dose of Veronal. Then upon waking the next morning, her head seemed to float several feet above the bed, and she could not bear the cooking smells. Three weeks had crawled past like this, with heavier doses of Veronal each night.

There was no question of writing. In Ospedaletti she had managed to produce something, but here even a letter to Murry cost her enormous effort, for she must strike a bright, breezy tone in order to prove to him that she had pulled out of the eddy of depression that had dragged her down in Ospedaletti. The clinic expenses were a constant worry. Every little bowl of orange marmalade, every pot of cream was another item on the bill which Jinny and Connie had not, as yet, offered to pay a penny of. Yet they had forced her to come here. She had not mustered the courage to enquire at the front desk if any arrangements for payment had been made, perhaps by her father, and she dreaded having to ask her cousin for money. Murry certainly wouldn't be willing to foot the bill.

Reading, too, was quite impossible. For nearly half the morning, her eyes just could not focus long enough to read more than a line or two, and at the very bad moments, all the words were double. She suspected that this distressing symptom was the effect of the Veronal, and now after three weeks of increasing nightly doses, her eyes were red and shrunken and when she got out of bed in the morning, her knees felt as though they were filled with jelly. The only respite was her cousin's visits. Connie and Jinny had kept their promise. Nearly everyday they whisked her away for a long drive in the sunshine. Ida rarely came. Jinny had found her a job at another nursing home and her duties there had quickly absorbed her. Alone in the evenings, Katherine often found herself missing Ida's company, though at first her absence had seemed pure bliss.

Coming down to breakfast one morning, she found a letter waiting on her table. Examining the Italian postmark, she smiled: it was from Lawrence in Capri. She sipped her tea scented with lavender, took a bite of a hot buttered roll, opened the letter and skimmed down the page. Lawrence's words hit her like a blow in the stomach, and she almost choked. A fellow at a nearby table turned to stare as she gagged and coughed.

"You disgust me, rotting in your disease like a loathsome reptile. I hope you die."

She threw down the letter in dismay and felt her face go red. There was no accounting for such a spewing of venom. The last time she had seen Lawrence, he had been so affectionate. Just weeks ago he had written from Florence, saying how happy he was there and what nice people he had met, begging her to join them. What in heaven's name could have happened in the meantime? Another quarrel with Murry? What had she to do with that? Or had he simply just lost control forever and slipped into madness? She crumpled the page, intending to throw it into the stove burning brightly in a corner of the breakfast room, then changed her mind. No, better keep it as evidence of Lawrence's deranged wickedness. She smoothed out the letter, put it in her handbag, snapped it shut.

Why was it always like this with Lawrence? He could turn upon one with such vulgar cruelty. This was the last straw! She would have to cut off from him, as so many others had done, as she had promised herself she would do countless times before, even though she knew she would miss his exuberance, his outrageous schemes, his passionate talk. Theirs had truly been a friendship of the mind uncontaminated by any sexual undertones, by any unrequited adoration, something so rare with a man. She had always had a special fondness for him for he was the only one who had comforted her when Leslie died. Ida was away in Rhodesia then and Murry had been so cold and unfeeling, as though he were jealous of her love for her brother. Only Lawrence had managed to console her, and the letter he had written to her after Leslie's death was perhaps one of the most moving letters she had ever received, conveying a deep and healing truth. *As one self dies, another comes into being,* he had written, *"it is your creative self." For us there will be a resurrection. We will be reborn.* How could he have written now, *I hope you die?* It was beyond comprehending, but she could not, would not, must not, allow herself to be treated in such a way. There must be something sordid and corrupt in Lawrence to make him think and write such unspeakable things. And Murry *must* defend her. She would write to him at once about it.

Her appetite had vanished. She pushed aside the teacup and the basket of rolls and signaled to the waitress to clear the table. Then, looking up, she saw Connie and Jinny coming in the door.

"My dearest, we have come to bring you home at last," said Connie, swooping down in her gray cape to kiss her, tickling Katherine's face with the ostrich feathers on her hat. Katherine allowed her cheeks to be kissed by both women. Their faces were fresh with the morning chill.

"And your English lady? Isn't she afraid of contagion?"

"Nonsense," Jinny trilled, "that was never the question."

"We have spoken to the doctor here who has informed us that you are much improved and are well enough to stay with us now," Connie reassured her.

"Our guest would have actually been very pleased to meet Connie's cousin, a famous authoress, but she has traveled on to Switzerland."

"And Ida?" she asked. She really would rather not have to share a room with Ida.

"We have found a room for her with a family in the village," said Connie, "where she will be quite comfortable I am sure. She is anxious for you to leave here and come to us."

"Aside from her work at the nursing home, I have also arranged for her to brush hair for some of our acquaintances, so she will have plenty to keep her busy," said Jinny.

"How exciting," said Katherine, then bit her tongue in remorse. Those few francs Ida would be earning were certainly not to be sneezed at, given their dire financial circumstances.

"I've told them to prepare your trunk and have it sent over to the villa. Now go and get your coat."

"But the bill..."

"You may settle it later. They will send it on to you at the villa."

The words burned in Katherine's ears. She would have to beg from her father and from Murry to pay the costs of this extravagant medical holiday they had obliged her to accept.

"We're on our way to the milliner's," said Jinny briskly, with a deft change of subject. "It's time you had a new hat, as well."

Katherine raised her eyes to the mirror hanging on the opposite wall of the breakfast room and studied her reflection with keen scrutiny. The brown velvet cloche pulled low on her forehead enhanced the drama of her probing, deep-set eyes. She had always considered it an extremely stylish little hat, and she was irked to hear Jinny remark,

"That little cloche would be fine for London, but here in the south of

France, I think you need something a little softer, and more feminine, with a touch of pastel perhaps."

Katherine went on gazing at her reflection. Illness had changed or was changing her. Who was this red-eyed woman with sunken, sallow cheeks and bluish pouches under her eyes?

"Very well, dear Jinny," she sighed, "I put myself in your hands."

VILLA FLORA

The maid had not yet finished putting all of Katherine's things away, but eager for a few moments' solitude, Katherine dismissed her. Collapsing onto the sofa, she looked around her new room with satisfaction, every pore of her skin glowing with pleasant exertion. It had been the most delightfully exhausting day, and it quite made her forget the rude shock of Lawrence's appalling letter at breakfast. They had shopped all morning, stopping for coffee at a roadside café under a row of tall mimosa trees abloom with great, fragrant puffs of yellow. At the milliner's shop, they had each tried on about two dozen hats, turning the shop inside out, with hats tumbling through the air. The milliner's assistant, a plump girl in pink, rushed back and forth on stubby little legs, with wisps of veil and snippets of ribbon and little birds that almost looked real, holding them up to their heads and saying, "With this *petit oiseau* Madame will turn every head in the street." And Jinny, who, when hatted, looked exactly like a dignified Houyhnhnm that had stolen someone's bonnet, kept saying in her awful French, "But I do not want to cause a sensation. I want a hat that sits *just so* upon my head," but none of the hats would sit *just so*, and kept sliding askew, no matter how many pins they stuck into her poor Houyhnhnm head. Katherine could not remember when she had last laughed so much for such silliness, and Jinny and Connie had laughed too. Connie bought a neat little cap with brown feathers for herself and two hats for Katherine, one trimmed with tiny rosebuds, the other with lavender ostrich plumes. The latter might have been a mistake, but Jinny had insisted on the plumes. Perhaps it was rather too showy, still this was the Midi, such things were the norm. At the apothecary's, Connie had bought them all creams, sachets, and perfumes, and Katherine had bought Ida a little cake of rose-scented soap. Then at the haberdashery, Connie had bought her gloves, stockings, and handkerchiefs.

A new hat, of course, required a new dress, and at the end of their shopping spree, Jinny had insisted upon buying her one.

"Just a little present to welcome the spring," Jinny had said, plucking a dress from a rack and holding it up against Katherine's slim frame: a confection of pale yellow chiffon trimmed in lavender.

Katherine had shivered at the touch of chiffon upon her bare white arms as the shopgirl helped her into the dress and did up her buttons in the dressing room.

"*Comme vous êtes maigre, Madame,*" said the girl, shyly fastening the dress at her waist.

Katherine studied her reflection. A month ago, in the bath at Ospedaletti, she had looked down on her naked body in the water and thought: *This is how I shall look when they lay me out in my coffin.* Ribs protruding, all knees, elbows, pale flesh veined in blue, shin bones as sharp as blades. She was plumper now; color had returned to her complexion. In this dress she felt like Persephone rescued from the dead. The girl stood behind her, smiling with painted lips and nodding at the mirror. The dress must be frightfully expensive. How could she accept such a gift?

As she stepped out of the curtained cubicle, Connie and Jinny uttered a cry of delight. Katherine sashayed three steps down the worn red strip of carpet in the middle of the shop, made a pirouette before them, twirling and swishing the chiffon skirts before the mirror's triptych.

"Your husband will fall in love with you all over again," said Jinny.

"I'm sure you haven't had many opportunities to wear such a charming dress over the last year. A woman your age needs little luxuries like this now and then," said Connie.

Katherine observed Connie's portly form. How many years had passed since she had worn such a pretty dress? Had she ever charmed young men or been crushed in a man's arms?

Jinny's blue eyes blazed into hers. "Accept this gift, with good graces."

Katherine lowered her eyes while Jinny ordered the girl to wrap the dress up. She was selling herself again, this time for the price of a pretty dress and the dream of reconquering Murry.

Now the dress lay spread upon the white satin coverlet. She would wear it to greet Murry when he came to visit... whenever that would be.

She wanted to write to him briefly now. She sat down at the desk which had been equipped by her hostesses with fine writing paper, leather blotter, costly fountain pen, and a pot of little white narcissus whose sweet, inebriating perfume filled the air. She penned a few lines. Searching for an envelope, she opened a drawer and was surprised to find a little black book bound in fine-grained cowhide. Curious, she removed the volume. Its weight felt satisfying in her hands. The frontispiece was inscribed "*to Katherine on her journey home, love, Jinny.*" A red ribbon marked a page. She opened and read.

"*God is our most passionate beloved. The kisses of his mouth are wine for the soul.*" Katherine groaned, shut the book, and threw it down on the desk.

There was a knock on the door and she rose to answer, as she was expecting Ida for teatime.

Stepping into the room, Ida glanced at the dress laid out like a sleeping body on the immaculate bedspread, at the hats set on stands before the gilt mirror, at the row of perfumes and creams in dark blue cut-glass vials and jars lined upon the dresser.

She lifted an eyebrow. "Katie, how much money have you spent?"

Katherine blushed and busied herself with putting away other packages.

"Hardly a penny. All presents from Jinny and Connie. And this is for you," she handed Ida the little cake of soap.

Ida sniffed it circumspectly and slipped it into her pocket.

"I hope you did not spend too much for this, Katie. I think your cousin and her companion are spoiling you."

"Don't you think I deserve a little pampering, after all I've been through?"

"Oh darling, of course I do, but remember everything has its price."

Noticing the book, Ida picked it up, but Katherine plucked it from her hand and shoved it in a drawer.

The maid knocked to tell them tea was served.

Down in the salon, twilight filtered in through the tall windows onto the red plush rugs. A fire was burning in the gilt-trimmed fireplace behind a brass screen. The warmth, the glow of firelight, the silence and sense of orderliness in the room satisfied a hunger in Katherine she had forgotten till now for the serenity of upper class domesticity. Truly, in such a house, she was at last in her element.

Jinny and Connie were seated at the table, chatting softly to a beefy-looking gentleman who rose to greet them as she and Ida approached the table. As he turned to them, Katherine noted the discreet white collar beneath the black tunic and repressed a grimace. Heavens, a priest!

Jinny introduced the visitor as Father Benjamin, adding that he was the author of a theological study she had left for Katherine in the drawer of her writing table, should she be interested in reading it. Then they all sat down to tea.

Katherine thanked Jinny for the book, saying that she had noticed it, but had not yet had time to examine it. "I am sure it is very interesting," she said with a conciliatory smile and promised to read it soon.

"We are ardent admirers of Father Benjamin's books," said Jinny, handing the tea.

"These ladies flatter me too much with their interest in my humble efforts. I would only be too honored, Miss Mansfield —"

"Mansfield is my nom de plume. Please call me by my real name, Mrs. Murry."

"Indeed, Mrs. Murry," he said with a gallant nod, "I would only be too honored if you should find the time to read my little volume. And of course I would be very pleased to discuss it with you once you have read it, if there is anything you would like me to explain to you in detail."

"Thank you. I shall certainly seek your explanation if the need arises." She modulated her tone with chilly cordiality.

"Perhaps after we have had our tea, you might like to hear Father read from his new work," said Jinny.

The priest beamed with pleasure at this suggestion, and removed an eyeglass case and a thick bundle of papers from his vest pocket and placed them on the table near his cup and saucer. Katherine noted the dense script covering the pages and exchanged a furtive glance with Ida. It was going to be a long evening.

After tea, Father Benjamin droned on, reading from his new work concerning the Virgin Mary as a model for modern women. Katherine suspected that the subject of this afternoon's reading had been chosen with her specifically in mind. Connie was listening with eyes closed; Jinny gazed intensely at the priest, hanging upon every word. Ida kept nodding off to sleep, jerking awake from time to time with a slight shudder and a startled widening of her eyes. To Katherine it looked as though Jinny were keeping the poor dear awake with an occasional poke.

When the clock struck half past six, Connie and Jinny leapt up and whirled Ida from the room, claiming that she would miss the next omnibus, and Katherine found herself face to face with the priest, who smiled with benign embarrassment.

"My child," he began with a clearing of his throat. "Your cousin tells me that you have been, that you *are* rather ill."

"The good Lord has seen fit to give me consumption," she said, then instantly regretted her aggressive tone.

The priest's smile faded. "Illness is a test for the soul..."

Indeed, what isn't a test for the soul? Loneliness, childlessness, poverty, unfaithful husbands? She had much to choose from.

"But your cousins are determined to heal you."

His words brought a chill to Katherine's chest.

"They have done much good work in the world. Miss Fullerton is an excellent nurse," the priest went on.

"May God wish it so," said Katherine in a husky half-whisper.

The priest peered at her closely, waiting for her to continue and at last she said, "Father, please do not be offended by what I have to say. I know my cousin and Miss Fullerton mean well, but I really am not ready to become a Roman Catholic."

They sat in a long silence as the windows darkened in the twilight, and the fire sputtered softly in the grate. The priest cleared his throat again, but did not speak, and gazed down at his well-manicured hands. Katherine felt the shadows deepening in the room, creeping across the walls and rugs; soon they too would be engulfed entirely. She fixed her eyes on a Venetian glass bird on the mantelpiece. Was it or was it not a phoenix? she wondered. The clock ticked discreetly, then on the melodious stroke of seven, the French doors opened and in stepped Jinny and Connie.

"Oh, I hope we are not intruding," said Jinny, eyes glinting as she came forward.

"No, not at all," said the priest, rising, "we were just having a bit of chat. I am sorry, Mrs. Murry we'll have to continue this very pleasant conversation another time." On the excuse of an appointment with a parishioner, he took leave. Connie accompanied him to the door. Jinny drew the curtains, then sat down on a sofa near the fire, folded her arms, and shot Katherine a puzzled look from across the room.

. . .

Katherine sat by the fire in the great hall, having breakfast alone. Connie had gone out on an errand. Down the stairs came Jinny in a lilac poncho, dressed for an early morning walk. Greeting Katherine with a hearty good morning, she urged her to join her for a stroll around the garden. When Katherine objected that she must first fetch her coat and her walking stick, Jinny replied, "A walking stick, at your age, my dear? I won't hear of it. But if you need an arm to lean on, do take mine."

The maid brought Katherine's coat, along with a pair of galoshes, for the grass was still quite wet at that hour, and helped her put them on. Jinny firmly took her arm and pulled her out to the garden where she escorted Katherine along a trail skirted by a boxwood hedge. There was a sharp but not unpleasant spring breeze.

Rounding the hedge on Jinny's arm, Katherine gave a gasp as a great lawn came into view, peppered here and there with hundreds of tiny bright blue hyacinths, swaying slightly in the breeze, shimmering with dew, exuding a heady fragrance.

Jinny's face shone as she stood looking out at the lawn. "I placed those bulbs there myself last autumn, hoping you'd be here to see them. One hundred and twenty bulbs in all! How my knees ached when I had finally finished."

Katherine's eyes brimmed with joy as she admired the flowers.

"Can't you just feel it—in this glorious sunshine—in these heavenly flowers sparkling with dew—that there is a Maker who has made all this—who cares for and thinks of every one of his creatures?"

Katherine turned her grave eyes upon Jinny's drawn face and studied the gaunt cheeks, the hard lines around Jinny's eyes and mouth now wrinkling into evidence as she smiled. Here was a woman who perhaps had suffered in ways Katherine could never imagine, and had found much needed comfort in God. Whatever sorrows and disappointments Jinny had experienced, they belonged to her past. Now she stood stalwartly, smiling at the sunshine, trying, in her own way, to help her. Must she criticize Jinny for that?

"Yes," said Katherine, "I do feel it. I really do. Differently than you do perhaps, but believe me, I do feel it," and she squeezed Jinny's arm affectionately, and began to recite in a low voice, "*Consider the lilies of the field, they spin not neither do they reap...*"

Jinny smiled, "Just so—there is a God to care for the needs of everyone. Just as there is a God to care for your own needs."

Katherine stifled a sob and Jinny embraced her, enfolding her in the wings of her poncho.

"Weep, my child. Weep. You will soon find comfort in the bosom of the great consoler. If only you would accept His love. If only you would come to Him like the little lamb you really are."

Leaning against Jinny, she suddenly missed Mother. How many times over these long years, had her body ached to stand like this, softly leaning against Mother and breathe in her perfume of Parma violets and rose water? And now Mother was gone. At this thought, tears streamed down her face.

"You are only too kind to be so concerned for me."

" I feel you are my own kith and kin," whispered Jinny.

Too moved to speak, Katherine wept for a few moments, then recomposing herself, reached into her pocket for her handkerchief, wiped her tears and said, "You and Connie are like my favorite aunts."

They walked back along the garden pathway to the villa. Jinny picked a daffodil from a flowerbed and gave it to Katherine who sipped the dew in its cup. When they stopped to look down at the glittering bay, Jinny turned to her and made a startling announcement. She and Connie were going to give up the Villa Flora.

"But we have our eye on another piece of property at Garavan, there just across the bay, a lovely villa, Villa Louise, with a guest house called Isola Bella. We hope you and your husband will accept our invitation for next year. We would like you to stay several months with us there."

This was an unexpected joy! A house of her own where she could be with family and with Murry. Surely she could convince him to join her for an extended visit. Walking back to the Villa Flora, she could already imagine the scene: the two of them alone in a small villa above the sea.

Stepping back into the hall with its vast, cold mirrors, Jinny touched her shoulder and asked, "You were married by a clergyman, I assume?"

Katherine was irked. Her mouth twitched as she replied, "No, we were married at the South Kensington Registry Office. Does it matter?"

Jinny gave a tired smile and patted her arm. " I suppose not, dear; I suppose not."

A bounty of mail awaited her. There was a fat letter from Murry and a package from Murry's brother, Richard. Opening the package, she found five copies of *Je Ne Parle Pas Français*, her short story which Richard had printed on the printing press Murry had just installed in the cellar of the Elephant. Like Virginia, she and Murry would now have their own press, named, at her insistence, the Heron Press, in honor of her brother Leslie, and Richard was learning to set type and engrave plates. The books were just as attractive as the ones that Leonard and Virginia printed on the Hogarth Press. She was pleased with the handsome binding and the illustrated title-page Richard had designed for her book. She decided to give a copy to Jinny and Connie immediately.

Murry's four-page letter brought wonderful news. He had negotiated with the publisher Constable to bring out a book of her short stories, and had obtained an advance of forty pounds. She was a paid authoress! This was real news; she was rarely paid for her work. Even the *New Age*, one of the most important magazines she had published in, had never paid a penny. Rather the joke among Orage's contributors ran: *New Age, No Wage* and that contributors paid Orage to be published. But forty pounds! That was a sum worth having. She still had the sanatorium bill to pay. She would have Murry send her the money at once. Her delight dissolved as she read the closing paragraph of his letter scribbled in a cramped space at the bottom of the page. At Garsington, he had met a woman, Betsy B., a gifted, intriguing young writer. She had invited him to a dinner party at her home to be given the next week. That was all Murry said but Katherine sensed a threat. She recognized the name: Betsy B. was an aristocratic friend of Ottoline's. Katherine did not know her well, but she had seen her once at Garsington: a fleshy young woman with a quick mind and a gull-like face, nearly swallowed alive in the coils of an enormous feather boa, with a fortune in diamonds winking on her florid bosom. Her older husband looked on while she entertained a crowd of flushed, tipsy gentlemen of state.

Connie stepped into the room with a bouquet of tulips freshly picked from the garden and Katherine put her letter away.

As Connie began trimming the tulip stems with a pair of scissors, she studied Katherine's face and said, "Bad news, dear? "

"Not exactly. I have just received a letter from Jack. The first part has brought wonderful news: my book is to be published by an excellent publisher and I have received an advance of forty pounds."

"Your father will be so proud of you." The snipping of the scissors was crisp, definitive.

"But then, in closing, Jack mentioned that a friend of ours has fallen ill."

"Oh dear," said Connie with sympathy, putting down the scissors, " Not seriously, I hope?"

Katherine felt herself blushing. She hated to be found out lying, even for something so insignificant. "I'm afraid I don't know how serious it is." This, at least, was *partly* the truth.

"Pray, my dear, pray for your friend."

Connie returned to her flowers, and Katherine watched her arrange them in a crystal vase set on a little lace mat probably crocheted by Jinny while sitting at the bedside of a convalescent. She envied the contentment Connie and Jinny seemed to enjoy with the simple things of everyday life: rearranging a bouquet, planting bulbs, knitting a scarf for a war orphan, making sure that the silver was polished and the floors waxed, that the hinges of doors did not creak. And behind this domestic harmony, loomed Father Benjamin and the Church.

"Connie, how did you decide to become a Catholic?"

Connie gazed at Katherine with earnest simplicity and her hand flitted to her breast. "I felt God in my heart and I instantly knew that the Roman Catholic Church was His true messenger on earth."

Katherine sighed. Why was it they all spoke like Father Benjamin's prose? It was not a language she could understand or speak. She longed for her own tribe, for people whose ideas matched her own and who spoke a language not alien to hers. She was quite willing to believe in a divine life force, in a timeless realm beyond appearances, but this language of sins and salvation, so black and white, baffled and repelled her.

L unch was spoiled by an extremely annoying episode. Just before the *entrecôtes* were brought in, Jinny sanctimoniously announced quite out of the blue that pure friendship between men and women cannot exist. And off they all galloped, on another one of the absurd arguments that occurred at nearly every meal. Connie and Jinny's ideas on life were obsolete and their tastes in art and literature, so philistine. Katherine could not force herself to remain silent when provoked, she had to have her say. What's worse was that on the few occasions Ida was present, she tended to agree with Jinny rather than defend Katherine, and today Ida herself had ended the debate with a ludicrous pronouncement, "Men will be men and I mean *all over,*" which, although it had greatly amused Connie and Jinny, had infuriated Katherine. She was sure that Ida's remark was a secret dig at Murry's infidelity and took it as a warning that she must beware of Murry's many admirers, to whom had recently been added the name of Betsy B. Another reason to return to England as soon as possible.

Coming down for tea later, Katherine found Jinny fuming, pacing before the fire. This was a truly unusual attitude. Katherine had never seen her angry or impatient. Her cousin's companion was all forbearance and charity. She was doubly astounded when Jinny informed her that she herself was to blame.

"What have I done?"

"This," said Jinny slapping a book down on the table so hard that the spoons rattled in their saucers. It was a copy of the volume containing her short story, *Je Ne Parle Pas Français*" which she had given to Jinny that morning - too daring a story, it seemed, for Jinny's taste.

"How can you say such a thing about the Blessed Virgin? I am sure it offended Her deeply. I am so glad Father Benjamin hasn't seen it."

Katherine was stunned. There was a reference to the pregnant Virgin Mary in her story, but she could not understand why it might be offensive. Still, she was appalled at her own blunder, at her inability to foresee Jinny's reaction. She ought to have realized that this story, in which she recast herself as the innocent victim of an ineffectual Murry and a predatory Carco, was too *risquée* for a couple of stuffy old spinsters like Connie and Jinny. Perhaps she had hoped unconsciously to shock them. But that it might have offended them not on moral but on religious grounds quite frankly amazed her.

Shamed and angry, her cheeks stinging, she apologized, saying she meant no harm, and that the immoral ideas expressed by the narrator had nothing to do with her own. Rather this story was her cry of protest against the evil of the world. Jinny stiffly accepted her apology. Then Connie had come in and tea had progressed as usual, but the atmosphere at the tea table was very quiet and strained, and Katherine was relieved when tea was over and she could retire to her room.

The next afternoon, sitting down to write a letter to Murry, she opened her desk drawer and found that Jinny's copy of *Je Ne Parle Pas Français* had been surreptitiously returned to her. She was deeply insulted. This was the last straw. It was time to leave their suffocating care. She must return to England and to her own people, to Murry and Kot and Virginia.

. . .

She lay on a rug in the soft grass on a hillside high up overlooking the bay of Garavan. She had driven over with Jinny to this side of the bay for what might be their last picnic, before returning with Ida to England. The tickets were bought, the berths reserved, the visas properly stamped in smeared blue ink. Their passports and tickets were safely locked in the drawer of her writing desk. On a blue canvas tarp spread out at a discreet distance from Katherine's rug, Jinny sat with her knees drawn up and her straw hat pulled low, staring down at the sea, a book abandoned beside her. Probably another one

140

of Father Benjamin's theological works, Katherine surmised, but she had not enquired. Jinny had presumably forgiven her for the blasphemy of *Je Ne Parle Pas Français*, for Connie had renewed her invitation to Katherine and Murry for the coming year. Not one word more had been said about Katherine's writing, and even the subject of religion had been scrupulously avoided in the last two weeks, though sometimes she felt Jinny staring at her after dinner, before the plates were cleared away, surely thinking, "Don't you think you'd like to have a little talk with Father Benjamin before you leave?" It was curious though, for now that the subject of faith had become taboo in her conversations with Connie and Jinnie, Katherine had begun musing on religious questions of her own, although she dare not confess this to anyone.

The April sun warmed her chest and scalded her cheeks with a rosy flush. A deliciously cool, not chill, sea breeze, perceptible even at these heights, freshened the air, tingling along her arms, tickling her neck. All around lay the remains of their picnic: a basket with cold chicken and asparagus pastries, an empty bottle of champagne, nibbled slabs of rich, crusty cheeses and a half-eaten loaf of fragrant bread. It had been a true celebration indeed. Propped up on one elbow, eye level with the tall grass, she observed the daisies, no bigger than pennies, scattered down across the slope, brightened here and there with a burst of purple or red anemones. A church faraway chimed the hours. It was four o'clock.

It was lovely to lie like this in the tender grass, to feel one's body melting into the earth and air and sky, while one's mind hovers motionless above. To take the air into her lungs freely without impediment was pure bliss. Gratitude rushed upon her towards Jinny and Connie for all they had done for her. She had put on weight again, was walking without a stick, and sometimes a day might pass without her ever coughing once. The doctor she had seen yesterday had seemed satisfied with her improvement. Her left lung was drying again. She might face the journey back to England, back to Murry, without undue concern. All this she owed to Connie and Jinny's care. It was true they were not really her sort, but they were *family*, even though they belonged to a different type of human being. It was not their fault if they did not understand her needs as an artist. She could not expect them to do so. She must continue seeking her own people, while striving to create a complete life for herself in a place of her own.

But what was a complete life? She had begun to ponder this more deeply. It was something more than having a home and a family and friends, more than having Murry beside her, more than writing and books and money, or the elusive dream of success. More perhaps than even having a child. Lawrence was wrong when he claimed that completeness could only be attained through one's lover and one's work. His own restless seeking, his hankering for Utopian islands showed that he really did not believe that work and relationships were all an artist may aspire to. He too was after something more, something indefinable.

Down below the fishing boats teased their moorings, heaving upon a gentle sea swell. Overhead islands unraveled into fibrous skeins against a shining sky. Sea birds darted down, silvery streaks in the sunlight. Closing her eyes, Katherine felt an electric surge of joy rushing through her body, fused with the radiance of sunshine, with the green glow of the grass, with the flashing anemones. Her joy brought with it a certainty of something that had been nudging at her thoughts for days but which had been long forgotten since the days of childhood. Quite simply: The source of all this bliss is God. He exists, *tout court*, and without Him nothing can make sense. *There*, she had formulated the thought: a long submerged belief had found at last admittance to the realm of words. The world might mock her, disbelieve her, shun her for such a statement. But it echoed solemnly within, encountering for once no resistance.

Hers was *not* the faith of Jinny and Connie, that was clear, nor could it ever be. Sorapure would understand her more intimately, perhaps. For Jinny and Connie, this divine force whose vital spark enlivens every creature, every rock or flame or drop of water, for them this force had become incarnate in Man in the gaunt figure of Christ racked in pain upon the cross. This was the mystery they demanded she must accept on faith: God was incarnated in human flesh. That was the obstacle. That was the catch. The other miracles: the immaculate conception, raising the dead, ascending into heaven, even resurrection were metaphors one could grasp and accept more readily. With Lawrence they had often talked about resurrection. He believed that death was not the end of human existence, and beneath it all Katherine secretly agreed with him, although Murry said that was rot. But the enigma of incarnation eluded her. Katherine felt a visceral sympathy and a chastening respect for the wounded body of Christ, for the ribs protruding through dead skin, the head lifeless, the mouth dripping blood, the terrible cry before giving up the ghost, for in a very tiny way, on an infinitely smaller scale, she had experienced a shadow of mortal suffering. Some people seem to sweep through life untouched or untried by debilitating physical pain and loss, while to others it is their daily bread and one never knows when or if, one shall find oneself among the ranks of the sufferers, in the camp where she had found herself stranded at such a young age. Sometimes she yearned for salvation, but salvation from what? From death, illness, pain, loneliness? From herself, perhaps? And here Jinny might reach out to her and say: Christ died for your sins.

Her sins! Could anyone really care about her sins? Oh, she had sinned, all right, she had shocked and outraged propriety, starting with Mother on down, but surely in the Book of Ages, her transgressions didn't amount to much. No God worth his salt could really concern himself with her sins. Yet she had wasted and destroyed, and she had paid a high price. Did that mean the score had been settled? Perhaps not. Now, Jinny had urged, she could lay her burden down at the feet of the Lord. If it were so easy, as easy as Jinny and Connie had intimated, what held her back? Why was she so different from the millions of human beings who had embraced the yoke of the Holy Roman Church? Surely she was not foolish enough to think herself superior? Perhaps this was the step she must take next. To accept simply as a child accepts the family name and language it is born to. Once you have made the first step: you have ascertained that you do believe in God, no, not the white-bearded fellow in a long white robe depicted in the primers of Sunday Schools, but a sacred force, a divine being... perhaps then the rest follows easily. She would demand of herself this intellectual effort of acceptance.

She made no attempt to restrain the unfamiliar tears of gratitude that bathed her face. She would not tell Jinny, or Connie, or Murry that she intended to follow Connie's example and convert to Catholicism. Once she was back in London, she was determined to go to Sorapure and ask him what she should do.

PART FOUR

Summer 1920

LONDON, 2 PORTLAND VILLAS

The stairs seemed so much steeper now, Katherine thought, gripping the banister to steady herself on her way down to her studio, but this was only one of the many subtle changes she had noticed in the Elephant since her return from France in May. Stepping into the house again after those months of absence, she had been struck by how small the rooms seemed, how shabby the furniture, by the fine cracks threading the plaster moulding round the doors, already in need of a new coat of paint. As the weeks had passed, the comfort of habit had not crept back to offset her sense of being out of place. Perhaps it was because strangers had lived there while she was away. Murry had rented out two rooms to help cover their household expenses. Upon her arrival, he had chased his lodgers out, but somehow their presence lingered in the atmosphere like an unpleasant odor. The first few days she had taken stock of the things missing, broken, rearranged, the curious additions. That ugly brown teapot that dribbled from beneath the lid whenever one poured, where had Murry come by that? And the faded red silk tie wadded up in the drawer of her bedside table? To whom did that belong? Her beloved Japanese doll, Ribni, had suffered a mysterious injury to one leg and had been relegated to a china cupboard where he clung mournfully to the handle of a chipped cream jug. Several books had vanished from the shelves, including a cherished volume of Shelley that had belonged to her mother. But these were all losses she could easily shrug off. Much graver ones were surely in store.

For Murry, too, seem changed. He had developed an unattractive stoop, despite the many sets of tennis he played with Brett. For hours every day he was out on the courts with her, panting and running and smashing the balls towards Brett's soft, sun-browned body, while she pranced across the lawn, showing off her legs beneath her whirling white skirt. He came home sweating and humming, bellowed a greeting from the stairs, and disappeared into the bathroom for a long, invigorating shower bath. Over dinner in the evenings when at last they met to talk, his eyes somehow seemed less transparent, as though a deposit of the finest sand had settled upon his cornea, filtering out a portion of the spectrum. Now that she was ill, she knew she must resign herself to the loss of his physical presence, the loss of his physical love; but his devotion, his mental companionship, his soul, whatever *that* might be, those she must continue to bind fast to herself even at a distance. Let him have a love affair with Brett, or whomever he might choose, as long as he remained tied to her alone in his most secret self. That was the real meaning of their marriage and the only thing that mattered.

Down in the kitchen she heard Ida clattering away with the pots and pans, and there came a ripish smell of onions and kidney. She stepped softly into the studio, snatched from her desk the little pasteboard sign inscribed *Engaged*, hung it on a nail outside the door, and shut the door firmly. This battle she had won at least. No one, especially Ida and not even Murry, was to disturb her when that sign was on the door. This was her time for herself.

She went to the window and looked out at the garden. This cool, wet August had plumped the blackberries on the bushes along the garden wall. She could almost taste their tartness with her eyes, but the leaves of the willows were edged in brown, signaling the end of summer. It would be time to wind herself up again for departure in a few days. Ida had already begun to pack their trunks. Ghosts of nightgowns and chemises, silk stockings and padded jackets were draped about Katherine's room, all needing some last minute attention: a button fastened or a hem restitched, before being folded in tissue paper, and placed in her trunk. All this packing, unpacking, assembling, disassembling - was there never any end to it? She thought of those garments strewn about like the dead skins of a snake. With each journey she shed selves, dreams, illusions.

This time, on Dr. Sorapure's advice, she was to stay away for two years so her lungs could thoroughly dry out. That odd expression doctors sometimes used made her think of her lungs as rotting sponges on a shore, bleached by salt and sunlight, crusty with sand. If they did not heal completely this time, he warned, she might be forced to consider a period of time in a Swiss sanatorium. At that thought, all the devils within her rose up in rebellion. She could not bear the idea of a sanatorium. Her brief stay at the Hermitage had been enough. In a sanatorium she would not be allowed to work and if she could not work, she would die. And Murry agreed.

There was no talk of Murry's coming with them to the continent, at least not at first; he could not leave his editorial work at the *Athenaeum*. He would join her later at Isola Bella, "Beautiful Isle," the small villa standing on the edge of the new property Cousin Connie and Jinny had bought across the bay at Garavan. How was it that the little villa she had glimpsed only as a blur across the water seemed almost more real than this house in Hampstead? She could picture it: pink stucco walls and dark green shutters; the jagged shadows of palm fronds on a hot brick terrace; gauzy curtains billowing in the sea breeze at night; a table set with blue and yellow crockery where, at either ends, sat Murry and herself. A house for lovers.

In Menton, on that bright afternoon last April as she stood blinking at the glare, trying to distinguish the villa that Jinny was pointing out to her across the shining slate of water, she had seen nothing but a spot of pink topped by a slanting line of darker red, surrounded by a mass of green. This, Jinny had explained, was the little guest house where Katherine and Murry were welcome to stay in the coming year. That vision shared with Jinny, with their eyes full of the glimmering sea, with the cries of gulls circling overhead, had been their truce after Jinny's repeated but rebuffed onslaughts of proselytizing. Throughout her stay in Menton with Connie and Jinny, they had battered her with their missals and prayers and rosaries, they had made a powerful appeal to the abyss of loneliness within her. Their influence had nearly seeped through to her most unconscious recesses, and in a moment of weakness, she had *almost* yielded to the temptation to convert to Catholicism. Once back in London, her religious enthusiasm seemed ridiculous, an adolescent's clamoring for meaning; exaggerated, maudlin. Conversion was not for her. Still, there was *something*; she had always believed in *something*, not the gods, those cracked and crumbling statues; in love perhaps, in some higher value, some sacred force. Looking out at the garden and at the heath beyond, she had a mysterious sense of lives dwelling within lives, myriad lives dwelling within the one great life which is *god*. Such ideas were surely heresy to Jinny and her priest.

Murry scoffed at Katherine's vague musings; Ida, such a simple soul, might understand. Yet she could not believe in a personal god who answered personal prayers. How many consumptives must have pleaded "God save me from my illness" promising heaven knows what in return, which they could never deliver, but she was not such a fool to bargain with God and his great opposeless will. Perhaps Lawrence was right after all: the closest thing to prayer she knew of was bound up in her work. How to eradicate the slave from one's soul? That was the question, and for the moment the only answer was by stripping away what was false in her writing. She could envisage no other possible salvation.

From another house nearer the heath came the sound of a piano, a tireless succession of scales, striving in a major key, then seeking in a minor one, softly muffled as though from under the sea. The monotony did not disturb her. It brought back memories of the Trowells' house in Wellington, where she used to sit in the shadows, her arms around her cello, half-dreaming it was a lover's body, waiting for her music lesson, listening to the student before her stumbling through a difficult passage. Then later, in London at Beauchamp Lodge where so many young musicians lived, there was always the sound of scales in the background, frothing in the treble on a keyboard or rumbling in the bass, or the low smooth thunder of a cello: a long deep note quivering in a room at dusk. Even the mere memory of that sound brought a shiver to her spine. To make that perfect note resonate took years of practice—and was writing any different? She too had her scales and exercises, her thirds and fifths. Sometimes she read a single sentence over twenty times aloud, weighing each word, smoothing over syntax, until the sentence hung before her, as perfect as she could make it, like a pure note sounded in an empty room.

She wheeled round to examine the study, to see if all were in order so she might get down to work, though today there would only be time for catching up on her correspondence. Virginia Woolf was due to arrive for a promised visit at half past eleven. Katherine received her writer friends in her studio, and she scrutinized it now to see if Ida had done a proper job of tidying the room. When receiving Kot or Walter de la Mare or Lawrence she might be slightly less exacting, but when Virginia visited, it was imperative that the Elephant make a favorable impression. No speck of dust or smudge of tarnish must sully the surfaces. Katherine's home could hardly compete, of course, with Hogarth House and its antique furnishings and rich Bokhara carpets. To the Woolfs' friends—the Bloomsberries, as Lawrence called them, Katherine and Murry were upstarts, hacks who must make their living by the pen while Virginia and her friends could devote themselves to literary pursuits as an expensive and eccentric hobby. Virginia would never know what it was like to sleep on a mattress on the floor, to use a packing crate for a writing desk or to wash her husband's socks in a communal sink etched with slimy green cracks, as she had done when Murry's magazine *Rhythm* went bust, and they had been forced to give up their flat and occupy the cheaper quarters of the former editorial offices until the lease expired. Katherine was proud of herself for pulling through those bleak moments. That she kept on working under such dire circumstances proved she was a real writer and no dilettante. But Virginia must not know of the poverty she had faced. She must see her always flourishing, charmingly housed and fashionably dressed, for the latter was perhaps her only edge on Virginia, a notorious frump when it came to clothes.

With approval Katherine noted the flowers Ida had arranged on her writing table: a bountiful bouquet of fragrant roses, lavender spears, starched zinnias, and effusive bachelor's buttons delivered yesterday in a cardboard box, fresh from Ottoline's garden. The three tall sprays of lilies in the Japanese vase on the mantelpiece were also a gift from Ottoline, but had been sent a few days ago. Since Katherine's return from France, Ottoline had sent flowers, invitations, loving notes, to ease her guilty conscience, perhaps, for entertaining Murry while she was abroad as though he were a bachelor, introducing him to the many literary ladies in town, including Betsy B. But these lilies! Katherine had developed a strange distaste for the formal, sensual pallor of these flowers, so

147

cool and waxen to the touch. The gaudy red stamen stained one's sleeves if one brushed too close. A spray of these could last weeks in a vase, blooms bursting open one upon the other along the thickly budded stem. Then almost unseen, a brownish patina crept across the creamy petals. They shriveled, dropped from the stalk while another bud burst open to the light. This morning a few withered petals lay strewn on the carpet in a pool of powdery red pollen. She sniffed the air and frowned. The lilies gave off a rank, sweetish smell like the odor of old flowers in a cemetery. She peeked into the vase where a green scum floated. Ida must have forgotten to change the water and the stems had begun to rot. She set the vase outside the studio door and called an order down to Ida to come and carry it away.

Sitting down to her desk, she penned a note to Lady Ottoline, thanking her for yesterday's flowers, but declining the invitation that had been brought along with the bouquet. Murry would have been disappointed to learn they would be missing out on another week end at Garsington Manor, so she had not even informed him and had slipped the envelope with the invitation in between the books on a bottom shelf where he would never find it. She would rather not meet Betsy B. at Ottoline's, and in any case, the literary soirées, the evenings at the theater, the dinner parties, the luncheons at the Café Royale Murry adored, had become a drain on her strength. Swathed in wraps of silk and wool, she would lounge on a sofa in the quietest corner of the room, receiving small groups of admirers waiting to speak to her. They too sucked her strength away, but Murry could not see that. He was delighted to see Katherine up and about London, attired elegantly as always, entertaining crowds with her funny stories, performing her role as the brilliant critic's wife. But she could not go on for long playing that part; she had made her choice in life, there in Ospedaletti that cold and crushing winter. Every free minute must be channeled into writing.

Still she smiled thinking of the parties she and Murry had so enjoyed before her illness, the charades and sketches they reveled in, the outrageous drinking and flirting and dancing. Once at Christmas years ago, Gertler had kissed her in a play they had written and performed together, and Lawrence had become furious with Murry for letting another man make love to her, even in the make-believe of a theatrical skit. After her performance, Lytton Strachey and Bertie Russell had flattered her with compliments. She laughed thinking of her vanity. It had meant so much to her then to be part of Ottoline's sophisticated circle but now she could hardly face them all put together in the same room. They sneered and simpered, making catty remarks about their friends. They aspired to lofty feelings and refinement, but harbored a coarse cruelty in their innermost natures. Were they not the true enemies of art? And as for Lawrence, where was he now? The memory of his last message *I hope you die* still scorched her like the touch of a flatiron to her skin. The force of his personality was such that he had made her feel she truly *was* that loathsome reptile and that was something she could not forgive him. Of all that crowd, Virginia was perhaps the *only* person of integrity, the only one with whom she still felt there was something to say.

She glanced at the cuckoo clock, impatient for Virginia to arrive. Last year, when she had returned with Ida from Paris, Virginia had come nearly every week, taking the train from Richmond, treading the shady Hampstead streets to knock at the door of the Elephant, proffering not only gifts: tea, cigarettes, chocolates and candied ginger but treasured hours of communion. Virginia's mind had such a glimmering quality, like sunlight shifting on the water. Katherine could discuss work with her as she could with no other writer, man or woman, and she came away reeling from those conversations, infused with a sense of purpose, ready to set to work again. Could Virginia, so phlegmatic and composed, ever understand how much those talks meant to her, and how she had missed them while in Italy and France last winter? And even how much she had missed them since her return to England last May, for Virginia had come only twice all summer, and today would be the last time she would see her before leaving for France with Ida once again.

Conversations with Virginia were agonizingly slow to ignite. One had to break through the cocoon of isolation Virginia spun around herself, with her perfect demeanor, her flawless chitchat, even those ludicrous hats and dresses she wore were a deterrent to keeping others from coming too close. Got up in a homely floral print, loosely clutching a bag on her knees, on her head a flowerpot or wastepaper basket adorned with feathers, she would sit across from Katherine, waiting, Katherine felt, for her to step across the barrier, staring at her with the watery blue-gray eyes of a seer, looking every inch the Sibyl of Cumae in disguise. But first there was a quagmire to trudge through as they enquired after each other's health, each other's husband, each other's house, exchanging their little, meaningless lies. Sitting across from Katherine with her hands folded demurely in her lap, Virginia at first always held back, murmuring monosyllabic replies until at last some droll anecdote Katherine related, some shrewd literary judgment randomly dashed off, or some heartfelt confession sparked Virginia's response, and then the real talk would begin.

There would come a moment, a long pause in which their eyes would meet. Katherine's probing eyes, alien to subterfuge, would peer into Virginia's otherworldly gaze. They understood each other then, somehow, Katherine was convinced; they understood each other's solitude. This was puzzling, for she always imagined Virginia as so complete, fulfilled, at peace, untroubled by the sorts of torments that plagued her: loneliness, Murry, illness, chronic lack of money. But when she looked into Virginia's forlorn eyes, she understood that her envy towards Virginia was just another fiction. When all falsity was stripped away, one thing must be acknowledged: she and Virginia shared something ineffable. Whichever way the worldly balance might tip between them, weighing fame, fortune, talent, or health, they were equals and would always remain so. There was something almost sacred about their special bond.

Yet she had risked all this by allowing Murry to publish her review of Virginia's latest novel *Night and Day* last autumn in the *Athenaeum*. Had she made a dreadful blunder? As a critic, she must strive to be impartial, choosing intellectual honesty over friendship, if it came to that, and sacrificing her hard-won place among Virginia's illustrious crowd to her sense of duty. She sincerely felt that Virginia's new novel had not only been a failure and bitter disappointment, but also, far worse, it had been an act of cowardice and deceit. After all their conversations on the new writing they were to create, after the *Voyage Out*, which Katherine had truly admired, *Night and Day* was a throwback to the romantic drawing-room fiction of decades earlier. It stank of preciousness. The war with all its horrors had been blotted out, as if it had never existed. How could Virginia have closed her eye to all those unending fields of graves in Flanders and in France? Virginia's new novel was a lie, as Lawrence would say, a lie in the soul.

Katherine was deeply convinced that nothing could ever be the same after this last war, and as artists, to feel otherwise signified a betrayal of their own integrity. Their only strength now lay in facing life and loss, shirking nothing: war, death, change, illness, and in finding new forms and styles to express the new situation in which they all found themselves after so much cruel destruction and waste. In ignoring the war, Virginia had broken faith with all those who were struggling to create new values in art and literature. Unable to voice such thoughts in her review, Katherine had ambivalently laced her criticism with praise. *Exquisite*, she had called it, *perfect*, but she knew Virginia had not been fooled. Her real feelings had shone through her final judgment on Virginia's novel in which she had emphasized its absence of wounds or scars.

Later her own words had haunted her, and she had begged Murry to let her rewrite the review, but he refused, for he quite agreed with her assessment. But perhaps she herself had not been honest. There were times when she sensed that Virginia had some tragic secret; she too was a fragile woman who had been wounded in her innermost being, and she longed to gather Virginia in a protective embrace.

During Virginia's last visit in June, an opportunity had arisen to make amends for the infelicitous review. While talking of their recent work, Virginia had praised her newly published story *The Man Without a Temperament*. "You've achieved something there."

Katherine had acknowledged this praise with a prim, restrained smile. Virginia could not guess the reserves of pain from which that story had sprung last winter in Ospedaletti. It was an elegy to her marriage, to losing Murry, so she said only, "Yes, it is the first in a new direction. *Prelude* by comparison is just a pretty little pastel watercolor."

A slight movement of Virginia's eyebrow, a folding of her pensive lip, betrayed her mild surprise. The Woolfs had admired that story enough to publish it as the third book on their list. Fifty unsold hand-bound copies still encumbered the cupboards of the Hogarth Press.

"But it will take me years of intense work. Success depends upon my health, and last winter I was wretchedly ill in Italy. I don't think I have ever been so lonely as I was in that drafty little chalet with grottoes underneath where the sea boomed all night long. I lay the whole day in bed with a pistol on the bedside table while strangers climbed in through the verandah window and stole my coat. And when I had hardly any money left and wrote to Murry begging for help, he sent me the balance sheet of his bank account to prove he had none to lend me.

"But writing is the only consolation, don't you find? You know, when I am away traveling, lying sleepless in a strange hotel, I amuse myself by telling myself stories, by inducing a sort of waking dream. I curl up on my right side and lift my left hand to my forehead as if in prayer and suddenly I am *elsewhere*. It is a summer evening, I go down to the wharf and breathe in the smell of fish and brine, and overhear the conversations of sailors and disembarking passengers... The vision could go on and on and the details are so vivid, and so much richer and realer than life. Then later when I sit down to my desk to write, I feel such pressure to get it all down before it vanishes." She had rattled on to Virginia about the birth of a new story and then she had demanded, "You must give us some stories for the *Athenaeum*."

"But do you think that I *can* write stories?" There was a little stab in Virginia's voice which Katherine chose to ignore.

"You are one of the very few who can. *Kew Gardens*! That was a real milestone. There you have seized on something new."

"But *Night and Day*?" Virginia had blurted it out the way a child might throw a stone at a cat on the wall, not wanting to harm it perhaps, but only startle it, to see its reaction.

Katherine was surprised, for she would never have mentioned the book. The rivalry between them was too prickly to confront directly. Realizing that her review had indeed hurt Virginia just as she had feared, she took the opportunity to revise her published comments.

"A truly astonishing novel."

"But I thought you didn't care for it."

"No, it is of the first cut! I confess, though, that I found some of the omissions rather perplexing, but I suppose this may be justified by the subject-matter and circumstances."

The words rang false and Virginia had gazed back at her, like a wary rabbit about to slip back down its hole.

Just then Murry had interrupted them, banging through the study door to show them some ugly candlesticks he had just purchased from a market stall--horrendous really, and Virginia stifled a very amused smile at his vulgar taste. When he had gone Katherine steered the subject from Virginia's book. "Did you like Murry's play, *Cinnamon and Angelica*?"

"No."

Katherine lit a cigarette, inhaled, then exhaled lengthily, suppressing a cough.

"Nor I! He is neither a poet nor novelist but he is a brilliant critic, one of England's best, yet he wasted months on that tedious play. Really—the title does sound just like an apothecary's remedy for dyspepsia. Amazing he can't see the facts himself."

"Seeing oneself and judging one's own work are the hardest things to do."

Katherine had been touched by this generosity. She knew that Virginia did not care for Murry. Then they had talked about loneliness, about how hard it was at times to participate in one's own life, how much effort it requires.

Virginia confessed, "So often I am silent in company; speaking with others seems so futile."

To Virginia she had said, "That is wrong—one should attempt to merge with people and situations just as they unfold before one."

"But if I am to write, I need to be invisible and anonymous."

Yes, Katherine had acknowledged to herself. *That* was the key: embracing the solitude and secrecy of a writer's life, but she knew she had not yet won through to that acceptance.

By eleven o'clock she had completed her correspondence for the afternoon post and made a few notes in her sketchbook. Then the bell rang and Ida called from the front door,

"Mrs. Woolf is here."

Virginia's silk dress swished and rustled as she entered the studio on her long legs whose loping grace always made Katherine think of camels in the desert. The summery straw hat she wore that morning, for once not too unbecoming —Vanessa must have chosen it, gave her an eighteenth-century shepherdess air. She carried a bag embroidered in *petit point* on a silver chain. On her feet were the sturdy pumps of a woman who enjoys brisk walks in town. As she bent to kiss Katherine, Virginia's body gave off a maidenly scent of talcum powder and rose water mixed with the faint musk of sweat. The alabaster skin revealed by her prim Tudor neckline fairly glistened with perspiration. She must have hurried on her way to the Elephant.

Settling herself on the chintz sofa, Virginia crossed her legs in a leisurely manner, displaying the tops of her stockings and a safety pin stuck in the hem of her dress. At this sight, Katherine suppressed a mischievous smile. That was just like Virginia to be so neglectful of such personal details. Once she had found a handkerchief wadded up and pushed in between the cushions of an armchair where Virginia had been sitting.

Ida brought the coffee at the appointed time and Katherine served her guest and herself. The two women sat, Virginia on the sofa, Katherine at the yellow table, silent and blank-faced in between sips of coffee; shy, darting glances; and banal comments—both impatient for the real talk to begin.

Pushing her cup aside and lighting a cigarette, Katherine said, "You know, this time I shall be away for two years, Virginia. I can hardly believe it."

Virginia poured herself a second cup of coffee from the silver pot and stirred in a spoonful of sugar. Katherine observed the effect of a ray of sun on Virginia's heavy gold ring set with an opal, imprisoning the light in its dull, pearly glimmer. Probably a family heirloom and worth a fortune.

"Where will you go this time, to Italy or to France?" Virginia asked.

"To France, I think, to a villa by the sea, where I shall take tea with a country doctor every afternoon on my terrace and discuss the progress of my disease."

"You must get well." Virginia chided, and Katherine was touched by her concern. Virginia's gaze came to rest on Katherine's slender figure bundled in thick wool, although the weather was warm enough that day for silk or cotton. Katherine was well aware that the bulky fabric could not disguise the frailty it clothed. It was no use keeping up a mask of pertness before these clairvoyant eyes.

"Illness undermines my solitude so I can't write. That is the only thing I fear. I have so much to do."

"Will Miss Jones be accompanying you, or Murry?

"Jones and I set out together; Jack will join me later, God willing. I confess I don't look forward to another period of loneliness."

"Yes, I suppose it is like being in exile for you. Like me in Richmond—though of course, it is only partially so for me. London is so near, and friends are always visiting, and there is Leonard. But still, at times one longs to be in the stir of things, not on the edge of them."

"Not I, Virginia. The stir of things consumes me. In some ways, despite its many horrors, Ospedaletti was bliss, for I lived only for my writing, with no distractions, except my own moods. If only one could control *those*, then the battle would be won. I think I shall be quite content to stand upon my terrace and contemplate the sea, rather than galloping to dinners and the theater.

"But I shall miss our conversations. It gives me such joy to think that you are a writer and that you live for your work the way I do. We share the same job, Virginia, and we are perhaps the only two women in England whose books are worth reading. Our little revolution will topple all those stodgy dons and hoary-bearded critics forever. And we must both do our part."

A spot of pink tinged Virginia's cheek. Katherine knew how she warmed to praise, yet Virginia merely said, "The only two women in England? Surely you are exaggerating?"

"Who else then? Tell me the name of someone—a woman—whose prose you admire."

"Someone surely."

"Lady Asquith?" Katherine teased. "Vernon Lee? Mary Butts, perhaps?"

A flash of undisguised horror appeared in Virginia's eyes.

"There! You see I am right," laughed Katherine. "There is only the two of us."

"It's true," Virginia murmured, "With you, I can talk directly. We seem to share an ease and interest so unlike what I find with other women, even clever ones. With you I seem to find an echo. I suppose it is because you care so much about writing, even though you care so differently than I. "

Leaning towards Virginia across the yellow table, Katherine said, "I have made a promise to myself, Virginia. I plan to keep a writer's diary while I am abroad. It will record the phases and processes of writing. It won't be one of those whining accounts of personal dejection. No, thank heavens, I burned all those years ago. This will be more objective: it will offer a glimpse into the secret laboratory of the writer's craft. I will send it to you to read, and you must keep a similar diary and send me yours."

"You'd be able to make nothing of mine. It's like a madwoman's dream, or like a deep drawer in an old desk where I collect shreds and scraps of my daily impressions which I later reassemble in obsessive experiments."

"My own journal is the same, of course, an exercise in scales and harmonics. But that's just it; that is what makes it real. And it must be real to have any value. It must be *dead true*."

"Yet, you will write it with a reading public in mind."

"Yes, Methuen is interested in publishing such a book."

"Methuen?" Virginia asked surprised.

Katherine detected a hint of jealousy in her voice.

"Most respectable. But will that not somehow falsify things, I mean, presuming a public? Can it remain dead true, as you say, in such circumstances?"

"Don't we always presume the presence of an external reader—someone other than ourself when we write?"

" Indeed," mused Virginia, "perhaps we do. I always do wonder: whom do we address when we fill a blank page?"

The clock struck one and the cuckoo emerged for a single chirp. Virginia would not stay for lunch; she must rush away again to meet Leonard somewhere. She rose from the sofa, looking suddenly taller and as regal, Katherine thought, as Athena. Smoothing the flounce of her dress and picking up her handbag, she fixed her bluish gray eyes on Katherine. "I shall miss you," she said.

A strange quiet had fallen upon the room. Outside the rattling of traffic and the brushing of leaves upon the window were quite vivid, but inside the silence now lay between them like a still pool of melted snow. Wading gingerly through that silence Katherine reached Virginia's side, put her arms around Virginia's waist, then standing on tiptoe, pressed her hot, flushed cheek to Virginia's cool one. Virginia stiffened, then yielded. Their lips almost touched. Katherine rested her head on Virginia's bosom and heard the rapid beating of her heart.

"It has been lovely," Virginia murmured, drawing back and lifting her hand to touch Katherine's shining hair, then her hot cheek.

Katherine let her arms drop and stepped back, looking up at Virginia with a penetrating gaze. "I think of you as a dear, dear friend. Don't stand there smiling enigmatically, with your head tilted to the side, keeping all your secrets to yourself. Rather think how rare it is to have someone like me for a friend, another writer like yourself, who wishes to be totally honest with you. "

"Yes, then," said Virginia, "I shall send you my diary. We shall be our own public of two," and with that, she clasped Katherine's hand again and glided from the room.

ISOLA BELLA

The trip had been blessedly without incident—except for when she had lost Ida at the station in Paris, and had to scream at her through the crowd, nearly bursting her lungs in the effort and causing her nose to bleed. Then she had to lie down with a compress of eau de cologne on her forehead for two interminable hours after the train chugged out of the station, keeping her eyes tightly shut so as not to see Ida's plump gray legs dangling over the edge of the upper couchette. As they swayed with the rhythm of the train, Ida's legs reminded Katherine of the horns of a monstrous snail, feeling out its prey, waiting to descend and gobble her up in one bite the moment she fell asleep

Later, while the snail snored and the train rattled southwards, she lifted the shade at dawn and spied orchards along the tracks laden with shimmering apples, and a man with a beret on an ox cart jogging down a country road, and she had felt the thrill and overwhelming relief of returning to this old country and its old ways. Lawrence was right about England, really, one had to give him that. The English countryside was rapidly vanishing under a huge black blot of coal dust and steam, but the French, despite their suave modernity, were wise enough to preserve the land by which they were so deliciously nourished. This was surely the reason for their sane solidity of soul.

At Menton, a fiacre had conveyed them to Connie and Jinny's new villa. Upon arrival, Katherine and Ida had been served a sumptuous tea, then promptly swept out again, escorted across the vast, well-trimmed lawn and shown to their quarters on the edge of her cousin's new property.

Stark on a cliff above the sea, two floors of pink stucco and a red-tiled roof, surrounded by a shady garden with an enormous terrace, Isola Bella surpassed Katherine's imaginings of the place. The garden frothed and foamed with flowering shrubs and trees: oleanders, crepe myrtles, bougainvillea, hibiscus, tangerine trees: purple, pink, red and orange. A high stone wall concealed this paradise from the road, so that one could sunbathe nearly naked if one wished, and from the terrace, the view of the sea was breathtaking.

A stairway led down the hillside from the terrace. From here, a path wound through fig and mimosa trees back towards the main villa, where white wrought-iron chairs were scattered on the lawn beneath pink-striped umbrellas. Unlike the isolation of the Casetta Deerholm in Ospedaletti, here company or assistance were always within call, yet upon greeting her this time, Connie and Jinny had seemed cooler and more distant than in the past. Katherine's disinclination to follow Connie's example in converting to the Roman Catholic Church remained an element of unvoiced tension with her cousin, and especially with Jinny. Despite their genuine affection and concern for her, Katherine sensed that her relationship with Connie and Jinny had been forever altered after those weeks together at Villa Flora.

But one must beware of false sentimentality and let go of the inessential; secretly this more formal arrangement quite suited her. Living too close to her cousin and Jinny would have racked her nerves and disturbed her writing. Indeed after leaving Ospedaletti to stay with them in Menton last spring, she had produced almost nothing. But now setting foot in Isola Bella, with its cool tile floors, and tall green shutters closed to keep out the afternoon sun, she knew at once that here was a place where she could write. The terrace would be her island haven and she immediately made plans to purchase a chaise-longue and to have an awning made, so she might lounge in the sun and work all morning long.

This heat was a blessing. To think in England in August she had been clad in wool and on some nights had needed a fire in her room. Although Ida drooped and sweated and complained, Katherine delighted in the weather. Every evening the dinner table was arrayed with the fruits of the late summer harvest: trays of green and purple figs, tart green grapes, spicy plums with blackish skin and golden flesh. It would all have been perfect save one thing: Murry was not there to share it with her. The plan was for him to come at Christmas—over three months away. She no longer asked herself how she would bear up; she simply knew she had to and that the time would be spent working.

Isola Bella came with a maid, Marie, a coachman's widow, a savvy little woman with kindly eyes; a neat, plump body tucked into a black crepe dress; a spotless white apron trimmed in St. Gallen lace and steel gray hair knotted in a tidy chignon. Marie's presence was a boon in every way. Ida was relieved of most of the housekeeping and cooking. Her duties during this sojourn were mainly to play lady's companion and secretary, run errands in town, and oversee the kitchen accounts. This was a vast improvement over their arrangement in Ospedaletti, when Ida had been burdened with nearly all the cooking and housekeeping in such primitive conditions. Here, at least Katherine hoped, their friendship might flower again under less stressful circumstances.

Connie and Jinny had explained to Marie that her new mistress was ill and must gain back her strength, and Marie took her task to heart. She was determined, it seemed, to put meat on Katherine's bones at all costs. Of course, that also meant putting extra pounds on corpulent Ida, but that could not be helped, and Katherine gladly abandoned herself to Marie's care. The kitchen was Marie's inviolable kingdom: down at the end of a long corridor, sealed off by double doors of heavy oak. Even Katherine herself hesitated to enter there. Opening those massive doors, she felt rather like a waif in a fairytale, trespassing into the realm of bounty, and could hardly believe that all this was under her authority as the mistress of the house.

Every detail in the kitchen might have served as a study for one of Brett's still lifes. A huge iron wood stove and fireplace occupied the west wall. The wall above the mantelpiece glinted with copper pots and pudding moulds burnished to a mirror's perfection, hanging alongside giant brass and earthenware platters. Dried herbs in bunches: *romarin*, *sauge*, fennel, mint, lemon leaves, bay laurel, all dangled from a beam by the fireplace, releasing a pungent fragrance in the warm air. In a corner stood a chest with many drawers containing flours, grains, and legumes. One drawer held red lentils like tiny coins of counterfeit gold; another, kernels of barley exactly like pearl buttons on a baby shoe. A smaller chest held round loaves of bread, each one as big as a baby, swaddled in white linen. On a sideboard beneath the window, aubergines and tomatoes were piled next to a fruit bowl overflowing with ruddy pears and purple plums nestled among fig and lemon leaves, where, to Katherine's joy, she would sometimes discover a tiny cricket clinging to the underside of a fig leaf.

A side doorway led down seven stone steps into a dark, cool larder. She loved the tangy, rich, earthy smell of the larder, mingled with the dampness of its stone walls. Here were the jars of olive oil and demijohns of wine, great wheels of cheese, slabs of butter, crates of *haricots verts* and *choux-fleurs*, heads of cabbage in scalloped bonnets and a wire basket full of glowing, brown eggs:

each one a world. Here were steel cans of milk, jugs of cream and a tall crock of old wine covered with a cloth, waiting to be transformed to vinegar, or was it the contrary? Marie was surely capable of such alchemy. Here hung the hams and bacon; yeast foamed in a jar. Burlap bags of coffee beans were stacked ready for the grinding. Opening a cupboard covered with a grating, Katherine would sometimes discover the limp, sad body of a plucked fowl or skinned rabbit for tomorrow's terrine, hanging from a nail, dripping blood into a basin.

She could not stay too long in this treasure trove, for the chill and damp sent a shiver through her knees. Shortly she was always found out by Marie, who, seeing the door unlatched, would call down the steps. "*Madame Jones, c'est vous là-bas?*"

Katherine would reply, "*Non, c'est moi, Marie.*"

"*Vous avez besoin de quelque chose? Un peu de chocolat, peut- être? Un petit morceau de pain?*"

"*Non, merci,*" she would say, slowly mounting the seven stairs back up to the sunny kitchen, "I just wanted to have a look at the larder."

"*Mais vous avez raison. Tout cela donne un sens de plénitude, n'est-ce pas?*"

"*Exactement.*" She and Marie understood each other very well indeed.

Katherine was fascinated by Marie's expertise in the kitchen. When in mid morning, interrupting her work schedule, she wandered into the kitchen to beg a *goûter,* she would observe Marie at *her* work: boning a chicken, scaling a fish, whipping up a sauce in a matter of seconds. Every course was prepared with the highest artistry. Her baked fish, served on a platter of clams and mussels, clutching a bouquet of *persil* in its jaws, looked just like a Dutch painting. Her meringues and mousses were so light, one feared they might float off the table and out the window before one could puncture them with one's fork. Even a simple tisane of lemon leaves or chamomile had a more delicate flavor and was more efficacious when prepared by Marie. How could one not admire the French for transforming the body's need for food—all its needs for that matter—into an art of the highest order?

As she sat at the kitchen table, nibbling a *tartine* Marie had buttered for her, Marie would tell her the town gossip, or relate the latest adventures of other dwellers in the house: the mouse in the larder or the stray cat who came to beg milk at the kitchen door. How the mouse devoured a napkin; how the cat made off with a fish from the kitchen sideboard and refused to eat the mouse. Katherine would laugh, for these stories delighted her; they were the sorts of stories a maid in a Tolstoy novel might tell.

Other times Marie bemoaned her widowhood and beat her breast as she recalled walking the promenade in Nice at her husband's side. But she waxed warmest when speaking of Monsieur, of Murry, who must be a very important man being a writer and publisher of a magazine, and of the recipes with which she would regale him upon his arrival at Christmas. At night when Katherine sat at her writing desk, scribbling a few lines to Murry before bedtime, her letters were full of Marie.

It pained her that Ida and Marie did not take at all to one another. Ida distrusted Marie and Marie's face clouded whenever Ida ventured down the corridor toward the kitchen doors. Shortly after their first week at Isola Bella, when Ida examined the stores and the accounts, she had begun to grumble that their cook was too lavish with expenses. Pounds of butter and sugar and nearly half a ham had inexplicably disappeared from the larder in a matter of days and Marie was always demanding money to purchase more. Ida had decided to keep the key to the larder herself, so that she could check how much food Marie was pinching from their stores, but Marie soon rebelled, as any cook would, and Katherine decreed that the larder door be left unlocked. When Katherine questioned the old woman or asked to see the receipts from the grocer, Marie would decry the rising price of cauliflowers and beef and insist that as Madame was ill she must have only prime quality eggs, butter, and wine, *et vous savez bien, ça coute très, très cher* because the last war had ruined prices in France. To Katherine it was obvious Ida's suspicions were correct. Marie was probably helping herself freely to the supplies in the larder, but she was inclined to let Marie have her way, for never had she felt so pampered, and with such chic and luxury. And when Marie invited the gardener or delivery man into the kitchen for a glass of wine, Katherine pressed her lips together and looked the other way, uttering a prayer and an exhortation under her breath: Let there be bounty in her house as long as the money held out!

. . .

Within two weeks of arrival, she fell ill again, this time with dysentery and high fever, and then her cough returned worse than ever, with its ominous heaving rumble. Ida had to go out into the night to fetch a doctor, and a remarkable little man had come into their lives, Dr. Bouchage. Having served in the war in a British occupied area, he spoke English more than tolerably well. Thanks to his cures and many housecalls, her fever had dropped after six days, thanks also to Marie, who labored up the stairs several times a day with bowls of soup, broth, and tisanes. Her recent bout of illness had left Katherine nearly two stone lighter; with trembling legs, a touch of jaundice, and a distressing pain in her neck where a gland had swelled to twice its previous size. Since the fever had not yet abated, Dr. Bouchage ordered her to remain in bed for another five days. Who could tolerate such a punishment, while outdoors on the terrace lizards leapt along the garden walls? She could hardly bear to spend another five minutes in bed, as comfortable as it was, with its cool linen bedclothes.

The walls of the room where she had lain these long days were painted shell pink, and a pink-tinted glass globe fringed in ruby beads hung suspended over the bed. Once she had glimpsed it ablaze in her fever, and had mistaken it for a fountain of blood. Now the light was switched off and the shutters of the tall windows were closed. She could just make out a gilded bar of sunlight through the slats. It must be late afternoon, for the sun beat on that side of the house only after four o'clock. Through the slats she could also detect a slight movement of dark green leaves. She longed to be outside again.

On the bedside table stood a lamp with a rosy shade, medicine bottles and a glass, and a stack of beloved books. The red was Dickens, *Bleak House*; the dark green volume was Keats' letters which since last winter she always kept within reach for sleepless nights. The worn muddy brown was her Shakespeare, where a white rose pressed flat marked the sheep-shearing scene in *The Winter's Tale*, but she hadn't read a word since she had been ill, and of course, had written nothing. God knows what Murry must think, she had sent him only one book review since her arrival at Isola Bella and she had promised to produce a steady stream for the *Athenaeum*. Indeed, if she didn't provide book reviews and stories for him to publish in every number, the quality of the magazine fearfully diminished. How could she possibly get back on schedule after such a setback? Besides, she and Ida needed the money from those book reviews. She was paying rent to Connie and Jinny for the villa.

Now that she felt strong enough to sit up, she thought she might note down a bizarre dream about Oscar Wilde she had had while dozing, not wanting to forget it entirely. Propping herself up on her pillows and reaching for her copybook and pen, she was surprised to discover they were not in their habitual place with the other books by the bed. She opened the drawer of the bedside table; her comb and mirror were there, her lip rouge; even her pistol was still there wrapped in a black scarf with silver lozenges. But pen and notebook were nowhere to be found, and she concluded with some irritation, that Ida must have taken them away. It was absurd that Ida considered pen and paper more dangerous than a gun which she might have fired in a moment of delirium. No doubt it was Dr. Bouchage's doing; he had forbidden her to work until she had completely recovered. What she was going to do now wasn't exactly work. Now where had Ida put her copybook?

She peered across the room at the writing desk beneath the window. There among the pile of deadly books she had promised to review for the *Athenaeum*, was her favorite notebook, handsomely bound in Florentine paper; her inkstand; and a jar of pens and pencils. She threw off the sheet, swung her legs over the edge of the bed, touched ground, slid her *derrière* off the high mattress and pushed herself up on wobbly knees. The exertion quite knocked the wind out of her and she grabbed hold of the bedside table to steady herself. Then regaining her breath, she lifted her head to the gilt mirror on the opposite wall where a stick of a woman in a muslin robe stared back at her with glinting yellow eyes. The effect was nothing less than electrifying. Good God, what a hag she had become.

She took as deep a breath as she could muster, deliberately turned her head away from the hag in the mirror and calculated the amount of effort required to stagger towards the desk, retrieve her notebook and pencil and return to bed. It clearly would take far more energy than she had at her disposal and she was also uncertain now as to how she might maneuver under her own steam back into the bed, which was rather high. She was quite stuck, and might have to remain poised like that, clutching the bedside table until she collapsed on the floor. *If* there were any puff left in her, she *might* try to call for help, but that for the moment was impossible. She wanted to laugh in sheer desperation, but all that came out of her mouth was a hoarse sob.

The door opened. Ida appeared in the great gilt mirror above the mantelpiece opposite the door, a towering figure bearing a tray with a bowl of steaming broth.

"Katie, my dearest what are you doing out of bed? Do you need the bed pan? I'm afraid I took it away to sterilize it. I thought you were still asleep. I'll have it brought immediately."

"Jones..." she croaked.

" You shouldn't be out of bed, you know, " Ida advanced with the tray, a stern look in her eye. "Now just hop back in this minute."

" I—cannot—possibly—hop," she panted. Her strength gave out and she sank to her knees on the carpet.

"Oh Katie—I hardly realized, how stupid of me!" Slamming the tray down on the dresser, Ida rushed to help her. "Here, hold tight, slowly now. Thank goodness you didn't hit your head." She hoisted her back up onto the mattress, and helped slide her legs beneath the sheet.

"Just the sheet—thank you,—it's so —warm—today." Katherine lay back on the pillows and struggled to get her breath back. Ida closed her eyes at the grating sound. Then, when she was finally able to speak again, she peered intently at Ida who gazed anxiously back.

"Thank you, Ida. If you hadn't come in just then, I don't know what would have happened. And now Jones, if you please, my copybook and a pencil," and she pointed to the desk.

"I shan't hear of it. Broth is what you get, made by the precious hands of our butter thief." Ida pulled a chair to the bedside, picked up the tray from the dresser, and sat down. "Open your mouth," she ordered, and brought a spoonful of broth to Katherine's lips.

Katherine tasted and swallowed, then commented huskily, "It's rather warm today for broth, but this *is* delicious. Please Ida. I am quite capable of feeding myself."

Ida ignored Katie's remark and lifted the spoon to her mouth again. "Made with wine, I suppose, like everything else she cooks so lavishly."

Katherine downed another spoonful, then lay her hand on Ida's wrist. "Please Ida. Let me feed myself. If we must discuss Marie, let's do it some other time, when I am feeling better, shall we?"

"Very well then," pouted Ida, placing the tray in Katherine's lap. Katherine took a few more spoonfuls under Ida's observation, and then asked, "Has the postman come?"

Ida nodded, tight-lipped.

"No letters?"

Ida was silent.

"He's waiting ,you know, for me to send him my reviews."

"Save your breath. Don't talk. Eat."

" I promised to send him..."

"Give up writing those reviews, Katie. If you must work, do your own writing. Dr. Bouchage thinks you mustn't overtax yourself."

" Jack needs those reviews, and I *need* those few pennies. Life is so expensive here."

"That's why we can't have the cook making off with butter and ham and pounds of sugar every week."

Katherine closed her eyes to concede Ida's point. "But I find her so satisfactory in so many other ways. I'd hate..."

"Satisfactory? When the butcher overcharges me a few pennies for a cut of beef, you take me to task for it. You accuse me of mishandling our money, and it is true, I am not good at accounts and inventing tricks for saving us money. But when this woman *steals* from us, you smile and close your eyes, simply because she can make a tasty chicken stock and roast a leg of lamb."

"Don't be silly."

"When your cook in Hampstead nipped at the brandy in the liquor cabinet, you sent her away, but when Marie offers gallons of wine to the neighborhood workmen..."

"It's not the same thing."

"Katie, you have lost your head over that woman; she is sucking our finances dry, and you don't want to see that. She means more to you than I do, I think"

"Now that's ridiculous, Jones."

"Well, what am I to you, then?" Ida crossed her arms on her bosom and glared at Katherine, waiting for her reply.

Katherine pushed the tray away, sank back on the pillows and groaned,

"You are my jailer, Jones; my jailer, my cross and my albatross--"

Ida, furious and in tears, reached for the tray before it slid off the bed.

Katherine folded her hands on her breast and stared up at the ceiling. "And of course—my wife. A perfect—one."

"What nonsense!" Ida jumped up and bustled from the room, but as she banged through the door, Katherine caught sight of her face ablaze with triumph.

. . .

She lay on the chaise-longue, with Murry's infelicitous letter in her lap, frowning out to sea, brooding on how she should reply. Thank goodness Ida was not home this afternoon to pester her. She needed time to be alone and think, and the sea for once was a soothing presence. Today a veil of white mist hung on the water as far as one could see. Her eyes were fixed on a sailboat bobbing and tipping on the horizon. Just another strong gust and it would capsize. *There! Over she goes!* She could almost feel the shock of cold water; the hapless skipper soaked to the skin, gasping for air as he clambered to toss the boat over and climb back aboard, the sting of salt in his eyes. *There!* Now she was upright again. No, *down* she went again, then righted herself and skimmed away into the mist. Heaven knows, getting drenched was probably half the fun.

Her thoughts returned to the letter, which had been as much a shock to her as being dunked in a cold sea, but certainly had not been amusing to read. These few weeks at Isola Bella, Murry's silence had been appalling. She had ached, she had burned for news but not even in this wretched letter had he acknowledged the review she had posted to him before falling ill, or had he sent any news from her publisher, Constable, although her book *Bliss* was due out within days, if it were not out already. She must know how the press had responded, if Virginia had agreed to review it for the *Athenaeum. That* had been a bold request, after she had dismissed Virginia's *Night and Day*. Still, the only person in England who might really understand what she was about in *Bliss* was Virginia; that was why she was counting on Virginia to review it. But Murry, maddeningly mentioned neither *Bliss* nor Virginia Woolf.

She picked up the letter again in a listless hand. All the strength seemed to have gone out of her fingers and wrists, still tender from the effort of holding a pen earlier in the day. A week had passed since her fever had ebbed, but the illness had left her shaken. She could not negotiate stairs without assistance, and even a trip to the other end of the bedroom carpet required the aid of a walking stick. Since last week, against doctor's orders she had been out again lying on the chaise-longue under the awning, working on her stories in the mornings, grinding out reviews for the *Athenaeum* in the afternoons, and waiting for the postman who had finally just brought news from Murry. She knew she must answer him straightaway, but a hasty note dashed off before teatime would not do in the least. Her reply must be pondered, formal, chillingly definitive.

In truth, she had had a presentiment as to why his letters had been so infrequent. As she lay tossing in bed with fever, she had been tormented by a casual question Murry had launched one evening after dinner shortly before she and Ida had left for the continent.

Sitting across from her at the table, looking ever handsome in his brown corduroy jacket which brought out the greenish-glow in his eyes, he had said, "Would you mind if I moved in with Brett while you are away in France? She has two rooms to let and I could let the whole of the Elephant to Milne. It would cost far less to live at Brett's than at the Elephant, and I could pay all the expenses on the house with the rent I received, and even have some left over to live on. We'd save a lot, you know, and then when you return, I'll send him away."

She had cringed at the thought of strangers handling her things, lying in her bed again. "But all my clothes and books and things are there."

"I'll have them packed away safely," he had said, plucking a pear from the fruit tray, and proceeding to peel it absent-mindedly. This had infuriated her. How could he contemplate her absence so coolly? But she had made an effort to consider this proposal impartially, from all its angles. It was important for Murry to save money. But to move in with Brett?

"No, Jack, I don't want strangers in our house again and what's more, I'd rather you not live with Brett."

"There's nothing between us, if that is what worries you, Katherine. I admit there was a brief intimacy. It's over now. You know I wouldn't want you to be hurt."

"I know you are irresistible to women. I know you must have your needs. I wouldn't want to be a drag on your happiness. But no, I would rather you not." She had been unable to speak the words most crucial *"whatever you decide, don't tell me about it."*

During the long feverish hours at Isola Bella, lying in bed, staring up at the red fringed lamp, she had wondered if he had let the house anyway, despite her objections and simply had not told her. This letter dispelled all doubts: he was still at the Elephant for it was no longer Brett who had captured his attention. More or less, he had almost confessed he was about to embark upon an affair with a friend of Ottoline's. Why must he tell her outright about his love affairs? But that was only one of the unpleasant matters addressed in his letter. Another problem had come knocking at the door, rattling an alms can: Floryan Sobieniowski, a problem which required even more urgent attention than Betsy B.

It had been several years since she had heard from Floryan, but his surfacing now from some dark corner was no surprise. He had probably heard her new book was about to come out and that it was rumored to bring her at last fame and financial success.

Floryan! How had she managed to let herself get sucked in by his decadent charm? Of course they were both young then. He was a harmless dreamer in those days, and had not yet taken to blackmail and other illicit means of self-support. Harmless, perhaps not quite.

In Bavaria, after her miscarriage, by far the loneliest moment of her life, Floryan had helped her recover from depression. Haggardly handsome, with a soft Slavic accent, a devilish beard and a shock of silky brown hair falling into his eyes, he had introduced her to Chekhov and other Russian writers in between kisses on a secluded bench in a lonely park. She had fled Bavaria in Floryan's company. Off they had gone to Paris, taking adjoining rooms in a seedy hotel, planning a trip to Russia, but in a few weeks she had tired of him. Early one morning without informing him, she had gone to the station and taken a train to Calais where she had posted him a letter of farewell from the docks before crossing the Channel. Somehow he tracked her down in London and they had remained in touch for awhile. Murry had even published a couple of his translations in the *Athenaeum*. Some years ago, when she and Murry were living in the country at Runcton Cottage, he had shown up at the door with two trunks full of books, demanding hospitality. All night he strummed on his guitar, yodeling melancholy Polish love songs to the starless sky. In the end, Murry had offered him money to make him go away. *That* had a been a wrong move, as was now obvious, for as Murry informed her, Floryan had written him demanding *forty pounds* for the return of her letters. A fifth of her yearly income!

Silly letters they were from a girl in love with the idea of romance. Effusions, promises, intimate confessions, all insignificant in themselves, but now with her book coming out, they could possibly do great damage if handed over to the press, where she had, God knows, enemies. What would Beatrice Hastings make of them? No, she must get them back. Murry did not intend to pay, and with all the expenses of living abroad, and doctor bills, she hadn't a penny left. She would have to get the money from Ida.

Returning in late afternoon from her errands in Menton, Ida found Marie stepping out to the terrace on her way to take Katie a tray with tea and refreshments. "I'll take that now," she announced, whisking the tray from Marie's hands. Marie appeared rather startled by Ida's haughty manner, but Ida checked any protest with an icy glare. Katie was *her* charge and companion. Marie was just a servant and had better learn to keep her place.

Katie sat on the chaise-longue with her knees pulled to her chin, a wool shawl tucked around her, staring out to sea. The awning had been cranked up so she might benefit from the last golden rays of the autumn sun. Seeing her approaching with the tray, Katie smiled wanly and waved a limp hand. Ida frowned at this tepid greeting, so unlike Katie, who was always either effusive or irritated, but never bland, and thus deduced that Katie must still be feeling out of sorts. Indeed, despite Marie's rich soups, roasts, puddings and jellies, Katie had gained no weight at all since recovering from the recent fever that had melted her away like a candle. But it was not the climate or the food that did not agree with Katie. The problem was, most assuredly, Murry.

Noting a pile of letters on the folding teak table beside the chaise, Ida surmised that Katie had received some bad news. Hastening towards her, she stumbled on an uneven brick in the terrace and nearly dropped the tray, but Katie did not notice. "Back so soon?" was all she said.

Setting down the tray on the table next to Katherine, Ida was aghast to see that a fly had fallen into the cream jug. It had to be removed at once before Katie saw it. Katie had a horror of flies, of anything unclean. But alas, Katie's hand was already reaching for the jug, for she always poured the cream into her cup first before pouring in the tea.

"Wait, Katie!" Ida shrieked.

Katie glanced up in alarm.

"There's a fly in the cream!"

"Is that all?" she asked. "You shouted so hysterically, I thought perhaps you had poisoned the tea and then repented."

"I'll dip him out," said Ida, seizing the teaspoon.

"No, wait a minute. Let's see if he can do it by himself."

They both peered curiously into the jug and watched the fly as it crawled up the slick side again and again, slipping down with a tiny splash into the cream before it reached the rim. Ida was sure the poor thing would drown before it could escape. Why subject it to torture?

Katie watched in fascination, then after observing several doomed attempts, fished it out with a spoon and plopped it on a napkin. The fly stumbled half-drowned on its minute legs along the edge of the table, then shook its wings and buzzed away. Katie poured herself a cup of tea with sugar, but added no cream.

"Too much for him I expect," she said in a tired voice as she stirred the tea, "I know exactly how he feels. *As flies to wanton boys...*"

"I see the post has come," said Ida, eyeing the torn envelope on top of the pile of Katie's letters. She recognized Murry's handwriting. Sitting down across from Katie, she peered into her face and asked, "Any interesting news?"

Katie did not seem to have heard. Her hands clutched the cup, but she did not drink. Her eyes were focused on a spot far out at sea. There was a quizzical half-smile on her lips, and a crease between her eyebrows. Ida knew that look belied deep worries and she longed to kiss and smooth that crease away, along with all the troubles it denoted.

Katie sipped her tea, then turned to ask abruptly, "How much money have you got?"

"I think about five francs," said Ida, "Let me go look in my handbag. I left it in the hall." She started to rise from her chair, but Katie reached out and touched her sleeve.

"No, Ida. It isn't five francs I need. I need... *we* need... Jack and I desperately need forty pounds. Can you lend me that much?"

Ida sank back in her chair, astounded by Katie's request. "Where would I get forty pounds?"

"I have just paid the doctor, and I cannot ask Connie for any more money or draw on my allowance in advance, as you know. From your sister perhaps? Or perhaps you could write to Dolly Sutton? Or even to Mrs. Sally?"

Katie made it sound as if forty pounds were the easiest thing in the world to come by, but for Ida it might as well have been four hundred.

"And you know how expensive the food is here." Katie's eyes fastened upon Ida's waist. Under her scrutiny, Ida felt the waistband of her skirt binding even deeper into her stomach. With Marie's rich cooking, she had been putting on weight since the day they came to France, though Katie remained as thin as ever.

"Katie, I'll do what I can. But why do you need forty pounds?"

"You remember Floryan?"

Ida nodded. She had never liked that shaggy-haired Pole whose peasant hands were always stained with ink and cigarettes. The thought that those hands had once touched Katie filled her with revulsion. It had been years since they had spoken of him.

"He has asked me to give him forty pounds to return some letters I wrote him years ago, which if they were to be published at this time, might ruin my literary career forever."

"Does Jack know?" Ida half-whispered.

"Of course he does. We have no secrets from each other."

Ida raised an eyebrow and Katie corrected herself, "Or almost none. And in any case, he wrote to Jack first, demanding money and Jack has just written to me."

"If it is so important to you, I shall do my best."

"It is only a loan. I shall pay you back immediately when the royalties from *Bliss* begin to roll in, as you know they will."

Ida nodded. She had no doubt her Katie would soon be rich and famous.

Yet forty pounds was a formidable sum. Who could she ask for such a loan?

. . .

It took weeks for the letters to arrive but at last a parcel came from Murry. Katie did not deign to glance at the contents. She was satisfied to read in Murry's accompanying note that he and Floryan had met in the offices of a notary public, where in exchange for Ida's forty pounds, her former lover signed a statement swearing he would never contact them again. "I really don't want to remember that time," was Katie's only comment, and she handed the package to Ida and ordered her to burn the letters.

A sweet, resinous smoke curled up from the pinecones as they kindled in the sitting room fireplace. One by one, Ida fed the letters into the flames with all the solemnity of a vestal virgin tending her sacred fire. It was not the first time she had burned letters on Katie's orders. They had had a good bonfire in the garden in Hampstead with a pack of letters Katie had written to her in their early days, though Ida had been sad to see her precious missives go up in a blaze. But Katie had been adamant. They must be destroyed.

Katie sat near the hearth, half-mesmerized by the flickering firelight. They were both spellbound by a curious optical effect. The ink burned more slowly than the paper, so that a ghost of her handwriting remained still visible on the charred paper for a moment before the ashes fell to pieces in the grate. "Here lies one whose name was writ in ashes," she murmured after the last letter had disintegrated in the fire. Her voice was so mournful it sent a quiver up Ida's spine.

"When I am dead, Ida, make sure all my letters are burned. Everything personal must be destroyed. I don't want my laundry lists and chemist's accounts picked over by vultures. Only the stories, the finished ones, must remain. Please make sure Jack obeys."

"Why do you say these things, Katie? You are here to get well, and you mustn't give yourself up to gloomy thoughts."

"You know as well as I do that I am no better than I was in London. Doctor Bouchage reassures me that this is the right climate for me, but I do not believe it so. My blood hammers in my veins day and night. Every breath is an effort. I often feel as though my lungs have collapsed. I tell you, I have quite lost faith not only in doctors but in everything—even in Jack."

"But it won't be long before his visit. You'll see how quickly the time will fly and soon he will be here for Christmas. Then you will feel differently about everything, I am sure."

"Yes, *if* he comes as he promised, but that was before his affair with that woman. He has made me, rather *us*, the scandal of London. That rapacious bird of a woman, fattened with crumbs, has been sweeping down upon Murry's loaf. I can just imagine how Ottoline enjoyed the gossip, though for Brett it must have been a shock to lose her tennis partner."

Ida was silent. Murry was a man she would never understand and could never condone.

"Oh, I wish I were back in our Hampstead house, lingering on the top landing, looking out to see if the lemon verbena has lost all its leaves."

"I expect it has, Katie," said Ida brightly, grateful for a change in the topic of conversation. "Lemon verbena is a perennial, though it loses its leaves in winter, it comes back in the spring, fragrant as always."

"Oh Ida, you are a remarkable store of useful knowledge," she snapped, "What would I do without you?" She tossed a pinecone into the fire and the flames sizzled and sputtered.

As she stared numbly into the flames, Ida felt Katie seek her hand and squeeze it penitently, like a naughty child might do.

"I dreamed I died," Katie began softly.

"Stop it, Katie!" Ida tore her hand away, seized the poker, and began to stab the coals.

But Katie was relentless. "I dreamed I died, but there was nothing fearful in it. And I walked on a heath glistening with dew."

Ida burst into tears and threw down the poker. She would rather have Katie raging and shouting than speaking in this melancholy tone she had adopted of late. "Then I shall die too, and follow you to heaven."

"God forbid!" laughed Katie, tucking a straying lock of hair behind Ida's ear, "That is the last thing I want. And in any case, to prove to you there is *no* heaven, *no* immortality, after I am dead, I will send you a coffin worm in a matchbox."

"Not a coffin worm Katie! You know I hate worms."

"Well, then, an earwig. Look for it in Jack's desk drawer."

"Katie, you mustn't make jokes about such serious things!"

Katie kissed her cheek and went up to her room, while Ida sat in the dark, waiting till the last coal was extinguished.

Katherine sat down to her desk and took out pen and copybook. She left the gauzy curtains undrawn, so she might see the lights twinkling along the waterfront. Out in the bay a fishing boat was heading out for a night's work. She felt akin to those fishermen. She too now must try to net her catch. If only she were a real writer, dedicated to her work and to it alone. How often she failed. No one knew better than herself exactly where and how she failed time and time again. She never quite captured the range and complexity of impressions her observations allowed her when a certain mood descended upon her like grace. From that mood, call it a *strange mode of being*, like Wordsworth's *spots of time*, all her writing stemmed. Certainly there was nothing like it: to be divided always into two or more, a multitude of selves. To be the detached observer, sitting in a carriage, driving along the sea, clinging to the cold handle of the carriage door, smelling the tang of salt in the air, and at the very same instant to hang suspended in the silver flash of rain against a smoky sky, to be scattered in the foam blowing along the strand. To feel this multiplicity of selves all at once, within and without oneself, to be a world complete, *that* was bliss. Passenger and driver, the little boy in a blue cape, nibbling strawberries at the roadside, the high-stepping horse and the roiling sea were all parts of herself. But how to describe the mystery of those moments? Sometimes she held her pen for an hour or two before the words came. Then there was no stopping the rush, she drove herself mercilessly till the flow dried up. Yet that shifting fabric of words was merely the shadow of what she saw so clearly in her mind, what she felt in the sensations of her body when in that state of rapture from which her stories stemmed. It was just like being possessed.

Tonight she must write. Not the diary she had promised to keep and send to Virginia. After her first few days in Isola Bella, she had abandoned the idea entirely. She dared not tell the truth. The only way to tell the truth was to disguise it somehow. Truth could only come through fiction. Of this she was convinced. That was the challenge: to make a fiction which is true, even truer than personal experience. Nothing she had written yet—except perhaps, moments of *Prelude*, *Je Ne Parle Pas Français*, and *The Man without a Temperament* even approached her intention. She could not bear the thought of leaving only these fragments, mere snippets of the real work she had only just begun to envisage. Ten years. That is all she asked, the minimum needed. Ten years, if she could be assured that, perhaps she wouldn't mind dying at the age of forty-two.

Another story was bubbling in her brain and she must get it down. But getting the tone just right, capturing the atmosphere, this was the challenge facing her now. *The cherry orchard has been sold. They are chopping down the trees.* There is no going back from this point, we must row bravely on through the thickening darkness. *That* was the tone she sought. Chekhov was a master at creating a sense of imminent upheaval, every word so cutting and precise. Her new story would share that clarity of vision. It was born from a sketch of Ida and of her tyrannical father, Colonel Baker. It would begin and end with a promise of life, yearned for, sacrificed, then irreparably lost, like a desert flower closing its petals at dusk. For that was Ida's life. And yet there was beauty, there was solemn truth in the opening and shutting of the flower.

On she wrote all evening and into the night, avidly covering page after page in her copybook with her fine dense script until her head throbbed and her fingers ached. A clock chimed the hours, though she was hardly aware of anything but the words trickling, then streaming out upon the page. At three in the morning she had finished. Rising from the table on cramped legs, she furiously rang the bell for Ida.

Half-drugged with sleep, Ida appeared in the doorway in her flannel nightgown, her hair in a plait.

"Katie, are you ill?"

"It is done, Jones! We must celebrate with tea! I am famished."

Ida shuffled off to make the tea. The first rays of dawn found them sitting on Katherine's bed, with a picnic spread on the counterpane, sipping tea and nibbling hard boiled eggs with brown bread, as they used to do years ago at school.

"Is that me?" Ida asked timidly, after Katherine had read the story aloud to her.

"You and not you. It is art. You shall be as immortal as Hamlet or Ophelia!"

"Oh Katie! You mustn't tease me so." Tears glinted in her eyes.

. . .

A single letter lay on the little round marble table in the hall where Marie always left the post for Katie, when she wasn't already lurking on the doorstep to snatch it from the postman's satchel. It must have been delivered in the early morning post, and Marie had left it there before stepping out to the market. The envelope lay on a burnished brass tray next to a Chinese bowl where every morning Marie arranged some small offering from the garden: late roses imperceptibly frost-browned or a spray of ruddy hawthorn berries. Today it was a plump rust colored chrysanthemum surrounded by a nest of ferns. There was something typically French about this corner of the house, which reminded Ida more of a stage set than of a room in a real house where people lived and went about their business. Next to the table stood an ornate gilt chair with red velvet upholstery, like a small throne, where no one, absolutely no one, ever sat or could ever dream of sitting. The chair was far too frail to bear the weight of a solid human body, and very ill-placed in that dark corner, where the curtains were always drawn even in the autumn, against the bleaching effect of the southern sun. A chair for a ghost, for an invisible guest. A gilt-framed mirror hung above the table. Its silver slate was pocked and mottled with age, which only added to its value, as Katie explained, for it was two hundred years old and had never been broken. Ida was not superstitious, but she avoided looking into that mirror for fear of spying something unsettling. Like the phantom chair, that mirror rattled her nerves.

She picked up the letter to see who it was from, though there was no return address, only an embossed seal, some sort of coat-of-arms, but it had been posted in London. The envelope was of the finest quality paper, heavy and creamy to touch. The handwriting unfamiliar, nervy, haughtily elegant in its rounded strokes. Something important from someone important. Since the publication of Katie's book, *Bliss*, letters had been pouring in from all over England: letters of congratulations and admiration. Clippings of newspaper reviews. Young writers asking for advice. Offers from publishers and magazines. There was no dearth of mail these days, unless you counted the few letters from Murry. This was certainly not from Murry.

She slipped the letter in her pocket and went to the kitchen to fetch Katie's breakfast, which Marie had prepared before going out, leaving the coffee pot and a dish of rolls heating on the stove.

On this mild December morning, it was still sunny enough for a cold water bath which the doctor had ordered must be done before breakfast on an empty stomach. Katie stood naked in a broad square of sunlight before the open window of her bedroom, a black fan demurely held before her like a fig leaf, her nipples erect in the chill, gooseflesh visible along her arms. At her feet was a basin of cold salt water with a sponge.

"You're just in time, Ida. Please do my back properly," she called as Ida entered with the tray.

Obediently, Ida set the tray on the dresser, bent down, and seized the sponge, soaking up water from the basin. As she sponged the cold water across Katie's back, she noted that Katie was thinner than ever now, her flanks and buttocks as slender as a boy's.

At the touch of the cold sponge, Katie drew in her breath sharply, then turned her back to the sun, shivering as the drops dried on her skin, breathing deeply with a croaking sound. It was beyond Ida's understanding how dousing oneself with cold water before an open window in a draft could possibly cure consumption, but Katie assured her that it was so. The cold water draws the fever out, and the sun absorbs it, and the lungs slowly clear.

When the water had dried on her skin, Katie slipped on her beautiful dark green silk kimono, the one she had bought in London at the Japanese exhibit years ago. Plopping down in the armchair, she took the tray on her lap, and eagerly poured herself a cup of coffee from the silver pot.

Remembering the letter, Ida took it from her pocket and handed it to Katie. Curious, Katie examined it a moment before opening it. Ida went about the room, gathering up the paraphernalia from Katie's cold water bath. As she was folding Katie's towel, there came a hoarse gasp behind her, the clatter of cutlery falling to the floor, then a crash of china. She dropped the towel and wheeled round. Katie stared back at her, deathly pale. Even her lips were white. The cup lay shattered on the floor in a puddle of coffee at her feet. Ida's first terrified thought was that Katie had had some sort of attack: swallowed her tongue or burst a vessel in her brain. But no, the blank horror in Katie's eyes soon gave way to a more intelligible fury and she flung out her arm, clutching the letter in her hand.

"Katie, what has happened!" cried Ida, swooping to pick up the shards.

"That woman! "she hissed, flapping the letter at Ida, "Leave that for now. Read this!" she commanded.

Ida took the letter and skimmed through it, though she felt so confused she could hardly make sense of it, until she came upon the words, "*How dare you—an invalid, now living abroad, unable to give him any comfort or joy —How dare you keep him bound to you, depriving him of the life and love he deserves? The life and love of a healthy woman.*"

Ida was dumbfounded. How could anyone have written these words to Katie? And Murry was due to join them within days. She put down the letter, dazed.

Katie's eyes brimmed with malice. "Promise me you will never, ever, even when I am long gone, forgive Jack for what he has done."

"Of course, Katie," she said, though she could hardly make out exactly what it was Jack had done.

"Swear! You must *swear!*" she hissed.

" I swear."

. . .

Murry sat by the fire reading Milton. Six pairs of his socks dangled from the mantelpiece, drying in the warmth of the flames: a pair for each of the nights he had spent with Katherine here at Isola Bella. Now and then he looked up from his book to gaze at her while she dozed in an armchair nearby. After lunch today on his seventh day, they had reached a truce, but the first forty-eight hours of his visit had been perhaps the worst hours of his adult existence, barring an anguishing attack of gonorrhea when he was twenty-one. There had been no scenes, no shouting, hardly any tears. Katherine had simply shown him Elizabeth's letter and asked for an explanation. And he had given it, though he could not tell her the truth. For all their talk about honesty and sincerity, truth was the last thing Katherine wanted from him, and the last thing he intended to give her, for he could not bear to make her suffer any more than he had already done. The signs of that suffering were evident in her face, in her every gesture, and who was to be blamed but himself? He loved Katherine, but he did not need her in the way in she wanted to be needed. Could he be held at fault for that?

After these long years of caring for an ill wife, and being separated from her for months at a time, dependent upon letters and telegrams and unreliable postal workers to keep their love alive while bombs fell on them in London and Paris, he had begun to hunger for the comfort of a healthy, vigorous woman's love. The world might call him a cad, but beneath the world's hypocrisy blazed this simple and undeniable fact: he was a healthy man with a healthy man's needs and appetites, and then someone new had come into his life. Her very name was like a whispered prayer. How was it that she had chosen him? It always amazed him to discover that a woman he liked reciprocated his feelings, though that was usually the case. He seemed to attract women, to be, in fact, irresistible to them. Still, it always came as a surprise. He was, he knew, at heart, a timid man, and insecure with women. Yet how far he had come from the poverty and squalor of his youth to the white arms and blue blood of his new love. This fact held a charm for him which he could not deny. Perhaps if he had not been the editor of the prestigious *Athenaeum*, she would not even have looked his way, though, of course, she did not need his influence to have her writings published. Her name unlocked doors; she could be published anywhere she chose: in the *Times*, the *Dial*. She had craved his esteem and he had given it, for she was a very gifted writer. Not as gifted as Katherine; nonetheless, she had promise. Elizabeth was a talented, rich, well-bred and stunningly beautiful woman with whom he had had an exciting liaison. They supped on oysters and champagne in her bedroom after the theater, and discussed the state of novel writing in England, while sitting on an enormous bed surrounded by sumptuous curtains of cream-colored taffeta. He could but compare Elizabeth's bed with the ones he and Katherine had shared years ago. The mattress on the floor in Clovelly Mansions. The creaking settee in Old Church Street, too narrow for two and so short that his feet stuck out over the end of the bed whenever he lay down. He adored Elizabeth's body, her perfume. She was so much more female than Katherine. He had thought it extraordinary that she had not in the least been concerned about her husband discovering them like that in a tête-a-tête. The fellow might have entered the room at any minute. But it was over now. He had scrapped it all: the champagne suppers with Elizabeth, the *Athenaeum*, his editorial career. All of it. He had published Elizabeth's story in the last issue of the *Athenaeum* he was to edit, and had come abroad to join Katherine, forever. He had done what Lawrence had urged him to do years ago. Katherine perhaps did not realize how much he had given up for her. And he intended to be true.

"You promised me nothing would ever separate us!" Elizabeth had accused when he held her to his chest for their last goodbye. How could he have told her such a thing? His sexual urges had led him to transgress, to lie. He had never made such vows to Katherine, knowing that he could not keep them. Not because he was a philanderer, he considered himself more honest with women than most men, but because the world strews obstacles along one's way at every step. "How can I go on living without your literary criticism of my work?" Elizabeth had demanded in another letter, which Katherine, unfortunately had somehow discovered among his things. London echoed with the scandal, which he had made worse by confessing his desperation to all his friends and acquaintances. He was infatuated with Elizabeth, but he could not leave Katherine. At a farewell party he had organized at the Café Royale before coming over to France, he had poured his heart out to Virginia Woolf, who for once seemed sympathetic, while the others had snickered behind their drinks.

The clock struck nine, soon it would be time for Katherine to retire. He would have to help her prepare for bed. Ida was gone back to London, to close down the Elephant. Marie had been sent home early, straight after dinner. Here at Isola Bella Katherine sent Marie off on continual errands, so that the two of them might be alone in the house, and when there were no errands, Katherine sent her home, or to church, where she went most unwillingly, wondering why Madame wished to push her into the arms of the priests. On one of those afternoons, while Marie was out, he and Katherine had made love again for the first time in over two years, but a sense of doom had weighed upon him all throughout the act. Katherine's body was so slender now, with ivory ribs showing through translucent skin. He was afraid of hurting her. The erratic beating of her heart unnerved him, and he dared not kiss those lips ever again.

"You are and will always be my whole life," Katherine had said, clinging to him in the dark room, and they had wept together, bathing their pillows with tears. It was hard, so very hard to make a new life with a sick wife.

He thought often now of Villa Pauline, where they had been so happy six years ago—was it only six years? It seemed like a lifetime. Katherine was not ill. They had been poor, but they lived like kings on Katherine's small allowance. Champagne was cheap. Oh, the pleasures of the south of France! In the little garden, under a fragrant jasmine pergola, he had mulled over his book on Dostoevsky and written the first draft. That book had launched a career nothing short of brilliant. And across the wrought-iron table, her small stockinged feet resting on his thighs, sat Katherine writing *The Aloe*, her first mature masterpiece, in a blue copybook. Now he had been invited to lecture at Oxford on style and Shakespeare, and she was the acclaimed author of *Bliss*, and publishers were clamoring for more books. That just proved they were the geniuses he had always believed they were, despite all the cruel names Lawrence had called them of late—*mud worms, parasites, reptiles*.

Katherine coughed, stirred in her chair, spat into her handkerchief, and coughed again. The sound of her coughing made his spine prickle, as though a fine wire had been jerked up through his vertebrae. He buried his face in his hands.

LONDON, 2 PORTLAND VILLAS

Violet, the maid who had been engaged shortly before Katie left for France, had gone away to the country to visit her parents, so when Ida arrived on the doorstep of the Elephant at three o'clock, the house was all locked up. Luckily she had remembered to bring her key. Someone had been looking after the garden, for the rosebushes were properly pruned, though there were many tiny leaves from the willow to rake and dozens of pears had fallen to the ground beneath the tree, where they lay rotting in the grass. The cat was nowhere to be seen, though a tin dish rimmed with milk scum near the front steps suggested he still prowled in the vicinity. Later she would have to put out some food to lure him back, though she had no idea what she should do with Wingley. Taking him to France was out of the question, for Katie would soon be leaving Menton for Switzerland. If there were no one willing to take him in, her instructions were to have the poor animal destroyed. They could not leave him to starve on the street, once the Elephant was shut up and the maid sent away for good. Katie argued that having Wingley put to sleep would be more merciful than leaving him to fend for himself. Still Ida hoped the vet might be persuaded to keep him for a few weeks, if worse came to worse, giving her time to find him a new home, as she shuttled back and forth across the Channel.

Stepping through the green door, she nearly stumbled on a slim package that had been slipped through the mail slot. She picked it up. It was addressed to Murry, and from the feel of it, must be a book. She took it into his study and put it on Murry's desk near the brass lamp with the green shade, adding it to a pile of letters that had arrived since he had joined Katie in France. She returned to the hall, hung her coat on the rack, and paused to take stock of things. The house was all dark and dusty and it gave her a rather eerie feeling to be there alone. Violet certainly hadn't been doing a good job of keeping the place tidy. Murry's bachelor lodgers had gone, but they had left the rooms in disarray. There were whisky and gin bottles piled in a corner, stacks of old newspapers in the hall, and unemptied ashtrays along all the shelves. But it wasn't her duty to clean, she must pack up Katie's things, and the thought brought a lump to her throat.

The stairs creaked as she went up to the bedrooms. Despite the airless odor of a closed-up house, she fancied she could distinguish, ever so slightly, a trace of Katie's perfume in the upstairs hall. She went first to her own room, which had been occupied by Milne, a friend of Murry's, while she was away. The furniture had been rearranged, and the wallpaper was torn in spots, but the photograph of Katie and herself from their school days still stood propped against the mirror on her dresser. She dusted it off and gazed at it fondly. In those days Ida had thought of herself as a sturdy tree, or even a post, where Katie, an exotic bird of brightly colored plumage, could return to roost in between her exciting journeys and flights of fancy. And she knew then, as she knew now, that however high Katie might soar she would always return to her comfortable post. This had been their life now for nearly twenty years. Who might dare alter such a well established pattern? She slipped the photograph into her handbag. This was a treasure she would never part with again.

Peeking into the closet, she found her blue serge factory uniform still hanging on a nail. She changed into it now, carefully laying her plaid skirt and alpaca jacket on the bed, as Katie had taught her to do, then tied a worn paisley scarf around her hair. From her handbag she took the list of things Katie wanted brought to her and the instructions concerning what to put in storage, to give away, and to dispose of.

She went now to Katie's room and pulled the chintz curtains open to let in the last gleams of late afternoon. Compared to the rest of the house, this room was a miracle of order. Nothing much had been changed since Katie left; even the jars of powder and phials of perfume on the dressing table were lined up just as Katie had left them. It wasn't even very dusty, and appeared to be the one room in the house Violet cared about. Ida uncorked a phial on the dressing table and Katie's intoxicating scent of musk and oranges was unleashed into the air. She opened a drawer of the dressing table, pulled out a pale pink silk chemise, pressed it to her face. Yes, this was the perfume of Katie's skin.

Unlocking the wardrobe she sought the clothes Katie had asked her to bring. Her purple taffeta evening gown, her yellow chiffon dress, the one Jinny had bought her last year in Menton; her brown velvet jacket with silver buttons; her black wool cape with fox fur collar. Suddenly Ida found herself clutching the cape to her breast as tears filled her eyes. *They would never come back to this house again.* Katie talked of Switzerland and Paris as her next destinations. She could not stay for much longer at Isola Bella. Dr. Bouchage had warned them she must leave in the spring, for warmer temperatures would be enervating for her. He had suggested she seek the pure air of Switzerland, where she need not necessarily stay in a sanatorium. A cozy chalet at a high altitude perhaps near Sierre would be perfect. In any case, her cousin Connie had leased Isola Bella to other friends for the summer months, so by June they would have had to make new arrangements.

After Elizabeth's letter had arrived, Katie had told her that she was through with Murry. From then on they were to consider him a visitor, a very welcome visitor, but not someone to depend on or to take into account when making plans for the future. Katie had sworn that now and forever more, it would only be just the two of them, Katie and Ida, as indeed it had been all along for months, really, for years. But now that Murry had given up his liaison and the *Athenaeum* and had joined Katie in Menton, their crisis had been overcome.

Katie had changed her mind again and had told her she would have to go away now.

She and Murry intended to travel together searching for a new cure, then once Katie had recovered her strength, they would settle down somewhere in Europe, possibly in the south of France, making occasional trips to England in the summers. First they thought they would try Switzerland where Katie had contacted a doctor named Spahlingher who had developed a new series of injections. After closing down the Elephant and settling Wingley, Ida was to pop over to Switzerland to find Katie and Murry suitable accommodations for the summer. From there she was to return to Menton, to help Katie prepare for the move to Switzerland. It was unclear if she could stay long with Katie in Switzerland or if she had to go somewhere else. But where could she go?

Katie had warned her gently that the time had come for her to make a life of her own. They could not continue living together now that Murry had come back to her and had promised to stay for good. I am not allowed to have both a husband *and* a wife, she had joked, and had opted for a husband, if Murry could be described in such terms. Katie suggested she go back to Rhodesia for awhile, and offered to help pay for her passage. But what could she do there, and where could she go without Katie? Perhaps she *should* have followed Robert to Rhodesia when he proposed two years ago while on leave in London. By now she would have been settled in her own house, and possibly even have become the mother of a child. But that would have meant letting herself be touched, violated by a man's hands. Living with a man was absolutely impossible, familiarity with a man's body, so hairy and smelly, with that repulsive piece of flesh between the legs, was unthinkable. She had actually been forced to see one once in India as a child, when a half-caste had sneaked into a garden where she had wandered into a lonely corner to pick some flowers. There amid birds-of-paradise, he had exposed himself to her, commanding her to look upon the Serpent with One Eye and she had run off terrified, disgusted, and enraged to her nurse, too ashamed to recount the cause of her dismay. Thank goodness, her knowledge of adult male anatomy had ended there. No, marriage had never really been an option. She might go off to Africa, and apply for employment as housemother for an establishment where mission nurses lived, as a friend of Jinny's had suggested. Jinny's friend worked for a mission hospital, and had tried to convince Ida that her real place in life was helping the sick, but she could not imagine going so far away, and the mission might want her to convert. Another friend of Jinny's, a Swiss woman, Miss Suchard, had suggested she help her open a tearoom in England as she needed an English partner to apply for a license, but Ida knew nothing of business or tearooms. Her scones always came out flat as pancakes and scorched on the bottom. It did not seem a very practical solution. At the most she hoped Katie would not mind if she found a room somewhere not too far from wherever it was she and Murry decided to live, and would let her continue to visit her, slipping in and out as discreetly as a cat, so as not to annoy Murry too much. She found herself weeping again.

Digging into the pocket of her uniform, she found a grubby handkerchief, wiped her tears, and blew her nose. She must pull herself together. Folding Katie's clothes, she carefully packed them into a valise. Then she emptied out the drawers of the dressing table onto the bed, and picked through the pile, salvaging a few forlorn objects that might still find use—a comb with not too many missing teeth, a half-empty pot of lip rouge, a pink satin eyeglass case. Katie had told her to leave some of her pretty odds and ends for Violet, so Ida took an empty hat box from the wardrobe, and began to fill it with sundry objects: Katie's cream pots and perfume phials, some old underwear, stockings, and vests, and a pair of worn slippers with pointed Turkish toes not worth carting across the Channel. She had nearly filled the box half full when a chill seized her heart, *this is what one does when someone dies.* You clean out drawers and give things away to friends and to the poor. When her father died, she had not gone back to Rhodesia to help her sister unburden the house of Father's size twelve shoes, countless briar pipes, and patched shooting jackets. God knows what had become of all those things. Her sister had sent her a walking stick, the skin of a squirrel Father had shot, and an onyx signet ring that had slipped from her finger and had been washed down a drain while she was rinsing green beans in Katie's kitchen sink at the Elephant. But why these morbid thoughts? Katie would be furious with her for being so silly. *Katie was absolutely not going to die.* At least not for years yet. Sorapure promised she would be well in five years' time. From the box, she picked up one of the perfume phials again, uncorked it and dabbed it generously on her wrist and throat, then she slipped the phial into her pocket. Surely Katie wouldn't mind if she kept this for herself.

Next she rummaged through all the drawers and boxes of the wardrobe, checking to see if there were anything Katie might need. In a box she found a little black velvet belt with rhinestone clasp that Katie would surely want to keep, but her instructions had been brutal. Get rid of anything and everything that is not essential. Was this belt essential? She decided it wasn't, and put it in Violet's box, then remembering how nice it looked round Katie's trim little waist when she was wearing a black silk skirt, decided it was, and packed it in Katie's valise.

A chill draft teased the nape of her neck. Glancing to the window, she saw that dusk had fallen. A deep blue twilight gleamed in the tall window. She went to draw the curtains, and paused a moment, looking out at the heath as the streetlamps were illuminated one by one along the pathway. This had always been a special moment for her and for Katie; they used to watch from the balcony in Katie's room, as the lamplighter blazed his way along, making loops of fire with the tip of his lighter, moving from lamp to lamp. She peered down into the garden, looking for Wingley, but there was no trace of Katie's favorite feline. She pulled the curtains, turned to survey the room and shivered. The house had become quite cold, and she was also getting hungry. She would have to light the range in the kitchen and cook herself something but she hadn't thought of buying any food, and who knows if Violet had left anything in the larder? Perhaps an egg, or a piece of bacon or some dry biscuits. But she intended to finish her work first before venturing down to the kitchen.

When she had finished in Katie's bedroom, she fetched a few boxes from the attic and went to Murry's bedroom. It was a room she had rarely entered, except to strip sheets from the bed, sweep the floor, dust, and beat the carpet, tasks Violet had quickly taken over, for Murry preferred to be looked after by their pretty young maid, who had, however, quite neglected the room of late. Books and papers were piled everywhere, clothes were draped on the chairs. Ida picked up a pair of trousers and shook out the dust. A few coins jingled out on the floor along with a small cream-colored slip of paper, where the words *I adore you*, written in a feminine hand, most definitely not Katie's—appeared. Angry, she tore up the paper, then wadded the trousers up and stuck them in a box to put in storage with the rest of Murry's things. The only thing Murry had asked her to bring back to him were a few books from his desk. When she had finished packing up his clothes, she went down to the study to see about the books.

Aeropagitica by Milton, however one pronounced it, was a green book with gold lettering. Keats' *Lamia*. Something entitled *A Gift from the Dusk*, and a volume of Spenser. That was all. Murry had also asked her to bring any letters which might have arrived for him, and indeed a pile of letters lay on the desk. She checked through them quickly. Katie had ordered her to open any suspicious-looking ones and destroy them if they were from Elizabeth, but none of the letters seemed to be from her. There were two bills, a letter from the bank, a note from Murry's brother, Richard, and a letter from Italy, and then the packet that she had nearly tripped on coming in the door. She examined it now. It was from the *New Age,* the magazine edited by Katie's former friend, Orage, and was marked "URGENT" in red ink. It looked important, so she packed it along with the books in the valise she would take to Katie.

All the other books were to be put in storage, along with their pictures, Murry's clothes, their dishes, pots and pans, and cutlery, which were all to be packed up carefully in the boxes and crates Murry had left in the attic. He had also given her the telephone number of a man she must call to have those things taken away along with all their furniture and put in storage. Murry was planning to buy a cottage in Cornwall, where he and Katie might stay in summers when they returned from the continent. The house furnishings from the Elephant would be needed for the cottage.

Climbing up on a chair, she attacked the bookcases, tearing books down from the shelves, and dumping them into boxes at her feet. Clouds of dust billowed up as each book went smack in the box, making her sneeze continually. Now and then a photograph, a postcard, or a pressed leaf fell out from among the pages. There was a photograph of Leslie in uniform, which she tossed into the box with the books—it would only break Katie's heart to see it, and an invitation from Lady Ottoline, dated July 1920, which she threw away. Two hours later, the tall bookcases had been emptied, and she felt a queer sense of relief to see all that blank space where the books had been, but her hands and nails were black with dust. She scrubbed them clean in the little bathroom upstairs, then descended to the kitchen where she lit the stove and managed to cook herself some porridge. After this meager meal, she dragged herself upstairs to Katie's bedroom, took off her scarf and shook out her hair, then collapsed, still wearing her factory uniform, onto Katie's bed.

Katie had given her some money for the trip and had made her promise to eat a decent meal every day, so when Violet reappeared the next morning, returning from her visit to her parents, Ida gave her some money and sent her out for eggs, bread, milk and tea and a bit of mincemeat for Wingley. Then she telephoned the vet and managed to convince him to keep Wingley for a few weeks, while she joined Katie in Menton, to help her organize her move to Switzerland. Later in the summer, she would come back to London to make the final arrangements for the Elephant, and find Wingley a new home.

After Violet had returned with the groceries, Ida prepared a little dish of raw meat soaked in milk for the cat and set it on the front steps. Wingley responded to her call with a desperate meow, slunk out of the hedge, and pounced upon the food. Ida hung back in the doorway, observing the cat, hiding the traveling cat basket out of sight, waiting for the right moment to strike. She was distressed to see how scraggly Katie's beloved pet had become: so scrawny, his nose once as pink as a raspberry was now sickly yellow and large patches of his fur were missing. The poor thing must have gotten into a scrape with a much more ferocious beast than himself and he looked half-starved. Wingley did not seem to know her and when she reached out to caress him, he spat at her. When he had finished, he sat on the steps, cleaning himself, and as she grabbed for him, he scuttled back under the hedge. Crouching down on all fours on the gravel, Ida peered under the hydrangea bushes. He glared back, posed for defense. He attacked as she shot out her arm and as she pulled him out of the hedge, he pawed the air wildly, grazing her cheek with his claws. Ida plopped the squirming cat into the basket, slammed the lid shut, and buckled it tight. The cat stared out through his little wicker prison with haunted, furious eyes, and as she strapped the basket to her bicycle and pedaled off to the vet, Wingley's yowls of protest sounded distinctly human to her ears.

PART FIVE

1922

ESCAPE FROM SWITZERLAND

The little traveling clock sat on the ledge under the window, next to Ida's sponge bag and a deck of cards, but there was no time even for a quick game of Patience, the train was racing towards its destination. The heating in the compartment was turned up full blast, but the knob was stuck, and came away in Ida's hand when she tried to turn it down. Katherine fairly prickled in her heavy wool dress. She could feel the heat spots breaking out on her bosom. Pressing her hot cheek to the chill window, she looked out. Although it was only a few minutes past noon, the snowy valley where the track ran was already in shadow.

Once they reached Geneva there was a long wait for their connection, but they found a cozy corner at the station cafè, where Katherine curled up on a sofa, and wrote a letter to Murry. Then Ida brought tea and chocolates, and thus refreshed, they headed off down the platform in good time, long before the express train to Paris was due in. Katherine could not tolerate being rushed through crowds in her present state for she could barely drag herself along. Though the crystalline air of the Alps had helped dry out her left lung during her stay in Switzerland, where she and Murry had gone after leaving Paris, eight months at such an altitude had compromised her heart. She had been warned that the climate would not remain beneficial to her forever and that she must leave the mountains before the snows turned to slush and fog. On this bright January day she was now bound for Paris again where she hoped to reorganize her life for the coming spring.

In the black satin clutch bag laying on the seat beside her, she carried a letter from a doctor there, Dr. Ivan Manoukhin, a Russian émigré who had developed a new cure for tuberculosis by bombarding the spleen with X-rays. Koteliansky had given her the doctor's address, claiming that Manoukhin had cured many exiled Russian writers living in Paris, including Mihail Bunin, whose stories she had admired, and who had been a friend of Chekhov's. She had written and telephoned the Russian doctor at least three times before he had posted his reply.

Manoukhin had no doubts that his treatment would be 100% successful, and had penned that miraculous word *guérison* in his letter. It would not be an easy treatment, he had warned; it debilitated the patient before any signs of improvement appeared. It would also take time, and was very expensive. When she learned just *how* expensive, she felt an impulse to run screaming from the room: three hundred francs a shot for a cycle of fifteen weeks. She would have to remain in Paris for that whole period, during which she would require a good deal of assistance, bed rest, and a steady diet of steak, eggs, cream and oranges. A second cycle would probably be required six months later. The economic impact of all that was staggering, and she could hope to meet the costs of the treatment and of a lengthy stay in Paris only if she could keep on producing stories as rapidly as she had done while at Isola Bella. Had she enough puff left to keep fanning the flames? Lately, she had begun to borrow inspiration rather freely from wherever she could, frequently from Chekhov. Luckily she had engaged an agent, Pinker, Lawrence's agent, to handle her affairs, so she need only churn the stories out, at six guineas a piece, and let Pinker take care of all the rest. If Ida helped with the typing, that would make it all the easier.

Aside from the expenses of Manoukhin's treatment, food, and lodging, there were also the expenses of keeping Ida, but until she was truly well again, Ida's help was indispensable. She glanced across now at Ida intent upon a crossword puzzle. Dependable as always, Ida had agreed to accompany her when Murry had refused to come along with her to Paris. He was so enjoying the winter sports in Switzerland and couldn't bear the thought of returning to a city at this time, besides he wanted to finish his new novel. Ida had seen to the tickets and visas, packed the bags and the picnic basket, and once again they had embarked upon another journey. It was daunting to think how many miles on the map of Europe the two of them had covered together over the last four years, sitting hours and hours on these dirty trains.

It would only be a brief stay in Paris. She would see Manoukhin and make arrangements to begin his X-ray treatment in May, which was when the lease on the chalet where she and Murry were now living ran out, and they would have to recamp again. After seeing the doctor, she would hurry home to Switzerland and stay there till just before the spring thaw. Then she and Murry would head down to Paris again, and she would cast herself into the Russian's hands. As for Ida, she would just have to find somewhere to go. They could not go on forever being a threesome now that Murry had returned. Ida had told her about a Swiss girl who wanted to open up a tearoom somewhere along the south coast of England and needed an English partner to apply for the necessary licenses. The girl had begged Ida to throw in her fate with hers and help her establish and run the tearoom. It sounded like a feasible plan to Katherine. Keeping a tearoom was a suitably genteel occupation for someone like Ida and she thought she should encourage her. She could even help by giving Ida a little money to start out with, so she could buy herself some decent new clothes, caps and shoes.

When she was well again, Murry wanted to travel for an indefinite period, perhaps take a house in the Midi for a year, making occasional trips to England. He also talked of building a house in Sierre or buying a cottage in Cornwall where they could stay while in England, and even a small car to get about Europe in, a prospect which excited them both. The freedom of the open road! Little roadside inns out in the country. But of course they could not build a house in Sierre, buy a cottage in Cornwall, and spend months at a time in the Midi. There would never be enough money for all that, no matter how many stories she managed to publish.

She sighed and stared out at naked apple groves crouching at the foot of the mountains, at terraced slopes of barren vines, at wide streams snaking through rocky beds of shale and ice. These rosy pictures of the future: a house, a car, traveling together, being well again, were only a self-delusion. Things with Murry were not really going well at all, and she was furious with him for not coming with her to Paris this time. Despite the domesticity they shared in Sierre, there had been stony silences between them and capricious, inexplicable absences. Above all she was tormented by a thought rotting in her mind that somehow Murry accepted her condition, that it suited him to see his wife as an invalid cocooned in blankets on a velvet couch.

He, too, considered himself ill and fragile; he thought of them both as two wayfaring pilgrims in search of the land of the sun. As for herself, she had not really walked for over six months. Oh yes, she could creep, and allow herself to be shunted back and forth by taxis and sleighs, but no more than that. On some days a single flight of stairs appeared to her as awesome and insurmountable as the slopes of Mt. Blanc. For months she had risen at eleven, gone downstairs at two, come up at five, and lay on her bed until it was time to crawl back into it at nine, while he perfected his figure eights on a frozen pond, or labeled botanical specimens gathered on his walks and pressed them in a German dictionary. Was that a marriage? Every evening for months, Murry had gone out after dinner alone, returning late. Where had he gone then? Where was he now? She imagined him trudging through the snow alone, twisting his ankle, stumbling into a crevasse and freezing to death. A shiver tingled down her spine. She pictured his body crumpled on the snow, alone beneath a pitiless sky. She shook off the image, astonished at herself. What made her think such hideous things?

She picked up the book on the seat beside her and leafed through it, searching for a passage she had underlined last night before falling asleep. This

185

little volume, *Cosmic Anatomy,* had been a constant companion for weeks now, and a source of ever-growing strife with Murry. Even its very title intrigued her, combining metaphysics and physiology. Orage had sent it to Murry to review for the *New Age,* and Ida had brought it to them along with Murry's bundle of letters when she had returned from London after closing down the Elephant.

It was rather odd that Orage had sent Murry any book at all. They hadn't been in contact for years, ever since Orage had published in the *New Age* some very venomous reviews of Murry's magazine, and of Katherine's own stories published there. But that was probably Beatrice's doing. She might very well have blackmailed Orage into printing those things. Katherine had forgiven them. Why keep a grudge for long? But Murry had not. Upon glancing at the book, Murry had dismissed it with utter scorn. He was baffled by the wave of occultism sweeping over London: the Royal Order of the Golden Dawn, Aleister Crowley, Madame Blavatsky, the Mahabharata, the Tibetan Masters, bodiless voices, and mediums spewing out yards of ectoplasm. He was unable to distinguish among these things and had even threatened to toss the book into the fire, when he saw how deeply it absorbed her. That too was so unlike him to bully her about a book. The ravings of a Theosophical lunatic, he had sputtered; but *Cosmic Anatomy* had set her thinking in a new way. It was like opening a window in a cramped, stuffy room and letting in a fresh breeze from the sea.

Your head and your heart are not in harmony, Lawrence had pronounced long ago over lunch at the Elephant. Your disease is born of *a lie in your soul.* And what was that lie if not her own infidelity to her innermost self, her innermost needs?

She had begun to wonder if there were a link between spiritual imbalance and physical health. Suppose it were necessary to be healed spiritually before the body can be healed? Did the body have a knowledge of its own, a consciousness of its own that animals have retained but men have lost? *Cosmic Anatomy* seemed to suggest this in the passage she had marked just last night. Here it was, boldly underscored with a red pencil: *Through evolution, we human beings have ascended our spinal cords up to the head, from where we look out upon the outsides of things. It is time we climbed back down and learned to look upon the insides as well.* Was there a way to contact this lower, more primitive, deeper self where perhaps the power of healing lay dormant? Perhaps the body could become an instrument, a servant—but of what? Of a mind more mature, more controlled -- or perhaps more receptive to the impulses of the universe? *When man opens his consciousness to receive a direct contact from the universe, he will not need to decide what he must do; his thoughts and feelings will obey the cosmic flow.* Lawrence would agree so whole-heartedly with that.

Here was yet another thought she found inspiring:

A casual event in the outer worlds may become a truly symbolic act, which means one in which two lines of events connect for a moment.

For Murry, this was mumbo jumbo, and perhaps it was. She did not really understand it intellectually. But still she did *feel* that she lived—one lived—on different planes of existence, and that from time to time, one rubbed shoulders with an angelic presence which was really one's greater self. There was this plane here in everyday life where one sits on a train and loses one's gloves and cries for a baby's death and coughs up blood. Then there is another plane where one finds oneself at times for unknown reasons, where the train, the baby, and the bloody handkerchief suddenly vanish in a vortex and eternity rushes down upon one straight down *vertically* through the brain. And these two planes, these two separate lines of time, intersect for a moment in one's consciousness, in a blinding, incandescent flash, in *bright shoots of everlastingness*. That was the meaning of epiphany. That was the moment of vision which she had tried to capture in so many stories. She felt this same striving in Virginia's work; it was what connected them most intimately. Lawrence also, though more darkly, seemed to be groping in the same direction. But he erred in reducing human love to a rutting animal's response to sexual stimulation.

Whatever one might think of *Cosmic Anatomy*, it posed a thousand new interrogations. Since those days in Menton, she had felt a widening rift between heart and head—between the emotional need to believe in God and the intellectual conviction that there is no God in which to believe. She sensed now that there might be a reconciling factor between the two. *Cosmic Anatomy* had pointed out a new path.

PARIS

Her cousin Elizabeth had recommended the Victoria Palace Hotel in Montparnasse, where she and Ida checked in later that evening and were shown to adjoining rooms on the top floor. Katherine's room was spacious and quiet, soberly furnished with a little burgundy sofa and a mahogany writing table. Under the porter's disapproving eye, she turned down the sheets to see how clean they were. Satisfied, she nodded to him, indicating that he might set down her bags, then dismissed him with a tip. Next, she sent Ida out on an errand to the chemist's before the shops closed. Relieved to be alone, she unpinned her hat and lay it on the dresser, tossed her embroidered shawl across the back of the sofa to add a spot of color to the somber room, and hung up her overcoat.

Ringing for the chamber maid to order a pot of tea, she sat down on the sofa to wait for the tea to be brought and stared at the tourist police notice pinned next to the mirror above the sink. How she despised hotels. They were exactly like the waiting rooms of train stations without the crowds or trains. How many stewed chicken wings had she consumed in rooms like these, brought up on a greasy tray? How many pots of lukewarm barley coffee? She was quite convinced she would die in a room like this one, sooner or later. They would find her stretched out stiff as a board in bed, done in by the combined effect of the hallucinatory wallpaper and the liver-clogging cuisine. Yet dying was not included in the list of tourist police regulations forbidding guests to launder clothes, cook, use paraffin stoves, or receive visitors who were not registered guests. Nowhere in the house rules was it stated that guests were forbidden to die. She ought to inform the management of this omission before it was too late.

She rose and went to the window where soft gray and lilac clouds massed low over the slated Paris rooftops, punctured by a forest of spires and chimney tops. On the balcony across the way, there hung a bird cage occupied by a single canary and a little pot of pink hyacinths was perched on the balcony wall. While she stood observing the canary, a woman in a blue-checked apron came out on the balcony, fed the bird and watered the hyacinth, then stepped back inside.

There was a story in that canary, Katherine mused. She took out a little notebook and pencil from her handbag and noted down the words "canary" and "hyacinth" and "blue-checked apron."

The maid knocked and delivered a tray with a pot of something that resembled tea but wasn't. She drank it anyway, sipping slowly, seeking strength and comfort from the tasteless brew, reviewing her plans. She wouldn't be seeing Manoukhin until tomorrow afternoon. In the morning she must get her hair washed properly and buy a new pair of gloves for her old ones were streaked with grime from the train. Perhaps she would stop at a flower stall near the hotel and buy herself a small bouquet of hyacinths to brighten up this cheerless room. Then after lunch she would get a taxi and go to the Trocadero for her three o'clock appointment.

When she rang the bell marked "Manoukhin," silvery laughter and a rustling sound could be heard from inside, and a pretty red-cheeked Russian girl opened the door to the street. Katherine was shown into a waiting room, where a few people sat talking animatedly in Russian. They stopped speaking just long enough to look her over once and greet her with a smile or cordial nod, then resumed their chatter. She took a seat in a worn leather chair near the window and with alert, amused eyes studied her fellow patients: a man who looked like an artist from Montmartre with traces of yellow paint round his nails; a fellow in a corduroy cap and shabby tweed jacket who might have been a coachman or a gardener in his Sunday clothes; an older woman with a double chin and a paisley scarf tied round her head *babouchka* style, and a thin, fashionably dressed matron with two delightful small boys who ogled Katherine outright. When no one was looking, she stuck her tongue out at them, and the younger one, no more than three, turned away, outraged. In a corner by the door sat a very pallid, willowy young girl with troubled eyes who looked exactly like she had always imagined Marie Bashkirtseff to look. They all might have been characters in a Chekhov play. Even the place looked more like a stage set than a waiting room in a clinic. A samovar bubbled away in a corner near the door, exuding unhealthy puffs of charcoal smoke. People helped themselves to glasses of tea and went on talking.

After an interminably long wait which had taxed her patience to the utmost, when nearly all the other patients had gone, her name was called and she stepped into the doctor's office. Seated at a handsome inlaid desk was Dr. Manoukhin, a tall, dark, reserved-looking man with a chiseled goatee and darting Slavic eyes. All the trappings on his desk were made of polished silver: pen, inkstand, picture frames, and paperknife. In a corner stood a cubicle partly closed off by a white curtain where, through the gap, she glimpsed a mechanical contraption made of steel and iron. The X-ray machine looked more like an instrument of torture than a means of modern medicine.

She sat across from him, looked up with hopeful candor into his eyes and smiled as yet another examination began. Katherine expounded her case history, the many cures she had tried, her recent stays in Switzerland and her fears for her heart. She then proceeded with the list of secondary illnesses and health conditions from which she had suffered, holding nothing back. As he followed Katherine's recitation of her medical history, the doctor stared at her with probing eyes, nodding pensively now and then, arching an eyebrow, pinching, once, his thin lips. To her surprise, he did not make notes, take her pulse or even pull out his stethoscope. When she had finished her lengthy speech, Manoukhin swept all her words aside with a theatrical gesture. Cradling Katherine's hand in his, he gazed into her eyes and pronounced in heavily accented, guttural French: "I can cure you, Mrs. Murry. By summer you will be well again." He urged her not to wait till May to begin the treatment for there was no time to lose. She must begin immediately: tomorrow, if not then and there on the spot, and his eyes glanced towards the cubicle.

Katherine balked. She had counted on returning to Switzerland within days and staying there until spring, and now Manoukhin was suggesting she change her plans. Moreover, she was not quite ready to face the expenses of his treatment; there was still the chalet rent to pay until May. Would Murry be willing to join her, and if not, what would he say to her spending fifteen weeks in Paris without him? She had not brought with her nearly enough clothes and other necessities for a prolonged stay in Paris. If Murry refused to come, then her things would have to be sent, or else Jones would have to go and fetch them, and in either case it meant even more expense.

Still there was an alternative. She had discussed Manoukhin's treatment with a Swiss doctor in Sierre, Dr. Choue, who had treated her during the autumn. He possessed an X-ray machine and had informed Katherine that, if Dr. Manoukhin agreed to supervise him by letter, he might perform a first phase of treatment for her in Sierre. She could later come to Paris in May to complete the cycle with Manoukhin himself.

Manoukhin frowned at her query. He shook his head before she had finished, and explained, with some irritation, drumming his beringed fingers on the desk, that he could not take responsibility for patients undergoing his treatment in any setting other than his own clinic. If she wished to try his treatment, then she must do it in Paris under his personal supervision.

They chatted a few minutes more. Manoukhin complimented her on her literary reputation, of which he had vaguely heard, though he thought she was a novelist, and suggested he might introduce her to some of his Russian writer friends in Paris. He kissed her hand as she took leave, and begged her to telephone him in the morning to inform him of her decision, for he would have to find a way to fit her into a very busy schedule.

On the way back to the hotel, she stared out the taxi window at well-dressed women sauntering along the boulevards—so chic, so idle, so soulless—and brooded over her first meeting with the Russian doctor. She could not make up her mind whether her impression were a positive or negative one. When he had taken her hand in his and said those words, " I can cure you, Mrs. Murry," she had felt absolutely in her bones that he was the right man for the job. Truly he had been the ONLY doctor in years who had dared use that word, "cure," in her presence. It was, indeed, that word which had convinced her. Yet in another part of herself that looked out upon the world through some crack in her brain, she felt with equal, nay, stronger, conviction that the man was a fraud, despite Kot's glowing reports of his many successes. This inner discrepancy in herself was a source of true distress. Why was it that in the most important decisions of her life, she was always paralyzed by an inability to stick to one road, to one plan, to one impression? Optimism and enthusiasm for any one thing or person immediately gave way to the bleakest pessimism. Which attitude most closely approached the truth? It was impossible to say.

And what of the financial aspect? It frankly terrified her. Perhaps Father might help. Dare she enquire, perhaps through cousin Connie? And if Manoukhin were unable to fry her or broil her or dish her up in some other suitable fashion, that is, if the treatment should not work, why then, think of the money just washed down the drain, for nothing.

Yet she was so ready to believe. She sometimes dreamed that she was healthy again, able to run and leap and sing, but the fear of death weighed on her chest at nights now, no longer something abstract, dark, and rich; comforting as sleep;

soft as black feathers; sweet as clods of soil dampened by a spring rain; soothing the senses to oblivion. The reality was far different from Keats' poetic effusions of annihilation. Rather the thought of death was like the rush of a waterfall sweeping her over the edge in an overwhelming roar. She could not die, *not yet*, for so many reasons. Her work was unfinished. And there was Murry. And a thousand other things she could *not* part with, not just yet. No one could know the secret depths of her desperation. No one who had not experienced it directly.

The taxi drew up to the hotel. She paid the driver and got out, and pushed in through the revolving glass door, demanded her key, and took the lift up to her room, complimenting herself with each of these small accomplished gestures. She was still able to get about alone, on good days. Ida was out, but she had brought some tulips: red- tipped beaks still shut fast. Katherine rearranged the tulips, kissed their tips, and sat down to her writing table.

She had decided to go ahead with the cure, and must inform Murry that she would be remaining in Paris until the summer. He was free to do as he liked, to join her or to stay in Switzerland and continue his skiing lessons and his novel, but in that case, would he please send the following items she would need during her stay? And she began to make a list.

. . .

Katherine lay in bed in the adjoining room, resting from her morning session with Manoukhin. Through the open door, Murry could hear her labored breathing. Outside, a soft April sun was shining, but the shutters in the room were closed. After her treatments, Katherine could not stand sunshine, so they had to keep the shutters closed till dusk. Murry sat at the writing table, illuminated by a small lamp with a pink shade, working on his new book about Keats. Books, newspaper cuttings, notes, and papers were spread on every surface, including the floor. He knew that Katherine abhorred this clutter, but it was the only way he could keep his ideas in order and he was in the throes of a new essay.

He glanced at his watch. Damn! It was nearly lunchtime and there was nothing in the room to eat. He must dash out before the shops closed, otherwise he and Katherine would go hungry till dinner time. They could not afford to have food brought up on trays from the hotel kitchen for every meal. The watchword now was economize, economize, economize. Paris was amazingly expensive, and Manoukhin was bleeding Katherine dry. For lunch they made their own *foie gras* sandwiches or ate fruit and cheese.

It was such a struggle to keep the home fires burning by himself. He had to see that the rooms stayed tidy, that his own clothes and Katherine's were brushed and presentable, that the shopping was done and meals arranged and the chemist paid, and then he had to accompany Katherine to and from the doctor, as she was hardly even able to walk at the moment. These were things that Ida normally took care of, but he and Ida had changed places. Ida was now in Switzerland, where she had arranged to sublet the chalet to tourists, so that she could pay all the bills and the rent until the lease ran out, and even earn her keep. Katherine was delighted with this situation. For once Ida was financially independent, out of their hair, and had solved the problem of the chalet lease for them. But Ida's absence meant that Murry had to see to everything himself, and still find time for his writing. Katherine was all but incapacitated and spent nearly all her waking hours in bed, with the exception of a rare drive in the Bois at his side, when she felt well enough go out, firmly supported on his arm, half-drooping like a ragdoll.

He was glad they would not have to continue like this for much longer. Manoukhin's treatment was merciless. Katherine complained constantly of burning headaches, shooting pains along her spine, tremors, nausea, and palpitations. The good doctor saw nothing amiss in these disturbing symptoms, explaining such reactions were to be expected. The body responded violently at first and they must not be discouraged. It was a sign that the cure was working.

Murry had promised himself he would suspend judgment until the cycle was over. Katherine had even put on a bit of weight, but seeing her so debilitated in other ways distressed him deeply. It had crossed his mind that Manoukhin, like so many of the other doctors Katherine had seen in recent years, was little more than a crook and an impostor. He had been reluctant to send Katherine to Paris in the first place, as he believed the healthy life they had been leading in Sierre was her best hope for healing. But Katherine had been adamant about proceeding with the costly X-ray cure. Koteliansky claimed Manoukhin had cured an army of Russian exiles, and she was determined to see the first cycle through. It seemed to be her last hope indeed, and Katherine was doing her best to convince him that she believed it was helping, that *she would be healed*, that next year, they would go back to the South of France as they dreamed. But he no longer made plans or even thought about the future. This was life, *here* : this shuttered room, with his newspapers scattered everywhere and Katherine lying in the half-dark, stifling her cough so as not to grate on his nerves.

Yet the end was in sight. In two weeks her treatment would conclude, and they would be returning to Switzerland, and after a brief rest there, if Katherine were well enough, they would return to England in August. They'd been away for too long; there was business of varying kinds to tend to, and belongings and clothes from the Elephant to get out of storage.

He rose from the desk, slipped on his jacket, and noticed a book Katherine had left on the sofa. Her Bible, he called it, that *Cosmic Anatomy*. He picked it up and thumbed through it, shaking his head as he noted the passages underscored, marked in red, checked in green, X-ed in black and heavily annotated. He had never seen Katherine study any text so rigorously, not even her Shakespeare. She spent hours copying these same underscored passages into her notebooks, but they never spoke about it now, to avoid arguments. It was unaccountable that this book and its scatter-brained ideas had come between them. In matters of intellectual taste, they had almost always agreed on everything, but on this they were as polarized as cat and dog. Passionately she defended the author of *Cosmic Anatomy*, and he with equal fire scorned and refuted. His own vehemence actually surprised him. He might have just grumbled and let her be, but no, he found himself preaching and condemning with unwarranted violence, which only made Katherine furious, causing her to retreat into a world of her own.

She had been in touch with Orage again. He had seen the letters coming and going between the two of them. Doubtless she looked to Orage as a spiritual master who might explain the gibberish in that book. He had heard that Orage had gotten mixed up with an odd Russian fellow who had escaped from the Bolshevik revolution and was lecturing in London about a mind system, whatever *that* was. Katherine would surely be keen to hear his reports.

"Boogles," Katherine called from the adjoining room.

"I am just going out now before the shops close," he called.

"Boogles, come here," she commanded in her petulant, half-voice.

As he stepped into the darkened room, she reached out a thin, pale arm from the bed. Her frailty wrenched his heart. The treatments had a strange effect on her skin, making her veins show through with startling clarity. Her lovely child-like hands had become yellow and shrunken.

" I confess I am hungry." She smiled up at him with feverish eyes.

"Will it be foie gras or camembert?"

"Both, and *jambon* too, and a little pot of plum jam, if you will. I am starving today. That must be a good sign."

She tried to sit up, gave a groan, and sank back down on the pillows.

"I am so full of magical blue rays, I can hardly lift my head."

"Don't try then. Just hang on till I come back with the food."

"My noble hunter."

He turned away almost in tears.

She reached up and tugged the corner of his jacket.

"You don't mind, do you, Jack?"

He knew what she meant, but brushed it aside. Bells pealed out the window overwhelming their voices. "I must dash now... otherwise I shall find everything closed."

"Lock the door of course, I'd hate for anyone to come in here and see me in this state. And please leave me a glass of water within reach. I am sure I shall want it the moment you have gone out."

He went to the dresser, poured a glass from a carafe and brought it to the bedside table.

"Now go!" she laughed gaily, "and bag us that bacon!"

Turning the key in the lock, he heard her cough, a long sputtering then lacerating sound, followed by a round of wheezing.

He ran off down the stairs and into the bright street.

. . .

Katherine stood by the open carriage window, looking out over the hatted heads of the crowd, seeking Murry in the fray. The station had been invaded by a mob of young athletes from Provence on their way to a tournament. An army of scrubbed, pink faces and chubby legs in red knee stockings tumbled down the platforms, their blue caps and banners blotting out nine-tenths of the view. She twisted the pearl ring round and round on her slender finger, then glanced at the little traveling clock set on the ledge under the window of their compartment. Only three minutes left before departure. She scanned the crowd again.

That was so like Murry to leave her in the lurch like this. He had insisted on going off at the last minute to change some more money, when he could perfectly well have waited until they got to Geneva, and of course their tickets, and nearly all their cash were tucked into his pocket. What would happen if he missed the train—which seemed very likely—and she had no ticket? One minute, now, the carriage attendants were slamming the doors all along the train. Stragglers on the platform were urged aboard by conductors in gray uniforms.

A conductor passed beneath her window. Katherine leaned out and called to him.

"*S'il vous plaît... Je vous en prie.* My husband has been delayed. Can you please hold the train a minute more? Only one minute."

The conductor glanced up, frowned, shook his head. His moustache twitched in irritation. "*Mais c'est impossible, Madame...*"

"Please—only a minute," she entreated, then suddenly spotting Murry running down the platform, she shouted, "*Le voilà,*" but her voice was drowned out by the whistle of the train.

Murry bounded towards the train, his long legs scissoring the air in great leaps. He waved at Katherine and bellowed, "*Attendez,*" and nearly knocked a man down as he dived towards the carriage. The train conductor stared; the whole teeming station seemed to stop for a moment to admire the athletic if unpunctual arrival of the Englishman with his raincoat tails flapping. Then the conductor shouted to the stationmaster who waved a flag at the locomotive, and

194

the train in fact did not move, but only issued a long hiss of steam and seemed to fall back upon its haunches.

"Hurry!" Katherine tried to shout but it came out like a squawk. Her heart was pounding.

Murry jumped aboard. The whistle gave a second shriek and the door banged behind him. As the train shunted forward, he stumbled down the corridor to their compartment where Katherine, the sole occupant, sat with calculated composure by the window with a book in her hands, pretending to read.

Chest heaving, sweating profusely, Murry dropped to the seat across from her, took out a handkerchief, mopped his brow and smiled apologetically. "That was lucky." He looked around approvingly at the empty compartment. "Nice to have all this to ourselves, although I expect the train will fill up soon enough."

With studied slowness, Katherine marked her place in the book with a blue ribbon, closed it, caressed the cover with a shriveled hand, and lay the book on the seat beside her. She raised her eyes to his in a steady, probing gaze, as a tinge of scarlet brightened her cheek.

"What would I have done if you had missed the train? Without money or a proper ticket?"

Murry shrugged, "The fact is I didn't miss it."

"But you very nearly did. If I hadn't convinced that conductor to hold the train for you... You cannot imagine how agitated I am...You really mustn't expose me to such stress. It's terribly bad for my heart."

"There was a very long queue to change money, and then I stopped to buy a copy of the *Times* for the journey which I seemed to have lost in the rush." He groped in the pockets of his raincoat, but the newspaper was gone.

"You nearly missed the train for a copy of the *Times*?"

"Let's forget it now, shall we?"

Murry sighed, slipped his wallet from his vest pocket, removed a wad of money and counted it. Katherine leaned back against her seat, drew her traveling rug over her lap, and watched him from beneath lowered eyelids.

He counted the money again, this time aloud and in French, then exclaimed, "Damnation!"

"What is it now?"

"I must have given that cabbie five hundred francs instead of fifty."

Katherine made a grimace and shut her eyes tightly. "I'm tired darling. Wake me when we get to Geneva."

Leaning her head against the window, she felt the rumbling vibration of the train rippling throughout her body as they chugged out of the station. Imagine mistaking a five hundred franc note for a fifty! But it was useless to remonstrate. Murry lost things. His umbrella, his cufflinks, his fountain pen, his copy of the

Times. Shopkeepers cheated him; little boys thumbed their noses at him; hotel servants sneered. Yet he remained eternally winsome, oblivious to criticism or ill-fortune and always astounded to discover his own faults and shortcomings. Women loved him for this very ingenuousness. Perhaps they hoped they might polish this handsome hunk of rock into something more refined. But Murry resisted polishing. He lacked true tact or good manners, and he was completely self-absorbed. But the worst was that he had no consideration whatsoever for her condition. In moments like these, she wondered why she hadn't let Elizabeth just keep him? *Run back to your princess!* She had taunted him and at the time she had meant it. Why did he keep clinging to her, making things so difficult for both of them? Hot tears stung her eyes. She blotted them with her handkerchief and glanced over at Murry.

He had removed his raincoat, and now sat with legs crossed, hunched over a cheap French novel. His tortoiseshell eyeglasses had slipped down his nose, which twitched in an unconscious effort to keep them from sliding off entirely. The effect was so comic, she had to suppress a laugh. He looked just like a large, dignified rabbit in spectacles.

She picked up *Cosmic Anatomy* again, opened to the marked page and was soon engrossed.

Moments later, Murry interrupted her. "Why are you reading that rubbish?"

"I find it very illuminating."

He snorted. "I fail to understand what you see in that nonsense."

"It isn't the only thing about me you fail to understand."

Murry returned to his novel. She put down her book, closed her eyes, drew in a careful breath with no snags or pulls. At least she was leaving Paris on her own two legs, vertical again, if not exactly ambulatory. Manoukhin had been telling the truth when he had said that the violent reaction would be followed by improvement. And so it had, but the disease had not yet been eradicated and he had recommended that she undergo a new treatment in the fall. Before committing herself to that extraordinary physical ordeal and economic blood-letting, she must go to England to see Sorapure again and have her heart examined. He was the only doctor she trusted. He could tell whether there had been any real improvement or not. But she could not go to London until August. Exertion now was out of the question. The next few weeks were to be spent basking in the pure air of Switzerland, recovering from the strain of her recent radiation treatment, and Ida would be there to help soothe her nerves. Indeed, for the next few months, she did not intend to be separated from Ida, unless Ida desired. That question, at least, had been settled. There would be no tearooms or African missions for Ida, for it was clear to all three of them how much Katherine needed her now. Perhaps when she was finally well again, they might arrange things thus: six months with Murry and six with Ida.

SIERRE, HOTEL CHATEAU BELLE VUE

After an early breakfast, Ida stood in front of the mirror above the dresser in her room at the Hotel Chateau Belle Vue in a rare moment of self-scrutiny. She avoided mirrors except when absolutely necessary, for she was never pleased with what she saw in them, but at least today she noted with approval that her cheeks were less chubby. Her whole figure had slimmed down over the last few months. While in Switzerland without Katie, she barely had had the money, time, or inclination for a meal. Later in England she had spent hours on her bicycle combing the streets of Bath in search of a suitable location for a tearoom. All to no avail, thank God. As soon as Katie had beckoned, she had told Susie Suchard the tearoom business scheme was off. Anyway, she had never been able to imagine herself in a frilled apron and starched cap serving tea to strangers, reduced more or less to a servant. Susie Suchard would probably have turned out to be far more exacting a mistress than Katie even at her worst.

So she had given up the tearoom, as she had given up her job at the factory, all her friends there, and even Mr. Gwynne's esteem. She had given up that portion of property that might have awaited her in Rhodesia; she had given up Robert Wilson, no sacrifice, that, admittedly, the idea of a man's hands on her was pure terror. She had defied Jinny's attempt to pack her off to Africa to play housemaid and cook to Catholic nursing sisters and she had withstood all other attacks. Her only place was at Katie's side, wherever that might be: England or Switzerland or France, it made no difference, she would be there beside her.

This time Katie had promised her that she could come back to stay for good in a professional capacity to take care of her and also of Murry, if he wished. But whatever Murry wished or did not wish, it was the same to them. Katie had assured her she could consider her place as permanent. Murry, after all, did not understand Katie, did not love her as devotedly as she did. He was too self-absorbed, too fickle, too flighty. But men were like that. They were not born to be loyal.

She inspected her face critically. Her mother and sister had not aged well. She seemed to be following suit. Her pores seemed large, her skin waxen, with dozens of tiny wrinkles etched around her eyes. She patted and pinched her cheeks to bring a bit of color to her face, ran a comb through her hair, then from her pocket took a small pot of lip rouge and cautiously daubed a bit on her lips. There, that looked brighter! As she was fluffing up the bow on her pink-striped blouse, Katie's bell summoned her with a furious clang. She glanced at her watch. It was already half past nine, and Katie had asked her to come to her room early that morning to help her with some secretarial work. She hurried towards Katie's room where she found Katie wrapped in a voluminous afghan, sitting by the window with a pile of papers in her lap and a pair of Jinny's cast-off spectacles perched at the end of her nose.

Katie looked up from her papers. "What *have* you done to your mouth?"

"It's lip rouge, Katie."

"You haven't spent our precious money on such things, I hope?" She shuffled her papers about and peered suspiciously at Ida through her spectacles which enlarged her eyes in a startling way.

"Why no, Katie. I found a half-empty jar in your drawer in Hampstead, and thought you wouldn't mind if I kept it, instead of giving it to Violet."

Katie shook her head "No, of course I don't *mind*, but it doesn't suit you."

"Doesn't it?" she quavered.

"Not one bit."

Obediently, Ida took a handkerchief from her pocket and began to wipe off the rouge, staining her handkerchief bright red. Katie winced to see it.

"Not now," she said, "Do that later with cotton wool and cold cream. For the moment, we have work to do." She pointed to the desk where paper, pen, and blotter were ready. "I shall dictate, you shall write."

Ida was puzzled; usually Katie handled all her correspondence by herself. She wrote every letter personally by hand. Ida's main secretarial job was copying Katie's manuscripts with a typewriter and sealing them in envelopes for Katie's agent, Pinker. She rather dreaded having to write letters for Katie. She always seemed to make a mess with the ink, and her lines always ended up crooked. But Katie demanded her assistance, so she must make the effort. She picked up the pen, dipped it in the ink, and waited, pen poised.

Katherine took a deep, troubled breath, and began

"*I, Katherine Mansfield....* No, sorry, *I Kathleen Mansfield Beauchamp Murry being sound of mind and body*—mind, anyway, no—don't write that, —*on this day August 14, 1922 do intend this as my last will and testament.*"

A chill flickered across Ida's scalp. She put down her pen and raised her anxious eyes to Katie's impassive face, but Katie would not meet her gaze.

Katie continued, consulting notes written on a scrap of paper. "*I leave all manuscripts, letters, notebooks, and papers to my husband John Middleton Murry. It is my wish that he should publish only those finished writings he feels are worthy...* Jones," she broke off sternly, "pick up that pen!"

Ida bowed her head as a tear streamed down her cheek and plopped onto the page smudging the ink. "Katie, I can't....."

"Jones," she said softly, rising from the chair and approaching Ida. She lay her hand on Ida's shoulder. "You're the only one who can help me now. Please."

Ida wiped her tears with her spotted handkerchief, nodded, and gravely picked up the pen.

Katie continued, "*To Ida Constance Baker, I leave my gold watch...* Would you also like my Bible? The one with all the family marriages and deaths and births recorded in it?"

Ida imagined the Bible laying on her bedside table, with a ribbon marking the section of births and deaths wherein Katherine's own dates would be inscribed.

"Oh Katie, I couldn't...."

"Very well then," she said making a note, I'll leave it to Father. I also thought he would like my little brass pig. What do you think? Can't you just see it on his desk at the bank?"

She pictured Katie's brass pig on Mr. Beauchamp's marble-topped desk in the Bank of New Zealand, with the bank vault behind it holding thousands and thousands of pounds, and the image seemed to her so ludicrous, she gave an involuntary giggle, which, horrified, she tried unsuccessfully to stifle with a snort. Katie stared at her, astonished, then broke out laughing herself until she had a coughing fit, spitting up a bright blob of blood again on her handkerchief and Ida had to rush off to the kitchen for a bottle of mineral water.

After downing two full glasses, Katie collapsed exhausted into bed. Her eyes met Ida's and a long look of exasperation passed between them. Ida could not speak the words that weighed so heavily on her heart. *I would do anything, anything to make you well again...*

Katie sat up again, recomposed her face, and continued. "*To Anne Estelle Rice, I leave my embroidered Spanish shawl, to Samuel Koteliansky my walking stick, to Mrs. Middleton Murry, mother of John Middleton Murry, my fur coat* —it would never fit you Ida, you are too big in the shoulders, *to Richard Murry my pearl ring; I'd like his bride to wear it when he marries, and to the following people, I leave a book from my personal library to be chosen by John Middleton Murry: Doctor Sorapure, D. H. Lawrence, Walter de la Mare.*

Signed, KMM. There that's all, Jones. Have I left anything out? Are there any of my possessions you would like to have?"

Ida shook her head. She wanted nothing for herself. "But haven't you forgotten Lady Ottoline and Mrs. Woolf?"

Katie frowned. "No, I haven't forgotten. I lay awake half the night wondering about them, thinking about the last time I saw Virginia. Were they really my friends? I believed it so. But Virginia has not written for months. No. If you like, Ida, *afterwards...*" here she paused and Ida flinched and clenched her jaw when the meaning of that word sank in, "you may distribute a few mementos if you think it fit. Books perhaps if Jack doesn't want them. Now, please, read me what you have written."

Before lunchtime, three copies were prepared, signed and dated. Each was placed in a separate envelope and sealed with red wax. Ida held the dripping candle and Katie pressed her sealing ring with its Celtic knot into the soft wax. One copy was to be sent to Katie's solicitor in London, another was for Ida to keep, a third would be kept in among her papers.

"Promise me, Ida.... you won't say a word to Jack, until, the time comes... and then it will be up to you to make sure he obeys my last wishes...about my papers, I mean."

Ida nodded and turned away so Katie would not see her tears.

LONDON

Katherine looked out at the streets she knew so well as the taxi sped her towards Hampstead. It was odd to have no place of her own in London, to be a stranger here, dispossessed, with her books and clothes deposited in crates and boxes scattered from Cornwall to Sierre. Pieces of herself kept falling off the wagon as her life was pared down to the essentials. The only things she had brought with her on this trip were contained in her little scarred leather valise with brass nameplate, which at least had the advantage of weighing less than her beloved carpetbag. As she had no place to stay, Brett had offered her two rooms in her house in Pond Street, where she need not worry about too many stairs, while Murry had found lodgings with bachelor friends just down the street. Ida had gone to visit old friends in Chiswick for a few days.

When the taxi pulled up outside the gate to the little garden in Pond Street, she saw Brett standing in the doorway, still wearing her painter's smock of coarse blue stuff. Even at this distance, it brought out the startling cornflower color of Brett's eyes. As Katherine struggled out of the taxi, Brett ran down to the gate, flung it open, and nearly crushed her in a joyful embrace faintly perfumed with oil paint and turpentine.

She let herself be enfolded by Brett's eager arms, then stiffened slightly, partly afraid to soil her jacket with paint, still hesitant to resume full intimacy with her, though she had made her peace with Brett after two years' secret resentment. Yet Brett had once been her closest friend, apart from Ida of course. More than a sister, Brett was a member of her tribe, and unlike the sophisticated Virginia, Brett had always understood her pixie-ish humor. Katherine still smiled whenever she recalled their first meeting years ago at a party when she had slipped a handful of breadcrumbs into Brett's pocket as an impish overture of friendship.

Brett was still in love with Murry. But this thought no longer anguished Katherine. After Brett there had been other women, most notably, the plumed and boa-ed Betsy B. She had even come to accept the idea that Murry might marry Brett when she was gone. Certainly she would be a most satisfactory wife. It no longer appalled her to imagine Murry in the arms of another woman. Men replaced sick, then dead, wives. That was the way of the world, the world to which she felt her connection unraveling all the more she tried to cling. Since

Manoukhin's treatment had reduced her to this current state of fatigue, there was only the Now, and the Now brought with it a daunting string of challenges, descending from this taxi to the curb, maneuvering the garden path with its slippery pebbles, attacking a flight of steps.

She had spoken of this constant feeling of exhaustion, this sensation of ebbing strength in her arms and legs, as if the sap were being drained out of her, with Sorapure that very morning, for she had hurried to his surgery the moment she was back in London. He had allayed her fears by telling her that this disturbing sensation depended on the heat and on the prolonged stress of her stay in Paris. He had also reassured her about the condition of her heart, which he believed had not been weakened by Manoukhin's treatment. It was still ticking as reliably as ever. But Sorapure had questioned the efficacy of the treatment itself. Both lungs, in his view, were still seriously affected, and she confessed to him that after her initial improvement upon leaving Paris she had fallen ill again with pleurisy and fever in July while in Switzerland. She had begun to fear that Manoukhin was really an impostor after all, like so many of the other doctors she had seen in recent years. Still, she had promised herself she must wait until concluding her second cycle in October before passing judgment on the Russian doctor and his miracle machine, even though the thought of renewing his torture in the autumn was almost overwhelming. Nonetheless, Sorapure agreed it was worth continuing for another cycle, just to give it one last chance, if she thought she could stand it. There were no alternatives at this point, he had underlined, but retreat to a sanatorium.

Brett showed her to her rooms on the first floor, brought her a tray with tea and cucumber sandwiches, then left her to rest. Katherine lay down on the settee and fell asleep at once. Around five o'clock, she woke feeling refreshed. The house was cool and still. Afternoon shadows of foliage danced on the wall beside the settee. Brett had gone out. Murry would not reappear till dinner time. He had gone to the Café Royale to dig up his old cronies for a late lunch. She wondered if Brett had gone to the restaurant to join him. Ida was not expected back from Chiswick until the end of the week. Katherine was free to spend the rest of the day as she wished.

She managed to make herself a cup of tea on the gas ring, and sat sipping it by the window looking out on the garden where great puffs of pink and blue hydrangeas floated above a thick green hedge, dappled in the afternoon sun. She felt well enough to go out again and thought at first that she should take a walk through the neighborhood. She could manage fairly well on paved, flat stretches. The Elephant was not far, and though it had been leased to strangers, she had kept the front door key as a souvenir, or perhaps, as a talisman against homelessness. She was curious to know if the gladiolas she had planted with Ida two years ago had come up and bloomed again. But as she was slipping on her jacket, suddenly the prospect of seeing the place saddened her beyond measure. She must make an effort to give up the past. There was only one person she really wanted to see in London: Dick Orage and she decided to go and see him at once in his office off Cursitor Street.

On that August afternoon, no one was about the building but the char had just been there. A pungent smell of ammonia still lingered on the stairs as Katherine came in from the street, an odor mixed with the rank smell of tobacco that heavily pervaded the atmosphere wherever Orage prowled and with the tang of fresh printers' ink. Stacks of the latest issue of the *New Age* stood in the corridor, just off the press, waiting to be distributed. Stepping into the office, she saw that the secretary was absent so she walked straight in through the anteroom towards Orage's cubicle.

Through the open door, she saw him in profile, sitting at his roll-top desk piled high with papers, hunched over a manuscript, lips pursed, a blue pencil tucked behind his ear, shirt sleeves rolled up on his powerful forearms. A jacket hung on a nail on the wall beside him.

Hearing her light footsteps in the corridor, he looked up and a slow smile illuminated his face. His gaze seemed to hold her eyes threaded to his for a long moment.

Rising, he opened his arms to greet her as she stepped into the tiny book-lined room. She embraced him warmly, then dropped into an armchair near his desk, breathless again from just this one flight of stairs. She smiled apologetically, one hand on her heaving chest, and avoided his eyes as he examined her with concern. "It's nothing," she murmured, dosing her breath in small wisps, "just a bit of overexertion." She leaned back in the warm, worn leather chair and contemplated the objects on his desk: a typewriter, a half-empty bottle of whiskey, and a small ivory sculpture of a many-armed Hindu deity. Her eyes scanned the row of reference books on the shelf above his desk: The Oxford Dictionary, the Complete Works of Shakespeare, and the Bhagavad-gita, a Sanskrit dictionary. A hand-painted tarot card of the devil, whose face quite resembled Orage's own, brought a smile to her lips. The room was full of unemptied ashtrays. Yellowed cartoons papered the walls. Some she remembered seeing tacked up there years ago. In fact, nothing much had changed since she had last sat here, over twelve years ago, while he went over her stories with her, sounding out each sentence aloud as his blue pencil dipped down to strike out a word. It was he who had taught her how to write; but how far she had come since then.

Her breath regained, she smiled slyly and let her eyes travel across Orage's broad, ruddy face, where she detected a glint of something new. Though the office of the *New Age* seemed unchanged, Alfred Richard Orage was not the same man she remembered from twelve years earlier. Despite the graying tuft of hair, thinner now, combed low across a forehead finely hatched with wrinkles, he seemed somehow younger and more vigorous, charged with a charisma that almost tingled on her skin. Life had been treating him well. He looked like a man in love—or perhaps, like a man who has just won a thousand pounds at poker.

The old ease and intimacy she had always felt with him settled over her at once, and she found herself pouring out a vehemence of words, as though resuming an impassioned conversation interrupted only minutes before.

"I had a breakdown in Switzerland this time—Jack—well—it can't go on much longer. He needs a healthy woman and not an invalid. It is bitter sometimes to see how blind he is to my needs. Yet, I know he has his own although I did not understand till recently the depth of his need. There seems to be no solution to it. We have become like starved, selfish, resentful ghosts of ourselves."

Orage listened from behind closed lids and assented with a curt nod. She wondered if he were thinking of Beatrice's brutal desertion, of which she had heard various reports. Then in a peculiar voice that brought a shiver to her spine, he said, "Dwellers in Plato's cave."

This reference to Plato puzzled her and she fell silent. Orage opened his eyes and shot her through with a canny look. "It's not just Jack," she said, in response to his unspoken query, "It's everything. I haven't written a word since before the X-ray treatment. The flow has simply stopped. And when I go back and read the things I have written, I feel such a sense of futility. There is not one single story I would dare show to God. I have been a camera, nothing more, recording what I observe. But I could do more, much more. I have come to view my work as a river seeping through a marshland, dissipating in countless rivulets over a dark bog. I have tried so hard to put the full force of my being behind it, but the result is only a trickle. Writing must have purpose, but even that is not enough and yet I feel," here she paused, hesitant to go on, fearing she might sound too presumptuous or sanctimonious, but it was what she felt most deeply. She lowered her voice slightly, "I feel that writing might be an initiation into truth."

A long pause ensued, longer than comfort might allow. Then Orage rapped his pencil down on the desk and asked sharply, "What truth?" jarring her train of thought. "Which of many? Can you presume to know what truth is?"

She looked up startled into his stern eyes which seemed to emit a reddish light. She knew that look which flared in his eyes whenever the fervor of a new idea had seized him. She drew in her breath, shook her head with a timid half-smile. He had thrown down a challenge and she must take it up to see where he would lead her. "I have been thinking a lot about that book you sent me, *Cosmic Anatomy*—"

Again he interrupted brusquely, rudely she thought, certainly with impatience.

"Yes, that's a start, but only a herald, only the beginning—" He cut himself short and stared hard at her. "Perhaps to become a better writer, one must have a more complete knowledge of oneself, to have observed, scrutinized oneself in every nook and cranny of body, mind, and soul and to have understood what one has seen."

To Murry this remark might have seemed a platitude, but it struck Katherine with the power of revelation. Nodding, she waited for him to continue, her mind open, ready to consider.

He eyed her as though weighing her, as though trying to determine if she could be trusted with a secret.

"Generally we pursue the solutions to our problems through psychology, medicine, religion, and prayer at times. But these often fail for each one of these approaches addresses only one part of our self, one set of functions, and not the whole, complex man or woman."

Katherine pondered this statement and nodded again. She had the same reservations regarding the vogue for psychoanalysis. It did not really help one live better she thought. Lawrence himself was the proof of that.

"But in the Ancient World, from which Plato drew his knowledge, there existed a true psychology, or study of the psyche in a more complete form, transmitted orally through special schools, from time immemorial. Yet with Aristotle it was required to go underground, though it has been preserved in varied forms throughout the world in monasteries, ashrams, by secret religious orders, even by schools of arts and artisans. All great myths bear reference to it, all great religious texts speak of it in code. In western civilization it has been known only to a few—to the builders of the cathedrals, to the alchemists of the middle ages, to others we hardly know or guess, who have preserved this secret science of being intact until the present day."

The ardor in his voice made her heart race. His enthusiasm for ideas was always infectious, but there was something more than enthusiasm here. His passion ran deeper, rang truer.

"Sometimes in moments of great upheaval it comes to the surface and may be had for the asking by ordinary people like ourselves. And it has come to the surface now, in London, thanks to a fellow from St. Petersburg." He stopped abruptly.

Her eyes searched his face. He had always been a persuasive speaker, but the feeling he had instilled in her was not merely the curiosity fired up by an intriguing tale well- told. His words, or his enthusiasm, had awakened a thirst, a thirst of the mind, Quite simply there were things, incommunicable things, she must discover. Was this a key?

"A few of us—Dr. Maurice Nicoll and Dr. James Carruthers Young, disciples of the Swiss psychoanalyst Carl Jung, Dr. Kenneth Walker, a distinguished professor of the Royal College of Surgeons, along with a handful of others, have been attending a series of private lectures by a Russian philosopher, which are being held in a flat made available by Lady Rothermere who has joined our study group. Believe me, the study of these ideas makes all our other previous pursuits" he gestured at the books on his shelves, then at the manuscripts on his cluttered desk, "seem paltry by comparison."

Katherine hesitated a long moment before replying. The lengthening rays of sun cast a patch of yellow light on the floorboards which released a resinous smell of varnish mingled with the odor of musty books and old newspapers. The musty smell and the mellow light seemed to mix with the quality of the moment itself, which was somehow familiar and yet strange to her. There are moments when new things sprout and old things are shed, when doors open or swing shut—when the past or future hangs in the balance of a choice, of a word. This she knew was such a moment. She felt herself hovering before the offering, then she heard herself say distinctly. "I would very much like to hear what he has to say."

Orage scribbled an address on a piece of pasteboard. "Piotyr Damian Ouspensky, 38 Warwick Gardens."

. . .

She knew now that she had instinctively done the right thing in telling no one that she was back in London, which gave her a certain satisfaction as she sped towards her appointment in a taxi. Most of her friends would not approve of what she was about to do. She hadn't said a word to Murry or Brett about where she would be spending her evening. She had dressed soberly for the occasion in a charcoal gray sweater and black wool skirt. A bright orange silk scarf with lozenges of black and gold tucked around her throat provided that glamorous touch of color she never liked to be seen without. Rouged lips heightened her mask-like pallor.

Staring out the window as the taxi sped by Hyde Park, she remembered how much Virginia loved London at twilight. The city was like a young girl dressing for a fête, she always used to say. Once she had shared Virginia's exhilaration for the coming of evening, festive crowds and the lighting of lamps, but now these things aroused in her no enthusiasm. Tonight the street lamps gleamed on the rain-slick pavements. The few people about at that hour seemed to her like half-dazed figures shuffling through an unquiet dream. It came upon her forcibly then, looking out at the dirty London streets, just how much she hated London and how much she hated cities. It had taken fifteen years of bedsitters and unheated hotels with smelly pipes and bad food to convince her of this fact. Lawrence was certainly right about London. It was a sort of underworld peopled by the half-living. Where was Lawrence now? She had heard he was bound for

Australia. But would that help? Of all her friends, he might understand what had prompted her to come here tonight.

The taxi stopped at number 38 Warwick Gardens and she got out. The moment she swung her leg out of the cab and touched her foot to the wet pavement she felt a funny flicker at the base of her spine. Something had ended, something was beginning. Here she was, vertical again, alone on the empty street—a woman on her way to an assignation—with herself.

She felt awkward coming here unaccompanied, but Orage had another engagement that evening. Before entering the building, she glanced furtively left and right, like a thief or an adulteress, but no one was looking. Stepping inside, she was relieved that there were no stairs to climb. She rang the bell to one of the ground floor flats. The door opened and she entered a dingy vestibule with mauve walls and a maroon and gold damask curtain, where she was greeted by a flat-bosomed woman with spectacles, sitting at a desk. The woman pointed to a ledger on the desk, indicating that Katherine should write her name there. She skimmed down the long column of unfamiliar names under the date August 30, 1922 and signed herself in as Mrs. Kathleen Murry. Then she was ushered into a large salon where fifty people were sitting in straight-backed chairs gathered around a blackboard. To the right of the blackboard was a small table and chair. On the table stood a carafe of water, a glass, and a vase with artificial flowers which looked peculiarly stark and forlorn in that setting. The speaker had not yet arrived. There were only a few empty seats left. Katherine now made her way toward the closest one and took her place behind a plump woman in blue taffeta wearing a wide-brimmed hat, which seemed completely wrong for the occasion, and partially obstructed Katherine's view. There was a smell of carpets and chalk dust that stuck in her throat

There was also, she noted, as she slipped into her seat, an extraordinary silence. Not that faint buzzing murmur one usually hears at polite gatherings of distinguished persons. No one whispered, coughed, or rummaged in their handbag. Nor did anyone take any notice of her. One woman turned her head and raised her eyebrows, but that was all. Katherine did not recognize her, and she was unsure if the raised brows were meant for her or for the hat of the woman sitting in front of her. She recognized no one. She had hoped to see Lady Rothermere, Tom Eliot's patroness, but she was not among the guests.

A tall man in a black suit strode into the room and she knew immediately it must be Ouspensky. His face interested her at once: sculpted Slavic cheekbones set high in a feline face with a very broad forehead. His gray hair was shorn close to his scalp, a pince-nez fastened to his prominent nose. There was something soldierly about him and also something monkish. He would have looked equally distinguished in a cavalry officer's uniform or in a priest's swishing cassock. The light glared on his glasses so she could not see his eyes at first. He sat down at the table facing the audience and took a small piece of paper out of his pocket and held it up a few inches from his nose. During those five long minutes before he began to speak, the silence in the room grew even more compact and palpable, keen with expectation. Its invisible substance bore her up, kept her afloat. Then, with no preamble or clearing of his throat, Ouspensky began to speak.

The sounds he produced made no sense to her at first, for his accent was so thick she could not tell if she were hearing English or Russian or something else entirely. It struck her as strange talk. Murry, probably would have been appalled. She had to make an unfamiliar effort to follow his speech, then slowly his words sank into her consciousness where they echoed and burned. "*Your name is legion,*" Ouspensky was saying, "You are not one self but a hundred thousand selves, each one claiming to be I. Until the real I awakens, you are nothing but machines." Katherine found herself nodding in recognition. *Not one but legion*— Hadn't she felt that so often, put in different words, perhaps. "*Alone, you can do nothing,*" Ouspensky went on, "*To escape from prison, you must have help from someone outside the prison, from someone who knows how.*"

She listened and pondered. Ouspensky paused now and then to take a sip of water or consult his notes. Unperturbed, unhurried, impersonal—he reminded her of a statue of an Egyptian Pharaoh she had once seen at the Louvre. Or perhaps of a Japanese Buddha. He fascinated her in a unique way for it was not a physical attraction, though she felt drawn to him strongly. It was not merely an intellectual attraction, for it galvanized her being.

During the lecture, he drew a diagram on the blackboard: a diagram with suns and musical notes, The Law of Three, the Law of Seven. She reached into her handbag for the little notebook and pencil she always kept handy so she might copy the diagram, but the pencil slipped from her hand and dropped to the floor, making a discreet rattle as it rolled out of reach across the floorboards.

Ouspensky stopped speaking and stared in her direction. She saw his eyes then, mild gray with glints of steel, and although she supposed he was too nearsighted to make her out distinctly, she blushed crimson to the roots of her hair.

"It is not allowed to take notes," he said.

"I didn't know, I am sorry—" she began but the severity in his gaze stopped her from continuing. Any further explanation seemed out of place here. No one moved in the room, no one even turned in her direction. Ouspensky kept staring at her, then, to her astonishment, his lips twisted into a very faint but conciliatory half-smile. "Now you know," he said, "the taste of inner considering." He turned to the blackboard and began to discuss the diagram, but she understood nothing of his explanation, indeed she hardly heard his words. Inside she was roiling... why was she victim of such gratuitous attacks of embarrassment or anger? And what did that mean, "*the taste of inner considering*"?

When the lecture was over, no one greeted her. The group dissolved as unobtrusively as a cabal. The room emptied; the lights were put out; the door was pulled to; the flat-bosomed woman in spectacles vanished up the stairs; and Katherine found herself out on the deserted street where a taxi materialized almost at once.

In the fortnight that followed, she attended Ouspensky's other lectures, arriving early to get a better seat closer to the blackboard, though it was torture for her to sit over an hour on those chairs—four sticks and a plank that numbed her derrière—while trying to keep from coughing. The diagrams still made little sense to her, but as the days passed, the ideas she had heard had assembled in her mind into a fragmented pattern. They seemed to possess the ring of truth. For her *now*, at this time in her life. Not for Murry perhaps, she thought sadly; certainly not for Ida. And not for Virginia, or Lawrence, or even Koteliansky who were the three people with whom she felt the strongest intellectual affinity. All these years she had been *asleep*. She had merely followed the mechanical dictates of conditioning, of false dreams and false desires. Yet a deeper self lay imprisoned within, and now the time had come for it to awaken.

Orage told her that Ouspensky was the spokesman for another man—more mysterious, more difficult of access, who had brought these ideas to the West and had just opened an Institute in Paris. Here was her opportunity to make a clean sweep of things. She could return to Paris on pretext of continuing her treatments with Manoukhin—and in the meantime try to see if she could be admitted to this institute. But to obtain an invitation, she must speak to Ouspensky personally, and Orage arranged a meeting on the last day of September.

. . .

5a Gwendwr Road was situated in a genteel Victorian neighborhood in Kensington where the houses all had bay-windows and tidy little gardens with floppy pink petunias. She rang at a door with a stained glass panel and a solemn-looking young man answered and silently accompanied her to a study where Ouspensky sat at a mahogany desk, leaning low over a map, examining it with a magnifying glass. The desk was strewn with manuscripts, books, maps, photographs, a camera, a small telescope, compasses, other scientific instruments whose function and purpose were unknown to her. This assemblage of paraphernalia seemed to suggest the fervor of many intellectual pursuits all being carried out at once in preparation for a long journey. A cat snoozed on the windowsill in a patch of sunlight, perfectly at home, next to a window box where fat daisies grew alongside an herb that looked like chervil. Two chairs arranged upon a small red Bokhara carpet sat facing each other by the window. On a low table nearby were a few shot glasses, a tray of dill pickles and a bottle of vodka. Ouspensky rose from his desk to greet her, indicated the two chairs, then sat down across from her. The cat alighted on his lap, and he gently shooed it away.

As he sat waiting for her to speak, she found herself drawn up into a spacious silence for a long moment before words came.

"For some time now, I have felt like the survivor of a shipwreck. The ship is lost, and there will never be a return to the pleasant life of before. I want to make use of what little time is left to me. In these ideas I have found hope, but hope for what I do not know. I want to connect to the source."

There that was it, most decidedly, that was what she had come to say. She looked up at him and waited. His face impassive, he did not speak. His steely eyes were fixed on her with a peculiar intensity. She faltered now. Perhaps this was not the right thing to say. Perhaps she should embellish her words somehow, and yet she could not. An abyss had yawned. Her facility with words had abandoned her. She stood, as it were, on the edge of a void. If he does not reply, she thought, I shall just get up from this chair and leave the room.

But he did not reply, nor did she stir. She sat in the silence, and with uncustomary calm, turned her attention upon the words she had spoken and then upon the need from which those words had arisen. Yes, she could not, must not add anything more. All she might do was make a clearer, more direct request.

"I am about to leave for Paris to undergo medical treatment there. Can you put me in contact with someone there who shares my ideas?"

A silence passed again as she waited for his reply, but this time her anxiety had lessened. One moment? Ten minutes? She felt inundated by a clarity of mind so natural and luminous she wondered why she did not always dwell in this state.

He spoke now, "Do you know what it means to possess true individuality?"

Katherine shook her head and looked down at her feet in her black shoes upon the Bokhara rug. Her feeling of clarity seemed to be draining away and she had to make an effort to cling to it just a little longer. She raised her eyes to his face again.

"It means possessing consciousness of will. Being conscious that you *do* have a will and that you *can* act," he continued.

Something snapped, time resumed its normal pace. The cat rubbed against her ankles and purred. The tang of dill tingled in her nostrils. Ouspensky rose and went to his desk, scribbled something on a piece of paper, and handed it to her.

"*Institute for the Harmonious Development of Man, Fontainebleau.*"

"Orage will give you further instructions," he said, and led her to the door.

PARIS, OCTOBER 1922

Paris was soon behind them. Katherine sat very still and withdrawn, her eyes fixed on the window as the train rattled past the shabby little houses of the banlieu with their gray cabbage plots brightened here and there by yellow bursts of chrysanthemums, then on across charred fields where peasants were burning off the wheat stubble. In the distance up ahead lay the forest of Fontainebleau, a dark streak on the horizon.

On the seat beside her lay a pair of dove gray gloves and a wilted bouquet of cyclamen Ida had insisted on buying for her from a beggar girl at the Gare du Lyon. At her feet, her leather valise containing only the essentials for an overnight trip. Her hat box and steamer trunk had been left behind at the Select Hotel for she had been invited to spend only one night in Fontainebleau at G. I.Gurdjieff's Institute for the Harmonious Development of Man. If Mr. Gurdjieff accepted her as a pupil and allowed her to stay, she would send Ida back to Paris early in the morning to fetch her trunk and other belongings. The question was: would he say yes, and would he let her stay for as long as three months? That ought to be enough, she thought, though enough for what exactly, she was not sure.

Ida sat across from her, looking distraught, puzzling over a handful of coins, counting and recounting francs and sous. This journey, like so many others, would have been impossible without her assistance, and Katherine knew she should be grateful, yet Ida's every awkward gesture, every little blunder jarred her nerves. She watched Ida fumbling in her pockets, pulling out more change. The train jolted. A five franc piece tumbled from her hand, rolled across the floor, and slipped, before their eyes, into a niche beneath a seat where it was now quite irretrievable.

"O Katie! Look what I've done! That was just what we needed for our cab fare."

Katherine shrugged and said nothing. Her dependence on Ida was one of those chains from which, she hoped, she would soon be freed.

A ray of sun flashed on the gleaming brass name plate of her valise. Katherine stared at the engraved letters *KMM*, for Katherine Mansfield Murry. That was not the name printed on the passport she carried in the vest pocket of her overcoat, which was her real name, *Kathleen Beauchamp Murry*. But those were only two of a multitude: *Kathleen, Katherine, Kath. Katie. Katya, Yekaterina, Kass, Kissienka, K.M., Tig.* She had a host of names ready for any occasion and each one conjured up a different woman. Lately she had begun to wonder, which, if any, of these characters was the real I? *Your name is legion*, Ouspensky had said. Who was she really? Only a nameless pair of eyes, she often thought, absorbing the world into a pitiless gaze. To this thought she had returned often over the last few weeks: *I have been a camera*, a mere mechanical observer. At times it seemed to her she could even detach herself from her own body, as it jerked and coughed like a mechanical doll, while another eye looked down upon her from above, gilding all with a light from elsewhere. Was that perhaps the inner light of Self which Gurdjieff promised to awaken?

Now the train skirted a dense wood. It was a golden autumn afternoon. The woods were full of people out walking on pathways thickly carpeted with dead leaves. A fellow roaming with two ginger-colored hunting dogs waved at the train as it passed.

When does a journey really begin, thought Katherine, as the man with the dogs met her eyes, then slid away in the window. It was a little like falling in love or running into debt. The beginning is so subtle you may not notice, then suddenly there you are hurtling into the distance on a train. And there's no turning back until you reach the end of the line, until you have gone all the way through with it, burning your bridges if need be, and leaving everything tidy in case you never make it back.

She always did that before a journey, answered every letter, paid every bill, destroyed every useless or embarrassing scrap of paper. Last August, she had gone so far as to make her will, naming Murry executor and leaving her cherished pearl ring to his younger brother; to Ida, her gold watch. She had no other valuables to dispose of. She had accumulated little in thirty-four years: a brass pig, a walking stick, a broken Japanese doll, when she had once dreamed of owning houses, gardens, and an automobile.

This short trip today would somehow be decisive. To think this journey had all begun by opening a book months ago in Switzerland. How bitterly she and Jack had quarreled over *Cosmic Anatomy*, but reading that book had struck a low note of recognition in her, like the sound of a foghorn in the bay, signaling the presence of something portentous moving in the darkness, intoning a warning: *Wake up. Do something. There isn't much time.* And here she was, doing it, whatever it was, whatever it meant. By the time she had stepped through the doors of 38 Warwick Gardens to hear Ouspensky speak, she was already midway to Fontainebleau.

The train lurched as they approached the station. She glanced at the objects surrounding her: the leather valise, the dove gray gloves, the tired cyclamen, the maroon suede shoes on her small feet. She considered herself among these possessions: a woman traveling by train, her bag stuffed with cigarettes, pills for headaches and rheumatism, laundry lists, pencil stubs, notepads, a blood-spotted handkerchief, a rapidly depleting supply of French francs, and a small traveling clock ticking the minutes away.

Now she considered Ida, sitting across from her, peeling an orange and slipping the peels into her pocket for there was nowhere else to put them except under the seat, and offering her an orange segment, which she refused. Dear dull, dreamy Ida, with her red nose and dumpy bosom, her chubby calves and puzzled eyes. Once so lovely with blond hair hanging to her waist like a hank of silk. Ida her jailer, her slave, her shame, and yes, Ida, her sole relief. Katherine could hardly bear to look at her at times, overcome by disgust with herself at crushing Ida so completely; disgust, too, at Ida's willing submission. Fury at her own need for Ida's coddling and care. That dreadful winter in Ospedaletti, she had positively hated Ida for doing what Murry refused to do or never even thought of doing. Yet, she could never have written ten words over the last four years if Ida had not been there to make the tea, boil the eggs, rush back and forth with hot water bottles, however tepid, and keep her supplied with stamps and milk and bread, while she lay wrapped in blankets on the sofa or on a chaise-longue, scribbling in her notebook. None of her recent work, which she judged to be her best, could ever have been completed without Ida's help, and she knew that Ida understood this. It was Ida's secret triumph, her reward. Through it all, Ida had been the perfect friend.

Where would she be today without Ida? She could not climb stairs unassisted, and there were days when she could not walk at all. Strangers thrust chairs at her when she stepped breathless into a shop. Old women offered her their arms on street corners. It was appalling to be so ill, to be so dependent.

She often wondered what her relationship with Ida would have been like had she not fallen ill. Might they have had a cooler, more civil friendship conducted at a distance? Would Ida have married Robert Wilson, returning to Rhodesia to have a brood of children? Would she and Murry have played doting aunt and uncle to Ida's gangly sunburnt bairns? Impossible to imagine, though it was a great loss that neither one of them had experienced motherhood.

No one, not even Murry, understood their special friendship. It secretly amused and pleased her that no one seemed to see that Ida's devotion was by no means one-sided. They were like an old married couple, perfectly matched in their defects and idiosyncrasies, bound fast by habit, but also by a tough affection that nothing could erode. Ida was more than nurse, secretary, wife. In some very peculiar way, Ida *was* Katherine herself just as she *was* Ida. That was the miracle. But how would Ida adapt now the time had come for her to turn away?

. . .

Ida fidgeted on the seat across from Katie who had hardly said a word to her throughout the whole journey from Paris. The penny pattern book she had brought along with her lay abandoned on the seat beside her. She wanted to show Katie some new blouse patterns for the lengths of cambric she had bought, something to go with Katie's new tartan skirt, but she could see that Katie was in one of her moods and knew well enough not to disturb her.

As the train pulled into the station, Ida's heart gave a leap. She wanted to clutch Katie's hand, but instead she seized Katie's gloves and said, "Katie, look, we're here. Let's not forget these again."

The corner of Katie's mouth twitched, but she said nothing and took the gloves. As she put them on, Ida watched the pearl ring slide loosely round Katie's slim ring finger, and was terrified it might slip off and fall to floor, meeting the same fate as their five-franc piece, but the glove slid snugly over the ring without incident. Sticking the flowers into the breast pocket of Katie's overcoat, she straightened Katie's collar and smiled with approval. "It's just the touch you needed." Then Ida gathered up her own handbag and pattern book, reached down for Katie's valise and led the way to the exit where the stationmaster helped them down to the platform.

Dr. James Young from Gurdjieff's school was waiting at the station as they expected. Although the three of them had only met a few evenings ago in Paris, when he had come, at Orage's behest, to see Katherine at the hotel, he and Katie now behaved like long lost friends, making a fond show of greeting. He was a pleasant young man, tall, boyishly handsome with a penchant for tweed, a bit like Murry in that way, which Ida supposed was one reason Katie found him so charming. There were no taxis to meet the afternoon train, only a horse-drawn cab. Dr. Young helped them climb aboard, then hopped up beside the driver.

As the horse snorted with exertion, its breath plumed before them in the frosty air. Ida's skin tingled in the cold. She frowned as she watched Katie pull her coat closer around her throat and try to stifle a cough. Katie's face was flushed, her eyes shone with fever and excitement. As they jostled along, Dr. Young chatted to Katie about life at the "Institute" as he called it. It was still not very clear to Ida what sort of place it was and why Katie was so determined to be accepted as a pupil there. Murry had called it an institute of mental rehabilitation. Why did Katie wish to be mentally rehabilitated? But Ida knew better than try to dissuade Katie once she had set her mind to something. One could only comply or be left miles behind. She braced herself against the back of the seat and held on to the sides as the cab bumped across the railroad bridge and jogged down a country lane. A small wooden arrow painted white read *Valvins* and *Avon*. They passed under a dense canopy of tawny chestnut leaves. Saws wheezed in a nearby timber yard. The air was laden with the pungent sweetness of sawdust, wood smoke, and dead leaves. Then on the edge of a thick wood, the cab stopped beside an iron gate.

Dr. Young helped them down. While he paid the cabbie, Katie went to the gate and looked in, gripping the iron bars. There was a porter's lodge on the other side where a sign read "*Sonnez Fort.*" Ida peered in through the gate at an old monastery set back in among the trees, beyond a stretch of unkempt lawn.

She could make out seven windows set deep beneath a slated roof and a row of crooked chimneys. It reminded her of a witch's house in a storybook. She did not want Katie to stay here even one night. She had to bite her tongue to keep herself from blurting out, "Well, Katie, now that we've seen the place, why don't we look for a little café and have nice hot cup of tea and a pastry?" But it was too late for Dr. Young had vigorously rung the bell, and a swarthy gentleman with high cheekbones, wearing a gray overcoat came striding across the yard to greet them at the gate. As it creaked open, Ida surveyed the long pebbled pathway riddled with puddles and covered with leaves, leading to the entrance of the building. How would Katie ever make it? But to her surprise, Katie was doing very well, leaning on Dr. Young's arm as the swarthy gentleman led the way.

Ida hung behind. The path was wet in spots and globs of mud clung to the crepe soles of her sturdy brown shoes. She glanced anxiously at Katherine's feet, but Katie's suede pumps barely left an impress on the soft, damp leaves strewn along the way.

The garden had gone wild. Clumps of red begonias were overgrown with creepers, the big tiled fountain was drained dry, and a thick green scum grew along the rim.

"Looks like you could do with a good gardener," said Ida.

"Mr. Gurdjieff just purchased the property in July. We haven't had time to tackle the gardens yet, but we shall soon ," said Dr. Young. "We're doing the work all ourselves, you know, all the painting and mending and plumbing and wiring."

"It must be handy to know how to do all those things. I'd certainly like to learn," Ida offered.

Katie shot her a monitory glance. They had discussed Ida's staying here too, but Katie was adamant. She intended to come here alone.

Ida stared at the man in the gray overcoat sauntering before them across the lawn. His coat hem was unstitched on one side and hung slightly askew. Could this be the mysterious Russian that Murry had warned Katie to stay away from? But no, as they walked towards the entrance, she heard him say to Katie, "Monsieur Gurdjieff is away at the moment. He will receive you this evening upon his return."

A red leaf sailed down from a branch, landing at Ida's feet. She retrieved it and studied it closely. Crimson with brownish stains, the branched veins blood red. What did it make her think of? The lines in a hand? A road map of France? She was about to show it to Katie and ask what it reminded her of, but then suddenly she knew. The red leaf reminded her of a piece of chicken lung scraped out of a chicken's carcass. She put the leaf in her pocket. It was an omen, but of what she was not sure.

Once inside, Katie crept up the stairway, gripping the worn wooden banister, pausing several times to catch her breath while Dr. Young hovered at her side, frowning with concern. Ida noticed the musty drapes, the moth-flecked animal skins hanging on the walls, the dark 18th century still-lifes of bronze fruit and dead, swooning poultry in heavy gilt frames badly in need of dusting. She resisted the temptation to run her finger along a dust-furred windowsill. Katie, so fastidious, coming to this place?

. . .

Dr. Young vanished down a stairway, leaving them alone with their host who led them to a door along a dark corridor where he stopped and produced a key. Katherine smiled with delight as the door swung open into a stately chamber with pale blue drapes emblazoned with stars. Her eyes took in a double bed, a cheery fire flickering in the hearth behind a brass screen, a marble washstand with pewter pitcher, a dresser with Empire mirror set opposite the window. While he set her valise in a corner, Katherine went to the window and looked out over the front lawn towards the gate. An enormous plane tree with broad yellow leaves fluttering against a bright blue sky partly blocked her view of the horizon. Gazing out at the massive trunk and at the space of sky and grass stretching on before her, she felt her lungs expand in a spasm of joy. She closed her eyes and savored the faint autumn sun on her eyelids, on her chest.

"I expect you'd like to have a rest after your journey," the man was saying. "At four o'clock, I will send a girl up with tea." Now he addressed Ida, "Your room, Madame, is upstairs. Please come with me."

Dismay welled up in Ida's eyes, but Katherine smiled wanly at her, laid her hand on Ida's sleeve and promised to call her when the tea was brought. Ida nodded and followed the man out of Katherine's room.

Katherine sat on the bed and breathed a sigh of relief at finally being alone. She ran her hand across the smooth blue satin quilt. She had not expected such luxurious accommodations. She would have to thank Dr. Young and Monsieur Gurdjieff for this courtesy. The thought that she would soon be face to face with Gurdjieff excited her, but also provoked a quiver of sheer terror.

She knew so little about him, except that he had come out of Russia, like Ouspensky, safe through the turmoil of the Revolution. In his youth, he had journeyed to inaccessible places which to her existed only in fairytales and on old engraved maps: Tibet, Beluchistan, Samarkand. He had brought to the west a philosophy of self-knowledge, a method for bringing oneself into harmony. It included the whole person, not just the head, but the body and emotions as well. A complex cosmological and psychological system lay behind it which Ouspensky had illustrated on the blackboard with his diagrams. Despite their abstractness those diagrams and ideas had echoed something she had long felt in herself, and many of the ideas she heard from Ouspensky were the confirmation of her own musings and discoveries.

For example: *There is no permanent self.* Or rather, what is permanent is buried beneath a dross that must be burned away. She knew something of this burning, now that she was ill. It was a truth she had seized on long ago. Certainly it was nothing new. Keats too had grappled with this absence when he wrote: *A poet has no identity.* He becomes whatever his attention fixes upon: a flower, or stone, or the sun, a child running through a field. He is merely a parade of phantom selves, but beneath this shadowy procession, something else lies dormant, which must awaken. "*Call the world if you please,*" Keats wrote, "*the vale of soul-making.*" And what was the soul if not the real essence of a person, complete and mysterious, impersonal and permanent, untouched by outer circumstance, struggling to force its way up through darkness, to unfold and know itself in the light of the sun? She knew this to be true and even her rheumatic bones vibrated to the sound of it. But it was a truth she could share with no one, except Orage and sometimes with dear Leslie, dead these seven years, with whom she still held long conversations at night before falling asleep.

The others had all tried to keep her from coming here. Her cousin Elizabeth had warned her not to believe in miracles. Murry was disgusted at her new interest in occultism, as he called it, as if he imagined her decked out in a black robe, muttering spells in Gaelic while tossing incense into a brazier and waving a sword through the smoke. Ida was maudlin at being abandoned. Why were they all so blind to her real needs?

She got up and took a few things out of her valise. Her traveling clock. A bottle of Parma violet cologne. A burgundy cashmere shawl with beaded fringe. A copy of Ouspensky's book, *Tertium Organum.* Pen, ink, and a few sheets of paper, but she did not intend to write a word until she had seen Gurdjieff. She had also brought a small photograph of Murry, which she placed on the bedside table. She lay down on the bed and tucked the shawl around her legs. Propping herself up on one elbow, she studied the photograph of her handsome husband.

Just that morning, she had posted a letter to him, telling him that she was coming to Fontainebleau, but not divulging her plan to stay three long months, a prospect that frightened and exhilarated her. For once alone, without Ida. And without Murry, but then she was used to his long absences. They loved each other better in their letters than in the flesh. Yet why did it have to be that way?

It was odd how everything was interwoven, like the strands of a spider web. Touch one strand, and the whole construction vibrates. After writing her last story, *The Fly*, that stank so of bitter truth, she had come to feel that her contact with some vital source had been severed. All her difficulties and sorrows: with Murry, with Ida, with her writing, with herself, derived from that one interrupted contact.

And yet, she sensed this mysterious source of nourishment quite near, all around her. Just out of reach, something abundant and changeless abided, waiting to be awakened, yearning to be embraced. She felt it most intensely when she was writing, in the silence of solitude and concentration. She had felt it many times in Menton while contemplating the sea at dusk. She felt it now, lying in this unfamiliar room in the fading light of afternoon, but it eluded her except for *glimpses*. Orage had understood her perfectly when she had spoken to him of *yearning*, of *glimpses*. The others did not, but then they were not ill. Perhaps it was an inexorable law. *A healthy person cannot understand someone who is ill. A full man cannot understand a hungry one.*

. . .

Ida's room was a narrow nun's cell on the floor above Katie's, furnished with an iron-framed cot shoved against the wall, a writing table with tarnished brass candlestick, a worn blue rug. A fire had been lit for her in the hearth, and the room, though Spartan, seemed clean and cozy enough. As soon as she was alone in the room, she checked under the bed and in all the corners for spiders, but found none. The sheets were fresh and the room had been properly dusted unlike the dim stairway. She had certainly slept in worse rooms while traveling with Katie. And many were the nights years ago she had spent huddled on the doorstep of Katie's flat in Old Church Street, not wanting to disturb her while she was inside with Murry. She took a small bundle out of her handbag containing a toothbrush and comb wrapped in a piece of muslin, for she had brought nothing else for the night, and put it on the table before the window overlooking the grounds to the rear.

Peering through the thick, bubbled pane, she surveyed the tangled shrubs of a formal garden gone wild, an orangery in need of repair, a ragged lawn of unclipped grass, and further on, a thick wood. A clearing had been made in one area of the wood where a huge shed was under construction. It looked like an airplane hangar. She wondered if Mr. Gurdjieff kept an airplane and if he would take Katie flying in it. It was a dreadful thought.

Over twenty people were at work on the grounds, mostly men, but she spotted a few women among them. Some people were digging, others clearing away brambles and debris and piling it in a corner of the yard, still others were hammering away on the roof of the shed. Surely Katie would not be expected to do anything so strenuous.

Although she was not tired, Ida lay down on the bed with her arms crossed on her bosom and stared at a spot on the ceiling, wondering if it were a bug or just a stain. She closed her eyes and was relieved to see upon opening them again that the black spot had not moved. She knew that this room should hold no terrors for her, and yet something mournful hung heavy in the air. It was not the fact of being sent away from Katie's room. She was used to that. It was not just the forlorn feeling of having to go back alone to Paris tomorrow, being separated from her once again for who knows how long. It was something deeper which she could not quite bring herself to peer into. Just a quick glance into that vortex was enough to make her head spin and she had to close her eyes. It was almost like being back on that omnibus in Ospedaletti, skirting the edge of the precipice. But Katie was never afraid to look down; it thrilled her to be poised above those crashing waves.

Too restless to lie still, Ida got up, went to the window, and leaned her forehead against the cold glass. Down in the yard they had set fire to an enormous pile of rubbish from the garden. Leaping flames enveloped the pile; a tall plume of gray smoke curled into the air. She fancied she could feel the roar and crackle of the blaze, the sharp smell of green wood burning. She thought of the funeral pyres she had once seen in India as a child, where devoted wives committed suttee. As she stared into the pyre, she realized why Katie had come here. Quite simply, she had come here to die. But why here and among these strangers? And how could she go on living without Katie?

. . .

The clock ticked loudly in the chill room. Nearly four o-clock. They would be bringing the tea soon. Katherine, still lying in bed, propped up on blue velvet pillows, frowned at the gleaming white clock face with its neat black numbers trimmed in gold. How much time did she really have left? Just one year ago on her birthday, she had calculated at least another ten years. But that was before Dr. Manoukin and his miraculous X-ray treatments.

How eagerly she had submitted at first beneath the rays of his infernal machine as it wheezed and rattled, her naked back flattened against a cold slab of steel, at three hundred francs a shot. Yet, after the second cycle had begun, she feared that the X-rays themselves would shorten her life. Her blood had boiled for hours after each session; her head throbbed; her heart fluttered in the pit of her stomach. When she told Dr. Manoukhin of her decision to interrupt her treatments and move to the Institute, he was horrified and came in person to her hotel hoping to dissuade her. They sat in the salon on the dusty chintz sofa and she offered him a glass of port.

"I can still heal you," Dr. Manoukhin had promised, "but if you go to that place you will be dead before winter's out."

How she had laughed at that! "But I must go Monsieur," she replied, "for I am sure that this dreary hotel will kill me if I don't escape first," and she pointed to the ghastly wallpaper and rolled her eyes.

He had not appreciated her humor. "I will write to this Monsieur Gurdjieff and inform him of your condition. And I will beseech him not to admit you on any pretext."

With that he had drained his glass, picked up his hat, and took his leave with a stiff bow.

Now she wondered. Had he carried out his threat and written to Mr. Gurjdieff? And what would he make of such a letter? She would say nothing about it, in any case, unless Mr. Gurdjieff brought the subject up himself.

A claxon honked in the yard, a motor sputtered. She got up, tossed the shawl around her shoulders and went to the window. A car was nudging through the gates and a young boy was running toward it from the great house. The car pulled up near the porter's lodge and the boy rushed to open the door for the driver. A man got out. Despite the distance, she could make out a few details. A robust man of medium height, dressed in a dark suit, a hat set at a jaunty angle, a cigar or perhaps a cheroot clenched between his teeth. There was nothing remarkable about him, except, perhaps, the suppleness in his movements, his erect carriage, the brisk tempo of his gait. He strode across the lawn, stooped to pet a dog that loped toward him, and then, with the dog trotting at his heels, disappeared around the corner.

There was a knock at her door. Opening it, she found James Young, now in patched and paint-spotted work clothes, and behind him a young girl bearing a tea tray.

. . .

The tea was served Russian fashion, not in cups but in tall glasses and not with milk, but lemon, just the way Kot always used to drink it. She thought of him fondly as she dropped a slice of lemon into her glass. Perhaps he might understand why she was here.

Dr. Young sat cross-legged on the carpet, like a Turk. Ida, summoned from her cell, sat on the bed next to Katherine. Adele, the young girl who had brought the tray, was seated by the window on a low stool, where she sipped her tea but did not talk. Katherine found her entrancing. Tall and gracious, with pinkish cheeks and pale blond hair, dressed in an embroidered peasant blouse, green dirndl and a white apron, Adele looked exactly like a Russian doll.

It was strong black tea with a smoky flavor, probably boiled up in a samovar. The tangy scent reminded Katherine of gunpowder and made her think of campfires and caravans across the steppes. There was a rich chewy cake, almost black in color, made with poppy seeds and walnuts, a plate full of lemon slices, and a little pot of thick whipped cream.

Spooning some whipped cream onto his cake, Dr. Young informed them that all the milk, butter, and cream served at the Institute came from their own cows.

Katherine spread some cream on her cake, "Tell me," she said to Adele, trying to draw the girl out, "Are you the milkmaid?"

Adele blushed. "Milking cows is one of my chores."

"You must have been with Mr. Gurdjieff in Russia."

Adele nodded.

"If only I could have been with you then." Katherine closed her eyes, bit into the cake and filled her mouth with dark sweetness. She imagined the two of them, Adele and herself, sitting on a carpet spread on the ground, drinking tea out of tin cups. The bells of wandering herds—sheep or maybe camels—tinkling in the distance.

A bell rang in the corridor and a woman's voice calling out in Russian echoed along the hall. Adele jumped to her feet to announce that she was wanted in the kitchen, but promised to return for the tray.

After she had gone, Dr. Young told them Adele was one of Gurdjieff's dancers in the performance they would watch that night, "The Initiation of a Priestess."

Katherine was duly impressed. "Oh Ida, isn't she a wonder? "

Ida, discreetly trying to dislodge a poppy seed from between her teeth with her tongue, repressed a stab of jealousy at Katie's praise for Adele and was relieved when the girl had gone. Eager to lead the conversation away from Gurdjieff's pretty dancers, she asked Dr Young about the shed she had seen in the forest.

"It is to be a study house, for lectures and dances. A sort of dervish lodge," he explained and offered to show Ida the grounds in the morning.

"Why not now? It's not quite dark out yet," asked Katherine. "Tomorrow I expect Ida will be returning to Paris rather early. This may be her only chance to see it. I would love to come, but I must stay here and wait till I'm called."

Ida stared at Katie. Once again she was being sent away. No doubt as soon as she had left the room, Katie would find an excuse to call Adele back for a longer chat. Her eyes misted over as she thought that someone else would be sharing Katie's adventures from now on.

Dr. Young had finished his tea. He stood up to take his leave and told Ida he would be glad to show her the study house.

"Katie, can't I stay here with you?"

"But I'll be seeing Monsieur Gurdjieff soon, and I would like to collect my thoughts."

Ida rose, lips pinched. "I must fetch my coat." Stepping out into the corridor with Dr Young, she caught sight of a figure clad in flowing white robes disappearing round a corner of the dim hallway. "What was that?" she whispered.

"Just a dancer in a costume," chuckled Dr. Young, "No ghosts here, never fear,"

Ida frowned. Dr. Young was quite mistaken about the ghosts. The place was full of them.

. . .

The fire was dying. Dusk had fallen. Katherine sat before the hearth, wrapped in her shawl. Her feet and hands were numb. There were no more logs to add to the fire. It was growing late and still no one had come for her. Surely Monsieur Gurdjieff had not forgotten she was still here waiting? The house seemed so silent. She went to the window, opened it wide and leaned out into the cold. No lights burned in the other windows. The lawn and the porter's lodge were deserted, then from far away came the sound of a piano, an insistent rhythm, an eerie melody.

She stood transfixed by the music. There was a sadness in it as old as time itself. Then it suddenly changed, the rhythm grew jarring, syncopated, vigorous. It stopped abruptly, and after a pause, began again, a few lonely notes seeking out a simple melody in a minor key, floating like the sound of a flute in the mountain air. But surely she would catch cold leaning like this into the dusk. She closed the window and turned to the mirror, picked up a comb and passed it through her sleek hair, for the slight wind had disarranged it. She examined her neat body, her white face with its almost Chinese allure, her huge eyes, her shining fringe. Here she was, at last. She held the soft cashmere shawl up to her face and complimented herself on the choice of color. Dark shades of red and violet were so becoming to her complexion. She swathed her head with the shawl, like a Muslim woman in chador.

What was Gurdjieff like as a man she wondered? Was he attractive? She had heard intriguing stories of his charisma—that he could give some women very particular sensations only by glancing at them from across the room, but that was probably just a silly tale. Would he find her attractive? But how could he not? With her gamine charm and her womanly sensuality, she knew that Katherine Mansfield was irresistible to most men and to many women, too, more than would care to admit—despite her rotten lungs. She pictured those lungs to herself now, made of cracked and flaking leather, sewn inside a ragdoll's body with small perfect breasts. She laughed at this self-description, puckered her mouth, made a wry face in the mirror, then pulled the shawl away from her head in a gesture of disgust. Would she never tire of play-acting? And when all the masks and costumes were stripped away, was there anything underneath worth keeping?

There was a knock at the door and she stiffened in panic, but it was only Adele come to take away the tea things.

Katherine pointed at the grate and told the girl to bring more logs. "Feel how cold I am!" she said, seizing Adele's hand, but the girl recoiled slightly from her icy touch.

"It is not allowed to take logs without asking permission, but I will try to find something," Adele said as she took the tea tray away. She returned shortly, carrying three huge logs and some twigs wrapped in a piece of old blanket.

"Please don't tell that I have stolen logs from other rooms," she said with a smile of conspiracy, putting down her bundle. She knelt before the hearth and poked the embers. "But I have not brought any paper."

Katherine took a newspaper out of her valise. She had not even opened the latest *Literary Supplement* Murry had sent her, but what did it matter? She must have warmth. She handed it to Adele who tore it into strips, wadded them up, arranged them in the fireplace, and blew on the coals.

The blaze quickly revived. Katherine stood at the hearth and held her hands a few inches from the flames. Adele still knelt by the grate, staring into the fire, her face flushed by the heat, her cheek smudged with cinders. She looked so fetching Katherine had to restrain herself from bending down to kiss away the smudge. Together they watched a pine twig ignite, flames traveling to the tip of each needle. The twig snapped, glowed, and sank into the grate. It was, thought Katherine, a fitting symbol for herself. Soon enough, she too would be consumed in a burst of sparks.

"Monsieur Gurdjieff says that fire is the light of the sun returning," Adele murmured.

"I have not yet met Mr, Gurdjieff. You must tell me what he is like."

Adele considered this request at length, then said, "Mr. Gurdjieff is a man with a very strong being."

Katherine was puzzled by the girl's quaint expression. "What do you mean? Physically strong? Or a strong character? A strong will?"

Adele shook her head, flustered. "My English is not good." She brightened, "But when you see him, you will know. It is his eyes. They see you in and out."

"When I am well enough, will you teach me Mr.Gurdjieff's dances?"

She shook her head again. "I cannot teach them yet, but one day I hope to be able to. That is my wish. Mr. Gurdjieff says everyone must have a strong wish." She stood up, smoothed her apron, and smiled at Katherine. "And you, Mrs.

Murry, what is your wish?"

Perhaps it was only a trick of the firelight flickering in the dim room, or of the gleams reflecting from the polished brass screen, or perhaps it was the power of the question itself—suddenly the room, and with it, Adele vanished, and Katherine was alone before an interrogation to which she found no immediate reply. She lifted her eyes to the window and understood in a flash of revelation, that this was the key to all that was missing, to all that she had lost. She was afraid to know and speak aloud her one real desire.

A coppery sheen drained away behind the dusk. Above a tangle of branches, one lone star shone through the blue. She saw at that instant she was all this: the tree, the star, the night itself, the steadfast center of the whole and yet an atom whirling on the fringe. She knew then what it was she had always wanted—but could confess to no one—that this moment, this night, this breath would never end. She wished with all her being that she could live forever.

THE END

Bibliographical Notes:

The following is a selected bibliography of some of the materials used in creating this slice of Mansfield's life. It is by no means exhaustive.

Mansfield, Katherine. *The Journals and Letters*. ed. C.K. Stead. London: Penguin, 1977

Mansfield, Katherine. *Letters of Katherine Mansfield*. New York: Knopf, 1929

Mansfield, Katherine. *The Scrapbook of Katherine Mansfield*. New York: Knopf, 1939

Mansfield, Katherine. *The Collected Short Stories*, London: Penguin, 2001

Baker, Ida Constance. *Katherine Mansfield: The Memories of LM*. New York: Taplinger, 1971

Murry, John Middleton. *The Autobiography: Between Two Worlds*. New York: J. Messner, 1936

Lawrence, D.H. *Selected Letters*. London: Penguin, 1950

Ouspensky, P.D. *In Search of the Miraculous: Fragments of an Unknown Teaching*. London, Routledge & Kegan Paul, 1947

Woolf, Virginia. *The Diary of Virginia Woolf*. London: The Hogarth Press, 1978

Boddy, Gillian. *Katherine Mansfield, The Woman and The Writer*. London: Penguin, 1988.

Carswell, Catherine. *The Savage Pilgrimage*. London: Secker & Warburg, 1951

Carswell, John. *The Lives and Letters*. New York: Norton, 1982

Meyers, Jeffrey. *Katherine Mansfield, A Darker View*. New York: Cooper Square Press, 2002

Moore, James. *Gurdjieff and Mansfield*. London: Routledge, Kegan Paul, 1980

Nott, C.S. *Teachings of Gurdjieff: The Journal of a Pupil*. NewYork: Weiser, 1974

Also of interest:

Johnson, Alexandra, "A Public of Two," *The Hidden Writer*, New York: Anchor Books, 1998.

Stead, C.K, Mansfield, London: Harvill,2004

Tomalin, Claire, "The Winter Wife," Nick Hern Books, 1991

A variety of invaluable documents concerning Mansfield and Gurdjieff is available at
www.gurdjieff-bibliography.com   edited by J. Walter Driscoll
www.katherinemansfield.org.uk

End Note

Katherine Mansfield died in Fontainebleau on January 9, 1923
and is buried in the cemetery of Avon.

Author's Note

Linda Lappin is the author of *The Etruscan* (Wynkin deWorde, Galway, 2004) hailed by critics as a new classic in American writing about Italy. Semi-Finalist for the 2000 Three Oaks First Novel Prize awarded by Story-Line Press, in Oregon, *The Etruscan* was selected as a Book of the Week by *Book View Ireland* and praised by the *Literary Review* as "compelling, haunting, intriguing," and by *Prairie Schooner* as "gorgeously detailed, wickedly fun." She is also the author of *Prisoner of Palmary*, an experimental historical novel set in 18th century Italy, short-listed for the Mid-List First Novel Award in 1999. Her essays, poetry, reviews and fiction have appeared in a wide variety of US publications, from the *Kenyon Review* to the *Kansas City Star*. She has twice been nominated for a Pushcart Prize. The last chapter of *Katherine's Wish* was short-listed for the Hoffer short fiction award in 2007 and was published in *Best New Writing 2007*. She teaches Creative Writing for the U.S.A.C. Study Abroad program in Viterbo. She also directs the Writing Center of Centro Pokkoli www.pokkoli.org

Her websites are www.lindalappin.net and www.theetruscan.com Her forthcoming books include *Signatures in Stone*, a mystery novel set in Bomarzo, Italy, and *Spirits of Place*, a creative writing textbook.

For information on other Wordcraft of Oregon, LLC,
titles, please visit our website at:

www.wordcraftoforegon.com